Praise for *Everything Here Is Beautiful*

"There's not a false note to be found, and everywhere there are nuggets to savor. Why did it have to end?" —*O, the Oprah Magazine*

"A bold debut . . . Lee sensitively relays experiences of immigration and mental illness. . . . A distinct literary voice."
—*Entertainment Weekly*

"Extraordinary . . . If you love anyone at all, this book is going to get you." —*USA Today*

"Lee's debut novel is a profoundly relatable drama about how far you would, or should, go for family." —*Marie Claire*

"Sisterly ties take on brilliant nuance in Mira T. Lee's shattering debut about love, loss, psychosis, and what we owe ourselves and the family we love. . . . Beautifully written." —*The Boston Globe*

"This exquisite book is one that will hurtle past all your expectations."
—*Bustle*

"Deftly dealing with big issues such as mental illness and immigration, this debut is a powerful look at love and family."
—*POPSUGAR*

"[A] gorgeous yet heartbreaking debut." —*Real Simple*

"*Everything Here Is Beautiful* is filled with unexpected, fragile moments of beauty." —*Shelf Awareness*

"[An] exciting debut about two sisters . . . the unpredictable changes of their lives, and the necessary sacrifices and important gifts that sisterhood brings." —*Southern Living*

"[A] promising debut . . . Lee handles a sensitive subject with empathy and courage. Readers will find much to admire and ponder throughout, and Lucy's section reveals Lee as a writer of considerable talent and power." —*Publishers Weekly*

"A heartfelt story about sisters, family bonds, immigration, love, and an unvarnished look at how mental illnesses impact the lives of the person living with them and those who love and try to understand . . . In Mira T. Lee, mental health has found a new novelist champion." —Pete Earley, *New York Times* bestselling author of *Crazy: A Father's Search Through America's Mental Health Madness*

"A luminous testament of loss and reclamation and the painful necessity of love." —Ron Powers, *New York Times* bestselling author of *No One Cares About Crazy People: The Chaos and Heartbreak of Mental Health in America*

"This heart-wrenching, delicately drawn novel is filled with family love, passion, pain, and forgiveness. Mira T. Lee spins a story spanning oceans that draws us ever closer to her characters' generous, flawed hearts. Powerful and unforgettable." —Jean Kwok, *New York Times* bestselling author of *Mambo in Chinatown*

"This book took my breath away. Lee has an incredible gift for empathy—I found myself rooting for, and caring deeply about, all of characters, even when they couldn't stand each other. I especially commend her nuanced, compassionate depiction of mental illness and how it impacts families. *Everything Here Is Beautiful* is an insightful, generous celebration of our capacity and complexity as human beings." —Mark Lukach, internationally bestselling author of *My Lovely Wife in the Psych Ward*

"Everything about this book is beautiful. It's a sisters story, an immigrant story, and, more than a story of one family, it's an unflinching reflection of the fast-changing American Family." —Ron Fournier, *New York Times* bestselling author *Love That Boy*

"*Everything Here Is Beautiful* vividly captures the kaleidoscope of emotional contradictions within our bonds to family and country. Mira T. Lee's powerful debut crafts an elegiac journey: uplifting, disturbing, and—proving its title—beautiful."

—Matthew Pearl, *New York Times* bestselling author of *The Last Bookaneer*

"Mira Lee has crafted an eloquent, vivid story not just of mental illness, but of passionate longing and family love in which there are no perfect choices but always a pulsing light of hope."

—Lucy Ferriss, bestselling author of *A Sister to Honor*

"I was steadily drawn into this beautifully written story of enduring love and family, however family is defined. Mira T. Lee's characters are captivating and very real, illustrating how intractable mental illness marks everyone in its sphere and renders the quotidian both beautiful and threatening. A compelling read."

—Daphne Kalotay, bestselling author of *Sight Reading*

"Charismatic and electrifying. Lee makes vivid the messiness of life and the way we tie ourselves in knots just trying to do the simplest things: love and be loved in return. A knockout."

—Rufi Thorpe, author of *Dear Fang, With Love*

PENGUIN BOOKS

EVERYTHING HERE IS BEAUTIFUL

Mira T. Lee's work has been published in numerous quarterlies and reviews, including *The Missouri Review, The Southern Review, Harvard Review,* and *Triquarterly.* She was awarded an Artist's Fellowship by the Massachusetts Cultural Council in 2012, and has twice received special mention for the Pushcart Prize. She is a graduate of Stanford University, and currently lives with her husband and two children in Cambridge, Massachusetts. This is her debut novel.

Look for the Penguin Readers Guide in the back of this book.
To access Penguin Readers Guides online,
visit penguinrandomhouse.com.

Everything Here Is Beautiful

❧

Mira T. Lee

PENGUIN BOOKS

PENGUIN BOOKS
An imprint of Penguin Random House LLC
penguinrandomhouse.com

First published in the United States of America by Pamela Dorman/Viking Penguin,
an imprint of Penguin Random House LLC, 2018
Published in Penguin Books 2019

A Pamela Dorman / Penguin Book

ISBN 9780735221970 (paperback)

THE LIBRARY OF CONGRESS HAS CATALOGED THE
HARDCOVER EDITION AS FOLLOWS:
Names: Lee, Mira T., 1970– author.
Title: Everything here is beautiful / Mira T. Lee.
Description: New York : Pamela Dorman Books, 2018.
Identifiers: LCCN 2017025306 (print) | LCCN 2017037970 (ebook) |
ISBN 9780735221987 (ebook) | ISBN 9780735221963 (hardback) |
ISBN 9780525558231 (export) ·
Subjects: LCSH: Sisters—Fiction. | Mentally ill—Family
relationships—Fiction. | Life change events—Fiction. | Psychological
fiction. | Domestic fiction. | BISAC: FICTION / Contemporary Women. |
FICTION / Literary.
Classification: LCC PS3612.E3465 (ebook) |
LCC PS3612.E3465 E82 2018 (print) |
DDC 813/.6—dc23
LC record available at https://lccn.loc.gov/2017025306

Printed in the United States of America
3 5 7 9 10 8 6 4

Set in Janson Text
Designed by Nancy Resnick

For the families

Empathy: because the commonality among human beings is emotion, and the only way we can bridge our vast discrepancies in experience is through what we feel. Let us be humbled in the knowledge that one may never fully understand the interior lives of others—but let us continue to care.

Everything Here Is Beautiful

Prologue

A summer day in New Jersey. A house with a yard. The younger one, four, likes to fold her body over the seat of her swing, observe the world from upside down. She circles her feet, twists the pair of steel ropes until they're all the way wound. She kicks up her legs. The swing spins. She likes the sensation of dizziness.

The older one, eleven, in the kitchen, chops ginger and scallions, puts on the rice. Sets out a small plate of pickled radishes.

It is early morning. Their mother is still asleep. On Mondays and Thursdays she attends night classes at the local college. On Fridays she works at the accounting office until late. "One more year," she has said, though she has promised this before. She has come a long way since her husband died and she was forced to come alone to America. The mother will soon sit for another actuarial exam. "An excellent profession," she tells the girls with pride. They know only that it involves a lot of math.

The older one sits at the kitchen table. Opens her tin pan of watercolors, paints with quick, smooth strokes. She will try a still life today, that bowl of peaches, or a vase of Shasta daisies fresh-picked from the garden. She likes the feeling of focus. When the rest of the world falls away.

"*Jie!* Come look!" her sister calls from outside.

The older one doesn't look up.

"Come here, I found something!"

She sets down her brush, heads out to the yard. The screen door slams shut behind her.

"Can you see it, Jie? There."

In the corner, by the fence. Wet grass tickles her feet. The younger one points to something in the low branches of the dogwood tree.

"It's a spiderweb, Mei-mei. See how its threads stretch from this branch to that one?"

It is their first summer in New Jersey. Their first house with a yard. Before, they lived in Third Uncle's basement, in Tennessee.

The younger one's eyes, wide.

"Don't worry, Mei. You don't have to be scared. Spiders won't hurt you. They catch flies and mosquitoes and all kinds of other insects. See the web? The spider spins it with a silk from its body. It's sticky. The bug gets caught in those strands and the spider eats it. It sucks out the blood."

The younger one nods, ponders this information. The older one turns to go back inside.

"But . . ."

The older one, impatient, though she isn't sure why. "What, Mei?"

Her sister is pointing to the web again. It shimmers in the sun. Catches the morning light.

"Look, Jie. See? It's beautiful."

Part One

Part One

1

Miranda

Lucia said she was going to marry a one-armed Russian Jew. It came as a shock, this news, as I had met him only once before, briefly, when I was in town for a meeting with a pair of squat but handsome attorneys. His name was Yonah. He owned a health food store in the East Village, down the street from a tattoo parlor, across from City Video, next door to a Polish diner, beneath three floors of apartments that Lucia said he rented out to the yuppies who would soon take over the neighborhood. He had offered me tea, and I took peppermint green, and he scurried around, mashing Swiss chard and kale in a loud, industrial blender, barking orders to his nephews, or maybe they were second or third cousins (I never knew, there were so many), because they were sluggish in their work of unloading organic produce off the delivery trucks. He yelled often. I thought, This Yonah is quite a rough man.

He dusted the wine, mopped the floor, restocked packages of dried figs and goji berries and ginseng snacks on the shelves. He was industrious, I could see, intent on making his fortune as immigrants do. Lucia said he played chess. I'd never known my sister to play chess, though she was always excellent at puzzles as a child. Yonah didn't seem to me the kind to play chess either, nor to drink sulfite-free organic wine or eat goji berries. But as they say, love is strange. And I wouldn't begrudge my sister love, nor any stranger, not even one who smoked, and was the kind of man who looked disheveled even fresh after a shower, and would leave his camo briefs lying around on the bathroom floor. I admit I was disturbed, creeped out, by his prosthetic arm, which he wore sometimes, though more often I'd find it sitting by itself in a chair.

Lucia brought him to visit our mother, who was dying. Our mother was tilted back in a green suede recliner, wrapped in cotton blankets, watching the *Three Tenors* video we'd given her the previous year. She took a long look at this man—his workingman's shoulders, his dark-stubbled jaw, his wide, flat nose. Her Yoni had the essence of a duck, Lucia said (endearingly), or maybe a platypus, though she'd never seen one up close. My sister liked to discern people's animal and vegetable essences. In fact, she was usually right.

Our mother winced as her gaze settled upon his left arm, a pale, peachy shade that did not match the rest of him. "What happened to your arm?" she said.

"An accident, when I was twenty-one." He said it quietly, but without any shame.

"In Soviet Union?"

"In Israel. I moved there when I was teenager."

"You are divorced," she said, and I tried to read his thoughts in the fluttering of his blue-gray eyes. I wondered if Lucia had warned him that our mother was like that. I wondered what had been shared, what omitted, when the two of them exchanged stories over chess, over wine. I wished to say to this man: *Do you really think you now know our Lucia?*

"Thirteen years," he said. "I have been divorced for thirteen years." Our mother winced again, though it could've been from the pain shooting through her bowels, or her bones, or her chest.

"You are Jewish," she said. "Jewish are so aggressive. You have children?"

"Two," he said. "They are with their mother, in Israel."

At the mention of the other woman, our mother spat. Once, I suppose, she would have wanted to know more, like what did he do, or how old were the children, or what were their names, or did they play musical instruments, and we might have told him that Lucia could recite twenty Chinese poems by the time she was three, or that she was a real talent on the violin, or that she'd suffered a terrible bout of meningitis at age six and nearly died.

"Why are you divorced?" she asked.

"We were married too young," he said. The skin of his face seemed to hang off his cheekbones. A basset hound, I later said to Lucia.

"This is life," he said to our mother.

She did not seem quite satisfied with this answer, though she nodded, expelled a heavy sigh. "Take care of my daughter," she said.

But she was not looking at him. She was looking at me.

She fell asleep. Two weeks later, she was gone.

꘎

"Three piles," said Lucia. "Everything in three piles."

Keep. Salvation Army. Trash.

This was our strategy, tasked as we were with selling the house in New Jersey, as specified by our mother's will (our childhood home, marred by death, now considered "inauspicious"). So we sorted CorningWare and gas bills and soy sauce and ice trays and Cabbage Patch dolls and garden hoses and yarn and frying pans and Maurice Sendak books and twin bed sheet sets with faded Raggedy Ann and Andy pillowcases. Keep. Trash. Keep. Keep. Salvation Army. Trash. And when we reached Ma's bedroom, a hallowed hush, as if to acknowledge the finality in this sacred act of disturbance on which we now embarked. The desk where she'd worked, pencil in hand; the throw pillows Lucia sewed one year in home economics class; the portable radio; the clock; her *Reader's Digest*s; the bed where she'd lain tethered to her morphine drip, eyes closed, silent, body slack at last.

"Fashion show?" whispered Lucia.

"Well . . ." Why not?

We peered in the closet, the one we'd raided often as impish children. We picked out two vintage cotton sundresses, one with chevron stripes, the other, zigzags. "Twirl!" said Lucia. "You," I said, and in unison, our skirts puffed out like upside-down tulips.

We burst into tears. Twelve cycles of chemotherapy, three surgeries, three courses of radiation, two clinical trials, three remissions, four recurrences, over nine grueling years—yet the permanence of Ma's absence still came as a shock.

We worked until late. At two in the morning, we decided to bake. We blasted Abba and Blondie and the Rolling Stones, broke out in song as flour and sugar flew everywhere. "Almonds!" said Lucia. "We need almonds!" Chinese almond cookies were Ma's favorite, so we set down our spatulas, drove to the twenty-four-hour pharmacy to shop for nuts.

We'll be roommates someday in an old folks' home! We'll be cranky and play bridge and complain to the nurses about our hemorrhoids. Ha ha, when you're eighty I'll only be seventy-three!

No doubt the grief made us giddy. The late hour. The fatigue. But it was like that, to be with Lucia.

We fell asleep in the family room, the house buttery warm, the waffle-weave of sofa cushions imprinted on our cheeks. And then morning came. And with it came Yonah, roaring up the driveway in a giant rental truck.

They married quickly, in City Hall. Lucia wore a sparkly tank top with pink bicycle pants, silver hoop earrings. She beamed, like a bride. Yonah wore his best khakis, a wrinkled white shirt, a bright red tie. I thought, *This* is who my sister is marrying: a man the shade of gravy, with a missing limb and a spaghetti-sauce-colored tie. I'd never expected my sister to marry a more conventional man, or a Chinese man, or a highly educated man with a spotless résumé. Lucia had dated a Greek boy in high school, chosen NYU over Cornell, rejected math and sciences for English, all to our mother's dismay. And while her college dormmates had busied themselves with one incestuous hookup after the next, Lucia met a soft-spoken drummer who lived with four other musicians in Tribeca, ditched her violin for electric bass. She found her wanderlust, too, forgoing the air-conditioned offices and suits our mother and I were both familiar with to teach English in Ecuador, tutor in Brazil, volunteer at an orphanage in Bolivia. In her early twenties, she worked as a travel writer in Latin America for a small start-up firm, before returning to study journalism. She wrote feature articles now for a newspaper in Queens—the next best thing, I suppose, as there she was friendly with halal butchers, Egyptian barbers, Salvadoran cooks and the old Chinese grocers who sold dog penises and exotic mushrooms for six hundred dollars a pound.

Still, I had not imagined this.

Yonah beamed, like a groom. He beamed with the whole of his wide, duck face and his wiry brows and his small, sticking-out ears. "Take picture now!" he barked, and I followed him through the rectangular window of my camera, trying to see what Lucia could see, and yes, he was rugged, fit, masculine. Attractive, one could say. I'd never thought of Lucia marrying before me—after all, she was younger by seven years. My *mei-mei*.

They had signed prenuptial agreements, at my insistence. I did not think Yonah was marrying for our mother's money (not a fortune, but far from meager), nor for Lucia's American citizenship, but I felt my concern was reasonable. "Take more picture!" he said. I did not like how often he spoke in imperatives, though I understood that English was not his native tongue. We had that in common. I did try to like him, I did.

After the two-minute ceremony, he hugged me fiercely, strong as a bear. "*Sister!*" he said. "*Achoti! Hermana! Sestra! Belle soeur!*"

"*Jie,*" said Lucia.

"*J-yeah!*" he said in a remarkably accurate third tone. He laughed from his belly. I liked that about him. Then he scooped up Lucia with his good arm and carried her down seven flights of stairs, out to the plaza where spring blossoms danced and songbirds chirped and a rainbow might have appropriately appeared. He spun her around and around and Lucia shrieked with delight, her arms outstretched, head thrown back, bobbed hair and sharp chin shining in rays of new sun. "My wife, she is beauuuu-ti-ful," he sang, and Lucia's eyes shone with such clarity that even my most shrouded worries burned off like a morning fog. They were in love. Our mother, I was sure, could know this safely, from wherever that place is where the dead view the living.

He welcomed me to their home. It was cramped: a two-room apartment adjacent to the kitchen of the health food store. It smelled like cigarettes. In the windowless bedroom, four black-and-white security monitors sat stacked on a large, steel desk cluttered with paper cups and ashtrays and framing nails and remote controls and piles of Lucia's small, girly clothes. Lucia decorated their marital bed with oddly shaped pillows—clover, heart, frog, banana. She loved to lie there snacking on pita chips or yogurt-covered pretzels, watching the store. "That's where he first saw me eating macadamias," she said dreamily, pointing to the bulk nut bins on security screen one.

In the living room, a twin mattress was laid out on the floor. It served as a bed for Yonah's visiting nieces and nephews or cousins or uncles, whoever was passing through. Lucia loved the bustle, the chaotic, hostel-like feel of the place. The Organic Kibbutz, she called it. And now it was her home, too.

"Do you believe in happily ever after?" she asked me that day, as we sipped peppermint tea from our paper cups. I recalled the stone-faced art professor I'd recently dated for six weeks, felt a slight, involuntary jerk of my brow. Slight, but noticed, because Lucia noticed these kinds of things.

"Oh, Jie." She sighed. "You could at least *try* to believe." She reached over to hug me, patted my head, like she used to as a child.

That night I lay on the twin mattress and listened to the sounds of the two of them panting and moaning, gooey and fucking like rabbits. My sister was officially a newlywed. A wife. It came to me suddenly, as a blunt ache inside—I'd never felt more alone.

Yonah was frugal; our mother would've approved. Every other Sunday he dragged in furniture from that Middle Eastern flea market on Twelfth and B. "Listen," he said. That's what he always said: "Listen. You wanna know something? The yuppies, they love this stuff. You know how much this cost?"

I examined the three-by-four-foot tea-stained mohair rug.

"Twenty bucks!" he said. "Secondhand store, you pay two hundred; this one you clean, it's like perfect."

"Perfect!" said Lucia.

She painted the bench outside the store a bright berry red. Bought a dozen tropical-looking plants to decorate the café area, which had been recently expanded to include a fancy soup and salad bar, and now all the neighborhood characters came to mingle in the exposed-brick aura of their urban oasis, lounging to trip-hop or Moby or Ella Fitzgerald (Lucia promptly declared them her favorites) while young people huddled over soy milk beverages, many of them lesbian hipsters or drama students or aspiring environmental activists.

I cannot say I particularly liked the way my sister behaved around her new husband or how he'd speak to her often as though she were a child. "Lucy Goooosey," he said (she'd hated that nickname all her life), "I made you your favorite food in all the world . . . shakshuka!"

Shakshuka?

Lucia loved our mother's spare ribs—yes, those tender pork spare ribs marinated overnight in honey and garlic and five-spice powder. "I love you Lucy Goosey," he said, scooping runny egg and tomato into her mouth. He kept kosher. Our mother would've been disappointed; she would not have trusted a grown man who was coarse like a rhino but who ate like a bird.

I did like how he always made efforts to welcome his customers: "*Hola!*" to Juan Carlos, the Colombian guitarist, "*Guten Morgen!*" to redheaded Mikael, "*Konichiwa!*" to Mrs. Sato and "*Chow chow!*" to Mrs. Sato's long-haired Pomeranian. They liked him. They liked to stop and chat at his store. Later, Lucia told me, "Yoni, he can't read or write English."

"What?" I said. "What do you mean?"

Lucia shrugged. This saddened me, because my sister had always loved words—their sounds, their rhythms, the moods they conveyed. As a child, she'd sit for hours on the toilet with a dictionary in her lap, circling her favorite words with a stubby red pencil.

"But how does he run the store?" I said.

"He has business partners, *cousins*," she said. "Uncle Leo does the bookkeeping. Cousin Abby does the ordering. Yoni manages the workers. He's a *people person*." She would teach him if he wanted to learn. Later she said maybe he didn't want to learn.

"But he reads and writes Hebrew," I said.

"Sometimes." She shrugged again. "Do you know how many words I write down in a day?" She took out her tall, spiraled reporter's notebook and flipped through page after page of meticulous notes and lists. "I write down *everything*."

"So?" I said.

"Yesterday, Yoni wrote down six Hebrew words."

"Six words?" I said. I did not understand. I worried about her then. I tried hard to read her tiny handwriting, and her face.

"Six words," she said. "Some days one. Some days none."

"So what?" I said.

"Can you imagine?" she said. "He organizes everything in his *brain*."

Yes, this was pure Lucia.

She found an immigration lawyer, filled out duplicate copies of form after form, gathered glowing letters from the lesbian owners of the tattoo parlor down the street, the manager of City Video, the Polish chef next door, and within six months Yonah became a proud green card carrier. Lucia could be resourceful like that; efficient, like our mother. And then she was determined to help him quit smoking. She brought home pamphlets and read them aloud, signed him up for support groups, bought nicotine gum, hid his ashtrays, then his Marlboro Reds (until he roared), and made him watch videos of blackened, cancer-infested lungs. She monitored his cough, and when it didn't go away for four weeks she made him his first doctor's appointment in ten years.

Occupying the twin mattress that winter was Yonah's aunt's best friend's son, Chaka, fresh from Haifa, so when I came to the city for a business meeting I offered to stay with a friend, but Yonah huffed, *Ridiculous!* He moved to a long, cushioned bench in the café so I could sleep with my sister and I said thank you and tried to ignore the cigarette burns on the sheets. Lucia and I lay awake, propped by pillows, snacking on egg tarts and pineapple buns from our favorite Chinese bakery on Mott Street, watching episode after episode of *Sex and the City* (Lucia had faithfully recorded them for me on videotape). In the morning we watched Chaka chop celery and flirt with Noemie, the busty new Puerto Rican girl on the register who wore tight, cap-sleeved shirts. "Great Dane," said Lucia, pointing to security screen two. "Right," I said, watching Chaka wave a paring knife with his graceful young limbs. "What a heartbreaker," said Lucia. "Look at those eyes." "Watch out, new girl," I said. "*Aiyaaaa*," said Lucia. We laughed.

She asked me to take Yonah to see the doctor. She had an interview with a prominent food critic in Astoria (for which she trotted out a vintage pair of Mary Jane pumps, red suede). Yoni hated doctors, she said. She'd found him a woman doctor who spoke Hebrew with an office only six blocks away. I was touched. I couldn't remember my sister being so thoughtful in the past.

He made me peppermint green tea that morning. "Shakshuka?" he said.

"Oh, no," I said, "that's okay."

He brought me vegan chocolate-orange pound cake. "Lucy's favorite," he said. I tasted it, and it was surprisingly moist. That might have been the first time I was alone with him. We walked quickly, without saying much, though when he spied an old boom box awaiting disposal, he whipped out his pocketknife, pried out the batteries, dropped one onto the sidewalk. "No bounce, you see? This one is good." "You could take the whole thing," I suggested. "Nah," he said. "I got boom box. Better one than this."

At the doctor's office, the secretary handed him a clipboard full of forms. He handed them to me. "Please," he said (quietly, but without any shame). "Name," I said. "Birthday. Symptoms," I said. "Family medical history, check all that apply." That's when I found out Yonah's father had died of lung cancer at the age of forty-four. Yonah's age.

Our mother had died of lung cancer, too, though she smoked only two months, back when we first emigrated from Shanghai to Tennessee. Lucia never knew how it was, stuck in Third Uncle's house, banished to the basement, Ma gagging because it smelled like feet. My sister was a colicky baby, howling, red-faced—to calm her, I'd aggressively belt out Chinese lullabies, or the Popeye theme song, or one of the old southern spirituals I learned at school, so strange to me as a child:

> *Ezekiel connected dem dry bones,*
> *Ezekiel connected dem dry bones,*
> *Ezekiel in the Valley of Dry Bones,*
> *Now hear the word of the Lord!*

I'd never heard the Lord say a thing, but a girl at school said if I prayed to Him, I might get what I wanted. So I prayed for Him to strike down Third Uncle so he would no longer assail us with profanities, or insult Ma's cooking, or throw dishes down the stairs when the baby cried. These were the years our mother's lips remained pressed into a tight, thin line. Every morning I was called up to Third Uncle's room to wash his feet and rub his bunions with tiger tooth liniment; every afternoon I'd run home from school, study quickly, so I could care for Lucia when our mother left for her night classes. *Ma, why did we have to come to America? Aiya, Nu-er, very complicated. Family matters. Your Ba thought it was good idea.* But our father had died in a car accident six months ago, when we were still back in China. I did not understand family matters. Day after day, I sat alone in the cafeteria, picking at the grains of rice in my thermos, afraid to look up. Only eighteen months later would I meet a girl in Art Club who shared with me her brand-new Cray-Pas, then her Mallomars, even invited me to her house to show me her Vidal Sassoon hair dryer, and how to blow out my hair and set it with hairspray instead of always wearing it in a single braid down my back. Tess Carter, a true blue-eyed blonde, who would transform those years into something bearable. And on the last day of fifth grade, when Ma announced she'd accepted a job in New Jersey, Tess and I had wailed and sobbed, swore to write every day on the Hello Kitty stationery we picked out together at the Hallmark store—and though the letters dwindled, we would reunite, fortuitously, in New York City, for college at Barnard. My first American friend would last for life.

Yonah was in the examination room a long time. When he came out his face was red and he paid the receptionist quickly from the thick wad of cash he always carried in his pocket. "Is everything okay?" I said.

"Listen," he said. "I'm gonna tell you something. Doctors, they don't do nothing. Never I had a lady tell me to cough and then squeeze my fucking balls!"

I laughed. I thought, Sometimes this Yonah is a funny man.

He came on vacation with us that first summer. Lucia and I liked to rent a cottage on Cape Cod with a few of our friends. I invited Tess, who came from the city with her new boyfriend, the two of them all gushing and googly-eyed. Yonah invited his Uncle Leo, who lived upstairs and kept the books at the store. *"Avocado,"* whispered Lucia, and I recognized him instantly when I drove to fetch him from the bus station. Uncle Leo was short and stocky, wide at the bottom instead of up top, and wore round, rimless glasses and a yarmulke that covered most of his hair. He had unfortunately fat feet, I recall.

"So *you* are the sister," he said. He eyed me head to toe. "Where do you live, sister?"

"In Providence," I said.

"*Providence?*" He laughed out loud.

I found him rude. I did miss New York, but after Ma's third remission, I'd finally left the soulless midtown consulting firm where I'd worked for seven years, moved to Providence to help implement a new strategic plan for an arts foundation. "But what do you *do*?" said Uncle Leo, and I explained I mostly managed their finances. "A-ha," he said. "So you are good with money. Good at math." He nodded at me with new respect.

We went swimming. Yonah and Uncle Leo complained it was too cold. "*Hof Dor!*" said Yonah. "Now that's a real beach!" He spoke loudly about their houses in Haifa and Jerusalem, how they were furnished with antiques, and Uncle Leo spoke about how business was booming and how they could soon buy a new property in Williamsburg and expand the store. "This is America!" said Yonah. "Listen, you know about *air rights*?"

"Air rights?" said Tess.

"Greedy yuppie developers," said Yonah. "They want to build twelve floors of luxury apartments on the corner, where now is that car park. The neighborhood lets each building have six floors; they want more. But I have only four. Sure, they can buy two floors of my air!" He laughed, puffing rings of blue smoke.

"Two million bucks!" said Uncle Leo, slapping us all high fives.

"My wife will never have to work again!" said Yonah, grabbing Lucia's tiny waist.

You think you know my sister, I thought. My sister loves her work. She has no interest in being a rich man's wife. I thought, This Yonah is an arrogant man.

That evening he grilled pounds and pounds of kosher chicken breast and potatoes. "Kosher chicken is the best chicken," he said.

"Lots of paprika," said Uncle Leo, and we all murmured that it was indeed very good and very well spiced. After dinner, we retired to the screened-in porch, where I brought out a large bag full of canvases and tubes of acrylic paints. As a child, this had been my primary entertainment—hours and hours lost in colors and textures on twelve-by-sixteen-inch matte boards layered thick with experiment. Sometimes Lucia and I played crazy eights or Chinese chess. Sometimes I taught Lucia math as our mother had taught me—by sitting her in my lap, asking her to calculate how many chickens, how many pigs, in a barnyard with eighteen feet and six heads.

I pulled out a canvas of sunflowers I'd painted the summer before. "Jie!" said Yonah. "It's beautiful."

"Beauuuutiful," said Lucia. "Jie's always been an artist."

I blushed.

"You must hang your paintings in our gallery," he said.

"What gallery?" I said.

"We make a gallery in the café at the store," he said.

So now you think you also know art, I thought.

"Maybe you should paint something," I said. "Do you want to paint?"

"Yeah!" he said. He was enthusiastic, I admit; Lucia loved that about him.

I watched the two of them squeeze huge gobs of blue and yellow and red onto paper plates. "A duck," said Lucia. "I'm going to paint you, a duck." "A goose!" said Yonah. "Lucy Goosey, I'm going to paint you, a goose." He mashed my squirrel-hair brushes into the goopy plate and I winced. When he was finished, the goose was a yellow blob standing on thin, orange sticks, anchored by triangular-ish green blocks I recognized as similar to Uncle Leo's feet. Lucia's duck was muddy brown, with one orange wing. "Duck and goose!" She glowed. "We are duck and goose!" said Yonah, beaming, and they danced around the cottage and they kissed.

He entertained our friends, smoking late into the night. I coughed in my bed. Through the buzzing of mosquitoes, I could hear Uncle Leo telling stories of childhood in Moscow, eating stale bread and goulash, cold beet soup. They spoke, too, of Israel, their days in the Israeli army. I imagined Yonah dressed in camouflage, learning how to load a gun, disarm a grenade, living in a tin-can hut, rows of concrete bunkers looming on the dusty horizon. I knew nothing about Moscow, or Israel, or the Israeli army.

"Do you remember the tents?" said Uncle Leo. In the desert dark, it was cold. They were allowed their own pillows, and as homesick boys they squeezed them tight, as if to wring out their fear. They joked about Passover, about the matzoh, heavy in their bellies, that kept them awake and constipated all night.

That night I learned Yonah had trained as a marksman, that he'd lost his arm when he tried to remove a Palestinian boy's body from the path of an IDF tank.

In the morning I sat on the front porch in my Adirondack chair, reading a book, while he and Lucia panted and groaned upstairs. I wished to be glad for their happiness.

❧

One day in the fall, he called. He never called.

It was Lucia who called, usually once every week, to tell me about the poetry slam in the café where they'd served sulfite-free organic wine, or what they'd done for Rosh Hashanah, or the shakshuka she'd cooked for all the workers in the store (*three cartons of eggs!*). And Yonah would yell from the background in his singsong voice: "Jie! Come visit us soon!" Or, "Me and Lucy Goosey, we miss you! Everything here is beautiful!"

This time he whispered. "Listen," he said. "Something is happening." His rough voice wavered. "Lucia, she stops sleeping and she is laughing and laughing in the shower all night. This morning, she is crying. She is telling me I am filming her on the security screens, bad people are making movies of her in our room."

I was in the middle of preparing a chocolate soufflé, having been invited by a bungee-jumping financial analyst to his apartment for a third date. I turned off the oven, boarded the next train to New York, withholding fat tears I hoped our mother could not see from her grave.

"She needs a doctor," I said.

"I hate doctors," said Yonah.

"She needs a doctor," I said. This is how Lucia looked: Empty. Pale. Limp, like old celery.

"Why is this happening?" he said.

༄

It had happened once before, three years earlier, not long after she'd finished graduate school.

One doctor I'd spoken with explained that such episodes could be triggered by stress, or drugs, or trauma, or exhaustion. Or sometimes, nothing at all.

"Can't you *do* something?" I said.

"No," said the doctor.

"What do you mean, *no*?" I said.

No. Simply, no. Not unless her condition worsened significantly, such that she posed an imminent risk of harm to herself or others. Until then, no, we could not help her if she did not wish to be helped. All we could do was wait.

She lost her first real job with a newspaper in Connecticut. Worked as a coat-check girl at a trendy Manhattan bar, lost that job, too. For a while she came to stay with me in Providence, slept on a pullout couch in the living room. One minute she babbled on about serpents and spies, the next she fell mute like a shadow. When we hung out with friends, her tangential interjections turned every gathering tense. One weekend Tess came to visit and we went out to a club to see Lucia's old college friend's indie-pop band.

"How do you like living here?" Tess asked.

"I live on Earth, hello, and it's getting polluted," said Lucia. "Don't bother to breathe the air."

"Oh, pollution is bad," said Tess. "But Providence must be better than New York."

"They must be living in a recession," said Lucia. "Or regression." I could see Tess blink. "It's just math, it's not like everyone there's a genius."

"Have you heard the new Dave Matthews album?" I asked Tess, trying to deflect attention, and we exchanged opinions until our voices trailed off and Lucia murmured, "Matthew is a liar. He's always been a liar. He's just lying all the time until he wakes up."

Tess glanced at me, alarmed.

Is she okay? everyone whispered.

"No," I said. It was all I could say. She hardly ate, rarely bathed, but in the mornings she marched out carrying her reporter's notebook and in the evenings she returned.

One day she said she wanted to move back to New York. "I don't think that's a good idea," I said, but by evening she was already gone.

That episode lasted nine months.

It was a young jogger who alerted a policewoman, who brought her into the emergency room. She'd been sitting on top of a manhole cover in the middle of the street, cold and disoriented, singing at the top of her lungs. I took the next train into the city, rushed to the hospital, signed the papers for her involuntary commitment. Two psychiatrists signed in agreement; now the hospital could hold her against her will. When I found her the next day in the psychiatric unit, wearing blue scrubs and paper slippers, she shot me a look of blank hatred. *"You,"* she said. *"You* put me here." That day after I left the ward, I waited patiently until the elevator doors pinched closed. Then I broke down in tears.

Our mother came from New Jersey, bewildered. *What has happened, Nu-er?* she asked, but when I tried to explain, she shook her head, unable or unwilling to comprehend. In the tiny communal kitchen of the 38th Street Y, she cooked up a storm—fish congee, lion's head meatballs, *char siu* and shrimp fried rice. Twice daily she brought meals into the hospital, where doctors and nurses carrying clipboards came and went, ghostlike and evasive. Ma, brisk, removing Tupperware lids. *Mapo tofu and watercress, your favorites, Xiao-mei*—and if Lucia would eat, Ma would hover, scoop rice or fetch salt or a straw or a paper napkin to wipe the table, and if she did not, Ma would fret and dither, *You need to eat, Xiao-mei. Are you getting enough sleep? You leave this place we go shopping, I buy you proper bed, not that . . . that thing—you mean a futon, Ma?—Aiya, futon no good! Too soft no good, bad for your back! Too close to the floor, no good, give you arthritis!* And on and on she went, as if a flaccid mattress could be held accountable for Lucia's present condition.

Every other day I commuted to my office in downtown Providence, returned at night to the 38th Street Y, where the skinny window in our room faced a slab of brick wall. One evening I found our mother standing with her face pressed to the glass. From the portable radio that accompanied her wherever she traveled, the classical music station playing *Madama Butterfly*—Luciano Pavarotti, her favorite—and when she saw me, something burst inside. She wept, shoulders stiff, with quick, choppy breaths, and it shocked me; I had not seen her like this since we lived with Third Uncle. *The doctors will figure it out, Ma, it'll be okay.* Ma, inconsolable, and I wondered if I should not have tried so hard to shield her from Lucia's erratic behavior the past several months. But she'd been exhausted from her treatments; I had not wanted to burden her further. *Your sister, always such a happy child. Wild, yes, but so happy.* And then her gasps slowed, and her face went cloudy with that faraway gaze I still could not decode.

For one month we'd stayed in that dreary place. But slowly, my sister returned. Like a miracle. Our Lucia.

It was not my story to tell. But now it was clear, as I'd feared: Lucia had never told her new husband these things. Maybe she was afraid he wouldn't understand. Or maybe she'd wanted to believe, as I did, that nightmares could stay forever in the dark.

Yonah tried to calm her. She scowled. She pushed him away, and it hurt him, I could see. I tried to trick her. I said, "Lucia, you need to sleep."

"I can't sleep, not with them watching me."

I said, "You'll feel better in a place where you can sleep."

Finally Yonah said, "Listen to your sister, Lucy, no cameras there, no nothing, just quiet room for you to sleep."

She said, "Maybe I need sleep." In the emergency room she squirmed and Yonah cradled her head to his chest. When the nurse asked him questions, I answered and filled out her forms.

Yonah's mother's friend's grandson, Amit, was flopped on the twin mattress that night. His essence was a lump of boiled ham. Yonah let me sleep in the bed, and he slept on the long, cushioned bench in the café—though he hardly slept—and in the morning I lay awake by myself and watched security screens two and three, where long-limbed Chaka was kissing Noemie, whose tight pink cap-sleeved shirt now clung to her melon-shaped belly.

Lucia slept for eighteen hours, and when we visited the next day, she was livelier, less irritable, more herself, though her eyes still seemed cloudy, vague. Yonah brought her beet salad and ginseng snacks and her favorite pound cake. "Can she come home now?" he asked. He could not stand to leave her.

"No," I said. "I don't think so. Not yet."

She was stubborn. I did not remember her being so stubborn the last time. She said, "Doctors don't know anything about how I feel." She said, "I want to go home." She cried.

Yonah kissed her. He said, "Don't worry, we're gonna go home soon." That day he tried to feed her the small white pill himself, the one the pale, veiny nurse brought in a plastic cup. "You take this, Lucy Goosey, we go home, I make you shakshuka." When that didn't work he scolded her like a child. "Listen, Lucy, I am serious, no more playing games now." And when that didn't work either the pale, veiny nurse sighed, and when the same thing happened the next day Yonah said, "This is stupid. She sit here in this jail, and the doctors, they don't do nothing." He told the pale nurse and the doctor (a stallion, most definitely a stallion), "I am her husband. I am taking care of her, I am taking her home."

"Please, Yonah," I said. "You can't do that. She's not well."

"She's not an animal," he said.

"She's sick," I said.

"They lock her up, like animal."

"Please, be patient. It takes time."

"Three days she's here, they don't do nothing. This is stupid."

"It took a month last time. One month. But she took the medicine and got better. Really better." I spoke deliberately, as if to a simpleton, but he only shook his head.

"They don't understand her," he said.

"No. *You* don't understand. She has an *illness*." Lucia sat alone by the window, scanning the view with hollow eyes. "Look at her," I pleaded. "She's sick. That's *not her*."

"Jie. Listen." He lowered his voice. "I know Lucia. This place, these doctors, it's no good for her."

You know Lucia?

You?

I choked back my words, furious.

I pulled out a folder full of pamphlets and notes and clinical papers, which I'd saved for three years. *FAQs 4 Caregivers. Bipolar Symptoms and Signs. 25 Tips for Coping with Schizophrenia.* "She has a *mental illness*," I said. I brandished the folder like a weapon of proof. "This hospital is to help her. She needs help. Can't you see?"

"This hospital is *bull*shit," he roared.

I flung the pamphlets and notes and clinical papers he could not read in his face.

You are an ignorant, ignorant man.

"This is jail," he said, and in the end, he won. He was her husband. They had to listen to him.

I returned to Providence. I saw the bungee-jumping financial analyst. I apologized, explained. He stared at his dinner plate, chewed his lamb kebob laboriously, his discomfort seeping through the silences. I did not see him again.

I tried to contact Lucia's former psychotherapist, an astute young woman with whom I'd spoken several times after Lucia's first break. "Lucia has remarkable insight. This is encouraging," she'd said. *Encouraging?* "For prognosis. Because these kinds of illnesses are most often lifelong conditions," she said. I didn't believe her. Denial was easy, back then.

"Dr. Hassan no longer works here," said the receptionist.

"May I get her new number?"

"Dr. Hassan moved to London over a year ago." Click.

The line went dead.

That night I dreamed I was back at Third Uncle's house. His room, odorous, like dirty socks. Third Uncle, stretched out watching *Bonanza* on the television, spitting watermelon seeds into a potato chip bag. His short, stubby toes. Those thick, yellow toenails. The sound of his click-clicking teeth. *Ah, Nu-er, come help your uncle.* I watched in horror as the bunion on his left foot grew to the size of a small eggplant. I retched. High-pitched wails rang in my ears, like sirens. *Shut up!* yelled Third Uncle. *Shut up with all your crying, wang-badan!* I tumbled downstairs to the basement, found Ma crouched in the closet, eyes puffy and red. A door slammed. The baby shrieked. *Give her to me, Ma. I'll take care of her.*

Lucia said she did not like her work in Queens anymore. The subway was too loud. She said she would write from home, and Yonah let her work from their bed, which she covered with stacks of her color-coded papers. To me, he said: "Here always are people, in and out, and every day she stay in our room. She need rest. She need quiet. This city, it make people depressed."

I tried to talk to her, but this is what I sensed: something murky, a detachment, long pauses and gaps in her thoughts. She was still Lucia, perhaps, but muffled, disjointed, fractured into a thousand pieces. She refused to answer if I asked about her medications.

I blamed him. I admit, I did. But he brought her beet salad, cooked her shakshuka, bought her trinkets from the flea market, coaxed and joked and made her laugh. He indulged her, like a child. So what was I to do?

By this time, I, too, was in transition, with a rigid new boss at the arts foundation. *Your mother, your sister, yes, I know it's been difficult, Miranda, but perhaps it's time you considered a more family-friendly organization.* My insides deflated. My face burned. Though he was not altogether unkind. With his recommendation, I was able to find a fund-raising position up in Boston, where I soon met a tall Swiss urologist, introduced to me by a colleague as a potential tennis partner.

Our first match, the tall Swiss urologist played hard. He did not attempt to make small talk or flirt or humor me between points, but focused down on the ground, or up at the ball, or on the strings of his racquet, as if to look elsewhere would breach a seriousness he was required to sustain—though in the end, he lost, six games to four, and he approached the net dutifully with an outstretched hand. "You're tough," he said, shaking his head. "High school varsity," I mumbled, and for a moment I worried that I'd bruised his fragile male ego, that I miscalled a few shots, that he would refuse another contest (I'd enjoyed it, we were so evenly matched)—but then he reached an arm around my shoulders, the slightest embrace, and I caught him smiling a quick, private smile to himself, which I dared to interpret as a shy admiration.

His name was Stefan. Recently divorced, he'd come to Boston to consult for a global health organization. We went to an Irish pub, where he joked and flirted and looked me in the eye, laughed when I told him about the woman doctor who squeezed unsuspecting balls. A few weeks later, our first road trip to Maine, car trouble and rain left us stranded the entire weekend in a musty motel outside Augusta. Nevertheless, we'd ordered lobsters and French fries and dined in bed, watched the Wildlife Channel, learned about mating behaviors of the Congolese bonobos, had frighteningly good sex. Our last night there, I was stricken with food poisoning (as mortifying as it was wretched). He brought me fresh towels, ice, changed the sheets, and by the time I woke the next morning, he'd returned already from the convenience store, armed with bananas, Saltines, and ginger ale, along with two soft-bristled toothbrushes, the kind I liked.

On the long drive home, our conversation turned serious. I learned his wife had left him for a professional skier, moved to Austria with their son. "Your *son*?" Rafael, twelve, now in boarding school. "I'm sorry," said Stefan. "I really . . ." He drew a breath to recalibrate. "This was completely juvenile. I should have told you earlier, and I don't know why I didn't. I think I worried you would run away." Flushed, flustered, and I had not seen him like this, less than composed. "Do you miss him?" I asked. "I do," he said. "It's difficult being so far away. And my ex doesn't make things any easier." He reached for my hand. Stopped midair. "Are you angry, Miranda? If you're angry, I understand." But I could not say I felt angry or alarmed, deceived or betrayed—if anything, this news seemed to frame him in a softer light, and I found his contrition oddly sweet, his fallibility reassuring.

"What's his essence?" asked Lucia.

I pictured Stefan's steady brown eyes, his noble demeanor.

"Elk?" I said.

"Elk!" she said. "Is that like partway between a deer and a moose?" And she giggled and sounded mostly like herself, until the next time, when she would sound hard and vacant like a parking lot.

"Are you writing?" I asked.

"What?" she said.

"How is she?" I'd ask Yonah.

"She's perfect," he'd say, but not in his singsong voice. "Maybe we're gonna move to house upstate, when I find some more money. Maybe I sell the store." He sounded tired. I didn't ask what had happened to air rights.

That summer, Uncle Leo disappeared. "What do you mean, disappeared?" I said.

"Poof," said Lucia. "Vanished, like magic."

Vanished, like magic?

Later I learned he'd absconded with sixty-six thousand dollars, had been embezzling from the store for more than two years. Yonah flew immediately to Israel. I don't know if he found him. Lucia said everyone argued over whether to report Uncle Leo to the police. Yonah said no. Uncle Leo was family.

When he returned, his son, Jonny, was with him. Jonny was a handsome boy of eighteen; not tall, not short, but robust and athletic, with fiery eyes and dyed-black hair. He did not want to go into the Israeli army. He displaced Amit, the boiled ham, and lived on the twin mattress and helped prepare salads in the store (pasta with sundried tomatoes, black bean couscous, kelp with beets). He played video games and smoked and loitered with the neighborhood characters, and one night, after he had to be fetched from the police station for being drunk and high and harassing a lesbian at the tattoo parlor, Yonah slapped him across the face, and they fought, and when Lucia walked in, she saw broken glass and cigarette butts and camo briefs strewn across the floor. She withdrew into the bedroom, quietly closing the door.

"The yelling is everywhere," she said. "Too loud."

It was then that Lucia started to spend more time away; she liked Central Park, Coney Island, the beach at Far Rockaway, the Cloisters up north.

On her thirtieth birthday, she invited six of her friends to the store and made five pounds of our mother's spare ribs, basted with honey and garlic and five-spice powder. She baked them in the commercial oven, and when burning drippings set off the sprinkler system in the kitchen, Yonah cursed and roared. "Shit pig in my oven," he said. Then he cursed again, but in Hebrew, and not at her.

We mopped while Lucia sat in the café with her friends, and afterward Yonah disappeared into the bedroom until I came to inform him it was time for cake.

"Lucia, she wants a baby," he said.

A baby?

His prosthetic arm sat by itself on a chair. He closed the bedroom door to shut the twin mattress from our view.

"I am forty-five," he said. "I have two children. I love them, but I know myself, I'm done, I can't have no more. Jonny, he is lost, he need to find something for himself. I am his father, I need to help him."

He coughed and heaved. His body sagged. The left sleeve of his T-shirt barely covered his stump, and I found myself looking away.

He was a middle-aged man, struggling.

"She never say she want kids before," he said. "Jie, we need a different life."

It was true, Lucia had never been particularly maternal. Though she'd longed all her life for the slew of aunties and uncles and cousins we never had, she had not spoken about babies or children or motherhood with any kind of affection. Now she fawned over Chaka and Noemie's baby boy.

"Will you have a baby with the Elk?" she asked me.

I blushed. "I don't know," I said.

"I want a baby," she said.

My throat went dry.

I said, "Babies are a lot of responsibility."

Several months passed. Spring came. Yonah brought home a curly-haired black-and-tan puppy from a shelter on the Upper West Side. Lucia named him Lucky. "You could meet him," she said. "You could bring the Elk, too." The thought made me nervous, but I planned a trip—we would attend a gallery opening in Chelsea, visit the store afterward, I told Stefan. And when we did, there was Yonah, smoking outside on the berry red bench, and there was the curly-haired black-and-tan puppy, who trotted over to pee at our feet.

"Cockshit," said Yonah.

Stefan glanced at me. An enormous crane dangled above us. Yellow construction vehicles blocked the street. Jersey barriers lined the sidewalks in front of the store, and the Polish diner next door, and the swanky new wine bar that had replaced City Video. The air was swamped in dirt and noise. Lucky didn't mind; he licked his balls.

"Cocker spaniel–shih tzu," said Yonah. He grinned with his wide duck lips.

"Oh!" I said, bending down to pet Lucky's bearded face.

"Long time, Jie!" said Yonah, laughing. "Welcome, welcome." He embraced Stefan.

"They're really building up this neighborhood," I said. I shielded my eyes to take in the steel scaffolding rising up from the corner of the street. Apparently, the yuppie developers had finagled their six extra stories of air rights from someone else in the neighborhood.

"Is Lucia inside?" I asked.

"Lucy? She's not here."

"Oh. Where is she?" My casual words failed to hide my disappointment. Stefan squeezed my hand.

"She went shopping, I think."

Lucia hated shopping.

Yonah invited us inside, where the café tables were coated with a thin layer of dust. *"Konichiwa,"* he said to Mrs. Sato, who sat alone with her long-haired Pomeranian. *"Chow chow!"* I said. He brought us peppermint green tea and pound cake.

"Lucy, she want to move out," he said.

"What?"

He saw the shock on my face.

"What? Where?"

"I don't know. Out." He coughed. "She need something different, she is woman, she want a baby, this is what she says."

"But she wouldn't do that," I said. "She loves it here, she would never do that."

Unless she was crazy.

I did not voice this last thought aloud.

That evening Lucia called me from Long Island.

"Long Island? What are you doing on Long Island?" I said.

"I'm swimming!" she said, and in the background it wasn't her husband anymore, but the roar of waves. "I'm at the beach. Listen. It's beautiful here."

Our mother always said Lucia was different—restless, wild, born on American soil. (*Why does Chinese girl born in America want to visit poor countries all the time? Aiya.*) For years, I tried to defend my sister's free spirit as a tenacious form of American idealism, which I both respected and admired. But as of late, I could no longer decipher Lucia's motivations, what was happening inside her head. Perhaps Yonah felt the same. "She want a baby," he said. "I won't give her a baby. Who am I to keep her from going, Jie?"

Perhaps he was tired, or perhaps he was wise, or perhaps it was a permutation of love I did not yet understand—he made no effort to stop her. I made no attempt to change his mind.

I wondered if he was out of my life.

She moved out, up north, to a sleepy town in Westchester. She was determined to meet the future father of her child. I tried to reason with her: Parenting is difficult. All those sleepless nights. What about your life with Yonah, in the city? What about the store? What about your work, your writing, your career?

"What about it?" she said.

"The crying," I said. "Babies cry. Children are a lot of work. A lot of responsibility." I recalled Third Uncle's basement, Lucia squawking, red-faced.

She shrugged. Finally, I raised my voice. I called her rash, reckless, irresponsible.

"It's my life," she said. "I can love a baby."

She began to avoid my calls.

Nothing would change her mind.

I moved in with Stefan. We rented a cozy three-bedroom house in a suburb south of Boston. We cooked. We watched movies. We planted rosebushes. We built a deck. We read books in our lawn chairs, discussed over wine, spent Sunday mornings mulling over the crossword in bed. I set up an easel in the shady part of the yard, painted while listening to the Beatles or NPR.

I lived my own life.

And for months on end I did not speak to Lucia, the longest time without contact in our lives. I would cherish this luxury of finding contentment in the mundane, revel in it like a guilty pleasure.

༄

One day, Yonah called.

He said, "Lucia call me from hospital."

He said that was all he understood.

The policeman said when they found her, she was calling for a young girl to come down from a tree. She spoke in soft, soothing tones, switching from language to language. Chinese, the policeman assumed, and Spanish and maybe Hebrew and Portuguese. Except there was no young girl up in the tree. Lucia had taken off her dress and her tights, placed them on the grass and spread the sleeves at right angles, like an X. "*Lai, lai,*" she called. "Come down. *Ici.*" She waved, shivering in her underwear, pointing to the target as though a parachutist might land there. "Please, miss," said the policeman. "Pardon, Señorita. Do you speak English?"

She turned to the policeman and said, "Excuse me, sir, I speak Cyberspace." And then she screamed and screamed.

I did not tell Yonah that story.

I did not tell him because I was afraid he would fight me again, even though Lucia had already moved north and out of his life. I steeled myself against him. I would fight and he would not win this time.

He didn't fight.

When I visited the hospital, he was there. I don't know how he got there, to Westchester; he seemed so out of place in middle suburbia. It was the first time he had seen her in several months. She was thin. He'd brought her favorite vegan chocolate-orange pound cake, and she ate it with delight. She had taken a pill that day, and as a reward, or an act of good faith, the bony blond doctor wrote her a pass that allowed her to go outside. If you try to run, she warned, the police will come get you. It was a warm, fall day, I remember.

We didn't think she would bolt, we mostly trusted she would not, except for that small part of us that was afraid we didn't know this Lucia anymore, the things of which she was capable. So we clenched our teeth as she was released to the front lawn, and she dashed out at full speed, jumping into the piles of red and brown and yellow leaves the landscapers had left in neat piles. She spun around and around with her arms outstretched. "This is so beauuuu-ti-ful," she said, making herself dizzy. We clambered after her with long strides, breaking into a jog when she leapt too far ahead, like parents chasing after a child. We watched as she climbed a tree. Yonah hoisted her up so she could grab a low branch, and she scrabbled up the trunk with her feet. She sat on that low branch for a while, twisting her neck around like a bird, surveying from her new vantage point.

We sat on a bench. Yonah kept checking his watch. "Twenty more minutes!" he said. He did not want her to fall into disfavor with the bony blond doctor, and neither did I. "Fifteen minutes." She acted like she hadn't heard, humming to herself in the tree. "Ten minutes," he said. And I nodded at him, and we stood, erect like soldiers. "Lucy, it's time to go inside now," we said.

"Why, Yo-Yo, what's the time?" she said. A flippancy I disliked.

"Three-twenty," Yonah said.

"Ten more minutes," she said, as she swung her dangling legs. We were anxious. "Lucy, you shouldn't be late," Yonah said, in that paternal tone that used to infuriate me. She looked at him, leaned forward, bending to hug that low branch until her entire body lay horizontal, and then she lurched her legs and flipped over, landing two feet on the ground. "Perfect ten!" he said, and she slapped him a high five, beaming.

"Six minutes," I said. We escorted her back up the sidewalk path, past the security guard, up the elevator.

The bony blond doctor looked stern when we arrived. "What's this I hear," she said to Lucia, "about you being up in a tree?" Yonah and I looked at each other, confused.

"One of the guards said he saw you up in a tree."

Lucia's eyes dimmed. "I didn't do anything wrong," she said, and Yonah said, "She didn't do nothing wrong. She climb a tree. We was there. We was there with her, she didn't do nothing wrong," and I nodded, until the doctor raised her eyebrows, squinted her beady green eyes and said, Hmmph.

"*Ostrich*," he said, later.

I drove him to the train station, half an hour away, where he would take the Metro North to the 1 to the F. "Thank you," I said.

He hugged me. He said, "Take care, Jie."

Four days later, I was informed by a social worker that Lucia's treatment team was planning her discharge.

I drove immediately back to Westchester from Boston. Stefan came with me this time—and though I cringed at the thought of their introduction taking place in the hospital, I also did not want to go alone.

"She's calm," said the social, a plump but prim woman, pink and middle-aged. She led us down a maze of hallways to her office. The Ostrich was nowhere in sight.

"Is she taking her meds?"

"She's taken a few doses of Risperdal. On and off."

"Risperdal?" I shook my head, confused. "But she was on Zyprexa before. Risperdal hasn't really worked for her in the past."

The social frowned. "We often offer it as a first-line antipsy-chotic. She says she'll consider outpatient care."

"Consider?" I balked at the word. "But does she have insight? Does she understand what's happened? I'd like to speak with the attending psychiatrist, please."

"The attending is *indisposed* today," said the social. "Your sister is calm. We can't keep her here. Why don't you see for yourself."

We were shown to the visitors' lounge, where Lucia sat working on a jigsaw puzzle. When she saw me, a glint of light flashed in her eyes.

"Lucia, this is Stefan," I said. "Stefan, my sister Lucia."

"Nice to meet you," said Stefan.

Lucia's face darkened. She studied Stefan's outstretched hand but did not shake it. "So. This is the Elk," she said, with a silly smirk I did not recognize, and inside I felt my heart cave.

"I'm getting out," she said.

"Yes, I heard."

We attempted to make small talk. *Have you eaten lunch yet? What did you do in Group today? Have you been going outside?* Her answers, curt, though intelligible.

"And do you have a plan?" I asked. "For what you're going to do next?"

"A plan? I'll get a job." She folded her arms, tilted back in her chair.

"What kind of work do you do?" asked Stefan.

"Oh, I can do a lot of work. Mostly writing. Reading. Research. I ask a lot of questions, you know."

"I heard you worked in Bolivia for a while," he said.

"Yeah," she said, and her eyes relit as they chatted about the salt flats and flamingos and markets and *choclos* and the altitude in La Paz.

"Here's a question," she said. "A good one. Are you two going to make babies?" She pointed at us with two waggling fingers.

Now Stefan was taken aback, I could see, and my discomfort hung, tangible in the air, as Lucia scrutinized our faces and we said nothing.

"Wait. What? You're not? Well, that seems kind of useless."

A hardness behind her eyes I did not understand. What was it? Contempt? Arrogance?

By the time we left the building, I was on the verge of tears.

"That's not her, Stefan."

"What do you mean?" he said.

"It's not her. That's not my sister. I swear to you, Lucia has never acted that way to me, not ever."

"She wasn't that bad," he said.

"That's not her. That's her illness. And did you hear that social worker? She didn't even give a shit. What the fuck are they thinking, giving her Risperdal?"

I slumped to the curb, face in my knees. Stefan knelt down beside me, an arm around my shoulders. "You've done what you can, *Schätzli*. Honestly, she seemed all right to me."

"But that's not *her*, Stefan. One minute she's sweet, the next she's snide. She's not stable. It's like she's fighting some demon inside."

He did not understand. How could he? But he gathered me in his arms, pressed my head to his chest, kissed my hair. He let me cry and cry, unfazed.

That night, back in Boston, I watched the rise and fall of his rib cage as he slept.

Are you two going to make babies?

Guilt stuck in my throat. I closed my eyes, but images of Tennessee filled my head:

Luciano, ma'am? Are you sure? The filing clerk, a perky golden-hair with breasts like balloons.

Lucy, Ma. Tell them, Lucy.

What, Nu-er?

Like, I Love Lucy. The infant, sticky with drool, in my seven-year-old arms.

Ma'am? I'm pretty sure Luciano is a boy's name. You want me to change it?

What is it? I don't understand.

How about L-U-C-I-A? There. That's better, ma'am.

Ma, squinting. *Lucy-ah?*

Loo-SEE-uh, ma'am. Loo-SEE-uh. Oh, that's pretty, don't you think?

The baby began to whine and thrash.

Ma?

Okay, okay. Lucy-ah, good name. Thank you.

When I woke in the morning, Stefan was reading a book in bed.

"Sweetheart," I said. "I need to ask you something."

"What is it?" he said.

I drew a long breath. "Do you want to have more children?"

"Well . . ." I could see the Swiss in him strive for diplomacy. "My ex and I were so young . . ."

"Because I don't want to have children."

I blurted it straight out. Just like that. These were not easy words, nor easy emotions, demanding a self-evaluation I would have preferred to avoid. I clutched my blanket, cold and clammy with sweat.

"I just thought . . . I thought you should know."

He blinked, slowly. He took my hand. If it rattled him he did not show it. "Why not?"

But I did not know what to say. That I was cold? Unnatural? Perhaps I was selfish? That any maternal instinct I possessed did not come naturally, though responsibility had been sown in me from an early age?

"Your mother," he said, quietly. "And now, your sister."

I nodded. "This is worse." My voice, hoarse and strange. "At least with my mother's illness I knew what to do. This . . . this feels impossible."

His lower jaw protruded as he tap-tapped his teeth, a nervous habit I still found endearing.

"She seemed okay." He kissed my forehead. "I think everything will be okay, Miranda."

Jie, do you believe in happily ever after?
I wanted to, I did.

Two months later, Stefan asked me to move with him to Switzerland. My first instinct: to call my sister. I dialed her number, but quickly hung up. I wanted this decision to be mine, alone, and I wanted to *believe.*

ॐ

That winter, Lucia moved into a house full of Ecuadorians; the shared cooking and communal living suited her. I wondered if Yonah ever thought she would come back to him. One time she visited the store, on her way to Chinatown for a haircut, and he called me from her phone. "Guess who is here?" he said. He cooked shakshuka and brought her tempeh and beets and yogurt-covered pretzels. It was almost like old times.

One day in February, I was back in the East Village, having lunch with an old colleague. At the end of the street, the brand-new luxury apartment building was open, shiny with glass and chrome. It housed a gym on the first floor, where young people sweated on state-of-the-art elliptical machines. I walked past the store, then past it again in the other direction. I did this three times before walking in.

"Jie!" said Yonah, his smile stretched wide. He was bouncing Chaka and Noemie's little boy up and down on his chest. "Long time!"

"Yes, long time," I said. I gave him a quick hug. He brought me tea and cake.

The café was nearly empty. White icicle lights blinked from the tropical-looking plants. Ella Fitzgerald played. Yonah had lost weight. He said business had been slow, ever since the twenty-thousand-square-foot gourmet market had opened a few blocks away. "How's everything?" he said. "What's news?"

"I'm moving to Switzerland," I said. Stefan's start date had been confirmed. He would be working at a hospital outside of Zurich; we would leave at the end of the summer.

"Wow, Switzerland!" he said, his eyes wide. "You will go on a big adventure!"

"I think so," I said. I'd been once already, and Stefan's family were lovely and kind and terribly civilized, the sort of family who congregated for dinner every Sunday at Grossmuti's house. We'd visited Stefan's son, too, at his boarding school in Austria, an awkward scene, with Rafi clearly preferring the company of his Nintendo Game Boy to mine—until the suggestion of tennis was made. Then Rafi perked up, and we played one set while Stefan tried valiantly to remain impartial, including me in their fist-bumps and back-thumps, their affection sweet, even as Rafi emerged the victor, six games to four. But I struggled, too, because I would be the one to leave Lucia this time, an ocean between us. Stefan consoled me, insisted without reservation: *Miranda, you need to live your own life.*

"Have you heard from Lucia, how is she?" said Yonah.

I did not wish to worry him, so I said she seemed fine. I told myself it could be true. Her response to my news had been uncharacteristically flat—a *yeah, really?* with neither approval nor disapproval, only incredulity. She lived north of the city now, and was involved with another man—just a kid, really, a Latino no more than twenty-five, with smooth brown skin and strong cheekbones. He shook my hand sheepishly, lowering his eyes, the one time that I met him, and

I'd struggled, I admit, averted my gaze, tried like mad to bat away the unsettling images popping up in my mind—of him and Lucia fucking like rabbits. He did not offer me tea or cake.

"Yonah, how are *you*?" I asked.

"Oh fine, fine. Good, good, everything is good here," he said. "Some director and actors, they want to make a movie in the store. Maybe the store is gonna be famous soon!" He showed me the new countertop he'd built for the juice bar, the new shelves, new art. "I fix up the apartment, too," he said.

The twin mattress was gone. The bed had been moved to the living room. It was covered with a thick wool bedspread with a lion on it, and on the opposite wall hung a fifty-inch flat-screen TV.

"Where is Jonny?" I asked, and Yonah told me proudly that his son had just started this semester at a cooking school in Albany.

I looked around again. The old bedroom had been converted into a proper office, with a new desk and filing cabinets and a computer that Noemie used to keep the books. "See, I am learning English," Yonah said, showing me his pirated version of Rosetta Stone. I felt proud of him, though I eyed the ashtrays, which were still full, and he said he was trying, he really was, so I told him about a hypnotist up in Boston who was said to produce excellent results.

He opened a new closet with a mirrored sliding door. "See?" He pointed to the top shelf, where Lucia had left her collection of oddly shaped pillows, some shoes, some books, a bag of her small, girly clothes. His shirts and sweaters and heavy winter coat were organized neatly on hangers. "You want to see something?" he said. "Sure," I said. So he pushed the shirts and sweaters and coat far to the right, and there on the left wall of the closet, he'd carefully hung two paintings: the globby brown duck above the yellow goose.

"Remember?" he said.

"Yes," I said.

"Cape Cod," he said, and for one brief moment he could not

conceal the pain in his smile. I asked to use the bathroom. It, too, had been remodeled, with light green mosaic tiles, though dust bunnies stuck in the corners and his camo briefs still lay on the floor. When I came out, he was sitting on the lion bedspread, his head hung low. I sat down next to him, straight and still. Our mother might've said this: that immigrants are the strongest, that we leave our homes behind and rebuild. Everywhere we go, we rebuild.

We sat for a long time. We sat with weight in bent torsos. Without burden of words. And when at last he looked up, I caught his eye, and he reached over to place his good hand on mine, and it was rough and dry and warm.

"Jie," he said.

I'm sorry. My words, barely a whisper.

He did not say more, but it occurred to me then: *This Yonah is my family.*

We are bound, for better or worse.

2

Manuel

I met Lucia at the Big Apple Laundromat on Main Street. I was there to do my monthly wash. She was looking for a room. Carlos saw her first. Serge whistled. Hector yanked my head out of the dryer. "That one," he said, pointing.

She had short hair and peach skin, wore big silver hoop earrings. Browsed the flyers on the bulletin board, rubbing a pink panty to her chin. I noticed her calves, their shape, not thick like the white girls or spindly like the Latinas. And the smooth notches in her shoulders where the bra straps sit. And those *tetas*, just enough. Round and tender, the kind you want to test for firmness like a fruit, feel the weight of them settle in your fingers.

She said, "*Eres Ecuatoriano.*"

"*Sí,*" I said. "How did you know?"

She said, "I love Ecuador."

She had taught English in Quito once, tutored schoolkids in Guayaquil. "Happy times," she said. Smiled wide and her teeth were white and lined up straight so I knew she was an American. "Twenty-six minutes," she said. She licked her lips and I went rock hard. She pointed to a dryer. "Enough time for a drink," I said. "Why not?"

she said. I liked her pretty *Chinita* eyes, all shiny with surprise, like the world was still new or maybe she just bumped into something.

I ducked into the bathroom, scrubbed my hands, washed my face, patted my hair with baby oil. "Yee-ah, Manny," said Hector. Serge and Carlos pounded me on the back with their fists.

We walked down the street to the Dominican bar where they serve two-dollar beers and play bachata, and I saw she could move her hips.

I invited her to my house. We lived eleven of us in four rooms. Not all related, but we called ourselves Vargas. We said we were cousins. It made us feel safe. A week later, she moved into the fifth room, the largest, with sloped ceilings, on the third floor at the top of the stairs. We Scotch-taped her name to the mailbox. She paid one month's rent. Brought in a plastic-wrapped futon mattress, a metal dresser, two suitcases, a TV, a bunch of appliances packed in a garbage bag, three milk crates full of files. She went shopping at C-Mart. Filled the refrigerator with vegetables, the freezer with meats, her bedroom with banana plants. She put her rice cooker in the kitchen. The thing was shaped like an egg but opened up like a toilet, cooked twelve cups of rice at one time. She made tofu stir-fry with rice, fried rice with shrimp, sticky rice with pork. Shared with us, though Serge and Carlos didn't eat tofu and Susi didn't eat shrimp and Hector ate mostly beans. We made rice and beans with plantains, rice and beans with steak, *sopa de pollo* with cilantro and rice. We sat in the kitchen, eating. Watched the small TV on the counter next to the microwave. Carlos said, "No wonder we get along, Chinas and Latinos—inside we are the same, full of rice!"

A week later, I took her out on a date. Brought her to the Ecuadorian buffet. The place had no name, only a blinking red-yellow-blue sign: COMIDA TÍPICA. Inside it smelled spicy, like cilantro and cumin and vinegar. She made neat piles on her plate, a little of everything. Went back for seconds. Her favorite was spicy goat stew. Later, we stopped at the Dominican bar. They were playing salsa so I asked her to dance and Chinita was some great dancer—light as a bird, nailed the turns, responded to the slightest touch. Then we walked in the night and her dark eyes glowed and just when I wondered if I should grab her hand, she slipped hers into mine. All the way down Main Street I was sucked into that hand. She rubbed my thumb with her thumb, stroked my palm with her finger. The rest of my body dangled, like extra. We passed the Pizza Palace, packed with loud teenagers, and the hardware store and the barbershop and the Korean grocery that sold back-scratchers and flowers and toilet brushes, all in those tall buckets outside. El Pollo Loco was standing in front of the police station. *"Chiquita bonita!"* he said, bowing. Chinita dropped my hand to slap his wing a high five.

Pollo was one of those neighborhood characters, wore a giant chicken suit and walked up and down Main Street every day. His costume had no feathers. It was like rubber, pale, a bloated version of what you find in the poultry aisle: raw, sad, plucked. They said he showed up after the first Gulf war. I saw him wandering the streets, or down by the train station, or along the playing fields next to the river. It was some spectacular view there, especially at sunset, the Tappan Zee Bridge over the Hudson. Sometimes El Pollo Loco stopped to talk. Mostly he talked to himself. Once, on the hottest day of summer, I saw him take off that giant yellow chicken head, carry it under his wing like a helmet. That time I saw his face, it wasn't old or dirty, he was like handsome, almost, and then a couple of the local businesses started paying him to hand out flyers—pizza joints and sushi restaurants and Italian bakeries—places that didn't even *sell* chicken, but they made him keep his chicken head on. Some things don't make any sense.

"Está loco," I said to Lucia.

"Why?" she said. "Because he's friendly?" Her forehead creased right between her eyebrows. Sexy.

We crossed the street. This I noticed about Lucia: she was kind. And with her, instead of my usual slouch, eyes down, I noticed more of what was around.

First time we made love was up in her room, under her banana plants. She was good with her hands. Liked to give head. Then our bodies pressed together and it was like falling into warm, soft bread. After, we looked up, fronds above us like a lush green canopy. She said, "Imagine Esmeraldas." We would climb coconut trees, spear squid, lie in hammocks listening to waves. Never been to Esmeraldas, but I saw my youngest brother Fredy, born retarded, with a defective heart, and Mami chasing chickens, and Papi knee-deep in mud from the wet season.

One day Lucia said, "Come with me to Ecuador."

"I don't have papers," I said. I'd never told an American before. But this girl was *Chinita Americana*, different somehow. I trusted her. Anyway, it was no big surprise.

"Do you miss your family?" she asked.

"Yes," I said.

She looked at me like waiting to hear a story.

"I love my family," I said. "I have more *tías* and *tíos* and cousins than you can count. Like enough for an entire village."

"When I was little, I thought I had seven grandmothers," she said. "One on each continent."

"Why?"

"Why not?" She didn't say any more but she smiled.

Two days later, the phone rang in the kitchen. I answered it. She said, "I am in Ecuador."

"Ha, ha, bet you are," I said. She was joking for sure. Figured she was visiting friends in the city, but then she didn't come home that night.

Two days later the phone rang again. "I am in Esmeraldas," she said, and this time I believed her. "Manny, I am blindingly happy," she said.

"When are you coming back?"

She said, "Maybe I will stay in Ecuador forever."

One day a woman knocked on our door. She wore a dark blue suit. I was afraid. I thought she could be with police. She tapped her foot, stared at our mailbox, all the names ending in Vargas. She said, "I am Lucia's sister. Is Lucia here? Where is Lucia?"

She stood straight, her head seemed to float, hair scraped back so tight it stretched out her face. She looked too old and too serious to be Lucia's sister. But I knew she wasn't lying because she had Lucia's eyes.

I said, "Lucia is in Ecuador."

She nodded. Raised one hand to her chin. I could tell she didn't believe it.

"Is she all right?" she asked.

"I think so."

"Has she been acting strange?"

"I don't think so."

I invited her in, showed her up to Lucia's room. I'd been sleeping up there instead of with Carlos and Serge, so my clothes were everywhere.

"How long has she been away?" she asked.

"Maybe two weeks?"

Then she looked me up and down, squinting, like my body hid a clue. She dug around in her purse. Tore a sheet of paper from her notebook and wrote something down, pushed it into my hand.

"If she is acting strange, please call me," she said.

A week later two men knocked on our door. I opened it. They said, "We are police." They held up their badges. I was the only one home. They came inside, stamping dirt on the floor with their heavy black shoes. "Mind if we look around?" said one. I knew it wasn't a question so I didn't answer. Didn't say a word. I stood like a stone, next to a mop, in the corner of the kitchen by the pantry where it smelled like mildew and rice. Thought I could run outside, duck behind the hydrangeas, or jump into the dumpster in the back alley—I'd rehearsed these routes in my head before but they seemed childish and stupid now. I tried to pretend I wasn't there, that I didn't care. I listened to them clomp from room to room. Then they left. I didn't understand—unless it was drugs, not Lucia or illegals, they were looking for.

After, I stayed standing, frozen in the corner, for almost two hours more. Only after Carlos came back, I forced my ass to sit down. Then my whole body shook.

My Vargas cousins worried. Worried about *migras*. Worried about INS. Worried about rent. They hung blankets over the windows so the house was like night even when the sun was out. Every day it was time to put Lucia's things in boxes, put the boxes on the street. "Manny, she is not one of us," they said. I said, "Please, let's wait until the end of the month." But I understood, they were afraid of being sent back to their countries, the ones *Americanos* liked to visit so much.

We watched TV, local news. Hector liked a *chica* named Mindy Griffin who reported on channel 9. She had crazy blow-out hair that swooped around her face like a golden halo. Hector said she had a beautiful mouth, heart shaped, got off on the way she moved her lips. One day it was a seven-year-old girl attacked by a pit bull, then a gas leak on Main, or a three-alarm blaze pulverizing some old Baptist church in White Plains. *"The handiwork of an arsonist,"* said Mindy Griffin. "What is handiwork?" said Serge. "What is arsenic?" said Susi. Hector said bad news may as well come from a pretty face. Carlos said right. And blond hair and tight blazers and big boobs.

One day we found an envelope in the mailbox. It was full of cash.

I counted two months' rent, exact. "From Lucia's sister," said Mrs. Gutierrez, who lived in the basement apartment of the house next door. Mrs. G always wore the same terry cloth bathrobe and dark glasses and smelled like vitamins. "Be careful, Manny. Your *cariña* is trouble," she told me, when Lucia first moved in. I shouldn't have cared, but her words upset me, the way she said them so matter-of-fact. We shared the same landlord—a bald guy named Harry who wore little round glasses and owned a bunch of houses on our street. *Ñaño* knew we weren't cousins, but didn't care, as long as we paid rent on time. Mrs. G was the only one of us who dared complain to him, about the busted heat or clanging pipes or the heaps of garbage piled up in the back alley that never seemed to get taken away. Every morning she swept the sidewalk in front of our houses, chased the cockroaches and mice with a broom. "*Qué vergüenza*," she said. Disgrace. She coughed, tapped her chest with two fingers, complained of black mold in the walls. "Like a poison, making me sick." But she always waved to me when I left for work. She liked me because one time I helped make party banners for her grandniece's *quince*. "I gonna get things fixed around here," she said. "Don't you worry, Manny." For some reason that made me feel good, knowing Mrs. G kept eyes on everyone in the neighborhood.

My boss and I painted signs and shopwindows all over the county. I liked the work, but the driving made me nervous, though Boss almost always drove. The only one of my Vargas cousins with a real driver's license was Carlos. He got his in Oregon, using a fake social security number he'd bought from a guy at a Burger King. "I'll get you one," he said. "No big deal." But I wasn't all that comfortable with lying.

Every month, I sent money home to Ecuador. Cash, rolled in T-shirts with cracked logos or superheroes; Ricky and Juan liked X-Men best, Fredy got Teenage Mutant Ninja Turtles. Took weeks, even months, for a package to reach them. I always worried it would be lost.

But it wasn't only for money I was in the U.S. of A. Mami hoped I could find a way to bring my youngest brother to this country. Poor Fredy, born *retrasado*, but that didn't matter in America, Mami said. "In America, his kind are special. They treat them well." And no one accused a woman of carrying the spawn of the devil, and doctors would still give him the operations needed to fix his heart. "They take a piece of muscle from the leg and mold it like clay," she said. "Then they drill a hole in the chest. *Verdad!* I saw it on TV." I didn't tell her I'd never seen a doctor in America, not even the time I sliced my hand open, thumb to wrist, falling out of a second-floor office window. Boss drove me to the hospital, but I refused to get out of the truck. "I don't trust hospitals," I said. "It's just the ER," he said. But he could tell I wouldn't budge. In the end, he had to bring me back to the shop, wrap my hand in bandages himself.

One month later, Lucia returned. Chinita's skin was brown. She had a small belly. Rubbed it all the time. "At first I thought it was the water, I wasn't used to the water. But then I knew," she said. "Of course, I knew."

She'd vomited every day, she said. In the cafés of Quito, at the markets in Otavalo, on the bus to Atacames, in the sands of Súa, on the sides of the streets of Esmeraldas.

We made love. Her eyes glowed. Her brown skin, too. She was giddy like a breeze.

"What will she look like?" she said.

"How do you know it's a girl?" I said.

"She told me," she said, giggling.

I pushed my ear to her belly button. Didn't hear anything, so I licked it. Chinita slapped me, but we laughed.

I didn't really believe it. There was no sign of this human supposedly growing inside her. No proof it belonged to me. And Lucia was different from the other girls I'd been with before, confident she could get whatever she wanted. I supposed this was part of being American. I wondered if I loved her, but it didn't seem like the kind of thing that should take so much thinking. I always imagined I'd just feel it, and know.

"You have a big family?" I asked her.

"Just a sister," she said.

"Are you close?"

"We used to be," she said.

"And now?"

She was quiet. She patted her middle. Puffed up her cheeks and let out a sigh. "She doesn't approve of me anymore," she said. "She lives in Switzerland."

I remembered how the sister had looked at me, checking me out, like I was a bug under a microscope.

"And your mami and papi?"

Lucia shook her head.

Not sure why I didn't mention her sister's visit, or the envelope with the cash, but it didn't feel right. Clearly she didn't care to talk about her past. This much I understood about other people's families: They were complicated. You didn't pry.

When I was thirteen years old, I dreamed I would have six babies. In the dream I was chasing a rabbit, but it disappeared into the ground. I got a shovel, dug up the ground, but I unearthed a crying baby. Soon as I picked up the baby, the rabbit reappeared, so I dropped the baby and went chasing the rabbit again. I dug up three girl babies and three boy babies before finally, I caught the rabbit. I brought them all to my house with a wheelbarrow. While I boiled the rabbit to make soup, the babies crawled outside and cried. Then I fed them soup and they stopped crying, came in and sat around a big table. Multiplied until there were so many I couldn't keep track of them.

"That's really creepy," said Lucia.

"I love babies," I said. It was true. Ever since that dream I'd imagined it, six shiny faces around a kitchen table, slurping hot soup. This seemed to cheer her up.

"So you are happy?" she said.

"Are you?"

"Yes."

I squeezed her hand. But I was nervous. Afraid. I worried I could not be a proper father without papers.

❧

Fredy was Mami's last baby. She had two before him who died at birth: twins. The first was blue, coiled like an earthworm, not bigger than a mouse. The second was alive, a baby boy, six pounds on the butcher's scale. His mouth opened but he didn't cry, couldn't fill himself with air. Tía Camila cleared his nose with an eyedropper, pumped his chest, sealed his mouth with her lips, tried to inflate him like a balloon. His tiny limbs thrashed, his body jerked. A minute later, he lay still.

We buried the small one in the garden. Papi marked the site with a stone. Mami named the second one Alamar—it meant "to the sea." Mami loved the sea. She wrapped him in white linen, brought him to Canoa, where we hired a fishing boat. Papi and I rowed. Juan and Ricky couldn't yet swim, so Mami hitched them each to empty milk jugs, scared to death they'd fall in. When we were far enough out and people onshore looked like mosquitoes, Mami dipped the body into the water. I watched it drift away, bouncing on the waves. "Your brothers are a part of you," said Mami. "When one hurts, you all hurt." Her voice was quiet, far away. She sat in that boat, still as a statue, held my hand while Papi rowed. Juan hiccupped to hide his sobs. Ricky asked Mami what would happen to us brothers when Alamar got eaten by a fish. "Shut up, *pendejo*," I said.

When we returned to the beach, we made a picnic. Papi caught two bass, grilled them on a fire. Juan and I covered Ricky with sand. Mami pretended to be a monster, fingers creeping toward us as we sucked on sweet granadillas—she captured us, punished us with her tickles. When the sun got too hot on our sticky bodies, we ran into the surf. Ricky cried when he got stung by a jellyfish. "It's Alamar!" he said.

Five years later, Mami gave birth to Fredy at home in a round, wooden tub. Said he slipped out and swam instantly like a fish.

When he bounced up for air, his cry was so loud it startled her; she fell back and hit her head. Tía Camila grabbed the baby with a towel, handed him to Mami when she woke a few seconds later. "It's a boy," she said. Mami was so happy her baby was alive and breathing, she didn't notice anything wrong. Then Tía Camila showed her the gaping tongue, the flat profile, the up-slanted too-far-apart eyes. "He's not right," said Tía Camila. "Hush," said Mami. They brought him to a medicine man who lived up in the mountains. "Best, a dunce," said the man. "Worst, a deadweight. That child is a curse." Mami grew angry. What did he know, this old man who wouldn't even look her in the eye? But I noticed it, too, how the women at the market lowered their gazes whenever we all walked by. It was then, I think, the idea came to her, that I should go to America. "*Hijo*, a man's duty is to his family," she said. "You will help your brother. There is no such thing as a curse." I felt proud, full of purpose. I felt afraid, confused. But I nodded. I was fourteen years old.

༺༻

As far as I was concerned, pregnancy was a woman's business. I didn't need to know the details. Babies have been born since the beginning of time, in caves and fields and taxicabs, I figured they know what to do. "Stop joking, Manny," said Lucia. She punched my arm. Chinita was determined to prepare. She took special vitamins. Went to bed early. Weighed herself every day. She practiced breathing. Drank herbal teas. Joined chat rooms on the Internet. Every week she'd report something new she just learned. "The baby is the size of a grape today." "The baby has fingernails now." "Soon the baby will make pee." "Later, her body will be covered with fur."

Mrs. Gutierrez brought her rambutans. "Sour fruits are good for baby's skin," she said. "Backyard organic!" She bent down to pat Lucia's belly, which lately had seemed to become a public space.

"*Fantástico*," said Lucia. She inhaled. "Thank you." Mrs. G did

manage to grow an amazing assortment of tropical fruits and vegetables in the tiny patch of dirt behind her house. Sometimes Lucia
helped her pull weeds or spread fertilizer. She said it was good for
the baby to know the earth.

"The bugs, the mold, don't you worry," said Mrs. Gutierrez. "I
call Harry, I tell him he has to clean up this place. I put roach bait
all over but with that trash in the alley, nothing I do's gonna help."
She smoothed Lucia's hair. She seemed to have forgotten her earlier
warning to me. Babies changed people's minds. "With this precious
one, you be careful," she said, waving her broom in my direction, as
if already I'd done something wrong.

Lucia asked if I would come with her to see the doctor. I said I
didn't like hospitals. "It's a doctor's *office*, Manny," she said. "No police, no guards." But I was afraid the doctor would ask me questions.
Personal questions. "Trust me," she said, "it will be okay." I held her
hand in the waiting room. She was right. It was not what I'd expected. The room was painted a bright, cheerful yellow with vertical
white stripes, and two monkeys, a zebra and three giraffes. I liked
the animals, the way the room felt like a cage. "It's not a cage," said
Lucia. "What do you mean?" I said. She pointed out that the stripes
rose only partway up the wall. "It's a crib, you silly," she said.

A nurse brought us to another room. Pale green walls, with photos of pregnant women holding their naked bellies, smiling peaceful
smiles. "Who looks like that?" I said. "Not me," said Lucia. She
climbed onto the exam table, lifted her shirt. "Yoo hoo in there,"
she said.

A tall woman wearing a long white coat walked in. "Hello, Doctor," I said. I stuck out my hand.

Politely, she shook it. "I'm the technician. My name is Darlene.
I'll be conducting your ultrasound today."

She squirted a gel on Lucia's belly. Pointed to a screen. "I can't see
anything," I whispered. "Wait," said Lucia. The screen flickered like

the static on TV, then some grayish blobs rolled back and forth. And then, there it was: a baby. With a head, nose, toes. It floated and squirmed, bounced and kicked. Then it lay still, curled up, like it was lazing in a hammock. I laughed out loud. *Mierda!* Holy shit. It was real.

Darlene showed us its fingers, its spine, its fast-beating heart. "Do you want to know the sex?" she asked.

I looked at Lucia.

"Yes," we said.

"It's a girl."

"You see?" said Lucia, grinning.

A girl. My chest swelled. I wanted to tell Mami. I wanted her to feel proud. I wanted her to tell everyone about her first grandchild.

On our way home, Lucia said we should celebrate. We spotted El Pollo Loco by the Ecuadorian buffet. *"Hola,* Pollo," Lucia called out. A cardboard sign hung from a string around his neck: 2-4-1 EMPANADAS@PIZZA PAL. We slapped him double high fives. Then we went inside, stuffed ourselves with goat stew and plantains. When we'd eaten enough, Lucia announced it was time for peach ice cream and pickles. "You're kidding," I said. "I'm pregnant!" she said. We went inside the Korean grocery next door. She settled for vanilla and kimchi.

"To the three of us," she said, raising her spoon.

Suddenly it seemed very real, very serious. With or without papers, I was bound to this *chica* by this baby inside her. I tried to stand up straight.

And then my words slipped out. "Will we need papers?"

"Are you being romantic?" she teased.

"For the baby," I said.

"For the baby we need a piece of paper?" But I knew she understood what I meant. She knew I was always grinding my teeth at night, chewed on the inside of my cheek when I got nervous.

A few days later, Mami called. I told her the news.

"*Dios*, how many nights I prayed that you would meet a nice girl," she said. "*Una China Americana*. And now this!" I could hear her clapping her hands. "You will ask her, won't you? When will you ask her, *hijo*?"

In Mami's eyes it was our family's ticket. Fredy's ticket. Marriage to an *Americana*.

One day I went to work and my boss told me to go home. "Sorry. I hate to lose you, Manny," he said. But there had been crackdowns; I needed papers. "I can't take any more chances," he said. He had a friend who was hiring dishwashers for night shift. Paid a lot less than my old job, but it was a job. "I'm sorry," he said again. I knew there was nothing I could say, so I said, "Sure."

Mrs. G said she'd hook me up with her son-in-law, Maurice, who worked construction. "I tell him you're a good worker. Strong. Good body." I rolled up my sleeve, flexed my bicep. She tapped it with the end of her broom. "You like Maurice. He's a good guy. You hear about that *maniático*, burning down that candy store in Tarrytown? People are crazy." She coughed. I'd seen it on the news. Boss and I worked on that place last summer, painted it orange and white, a big gumball machine on the back wall. Mindy Griffin said the arsonist poured gasoline on old tires, set them on fire, smashed them through the shop's front window.

Maurice picked me up in a pickup truck. Typical *Americano*, with his buzz cut and twangy American voice, blasting thrash metal from an old cassette deck. I didn't like him. But I didn't complain. My Vargas cousins said in California, workers stood on street corners hoping for trucks to come by so they could work for ten dollars a day.

We drove north, through neighborhoods where the houses were mansions, the lawns smooth like golf courses on TV. Streets were empty except for trucks loaded with landscaping equipment:

mowers, blowers, trimmers, rakes, workers who were brown. We parked in the driveway of a big house. By the front door was a fountain where two stone fish spit water from their mouths. Maurice said this was a bath for birds. Dipped his hands and wiped them on his jeans so I did the same. We entered the garage. It clattered open when he swiped a plastic card, and the door inside was opened by a maid. Dressed in uniform, black dress with white lace collar and white apron, like she was out of some movie, and black shoes nice enough for church. She looked like Mami's age. The room was full of closets, with a shiny wood floor, bigger than any of the five bedrooms in my house. Maurice said this was a mudroom. I laughed. I thought of my hometown, Martez, where entire houses became mudrooms whenever it rained too hard. Maurice took off his coat and gave it to the maid. She handed us crumpled blue hairnets. I thought only cooks at restaurants wore these, but I put it on my head. Maurice snorted. He slipped his over his shoes. "This one is fresh off the boat," said the maid. I hated the way she laughed, high and thin, like I was lower than donkey shit.

We walked on thick plastic floor mats up the stairs, then down a long hallway to a bathroom. It was about the size of the mudroom, with blue flowered wallpaper, white floor tiles. A gold mirror hung on the wall above the sinks.

Maurice handed me a sledgehammer. Pointed to the tub.

"Does it leak?" I said.

He laughed. "Come on, *hermano*." Dropped his plastic glasses over his face. Then he climbed inside, took the sledgehammer from my hands, raised it high over his head. "Stand back," he said. "This baby's cast iron." He slammed the hammer into the middle of the tub.

The whole house shook. My ears rang.

"Now that," he grinned, "is satisfying."

I tried to copy what Maurice had done, but it took me six tries to make one serious dent. For the rest of the day I pounded away at the tub and the tiles and the walls. I learned this work was called "updating." To smash a tub to put in another tub. But it didn't feel good. I didn't understand the destruction of perfectly good things. The day was eight hours long. At exactly five o'clock we stopped, so the neighbors wouldn't complain. By then all that was left was loose wires poking out of studs. Whole room was in pieces, dumped in trash cans. We hauled them to the truck.

"So. What'd you think?" said Maurice.

I poked at a splinter in my palm. He grabbed it, dug with his fingernail, sucked and spit the thing out.

"Next time wear thicker gloves," he said. Pushed some bills into my hand.

It was less than I was expecting, but I nodded. Got home and I got straight into the shower. My hair was stiff with dust. The spray of water released pain from my body. I felt the hurt in my hands, my shoulders, my back, my lungs. When I spit or sneezed or coughed it came up black.

By her eighth month of pregnancy, Lucia walked like a duck, feet pointed out, one hand on her back like an old lady. Her T-shirts outlined the shape of her breasts but no longer stretched to cover her belly. She took special care to sleep on her left side, one pillow between her legs, three tucked around her like a nest. I was squeezed to the edge of the mattress, tried not to roll to the floor. She walked to the butcher to buy special meats, rode the train all the way into Chinatown to buy special herbs, boiled everything in a special clay pot with a curved wooden handle and spout.

My Vargas cousins complained about the smell.

"*Ay, chica,* let me guess . . . today's specialty is dead dog," said Susi, holding her nose.

"*Wet,* dead dog," said Hector.

"Chinese people eat cats," said Carlos. "I saw it on TV."

"That's disgusting," said Hector.

"Is it true?" said Susi.

"Oh, yes," said Lucia. "Dog penis is a great delicacy."

"You mean, you've tried it?" Susi shrieked, stuck out her tongue.

"No," said Lucia. "But I would. I don't see how it's any different from eating cow or pig or anything else."

"Mmm, pig," said Carlos.

"This . . ." said Lucia, "is pig's feet." She pulled a bloody hoof from its brown paper wrapping, waved it in the air. "It takes six weeks to prepare this soup." She put the pig's feet in her clay pot, along with a tub of black vinegar and a huge pile of ginger. She would boil this sludge once every morning and let it sit on the stove all day.

"In China, all mothers make this for their daughters," she said. "To drink after the baby's birth."

"But you are American," I said.

"*Cabrón*," said Susi. "Smart-ass. Don't listen to him."

Susi was eighteen, the youngest in the house, just a kid. Carlos said she escaped from a pimp in some beach town near Esmeraldas, but I wasn't sure if I believed him. Most nights she washed dishes at the Peruvian restaurant by the train station. Some days she cleaned houses with a service. She took an English class at the community center, too; Lucia had started helping with her assignments. The two of them sat at the kitchen table after dinner, Lucia kneeling on her chair, head bent over Susi's notebook, as Susi wrote her essays by hand. Sometimes I heard them laughing, snorting like donkeys, acting like they were sisters.

One night Susi came back from work, panting, hardly able to breathe. She said a man had followed her all the way up the hill from the station to Main Street, tried to grab her by her hair. "I bit his hand," she said, staring at her own like it was a diseased object.

"Good," said Lucia. I said maybe she shouldn't wear those shoes with the ridiculous skinny heels. Lucia told me to go away. She made Susi sit, hang her head between her legs. "Breathe," she said, patting Susi's back. She made her rinse her mouth out with warm beer.

The next night Susi said to me, "Does Lucia have family?"

"Why do you ask?" I said.

"It's a secret," she said.

"Come on," I said.

She frowned. "Does she have any friends? You know, girlfriends?"

"Is this some kind of game?"

Susi pouted. She was pretty, even though her eyes were slightly too small and too far apart, her nose too wide and too flat. But her body was tight, with those curvy hips, a perfect heart-shaped ass. She always wore her denim jacket over a miniskirt, and when she walked in those heels, it was like her body was trying to catch up to her head. A baby giraffe, said Lucia. Still, I could see why guys were hot for her.

"Can you keep a secret?" she said.

Susi had decided to throw a baby shower for Lucia. She made a cake with pink frosting, spread confetti on the table, strung up crepe paper streamers and hung balloons from the ceiling fan. Invited Celia and Ruth, our Vargas cousins who were hardly ever around, and Betty, her sister, and Mrs. Gutierrez, who put on a red-and-white-striped housedress for the occasion.

Lucia was surprised. She blinked her eyes. Rubbed her belly with both hands. She pulled ribbons off of presents. Onesies and bibs. Yellow pajamas with duck feet. The clothes, so small. A set of plastic bottles. From Mrs. Gutierrez, a bouncy chair that played tinny classical music. "It's Mozart!" said Lucia. From Susi, a teddy bear and a pink hooded fleece jacket with ears. *"Gracias, hermanita!"* said Lucia. They hugged, cheek to cheek.

I called Mami after the party. "Have you asked her, *hijo*?" she said.

"It's not so simple," I said.

The truth was, I couldn't tell if Lucia loved me. Wasn't sure if I loved her. Mami never talked about love. *Love is so American*, she would've said. I hadn't brought up the papers again. And I hadn't yet told Lucia about Mami's greatest wish: for Fredy to come to America to live with us and get his operations. It wasn't that I wanted to keep it from her, but I also wasn't ready to burden her with the hopes of so many.

Our baby was born with a round face and dark curls and two eyes like lying-down teardrops. Wrinkled, red and angry, she arched her back and shook her fists, screeched like this world was bloody torture. I could see Lucia was alarmed. "Is she all right?" she asked the nurse. The nurse bundled the baby in a blanket, put her in Lucia's arms, and immediately the body went limp. Her head rolled to one side, eyelids fluttered. She yawned, like a cat. Lucia and I laughed. I inspected her ears, her hands, her fingers, her toes, each tiny part perfectly formed. We named our daughter Esperanza Sylvia Bok. *Esperanza*. Hope. Sylvia, for my mother. Bok, Lucia's name. I was afraid to have her name connected to mine. We called her Essy for short.

We spent two days together in the hospital room. It felt protected, like we were inside a cocoon. "We are a family now," I said. "A beautiful family." The nurses brought us everything—blankets and water and juices and ice, and meals we ordered from a menu, like at a restaurant. They changed Esperanza's diapers, checked her weight and pulse, handed us a rubber pacifier when she cried. When Lucia slept, I held the baby, watched soccer on a television suspended from the ceiling, ESPN2. Never thought a hospital could be like this. I wanted to stay forever.

My Vargas cousins welcomed us at the house. Susi strung up yellow and white streamers, hung balloons. Carlos brought back a huge pot of spicy goat stew from the Ecuadorian buffet. We made rice and beans and *sopa de pollo* with cilantro. It felt like home.

When Essy was one week old, we took her to see a doctor at the Main Street Family Practice, between the barbershop and the Korean grocery. In the waiting room, Lucia filled out forms with the baby's name, and our names, and her birthday, and our birthdays, and landlords and employers and important contact information. She could see all the papers made me nervous.

A woman came and shook my hand. Her name tag said "DR. VERA WANG."

"Isn't that the name of a supermodel?" I said.

"Fashion designer," said Lucia. "Famous for her wedding dresses."

When will you ask her, hijo?

I fidgeted, annoyed. I didn't want Mami in my head just then.

Dr. Vera Wang made me nervous, too, the way she cooed and spoke with exaggerated gestures. She weighed our baby on the scale, measured her length, listened to her heart and lungs, checked her hips, counted ten fingers and ten toes.

"She's perfect. Congratulations," she said.

When we returned home that day, Lucia swept and mopped the entire house, top to bottom, while carrying our baby in a sling. She sang while she changed Essy's diapers:

> *Toe bone connected to the foot bone*
> *Foot bone connected to the heel bone*
> *Heel bone connected to the ankle bone*
> *Ankle bone connected to the shin bone*

All the bones. Then a Chinese lullaby. "So she will have a Chinese brain," she said. I wasn't sure what that meant. My Vargas cousins were happy that the house smelled like lemons instead of wet dog.

The next morning I found her on her knees in the kitchen, swatting under the refrigerator with the mop handle. "I found this," she said. "See?" She placed two small husks in my palm. They were brown, brittle, waxy, semitransparent. Weighed almost nothing. "Roach skins," she said. "What the hell! That's disgusting," I shouted. I threw them to the floor. "They shed," she said. "They spread disease." She wet a sponge in the sink, bent down, carefully started to wipe the floor. "I'm going out," I said. It was Sunday. She didn't look up.

When I returned, she was in the bathroom, scrubbing the tub with a toothbrush. "Bleach," she said. "We need more bleach."

"Looks clean to me," I said.

She didn't answer. Continued to scrub like she was on a mission.

"Come on. Let's go for a walk," I said. I took the toothbrush from her hand. I dressed Essy in her pink fleece hoodie with ears, snapped her in her stroller. We walked past the laundromat, the barbershop, the Korean grocery, turned the corner by the Dominican bar. Walked down the hill, past the train station, through the empty parking lots usually filled with commuters' cars, on to the path alongside the rocky pier. It was windy, warm, one of those freak days in January when the air is comfortable but the banks of the Hudson are still frozen. I put my arm around Lucia. My girl. I felt good. Instead of my usual slouch, I stood a little taller. We walked toward the playing fields where I saw my friends Mike and José and Santiago. Everyone was out today. "Hey, Manny," they called. "How come we never see you anymore?" They ran over, thumping the icy ground with their cleats. I used to play soccer every Sunday after church, some Saturdays, some evenings, too. Suddenly I felt self-conscious. I sucked in my gut. In spite of the labor I did with Maurice, I knew I was getting fat.

"I've been busy." I pointed to Essy. She was sleeping.

"*Felicitaciones!*" they said. "That's great, man. Hey, you gotta come back out soon."

"Sure," I said.

"You hear about Jimmy Prieto?" said Mike. Jimmy Prieto was a

friend of ours. A Mexican, and popular because he always volunteered to play goalkeeper.

"Busted," said José.

"What do you mean?" I said.

"Taken away. *Deportado*. Back to the beach."

I felt sick to my stomach. Mrs. Gutierrez was always telling us these
stories. Down by the Texas border, they dumped *Mexicanos* in the
desert without food or water. They took away the little scraps of paper
scrawled with their relatives' phone numbers. Left them with nothing.

"What happened?" I said.

"Broken taillight," said Mike.

"*Estúpido*," said José, waving his hands.

"Pay stubs. Double stupid," said Santiago. "They wanted five
grand just to post bond." I wasn't sure what that meant.

"He's got a kid, a boy," said José.

My throat hurt. "How do you know?"

They shrugged. "Everybody knows," said Mike.

My spine tingled, like a rope of ice.

Lucia and I continued on the winding path until we reached a playground. We sat on a metal bench. Our *bebita* napped in her stroller.
The sun warmed my face. The waves of the Hudson bounced and
sparkled, quietly lapped the shore. I stopped thinking about Jimmy
Prieto. I watched the bigger babies in bucket swings and the even bigger babies climbing steps, and then the ones who were not babies anymore, they were boys and girls jumping off slides. Our baby couldn't
sit up, couldn't bring her hand to her mouth, couldn't steady the weight
of her own head. She could not even focus her eyes yet. But she peed,
she drooled, she sucked, she breathed. She was alive, and she was mine.

I went to work with Maurice when he needed me. Demolition,
mostly, in the suburbs. A basement, a small bookstore to be converted into a Taco Bell, an old shed we tore down easily with our

hammers and hands. Maurice let me help his nephew with the painting of the bathroom at the Scarsdale house. After two months, he'd finally finished the "update," installed porcelain sinks with marble tops, a Jacuzzi tub, sconce lights, a white marble floor that warmed your feet. We painted the walls a deep purple. "Shit," said the nephew. It was his favorite word. "Shit, all that work and it's like taking a shit in an eggplant." But I thought it looked pretty good.

Evenings, I watched my baby discover her tiny mouth, her tiny hands, her tiny toes. Lucia dressed her in pink and yellow. Gave her baths every night in the kitchen sink, boiled water in a kettle to make milk from powder. Every three hours she got up to feed her and burp her and sing to her. Bounced on a big green exercise ball until Essy fell back to sleep.

One night, Lucia dropped the kettle and burned herself. Next morning the skin on her fingers turned black. She cried for more than an hour.

"It's okay. *Tranquila*," I said.

"Do you see this?" She held out her hand.

"Put ice on it."

"It's dead skin. Dead. It will never grow back." She cried again. Wrapped her hand in a wet facecloth, wrapped the wet cloth in plastic wrap.

That afternoon Hector suggested a barbecue. Sunday, NFL playoffs, and all our Vargas cousins were home. We threw steak tips and onions and peppers on the charcoal grill. It was freezing out on the back porch, but I warmed my hands on the fire. It felt kind of American.

I took a plate of food up to Lucia. She shook her head.

"You're not hungry?"

She poked at the meat with a fork. "It's all burnt," she said.

I went back to the kitchen. Everyone was already huddled around the TV. A referee threw a yellow flag. "What's *encroachment*?" said Serge. "When they don't throw the ball fast enough," said Carlos. "That's delay of game," said Hector. None of us really knew. A few minutes later Lucia walked in. Her eyes were red. She didn't look at us. She switched off the television.

"What are you doing?" I said.

"Electromagnetic waves are bad for the baby," she said. The baby was sleeping upstairs.

I could feel my Vargas cousins staring in disbelief, waiting to see my reaction. My hands shook as I switched the game back on.

"Don't do that," she said.

"You're tired," I said. I herded her out of the kitchen. Had to drag her up the stairs.

That night she cried herself to sleep. When I woke in the middle of the night, she was still crying. She wore socks over her hands like mittens.

"Are you cold? Why are you crying?" But she wouldn't answer. She looked pale. I thought she might be sick. I offered to change diapers. To get up at night and make milk from powder.

"There are bugs crawling on my body when I sleep," she said. She lay on her back, staring up at her banana plants. "I can't stand the crying."

"No one is crying," I said. Essy was swaddled, asleep in her bassinet.

"They are coming to take my baby away," she said.

"No one is coming," I said. But I didn't like the sound of her words.

One day I came home and our baby had tiny cuts on her face. I rubbed Vaseline on her cheeks, clipped her tiny fingernails. Lucia sat on her knees in the middle of the futon mattress.

"Why aren't you happy? Why are you crying?" I asked.

"They're talking," she said. "Manny, I miss Ecuador."

"Please, Lucia," I said. "Come have some breakfast. Hector is making pancakes."

"I'm not hungry," she said.

Later, I brought her a plate of pancakes. "Lucia," I said, "Essy would like to see you." I set the plate on the floor, held out the baby, whose face was puffy from crying.

"Not now," said Lucia. She shook her head. Sat cross-legged on top of her hands.

"She needs a diaper," I said.

"You do it," she said. "Television is not good for her."

That weekend, she stayed in her room at the top of the stairs, watching infomercials, volume all the way loud. She came out only to go downstairs to the kitchen, filled a small bowl with pig's feet soup, took the bowl back up to her room.

I didn't know what to do.

I brought Essy down to Carlos's room, the smallest one on the first floor, closest to the kitchen. Before I moved upstairs with Lucia, I'd shared this room with him. It had red-brown shag carpet, flowery paper on the walls above the wainscoting. I had just learned this word, "wainscoting," from Maurice. Dirty laundry rested in a heap on the mattress. I put a towel on the floor, put Essy on the towel, let her suck on my pinky finger until she fell asleep. I pushed aside Carlos's clothes, lay back, stared up at the peeling paint. Splotchy brown rings circled the ceiling light, like giant coffee stains. I couldn't recall if it was like that before.

And then I remembered: the piece of paper. The one Lucia's sister had placed in my hand. I dug through my wallet. Pulled it out. I studied it a long time, until I'd memorized the numbers. But I couldn't bring myself to call. Mindy Griffin's voice floated from the TV in our kitchen: three newborn puppies abandoned in a dumpster; brutality charges against a veteran police officer; a young couple injured in a hit-and-run.

Just the other day Mrs. Gutierrez told us six people on Cedar Street were taken during a raid. "*Drogas*," she said. "*Colombianos.*" My Vargas cousins were on edge. I understood. It worried them when outsiders got involved.

Susi said this happened to women sometimes.

"*Postpartum depression*," she said. She was proud to use these words.

"How would you know?" I asked.

"She has a hole inside her. *Gigante*. Where the baby used to be. Boom, bam." She clapped loudly. "You think a body can take this, like it's nothing? How can a woman be fine like this?"

I'd never given it a thought. Like being pregnant, it was what women did.

"I don't know how to fix such a hole," I said.

"First, you need to be *kind*," she said. I was being scolded by a child.

Her sister, Betty, lived in Pleasantville, had three daughters of her own. Susi asked her to come. Together, they scoured and scrubbed every corner of the bathroom, filled the tub with smelly water, bathed Lucia in herbs. "Calendula, plantain leaf, sea salt," Betty explained. Patted her with a towel warmed with a hair dryer, tied a wide, stiff band of cloth around her waist. "This is custom for new mothers, to wear the *faja*." They combed her dark, wet hair.

Lucia looked fresh. We sat in the kitchen drinking tea.

"Do you feel better now?" I said.

She nodded.

Betty patted her hand. "What is that smell?" she said. She wrinkled her nose, turned to me, like I was automatically the offensive one.

"What?" I said.

"Oh, that," said Susi. "You mean the wet dog?"

"Why are you looking at me?" I said.

"It's the soup," said Susi. "Right, Lucia?" She smiled. Showed dimples I'd never noticed before. Susi, she could be a sweet girl sometimes. She wanted to make things right.

"Esperanza talks to me," said Lucia.

"Yeah? She only screams at me," I said. I was trying to make her laugh.

"A mother knows her baby's cries," said Betty. "From the womb."

As if on cue, we heard Essy crying. I stood to go upstairs.

"Oh, Manny," said Lucia, grabbing my arm. "She's tricky. She says she's just fooling around."

"Tricky?" I said.

Her face, stiff with concentration, made me uncomfortable.

"Yes," said Lucia. "She communicates telepathically."

We heard Essy resume her screaming. Betty brought her down. "Her pajama is completely wet," she said.

I felt sick. Ashamed. My throat was dry, my tongue stuck to the roof of my mouth. The room started to spin. I took my daughter from Betty, grabbed tight on the railing as I brought her upstairs. I wiped her. Changed her. Wedged her floppy limbs into a clean long-sleeved onesie, fumbled with the too-many small snapping buttons. When I returned to the kitchen, Susi and Betty were busy peeling potatoes to make *locro de papa*, potato soup. I sat, holding my daughter in my lap. Glanced sideways at Lucia, who was still sipping her tea quietly. Chinita scared me now. I couldn't understand what was happening inside her head.

"Don't do that," she said. "Don't try to control me."

I felt in control of nothing. I didn't know what to say. Finally I said, "Babies are not tricky."

That night, the telephone rang. I picked it up. It was Mami. "*Feliz cumpleaños!*" she said.

"What?"

"One hundred days old!" she said. "I learned it is Chinese custom to celebrate, no? How is my *nieta*?"

"Fine."

"And Lucita?"

"Fine," I lied.

"You are lucky, *hijo*," she said. "Twenty-six years old and a father, a man. Why are you not asking her to be married?"

I didn't know what to say. I thought of my brothers, Ricky and Juan, that day on the boat in Canoa, before Fredy had even been born. Suddenly, all I wanted was to see them again.

"I have to tell you something, *hijo*. Hello? Are you there?"

"What, Ma?"

"It's about Fredy. He is not so well. His heart, his lungs. He is coughing all the time, he cannot get enough air."

The words, jumbled somewhere between my ears.

"I'm sorry, Mami. I can't talk right now. I have to go."

I hung up the phone.

One week later I came home and our baby was lying on the floor, naked and covered in shit. Lucia sat at the kitchen table, dressed in her bathrobe, socks on her hands. She sipped her pig's feet soup.

"Jesus Christ," I whispered. I ran to my daughter, took her up in my arms, sprayed her down in the kitchen sink. I cleaned her with wet napkins. Her face, her hands, her feet, her body. I dried her with a dish towel.

Lucia sat, motionless. "What?" she said.

I felt dizzy. Hot rage shot up my throat. I walked over to the stove.

"What are you doing?" she said.

I didn't know. But then I was picking up Lucia's precious clay pot by its curved handle. I smashed it on the floor. Lucia screamed. The baby cried. I felt clammy, hot and cold. My throat tightened. Neck greased with sweat. Lucia stayed sitting, didn't move. I knelt by her chair, grabbed her shoulders, leaned in so she could feel my breath on her face.

"*Basta*. Enough of this shit." My voice cracked. "What in hell kind of mother are you?"

I moved back into my old room, the one I used to share with Carlos. Carlos moved in with Celia on the second floor. I brought down Essy's bassinet, stuck it in the only place it would fit, between the head of the mattress and the wall. I boiled water to make milk from powder. I woke every three hours to feed her and burp her and rock her back to sleep. In the morning, the skin on the inside of my cheek was swollen. My jaw hurt when I spoke. I prayed to God. I asked Him to explain to me what was happening to Lucia.

Susi asked her sister to help. Betty agreed to look after the baby during the days.

"Betty is responsible," I said. "She is very good with babies."

"No one takes my baby," said Lucia. She planted herself on the kitchen floor, next to Essy, who gurgled in her Mozart bouncy chair.

"You don't take care of her," I said.

"No one."

"Please be reasonable." My throat, hoarse.

"I am her mother." Lucia folded her arms.

"*Óyeme mujer*," I said, loudly. "You can't even take care of yourself."

"I gave birth to her. Did you give birth to her? Did you carry her and grow her for nine months?"

"You sit all day with the TV on. You said TV isn't good for her."

"I am her mother," she repeated. "No one will take my baby."

I punched the wall.

"Manny!" cried Susi.

My knuckles hurt. I bit my cheek. I reached down for Essy. Lucia slapped my arm away. She scowled, lips tight, body stiff like an angry animal. "I will call the police," she said.

I hated her.

Susi knelt. She held Lucia's hand. "Until you feel better," she said. "Only until you feel better. Until you get some rest, Mama. Right now it is too much, you need to rest. You will feel better soon."

Lucia's face softened. Finally, she agreed.

Every morning she dropped off Essy at Betty's house, picked her up in the late afternoon, kept her clean until I got home from work. It was all I asked.

One Saturday, Lucia disappeared late morning and didn't come back until nine o'clock at night.

"Where have you been?" I asked.

"Gardening," she said. She often wore her padded green gardening gloves, even at home. "Where have you been?"

"Working," I said.

"Oh, yes," she said. "Gardening is a lot of work. I'm tired now."

It was snowing out.

Every evening, I gave Essy her bottle. I rocked her, sang to her, lay her in her bassinet. When she was asleep, I went to the bathroom to take my shower. One night, Susi was there, wearing two towels. One around her waist, the other on her head. Her breasts were full, her nipples wet and stiff. "Oh" was all she said. She blushed. But she didn't move. I couldn't resist. I unraveled the towels. She was soft and smooth and smelled like cocoa and rose perfume. I brought her to my room, closed the door. I combed her wet hair with my fingers.

She put her mouth around my penis, dug her fingernails into my thighs. I struggled to keep quiet. I rocked my hips, thrusting harder and harder, waiting for her to stop me—but she didn't, not even when she gagged. And then I no longer worried about Lucia, lying with her banana plants just two floors above, or Esperanza, sleeping miraculously through my cries. I closed my eyes and saw Sheetrock crumbling, collapsing pipes, the splintering of marble tiles. After, Susi massaged my back, my shoulders. She kissed my lips and blew life into my lungs. "Someone needs to take care of you, *mi amor*," she said. I immediately straddled her from behind.

Next day I couldn't look at her. When she spoke to me shyly I grunted, or pretended not to hear. But I lay awake late, listened for her footsteps, heels clicking on the kitchen floor. She got in after midnight. Smelled like sweat and soap, deep-fry oil and rose perfume. "Come," I said. I knew it was wrong, but I undressed her quickly. I locked my bedroom door.

One morning, a week later, Lucia came down from her room. Her hair was combed. She wore pink lipstick, silver earrings, a red sweater and white lace gloves.

"Smells good in here!" she said.

Hector was making pancakes. She smiled, eyes shiny. "I'm taking Essy to the doctor," she said.

"Why?"

"Three-month checkup. Don't you remember?"

She scooped Esperanza from her bouncy chair, carried her upstairs. The chair continued to chime. I wanted to kick it. Mozart was getting on my nerves. When she came back into the kitchen, Essy was dressed in a yellow sweater, black-and-white-striped leggings, a yellow bow tied in her hair. "My bumblebee!" Lucia threw a burp cloth over her eyes. "Where's my bumblebee?" she cooed. Essy pulled it off. And then she smiled. My baby's first real smile. She looked so much like her mother.

"Do you want to come?" said Lucia.

"I have to work," I said. But I smiled at her as encouragingly as I could. Remembered the first time we went to the Family Practice. Now I was just glad to see Lucia dressed. Maybe she was feeling better at last. I reached over to squeeze her shoulders. She slipped away, hummed.

I stepped outside to wait for Maurice. Pressed on my eyelids with my fingers. While I waited, I prayed to God. I prayed for Lucia. I prayed for forgiveness. I swore I would never touch Susi again.

"You're working hard, Manny," said Mrs. Gutierrez. She waved to me with her broom.

"Good morning," I said.

"You hear about the barbershop?"

"No."

"Burned. No more." She threw up her hands. "I could smell the smoke in the middle of the night." Mrs. G always slept with her windows open, even in the dead of winter. In summer we could hear her snore.

"Jesus Christ. No way." I sniffed the air, but all I caught were lingering hints of Susi's sex and rose perfume. "Was anyone hurt?"

"All okay," said Mrs. G. "Sure, okay, but completely ruined."

That day Maurice brought me to a new house, the biggest one I'd ever seen. Built like a castle, all gray stones with towers and spires. Iron gates opened to a circular driveway and another fountain, this one with naked angels spraying water from their penises.

"Rich people," said Maurice.

"Crazy bastards," I said. Guilt or no guilt, fire or no fire, I was in a damn good mood.

Maurice led the way through a maze of long hallways and stairs. We were headed to the guest wing of the house.

"Another bathroom?" I said.

"You think there's something better?" said Maurice.

I shook my head. I hadn't meant it like that.

"One time I did a trailer park demo, found a dead lady buried under her cats. No joke." He laughed like this was hilarious.

This bathroom was connected to a bedroom with a bed that was wider than it was long. I figured an entire family could sleep in that bed, including *tíos* and *tías* and cousins. Everything in the bathroom was white except for the black marble floor tile. Double porcelain sinks with sleek faucets, white marble countertops, sconce lights that were shaped like flowers. It looked a lot like the one we had just finished installing at the other house, except the other one was purple.

"This is for updating, too?" I said, confused.

"No," said Maurice, slapping the hammer into my hands. "This, my man, is for *style*."

This time it took me only two tries to break open the tub. By late morning, I was ripping up the floor tiles with a crowbar.

For lunch, we sat on the bed of the truck. I snapped open my carton of rice and beans. It felt good to be outside, even with the chilly wind.

"You got a girl?" Maurice asked.

"Yes," I said. But I was not sure why he would ask. It made me feel suspicious. When he chewed, I could see pieces of meatball in his mouth.

"How long?"

"Three months old."

Maurice looked at me funny. Then he burst out laughing. "Aw, shit, man. You have a *girl*, like a kid. I meant girlfriend, *chica*, you know."

"Oh."

"So you're married?"

I didn't answer.

"Aw, shit. You knocked her up."

I felt hot.

"Don't feel bad, kid." Maurice laughed. "Women know how to get what they want."

Late afternoon he came to check on me. I was sweeping up, re-sealing the plastic on the doorways with blue tape.

"It's for you." He held out his cell phone.

"What?" I couldn't imagine who would find me on Maurice's number. I took the phone from his hand.

"Mr. Vargas?" It was a woman's voice. American.

"This is Mr. Vargas." I felt strange addressing myself by that name.

"This is Dr. Vera Wang, from Family Practice."

"My baby," I said. My heart beat faster. "Esperanza."

"Esperanza is fine. Perfect. But it's your wife, Lucia."

"She is not my wife." I could hear the doctor cough, then cover her cough with her hand.

"Lucia needs help," she said.

"Our family helps us. Our cousins." I thought of Susi. Her dimpled moon face. The curve of her hips. Her heart-shaped ass.

"Mr. Vargas, I don't think you understand," said the doctor. "Lucia is not well. She needs medical attention. Serious attention. The baby is not to be left alone with her."

I was silent. My tongue like stone, the phone like a brick. "But where?" I finally said.

"The emergency room," she said. "If Lucia does not get proper help I will have to call CPS."

"CPS?" I did not understand.

"Child Protective Services. I'm sorry. It's the law." She hung up.

I still didn't understand. Couldn't think straight. I wanted to ask what just happened, where Essy was now, what Lucia had said or done. I knew Child Protective Services could take children away. I didn't know if they involved police.

Maurice was outside, checking the debris chute set up at the back of the house. "You look like shit," he said. My entire body felt rubbery and damp. I sat down on the pavement. "Come on," he said. "Let's get you home."

He drove fast. I asked him to slow down. When I stepped out of his truck, I knew right away something was wrong at the house. Even from the street, I could see lights on inside. This was never the case, since the windows were kept covered with blankets. I walked up the gravel path to the front entrance. Tapped the door, which we always kept locked. It swung open. "Hello?" I said. I peeked my head in.

Las cucarachas.

Cockroaches. They lay everywhere. Scattered by the refrigerator, ringing the sink, clogging the drain, dead on their bellies or flipped onto their backs, spiny legs squirming uselessly in the air. Must've been hundreds, all sizes, shiny and fat like beetles, narrow and spindly with long antennae still moving, just barely, so the linoleum floor seemed to writhe. I tiptoed and hopped to avoid their dark, oval bodies; they crunched like crackers under my boots. They'd come out of cupboards, closets, floorboards, walls, come out from hiding to die. From the hallway I peered into the first-floor bathroom. A handful floated in the toilet. A few lay lifeless under the sink. "Jesus," I said. Essy. I ran to my room. The bassinet was empty, except for the green pacifier we'd brought home from the hospital. I ran three flights of stairs to Lucia's room. Two of the bugs lay at angles on top of the comforter neatly covering her mattress, as motionless as if they had never lived. I ran downstairs, outside, puked.

Mrs. Gutierrez had appeared on her front stoop. She sat, broad and bulky from all the layers she wore under her terry cloth robe. When she saw me she smiled and waved excitedly. I walked to her. Saw she held a baby in her arms. My baby. Esperanza, bundled in a yellow blanket, asleep. "You see, I told you I would take care of things," she said. "I called the Health Department and that asshole Harry finally got the place fumigated. Finally!"

"Where is Lucia?" I said.

"*No sé.*" She shrugged. "She brought Esperanza to me and she left. You want to wait for her? I can make you a cup of tea."

"No, thank you," I said.

I grabbed Esperanza. I would not have my baby staying in that disgusting house. I walked five miles to Betty. Walked five miles back. By then Hector and Susi had come home. Together we swept and mopped and sprayed and wiped. We opened every door, every closet, every drawer in the house. We hunted dead roaches until every last bug was gone.

Then I remembered about CPS.

I went upstairs to wait for Lucia. She had covered her television with a batik cloth. I lay on her mattress, looked up at her banana plants. When I woke it was three a.m. I went downstairs. Climbed into bed with Susi. Lucia didn't come back that night. Or the next night. Or the next.

I worried. I took out the folded-up piece of notebook paper. It was dirty, creased. I didn't know what to do. Still, I was reluctant to call.

"But what if something terrible has happened?" said Susi.

"She's an American," I said.

"She could be hurt," said Susi.

"Maybe she is in Ecuador," I said, and for a moment I filled with hope. It was possible. It could be true.

"Or murdered," said Susi. Her eyes widened.

"Don't be ridiculous," I said. "You watch too much TV." She could be such a child. But I was afraid. Anything was possible.

"You must call. If you don't call, I will call," said Susi. She grabbed the piece of paper out of my hands, pulled out her brand-new flip phone. "Mi-ran-da Bok," she said. And then she was no longer a child. She was serious.

She went into the kitchen. I sat on the mattress. It sagged. I thought about how it had been in this room before I moved in, and before Carlos, Juno, and before Juno, Tina and Roby, and before them, who knew who else. Who knew how long it had been sitting here, with its tired springs and stains, its sad life of its own. Just as I lay down, I heard Susi's footsteps, marching back.

"It's Lucia's sister," she said, handing me the phone. "Lucia is in the hospital."

The words came at me in a stream that hardly made sense. *Postpartum* and *schizo* and *history*—history of this, history of that. *"She's sick."* And then, *"None of us want to involve Child Protective Services."*

CPS. I understood that.

"Should I go to see her?" I asked.

There was a long silence.

"Please take care of Esperanza," said Lucia's sister. "I'm sorry. I know this is a difficult situation. I promise I will call when there is more news."

The words swirled in my head. All night. All day. Lucia's past, this history, these behaviors that had complicated names. Night came again, but I couldn't sleep. I wrapped Essy in a fleece blanket, strapped her to my body in a sling, stepped outside. The wind howled but I felt strangely calm, welcomed the snow on my face. Most of Main Street was closed, dark behind metal gates. The barbershop was boarded up, but the smell of smoke and burned plastic remained. Only the laundromat churned with its bright yellow glare. I stood by the glass door, propped open to let in air, even in the dead of night. I stared for a while, hypnotized by the sounds of thumps and bumps and scrapes, the sizzling hum of fluorescent lights. As I turned to leave, I slipped on a clear patch of ice, nearly fell. Essy didn't stir. Inside the ice, cigarette butts frozen inside. The sight made my stomach churn. I spotted El Pollo Loco walking on the opposite side of the street. I thought to wave, but when he saw me he stopped, took up private conversation with a parking meter. I walked past the Ecuadorian buffet, the Korean grocery, the Dominican bar playing bachata. Thought to go in, but I liked how the cold air was clearing my head. I felt light, almost empty. Then I felt sad, then guilty, then dizzy with strange relief: I realized I was no longer worrying about Lucia. She had others to take care of her now.

"*Hijita*, I will take care of you," I whispered to Essy. Felt the heat of her cheek on my chest. Her long, dark lashes caught the snow. I zipped up my jacket, shielded her from the wind. I wanted to believe it, that I could be a good father.

⁂

I spent my days with Maurice.

"How's the wife?" he asked.

"*Loca*," I said. I bit my cheek. Tasted blood.

"Aren't they all?" said Maurice. He laughed like a sick donkey.

I did my best, but I had more dizzy spells. I kept grinding my teeth. All the time I had dreams I was taken away—by boat, by spaceship, by horse, by donkey. In one dream I was lassoed with a strand of spaghetti and drowned in sand. I worried my baby would end up abandoned on the street. With no father, no mother, what would happen to her? When Hector and Serge asked, I told them Lucia was not feeling well. "She is spending time with her family," I said. They seemed skeptical, but didn't say any more.

Mami called. She said, "When will you ask her?" The words didn't make sense. But I couldn't tell her the truth, I was too ashamed. Didn't even know where to begin. The closest I came, I said, "What if I don't love her, Mami?" She said, "*Ay mi amor*, you *learn* to love."

Every day after work I drove Lucia's car to pick up Essy from Betty's house. Always I started the engine first, then stepped out to check the signals and lights. I drove exactly the speed limit, no more, no less. When we got home I put Essy to bed. I cooked dinner. *Sopa*

de pollo with cilantro. Rice and beans. I sat in the kitchen watching
the small TV, watching the clock, waiting for the hours to pass until Susi would come home from the restaurant. Every night, she
would slip off her denim miniskirt, crawl into my bed, reeking of
soap and sweat and deep-fry oil and perfume. Some nights we made
love. Hot and furious, like wild animals. Some nights we slept, my
hands cupping her *tetas*, the left slightly larger than the right. Many
nights the baby woke every two hours, coughing. We took turns
bouncing her on Lucia's big green exercise ball; I was always afraid
it would burst. Susi laughed. Maybe this was the only time I laughed
back. "Why won't she sleep?" I said. "Is she sick?" My bouncing
slowed. My eyelids drooped. "A baby misses her mother," said Susi.
Some nights I wished Esperanza had never been born. Some nights,
I bounced and bounced until the weight of her tiny head finally
came to rest on my shoulder. My baby, content. It was magical. I felt
reassured, knowing I could love her so much it hurt. *Yo soy tu papi*, I
whispered. *Mi hijita, mi amor.*

Sleet. Not rain, not snow. I once tried to describe it to Ricky and Juan. Said it was God's spit. I'd lived through enough winters in New York, but this kind of cold still felt completely foreign, would never sit right in my bones. One morning after I dropped off Essy, I had to drive to a new work site up north. Sleet splattered down, thick and wet, loud like bullets on the windshield. When I got there, Maurice told me to go home. "Waiting on permits," he said. "Sorry. Don't worry. Take the day off, man. Relax."

I'd never come to this area before. I looked at my map, drove extra carefully. Stopped at a gas station to check all my lights. I decided to visit a coffee shop, ordered toast, read bits and pieces of the local newspaper. Police with new leads on the arsonist. Bingo fund-raiser to help rebuild the church. "Ugly day," said the waitress. "Can I bring you anything else?" "How about spring," I said. It was the last day of March. Heart of the wet season at home, and probably why I hadn't heard from Mami in a while. My coffee tasted good. The waitress was pretty. She flitted from one table to the next. Storm let up, turned to rain. On my way out I even saw a patch of sun. Maybe my surprise caused me to take a wrong turn. I found myself heading into a denser part of town, rather than to Route 9 which would take me back south. I passed a soccer field. A bunch of guys were out, mostly brown, not too organized. I turned around, parked on the street, sat and watched for a while until my calves started to ache. I took off my coat. It was foggy, drizzling again, when I stepped out of the car and walked toward the field. "You play defense?" said a guy in a red sweatshirt who was in charge. I nodded. He pointed to the other team. I spent the next few hours running in the icy rain, muddy, soaked to the bone. I charged, I jumped, I slipped, I swore, I slammed my body into frozen ground. The players were okay, but nobody got any traction. It was a sloppy game. I didn't care. It felt like heaven.

After, I sat in the car, heat full blast on my face. Found a towel in the backseat, took off my shirt. I liked the sensation of my winter jacket resting on my skin. I drove exactly the speed limit to Betty's house. Betty was holding the baby in her lap. "What happened to you, wet dog?" She pointed to my hair. Wet dog. I still had had no news of Lucia. When Essy saw me, she smiled. "Let's show your Papi something," said Betty. She plopped Essy on a thin blanket on the floor, where she sat, drooling. She *sat*. Straight up without sagging forward or toppling over or hunching down on one side. "She sits by herself," I said. Betty nodded proudly. This smallest of things seemed a miracle. Betty brought me a dry T-shirt and a pair of her husband's jeans, which were too tight and too short, but I didn't care.

"*Mi amor*," I sang. I had to sing loudly, so Essy could hear me over the rhythmic thumping of the wipers. Traffic was heavy for this time of day. Bumper to bumper, so I kept my foot on the brake. This weather caused accidents. Orange cones lined the middle of Main Street. Up ahead, a diamond-shaped sign. As I approached, I could read it: CHECKPOINT AHEAD. BE PREPARED TO STOP. Orange, the color of hazards. I cursed. Closed my eyes. I knew this process was to hunt drunk drivers, but I knew they also hunted people like me. For some reason I never imagined it would happen in daylight, not on such a miserable day. For some reason, my next thought was: *They will confiscate Lucia's car, and what will I tell Lucia?* The skin of my arms grew cold under my jacket. My armpits soaked with sweat. I would say I left my wallet at work. But my tongue was dry like sandpaper, stuck to the roof of my mouth. I saw the officer approach. He had a thin mustache, dark glasses on his forehead, wore a reflective orange vest like a construction worker. I rolled down my window. "License and registration," he said. He shone a flashlight in my face though it was day. I squinted. Opened the glove compartment. Started rummaging through Lucia's envelopes. He walked around to the passenger's side, his breath condensing on the window, still aiming the flashlight in my face. He opened his mouth and was about to say something when Essy let out a wail. I couldn't see my baby, she was strapped in her car seat, facing the rear. Lucia had insisted it was safest, though it made her carsick; for a while she'd thrown up almost every day. The policeman tapped at her window. She whimpered like an animal.

"This your baby?" he said.

"Yes," I said. "My daughter."

Now Essy's whimpers became grunts, then howls, like the monkeys in the rain forests of Ecuador.

"She doesn't like the car," I said apologetically.

"I can see that," said the policeman. He tapped the flashlight on the rear window. Then back up front near my face. "Sorry, you're not going to like this."

I was too frozen to answer. My chest tightened. I squeezed the steering wheel so tight it hurt my hands.

"She puked all over the place."

"Oh shit," I said. "I'm sorry."

"You'd better pull over and clean her up," he said. "Move along." He waved me through.

"Thank you," I said. I rolled up the window, turned down the next side street and stopped the car. My chest heaved. I dug out some wipes and cloths that Betty always kept with the baby diapers. Unlatched my seat belt and climbed in the back.

Essy was asleep again. Her face was wet. Her bib, her clothes, the straps of her car seat were all soaked with drool, sprayed with curds of spit-up, reeking of sour milk.

"*Gracias, mi amor*," I whispered.

When we got home, Mrs. Gutierrez was standing on our front stoop. She wore an oversize parka over her bathrobe, rubber boots on her feet. Still, she was holding her broom.

"I am sorry," she said.

"What is it?" I said.

She looked down at her feet.

"Is it Lucia?"

She shook her head. "They came."

"Who?"

She didn't answer.

"Lucia's sister?" I said.

"No," said Mrs. Gutierrez. "Light-haired. I don't know this lady." My heart sank.

"With *migras*. They took Susi," she said.

She explained that a woman had come to the door accompanied by two uniformed men. They asked about a baby. Susi refused to answer their questions.

"Assholes. They were assholes, that's all," said Mrs. Gutierrez. "They took Susi away, so rough. I will pray for her, she will not be mistaken for a *Mexicana*. *Mexicanas* they haul away in a truck, dump them in the middle of the desert."

"Stop," I said. "Please stop." I did not want to hear any more. My throat was tight. I sat down on the stoop. I hung my head between my legs and tried to breathe.

I told Maurice I needed to take a break. I couldn't bring Essy back to Betty's house. Betty no longer wanted to speak to me. I didn't blame her. I went to Dr. Vera Wang. "Lucia is in the hospital," I said.

"Good," she said, but she denied calling CPS. I didn't understand. My Vargas cousins asked around, but mostly stayed quiet, kept their heads down. No one wanted to be next. I gathered the belongings Susi had left lying all over the place, her clothes, her books, her high-heeled shoes. Couldn't stand to see them, so I brought them back to her room, the one she'd originally shared with Celia and Ruth. Her brand-new cell phone lay by her mattress. I slipped it into my pocket.

Hector found me a dishwashing job at a local diner. Carlos said his cousin Delia had two daughters, she could take Essy for a little extra cash. I worked. I slept. When I slept, I dreamed my coffee-stained ceiling collapsed and Lucia and Mami and Susi fell on top of me. I was too tired to tell them to go away.

One night, there was a catfight in the alley. One night, there was a trash fire in the alley. Mrs. Gutierrez called 911. I shoved Essy into her pink fleece hoodie with ears. Ran outside. I started walking to-ward Main Street. I didn't want to be anywhere near the house.

I walked and walked until I reached the police station. Sat outside on the front steps. It was dark. It was cold. My baby girl lay asleep in my arms. I thought, I can stand up now. I can reach for the door. Pull it open. I can walk in and say, *I give up. We don't belong.*

3

Crote Six

Lucia Bok was brought into the medical facility by the police at 10:05 p.m. A shopkeeper had reported seeing the young woman on Main Street, yelling and waving her arms at the traffic lights, wearing minimal clothing despite freezing temperatures. She was agitated, "difficult to subdue," the officer said. "They're going to take my baby," she repeated, again and again. When asked whether she lived nearby, she replied, "I live in the People's World."

Dr. Olga Watts, on-call psychiatrist in the ER, examined Ms. Bok, who responded only when addressed as "Lucy." Dr. Watts scanned the police report. "Who is trying to take your baby?" she asked. Lucy gestured like a schoolchild, zipped her lips with her fingers, threw away the key. "Has someone hurt your baby?" asked Dr. Watts. No. Had she hurt her own baby? No. Where was her baby now? At home. Who was taking care of her baby? Lucy fidgeted, poked at her cuticles, but eventually answered: her cousins. There was no reason to think these statements were false. Lucy was able to count backward from ten, correctly name several ordinary objects, including a pen, a bracelet, a pillow. She identified a watch as "a speedometer," a trash bin as "a velociraptor." Tangential, but clever, in a way. When asked what day of the week it was, she replied, "Mother's Day." Did she have any history of mental illness? Lucy shrugged. Had she ever been hospitalized? "Uh," she said, twirling her index finger by her ear. "Duh. I gave *birth*."

Throughout questioning, she remained calm. At times she stared at the blocks of fluorescent lights on the ceiling, cocked her head to one side, as if eavesdropping on an important conversation. She denied visual or auditory hallucinations.

"How old is your baby now?" asked Dr. Watts.

"Growing," said Lucy. "Every minute." She tapped her watch. She tapped her foot. Then all of a sudden, she stood up. "I should get going," she said, as if this interview were a mere inconvenience of which she had just now tired. She pulled a thick wool blanket over her hospital johnny, the one the police had given her when she was found.

Though Lucy Bok denied any thoughts of harming herself or her baby, Dr. Watts found herself uncomfortable. The girl was off, that was evident; whether she posed an imminent danger to herself or others was less clear. But those twiggy arms and legs, full breasts, and loose middle corroborated a baby's existence. The deadness in the woman's eyes made her ache.

"I'd like to call one of your cousins," she said, brightly. She would check hospital records. "Can you wait here, please?"

"I'd rather go," said Lucy. "This room makes me uncomfortable."

"It won't take long. Please, take a seat."

At this, Lucy Bok snapped. "I need to go now," she said. Attempting to leave the room, she pushed Dr. Watts aside with her hand, tripped on a rolling stool, which she kicked with her foot, sending it flying into the wall. "You're with *them*," she said. She narrowed her eyes. "It's time. I need to go." Her tone was sharp, bitter, carefully controlled, her previous placid demeanor erased.

Dr. Watts called for backup. Code Green. Lucia Bok entered the inpatient unit as an involuntary admission.

Nurse Bob was working intake for Crote Six, the sixth-floor ward in the east wing. It had been an unusually busy shift. One of the manics spiked a fever of 104.8, churned up into a delirium, had to be transferred to a medical unit. Several other patients, disturbed by the commotion, required sleep aids to settle down. Now, at 3:50 a.m., another new admit. He buzzed the security lock. Tall Paul Arroyo, largest of the safety officers, escorted Lucy Bok, one hand loosely grazing her elbow.

She looked familiar. Bob was sure he'd seen her before. A year ago, maybe two? Time passed with few markers in a place like this, and while at the beginning of his career he could recall the seasons by his patients' stays (the suicidal glee club singer that first summer, the manic cop who gambled away his house that first fall), by now they were mostly a blur. Depressives, psychotics, addicts, abusers, borderlines in search of three hots and a cot, especially after the holidays. It wasn't fair to label them, but he did. Everyone did. It kept things manageable.

"Good morning, Paul," he said.

"More like good night," said Tall Paul. "I'm off after this one." He palmed a yawn.

The next instant, the girl had twisted her body, ducked under Paul's armpit, caught the last crack of the closing door. "Ms. Bok!" he yelled. From Tall Paul's fingers dangled her johnny, by a sleeve, like Peter Rabbit's jacket on McGregor's fence. The shock froze them both for a half second while she slipped down the hall, fled through the stairwell door. Tall Paul shot after her.

Nurse Bob shook his head. How far did she think she'd get like that, practically naked on a bitter cold night? He tried to recall if she had pulled this kind of stunt before. He didn't remember her as a troublemaker.

Tall Paul returned a minute later with scratches on his forehead, a gash on his left cheek. He presented Lucy Bok in handcuffs, shivering. "We're going to take care of you here," said Nurse Bob, gently. With his island accent, smooth dark scalp, single metallic ball stud earring, he was an imposing figure, hard to forget, but the girl squinted without any sign of recognition. He administered a standard two-milligram dose of Haldol, handed her a toothbrush, paper slippers, a fresh pair of scrubs. "You'll feel better after you sleep," he said.

Coco Washington woke when Lucy was brought to her room. She bolted up in bed, positioned herself on all fours, arched her back like a cat and hissed. "Take it easy. Lie down," said Nurse Bob. Loco Coco, one of Crote Six's frequent flyers, returned every winter (same complaints, different hairdo).

Coco waited until Bob had left, popped up again. "Hey, psst, what's your name, baby?" she said.

"Where's the baby?" murmured Lucy.

"My babies are full grown," said Coco. "Except for my two-headed baby. It died. I gave birth to a two-headed baby once. In Jamaica. Hell yeah, that made me famous."

The two-headed baby usually sparked conversation. Coco's new roommate remained quiet, hugged her knees to her chest, rounded her spine like a shrimp.

"They said those babies were from Satan; they said I was a witch. But they were just two sad little boy babies stuck in one body. Poor souls, not made for this world."

Coco pretended to wipe away a tear. She reached into her nightstand drawer, pulled out a pack of cinnamon gum. "Want one?" Waved a stick in the air.

Lucy sat up, crisscrossed her legs. "I hate this place," she said.

"What's to hate, baby?" Coco snapped her powdery pink gum with her bicuspids. "You got a bed, your meals, the meds—all-inclusive, baby. It's the fuckin' Holiday Inn." She laughed, a cackly, high-pitched laugh. Slapped her cheeks with her frizzy dyed-orange braids. "We gonna be friends, right? I'll let you do my hair."

No response. Trust Bob to stick her with another dud. She watched as her roommate climbed out of bed. Then Lucy Bok collapsed to the floor.

"Jesus Christ," muttered Coco.

The body on the floor began to buck and writhe. "Help. Somebody help me, please." Tears spilled down Lucy's cheeks. Muscular spasms wracked her neck, her jaw, the left side of her face.

Coco gaped, horrified. "Holy babies. Shit, shit, shit." She jumped up and ran for help.

"It's the Haldol," said Nurse Bob. Side effects were common, but he rarely saw it get as bad as this. He gave Lucy two milligrams of Cogentin in a paper cup. She swallowed, too dazed to argue.

Returned to bed, Coco watched her roommate roll onto her side, stack her limbs, her body folded along its vertical axis. Such enormous dark eyes, like two gaping holes in her head. Pretty enough to be a movie star, at least in those foreign films.

"You okay now, baby?"

To her surprise, Lucy reached out her hand. "Can I have some gum?" she said.

A connection, thought Coco. Together they chewed, in near-dark.

"Helps the dry mouth," said Coco. "I got the dry mouth bad."

"Like cotton," said Lucy.

"You another suicidal?" said Coco.

Lucy glanced around the room, confused. She cupped her mouth with her hands. "I'm a mother," she whispered.

"Me, too," said Coco. "So we're gonna be friends, right?"

Lucy flopped back down, buried her face in her pillow. Coco lay wide awake. She watched Lucy toss and turn, settle finally onto her back, deepening breaths transitioning into slack-jawed snores. As gray light seeped in the cracks below the room-darkening shades, Coco grew alarmed. She tiptoed to her roommate's bed. With a hesitant hand, as if to pet a stray animal, she tilted Lucy's head to one side. Then slowly, carefully, using thumb and forefinger, she extracted the sticky pink wad from Lucy's mouth. Coco recognized a hazard when she saw one; she was determined to protect her new friend.

She hadn't been expecting it, exactly. But then it came as no great surprise, more a rush of relief, as though she'd been sucking in her gut for days, or weeks, or months without knowing, and could finally now exhale. The voice, slightly accented—Russian, perhaps?—the tone professional, yet kind. A doctor. A doctor? Miranda Bok rose from her chair. Doctors never called. This one was calling Switzerland. She was touched.

"My sister has a history," she said. "I'll fax it to you." She was prepared, this time.

But the doctor worked emergency. It was the end of her shift. Lucia would be transferred to Crote Six, one of the behavioral health units upstairs.

"I'll be there. Please don't let her out. Tell them I'll be there. Tell them she has a baby now."

"It's okay, Ms. Bok," said the doctor. "Stay calm. Breathe. Your sister will be in good hands."

"Thank you," said Miranda. "Thank you for letting me know."

From her bedroom window, the view: the clock tower in town, its copper-green cupola rising above sloped roofs, the cows dotting the hillside, the snowy peaks of Glärnisch in the distance. Day after day, it still felt unreal; she half expected Heidi to prance by with her golden pigtails. She stepped outside to the back porch, overlooking the bright blue waters of the Stöcktalersee. Sat in her wicker rocking chair next to her geraniums and her easel, pried open her laptop, checked her calendar. Two meetings to reschedule, including one with a health care nonprofit she'd been referred to by Stefan's colleague at the hospital. But it was doable. She booked a flight from Zurich to JFK, direct. Should she call Tess? But it had been so long since they'd last spoken, and such awkward circumstances, and Tess lived in Brooklyn now, and it was still some ungodly hour over there—she made a reservation at an inn on Route 9 instead.

She packed a small suitcase that evening. Her two sharpest work outfits, including her pearls, everything else for warmth. From her file cabinet she fetched a folder full of notes and clinical papers, pamphlets and guides. Despite their uninspiring titles (*Treatment Options*, *FAQs 4 Caregivers*, *Bipolar Symptoms and Signs*) she'd read every one of them multiple times, had *25 Tips for Coping with Schizophrenia* practically memorized.

1. You cannot cure a mental disorder for a family member.

She put it away, sighed.

"Do you really need to go?" asked Stefan.

They were eating dinner. Baked chicken with roasted potatoes and cauliflower. They had weekend plans. Tickets to a charity gala, for which he'd already rented a tux. His Grossmuti's eightieth birthday party on Sunday.

"I'm sorry," she said. "But if I don't, I'm afraid they'll let her out again." She recalled the incident with Yonah. How he'd interfered. But then that last hospitalization in Westchester when he hadn't dared, yet still Lucia had failed to be properly stabilized. She would not let it happen this time.

"For how long?" asked Stefan.

"I'm not sure. Maybe just a few days." The words, escaped, an optimistic puff in the air. She knew already it was a lie.

The next morning, she selected an outfit. Her most flattering jeans. A charmeuse silk blouse. No, the red wool sweater. No, the collarless black blazer. Her cream-colored, double-breasted bouclé coat, pink cashmere scarf, black knee-high leather boots with stiletto heels.

"How do I look?" she asked.

Her husband whistled softly through his teeth. "Pretty hot," he said.

She frowned. "Hot?"

"Okay, not hot. Stylish. Great. Slim?"

"Keep trying," she said.

The correct answer: Authoritative. Fierce.

Stefan laughed. "Miranda, here, I almost forgot. . . ." He snapped open his satchel, pulled out two rectangular boxes, neatly wrapped.

"What's this?" she asked.

"Chocolate. *Swiss* chocolate. Hospital food is the worst. Believe me, I know."

"Oh, Stefan. Thank you."

"I love you." He brushed her lips with his. "Tell her I say hello, okay?"

She nodded.

⚭

She was stuck in the middle. A gangly German to her left. A fat American to her right. The fat American said hello and the "o" smelled like pepperoni. "Want one?" he said, waving two sticks of Slim Jims. She declined. He produced a tin of peppermints from his pocket. "Oh, just take one," he said. "I'm trying to be polite." She minded, yes, she did—that blubbery face, his squishy elbow bumping hers. She accepted, out of politeness.

She hated airplanes. Always, since her very first ride. She could still picture him, that pudgy *gweilo* seated next to Ma, vomiting into a paper bag. The smell, making her queasy, and that terrible *sound*. She clamped shut her ears, breathed through her mouth, while Ma stared straight ahead, unblinking. Ma had changed since Ba died. Her face seemed wooden, and she rarely showed her teeth when she smiled. Partway through the flight, a spotty brown hand protruded from between the headrests. *Xiao hai, ni yao ma?* The *ayi* behind them waved a roast pork bun. Queasy still, but oh, the aroma! *Ma, I'm hungry.* But Ma maintained her waxy stare. She took Miranda's hand, placed it over her belly. *Shh. Be quiet.* Ma, pregnant. Full of Lucia, the size of a winter melon. *I miss him*, said Miranda. This whispered, meek, because it wasn't quite the truth, because her father had been too much a mystery, because he worked all the time, because he reported to the government, deployed to strange locales, and when he did appear she never knew what to expect—whether he'd come bearing cherries or wine gums or a gold bracelet for Ma, swing her around and around in circles (*higher, Ba! higher!*), or grunt and lock himself in the bedroom (*don't bother him, Nu-er, your Ba needs to be alone*). The last year, he'd mostly disappeared, and they'd moved from their small city apartment into her grandparents' house, and Ma and Po-Po had fought all the time. Until the day Ba died. Ma had woken her early in the morning, dressed all in black. *A car accident*, she said, and no one said more. Ma and Po-Po stopped fighting. They stopped speaking to each other altogether. And now she and Ma were by themselves, riding on an airplane to America.

Still, she thought it was the correct thing to say: *Ma, I miss Ba.*

Ma turned to her, still rubbing her hand on her belly. *Shh, Nu-er, don't be stupid.* That *gweilo* vomited six more times.

Miranda's cheeks flushed. She would not refer to her father again, and later, much later, when Lucia asked, the answer was the same: *Your father died in a car accident.* And Ma's lips would press into a thin, red line.

Charo Alvarez, social worker, was young, ambitious, new to the unit, determined to prove her worth. She disliked the sister immediately, found her pushy and abrasive. This job was about managing expectations.

"Did you read the notes I faxed over?" asked Miranda.

"We've had an extremely busy morning," said Charo.

Miranda bit her lip. She had been polite last time. With that German doctor, the Ostrich. She'd stepped aside and waited patiently for the updates from the nurses, for Lucia to accept the medication, for the professionals to do their jobs.

"*I* read them," said Nurse Bob. He held up the sheaf of papers. *Lucia Bok. Three previous hospitalizations. Disparate diagnoses. Schizophrenia. Schizoaffective disorder. Bipolar with psychotic features.* The notes were meticulous, included a detailed list of all previous medications as well as explanations of their outcomes. *Haldol caused her to shake. Cogentin blurred her vision. Zyprexa, 15 mg, clears her up quickly. Dislikes side effects. Abilify and Seroquel give her migraines. Risperdal, questionable effectiveness.*

"I remember you," said Miranda. "You were around last time when she was in that ward downstairs, with that German doctor. I know you tried to keep her."

Bob remembered, too. Miranda Bok had inundated Hobart Five with an unprecedented number of messages—phone calls, faxes, e-mails, letters—begging them to keep Lucy until she'd fully stabilized. But Lucy had been released. If a patient posed no immediate threat, they had no choice.

"Are you trying the Zyprexa?" asked Miranda.

"She's refused it. Says it knocks her out, doesn't like the weight gain."

"She's not entering a beauty pageant, for God's sake."

"The treatment team wants to try Abilify," said Charo.

"Abilify? No. She won't stay on it. It gives her headaches. It's in the note I faxed you." Miranda angled her body to face Nurse Bob. "I'd like to speak with the doctor about filing a medication over objection order. I know it can take awhile."

"Well, that's not possible," said Charo. "Such orders are only used as a last resort."

"I know that," said Miranda. "But Lucia is stubborn. And she has a baby now. This time she has a *baby*."

"The *team* makes the decisions," said Charo. "Dr. O'Hara is aware of the situation with the baby."

"Then you can tell him that if he lets her out and anything happens to that baby, I'll sue him and this entire hospital," said Miranda.

Charo glared at Nurse Bob.

"Well, a court order *is* a bit premature," said Bob. "It's usually best if they come to terms with the meds on their own."

"Part of managing their own illness," added Charo. She folded her arms across her chest.

"I'd like to speak with the doctor," said Miranda.

"Dr. O'Hara is very busy," said Charo. "He's only here in the mornings, and then he's busy seeing patients."

Busy. Miranda was used to this, socials shielding the docs, running interference. "Nurse Bob, please, my sister is stubborn, but once she's back on her meds, she'll be fine. The meds really work for her. She has insight. Properly stabilized, she'll be fine." She kept repeating it, as if unaware she spoke the words aloud: *She'll be fine.*

"Your sister's lucky then," said Nurse Bob.

"Lucky?"

"Sure. For some people, the meds never work."

"I haven't been able to get in touch with the husband," said Charo. She had tried Manuel at the house number several times, but no one answered.

"Boyfriend," corrected Miranda. "I think we should leave him out of it."

"Why is that? Is he abusive?"

"No, no."

"Negligent?"

"No."

"Is he employed?" asked Charo.

"Yes. But he's . . ." Miranda had no interest in involving Manny. He was young and immature and scared as hell, no doubt. Who wouldn't be? She fished for the right word. ". . . uneducated. About her condition, that is. He doesn't know about her illness or her history, and their relationship is . . ."

Charo's eyebrows arched.

"Delicate. And he's so busy working, taking care of the baby." That was true, too. A baby, crying all night, tested the most committed of mothers; what could be expected from a young, single male?

"But surely he should know what's going on?" said Charo. "She *is* the mother of his child."

"I don't see how it's necessary to involve him, at least while she's in here," said Miranda.

"I suppose so," said Nurse Bob.

Charo chafed. She didn't buy Miranda Bok's sudden sympathy for some young Latino kid. She would make recommendations to the team as she saw fit.

"Maybe when she starts clearing up on the meds," Bob added.

When, not if. Miranda forced a smile.

Nurse Bob liked Miranda Bok. He liked her energy. He liked that she still had the fight. Too many family members came through the ward already wrung out by the system, slumped in their chairs, panning the room with dull eyes. No opinions, no hope, no fight.

∽

"You sure you're not hungry?" said Nurse Bob.

Once again, Lucy had flatly refused her morning meds. Now she was refusing her lunch. She'd even refused the chocolates her sister had brought, donated them to the nursing station.

"You need to eat," said Miranda. "You're so thin, Lucia."

"Well, I *am* hungry. But this is probably drugged." Two triangles of tuna sandwich sat on Lucy's tray, untouched. The only food she'd consumed in four days came from sealed packages: three cartons of milk, three fruit cups, one bite of Saltine cracker, which she immediately spat out, claiming it tasted like mushrooms.

"They wouldn't drug your food," said Miranda.

"I slept for two days," said Lucy. "It was Friday, and then, poof . . ." She snapped her fingers. "It was Sunday. Two days disappeared, like that. I was drugged."

Miranda opened her mouth. Closed it. Recalled the *25 Tips*.

6. Listen. Empathize.

"That was the Haldol," said Nurse Bob. "Administered for your symptoms, and to help you sleep. I gave it to you. It wasn't in your food."

"Help me?" said Lucy. "I had a *seizure*. I went blind."

"Those were unfortunate side effects. I'm sorry." Bob felt awful. It had been listed in the notes.

"You see?" Lucy glared at Miranda. "I'm not making it up."

"Maybe your sister could bring you some food," said Bob.

"Of course," said Miranda, who perked up at the thought of being of practical use. "Is there something you'd like?"

"Well . . ." Lucy cocked her head to one side. "I suppose . . . sure. King crab legs. I could eat king crab legs."

"Crab legs? Did someone say crab legs?" Loco Coco called from her armchair by the wall of windows. She liked sitting near the potted plants—mostly spiders, jades, ficuses in plastic yellow buckets—the extra oxygen helped her asthma. "Who's got king crab legs?"

"My sister," said Lucy.

Coco shuffled over, dodging Big Juan Lopez's swinging paddle. Crote Six's Ping-Pong champion had just crushed one of the depressives. A new admit was next on the list.

"Sister. You ain't twins, are you, sister?" Coco snapped her gum.

"No," said Miranda.

"Me and Lucy here, we're like twins."

Lucy twisted her neck from side to side, showing off the pigtails Coco had braided for her.

"And I *love* Lucy." Loco Coco cackled. "*I Love Lucy.* Get it?"

"Yup," said Lucy.

"And you're bringing us king crab legs."

Nurse Bob watched the annoyance brew on Miranda's face. She exhaled slowly, drained it away. "King crab legs it is," she said.

"From the Golden Duck," said Lucy.

"Golden Duck?" called Big Juan. He set down his paddle. "Mu-shu pork, please."

"Mu-shu pork, got that?" said Lucy.

"Sesame chicken," said Hulk, the three-hundred-pound addict whose nickname derived from a tendency toward belligerence on the days he wore green.

A small crowd gathered. Scallion pancakes. Hot and sour soup. General Tso's chicken. Buddha's delight. Miranda pulled out an old shopping receipt from her leather handbag, flipped it over to jot down notes. Nurse Bob, pleased with the unit's sudden jovial mood, went to fetch Lucy's meds from the dispensary.

"The sooner you take this, the sooner we get you out of here." He offered her the small white pill.

Lucy's face clouded. She folded her arms, closed her eyes. "My body is my temple," she said.

"Don't mess with the temple," said Loco Coco. She stroked Lucy's hair.

"But the pills help you," said Miranda.

Lucy's eyes snapped open. "*You*. Don't *you* talk to me about pills. You and your Swiss doctor with your Swiss telepathy, putting me in this prison."

"Oh, Lucia. This isn't a prison. And I haven't even been in the country . . ."

"Oh, Lucia. Oh, Lucia. You think I'm crazy? You're the crazy one. You're PSYCHO crazy, putting me in here again."

"I didn't."

"What kind of person does that?" Lucy's voice rose to a squeak. "What kind of person locks up a woman who just GAVE BIRTH?"

"Lucia, please, all I want is for you to get better, so you can take care of . . ."

Nurse Bob found himself holding his breath.

"Esperanza."

"Es-per-an-za? So you know her name now? Essy is *my* baby. Not theirs. Not YOURS. YOU ordered it. You put me in prison."

"I didn't even know you were here until they . . ."

"They. THEY. You and the military strategists put me in this disgusting lockbox."

"Hey, come on, let's calm down," said Nurse Bob. He placed his hand gently on Lucy's arm.

"Calm down? Or what? You're gonna stick me with another needle?"

"Come on, baby," said Loco Coco. "I'm watching out for you. Everything's gonna be okay."

"Lucia, please . . ." said Miranda.

Lucy clamped her hands over her ears, squeezed shut her eyes. "LA-LA-LA-LA-LA-LA-LA," she belted, like a petulant child. She gestured with her chin in Miranda's general direction. "HER. GO. AWAY."

A delusion will not go away by reasoning and therefore needs no discussion.

Coco laughed, her high-pitched laugh.

"Don't take it personally," said Nurse Bob.

"But I don't understand," said Miranda. "I just don't understand why it's so hard for her to take those fucking pills."

Bob sighed. It was the million-dollar question. Why? *Anosognosia.* Impaired awareness of illness, also termed "lack of insight." Some part of the brain, anatomically damaged, such that it could no longer recognize its own malfunctioning. It wasn't an easy concept to grasp.

"How about this," he said. "What if I were to tell you, right now, that you don't live where you live? That your house isn't your house. You'd probably laugh and tell me to stop messing around. But then imagine you went home, only to be arrested by the police. The nice people at your address didn't want to press charges, so the police brought you to the ER, where a doctor insisted you take psychiatric drugs for your 'delusion' that you live where you *know* you live. Would you listen? Would you take the meds? Right now?"

Miranda shook her head.

"Of course not. Because you know who you are and where you live."

"Sure."

"But so does someone with a psychotic delusion. It's *that* real."

There were other reasons, too. Meds didn't necessarily revert a person to normalcy, though they might mute the symptoms. Some patients grew attached to their delusions, some ditched the meds as soon as they felt better, and the nasty side effects were for real. Blunted emotions, drowsiness, nausea, tremors, decreased sex drive, high cholesterol and diabetes, and weight gain, which especially devastated young women. "And then there's the stigma. High-functioning young woman like your sister, whole life ahead of her? She has her pride," said Nurse Bob. "So denial is understandable, too. Right?"

"But she can't even function now," said Miranda.

"That may be our opinion, but what if she doesn't see it that way?" Bob could see Miranda Bok struggling, still confused.

That evening, she called her husband in Switzerland.

"She hates me."

"*Schätzli*, what's going on?" It was two in the morning there. She could hear him yawn. "She doesn't hate you."

"Oh, yes, she does."

"She's just angry."

"At what?"

"Think about it. Wouldn't you be?"

It was true, anger and hatred were not the same, but Miranda often had difficulty distinguishing between the two.

"Were you sleeping?"

"I *was* sleeping."

"Sorry."

"It's okay."

"What's been going on? Anything new?" She wanted to listen, to bring her mind to a different place.

"I heard a good joke yesterday. What do testes and prostates have in common?"

"What?"

"Nothing. There's actually a *vas deferens* between the two."

She groaned.

"Come on, it's funny."

She laughed. "Kind of funny."

"Rafael has the flu. His headmaster called. Apparently, he's been missing a lot of classes this term. And Grossmuti's birthday party was a bit dramatic. Sophie slipped on a tablecloth and sprained her ankle." Sophie, his seven-year-old niece. A sweet, precocious girl, talented at piano, who Miranda was tutoring in English.

"Wait, what? A *tablecloth*?"

"Don't ask. My sister was not happy with this caterer."

"Is she okay? Sophie?"

"Sure. She'll be fine."

She'll be fine.

A freight train, struggling to punch through her sternum. He caught the strain in her silence.

"Miranda, maybe you should just let the professionals handle it now. The doctors. Take it easy for a day. Order some room service. Watch the Wildlife Channel." Their first trip together to Maine. The Congolese bonobos, the mating rituals, the nonstop sex.

"I haven't been able to speak to the doctor yet," she said. Peeved. "I'm getting screened out by yet another self-important social worker. How professional is that?"

"The one I met?"

"No. She's in a different ward now, thank God. But you know those *professionals* will let her out the minute I leave."

"But you've given them her history. You're communicating with the case manager. You're doing everything you can do. Right?"

This was Stefan. Always calm, always rational. Sometimes she wished he'd stop it, and just be on her side.

The next morning she drove to the hospital, attired in her gray pin-striped Calvin Klein suit, her pearls, her knee-high leather boots. But her neck felt stiff, her stomach tight. She willed herself to enter the building, that sea of white coats and green scrubs, creaking gurneys and antiseptic smells. She stepped into the elevator, stared at the button that would shuttle her up to Crote Six.

HER. GO. AWAY.

Breathless, she retreated. Into the foyer. Through the revolving glass door. Ejected to the cold, bitter gray.

Back in her hotel room, Miranda opened up a spreadsheet, closed it after ten minutes, unable to concentrate. She would take Metro North into the city that day. Then the 6, down, all the way to China-town, where she focused on the gum spots on the sidewalk, smells of durian and fried meat, expertly navigated her way through the crowds. She visited her favorite bakery on Mott Street, bought a sesame milk tea, four pineapple buns to go. She stopped at a souvenir shop to purchase an I HEART NY sweatshirt for Rafael, a snow globe for Sophie, baseball caps for the other nephews and nieces. Then she walked sixty-plus blocks up to Central Park, and then into the park, crunching on slush and ice, over and under bridges, across the Sheep Meadow where a group of rosy-cheeked coeds played Frisbee in the snow, past the band shell, the fountain, the frozen pond where aggressive mallards fought for tourists' bread crumbs. It was late afternoon by the time she stopped to rest on a bench, eat a pineapple bun, watch the pigeons, and her pulse, by then, was steady and calm.

She dialed Tess from a pay phone. Tess, her oldest friend in the world.

"Oh my God, Miranda! Why didn't you tell me you were coming to town?"

Embarrassed, she could come up with no good explanation, only excuses: *My sister . . . not sure . . . how long . . .*

They met at a coffee shop on the Upper West Side. Tess came through the door bundled in a short wool coat, and Miranda could sense her friend's new radiance instantly, even before glancing to verify the bump at her middle.

"Tessie, I'm so happy for you!" A sensation in her chest, an enormous swell, as if this was the truest thing she'd felt in years. And as Tess spilled the details: due date, sex (boy!), morning sickness, et cetera, she found herself prickled by only the tiniest hints of jealousy.

"And what about you? How's life in Switzerland?"

Serene, orderly, quaint. "It's kind of surreal. We're in a small town outside of Zurich. Lots of cows. I'm a bit of an exotic feature—people assume I'm one of those store-bought Asian brides."

"Ugh. That must be annoying."

"Yeah, though maybe it's also a little flattering." Miranda forced a wry smile. "Have you ever seen those Web sites? The women are gorgeous."

"They're probably eighteen!" said Tess. "We were gorgeous, too, twenty years ago. Remember Jamie Cabrera? I ran into him last week, he asked about you."

"Jamie Cabrera . . ." A Columbia debate champion Miranda had dated for a few months her sophomore year.

"He's a millionaire, founded some start-up company with Steve Lim. Steve asks about you, too."

"Steve Lim?"

"Still a sweetie pie."

"He was a good one."

"Single."

"Tess!"

"Just joking! Do you remember our first apartment, the one in Washington Heights?"

"The Dutch landlady who painted nine-foot Jesuses."

"In the front hallway."

"In oils!"

"And she didn't allow overnight guests, and you had to help me smuggle my brother in through the fire escape and he sprained his ankle."

"And Lucia, with her high school boyfriend."

"The Greek one, who brought us a box of his auntie's baklava. So polite!"

Miranda laughed. She missed her friend. She missed New York, the sheer wattage of the place, its mighty abundance, its chaos, its kinetic energy a comfort somehow. How long ago was it, those idyllic years, set free in the city to explore as she liked, to discover some cheap noodle shop or boho boutique or obscure sculpture garden tucked away somewhere in Queens? And her sweet *Mei-mei* would visit, and she'd wait on the platform at Port Authority, waving as the bus from New Jersey pulled in. And then they'd go find a museum or a free concert or some new art gallery, indulge in falafel or Gray's Papaya or Ethiopian *wat*. Life was simpler then. That was before Ma's illness. Before Lucia's.

"How's Stefan's family?" asked Tess.

"Nice." She searched for another word. "Dry. But nice."

"Nice is good. Better than crazy." Tess started to roll her eyes. "Oh, I didn't mean . . . I'm so sorry, Miranda. I just meant, in-laws. . . ."

"I know. It's okay."

"Have you gone to see your niece yet?"

"No." Miranda sighed. "I've been avoiding it. I feel awful for her father. I know I should go."

"You're amazing, to fly across the ocean for your sister. You know that, right?"

"I'm not sure Stefan thinks so."

Tess frowned. "Is everything okay?"

"Sure. Mostly."

"Mostly?"

"Oh, it's fine, don't worry." But Tess was already on alert, brows raised, skeptical. "It's just that Stefan never knew Lucia the way she was . . . before. All he knows is that she's a lot to deal with now."

"Okay, but what about his son? You're like . . . a stepmom. That's not exactly easy to deal with either."

"Rafi?" Miranda shrugged. "He's a typical teenager, I guess. Awkward. Listens to angry music on his headphones all the time. A bit dirty. His moods take up a lot of space."

"I can't even imagine living with a teenaged boy."

Miranda pointed to her friend's belly. "Um . . . ?"

"Mine will be perfectly clean. And polite, of course." Tess grinned.

"I think the trickiest part is trying to be a parental figure without having any real parental authority. But then acting like I'm his friend isn't quite right either. It's this strange in-between space. Though truthfully, I don't see him too often—he's mostly at boarding school. Stefan worries he's unhappy, but I think it's divorce-guilt. We played tennis a few times last summer, that was fun."

"And what about work?" asked Tess.

Miranda continued to muster up enthusiasm as she explained how she'd taken on a few clients of her own, smaller companies or nonprofits that needed help with their financials. She was working for Stefan's hospital, too, and hoping to talk to a couple of museums when she got back.

"A museum would be perfect, right?" said Tess.

Oh, Tessie. Ever positive. Miranda reached over to hug her friend. "You're going to be such a great mom," she said.

"You'll come visit again, won't you? After the baby comes? And you'll give me fair warning next time?"

"Sure," said Miranda. "And I promise to stay in better touch."

"Should we go buy some stationery?"

Miranda laughed. She still had those old letters in a shoe box somewhere.

"Do you think she really did that?" said Lucy.

Two triangles of tuna sandwich sat untouched on her tray.

"Did what?" asked Charo.

"Coco. Did she flush her baby down the toilet?"

Once again, Loco Coco had hijacked morning Group with theatrics about her famous two-headed baby, and she, Charo, had modeled respect, until Hulk came right out and said it, *You're full of bull crap*, and Coco had thrown another fit.

"Did Coco upset you when she said that?" said Charo. "Don't you have a baby, too, Ms. Bok?"

But the question triggered no sadness, no anger, no yearning, no pain. And though Charo knew, intellectually, that this numbness and detachment were woven into the illness, it still disheartened her.

"She's my friend," said Lucy. "She talks all the time. Her voice is loud."

"What does she say?" Charo couldn't be sure now whether Lucy referred to Coco or her baby or some aural hallucination.

"It's tiring."

"Why is that?"

"I'm protecting her," said Lucy.

"You're protecting your baby?"

Lucy rubbed her temples with her thumbs. "You don't know how tiring it is. I'm exhausted. Do you know Susi?"

"Susi? Susi is your baby?"

"Susi's my friend. She helps me sometimes."

Lucy released her gaze from her meal tray, focused now on something just behind Charo's head. Charo turned, but there was nothing. Only the wall of windows, the snow outside.

"Does Susi live at the house, too?" Finally, yesterday, she'd reached someone at the house. Not Manuel, but the gentleman had been polite enough, though he'd refused to give any information on his cousin's whereabouts. "Your baby is doing well. Do you know that? Your cousins are helping Manuel take care of her."

"Manny?"

Charo nodded.

"Well, the live-ins aren't really my cousins. If they were my cousins, wouldn't they be my sister's cousins, too?"

It was exhausting, making sense of people who didn't make sense, while concurrently trying not to offend them. "Ms. Bok." Charo summoned her most authoritative voice. "If you want to get out of this hospital to see your baby, the quickest way is to listen to the doctors and take your meds."

Lucy dissected her sandwich, separated the bread from the tuna, peeled off the crusts, picked out bits of celery. Charo glanced at the television. Game show reruns again.

"Half," said Lucy.

"Half?" said Charo, confused by Lucy's dismantled lunch.

"Half a pill."

"The treatment team wants you on Abilify," said Charo.

Lucy nodded. "Half."

Charo wanted to jump, shout, pump her fists. *Breakthrough.* She knew it. Had known it all along in her gut, that bringing up the baby and the boyfriend was the right thing to do. "Wait here," she said. She ran to find Nurse Bob.

☙

Coco watched as Lucy stuffed her belongings into a pillowcase. She didn't have much: four pairs of grayish-white socks, two tank tops, two sweaters, a pair of jeans, a six-pack of dowdy underwear her sister had brought, probably purchased from the Korean grocery.

"Ready to go," she said.

"*Mamacita*, you're crazy," said Coco. "Look at it out."

A flurry of fat, wet flakes. Reporters were billing it the Storm of the Year, forecast to go all day. Coco wrapped her blanket tight, glad to be inside. She pointed to Lucy's hospital slippers. "Like that? You gonna freeze your ass off, baby."

"Oh, yeah." Lucy scratched her head. "Where are my shoes? I don't know where my shoes are. Coco, can I borrow yours?" She dragged a red rubber boot out from under Coco's bed.

"You planning on making a run for it?" said Coco.

"Oh. No. Someone will come pick me up," said Lucy. "The social said I could go."

Coco raised her left eyebrow. Her roommate had taken a couple of pills, and blessed Jesus, she thought she was cured. "Well, good luck, I suppose."

Lucy frowned. "Did you really do it?"

"Do what?"

"Flush your baby down the toilet?"

Coco laughed. "Hell no, I never flushed no baby down the toilet. Is that why you leaving me now?"

"But you said you did."

Coco boiled.

"I'm sorry you're sad," said Lucy.

"We're all sad," said Coco, snapping her gum.

"Bye-bye," said Lucy. She flung the pillowcase over her shoulder, saluted with one hand, turned and marched out of the room. Coco scowled at the empty doorway. Bye? Just like that? She spat her gum at the bare white wall, satisfied when it stuck, ran to catch up with her friend. Rounding the corner to Hallway B, she collided with Miranda Bok.

"What in hell is going on?" said Miranda, wringing her soggy hair with her fingers.

"Lucy's leaving," gasped Coco.

"What do you mean?"

"She said she's leaving."

"Where is she going?"

"Out."

Miranda marched into Charo's office, Coco tight at her heels. "Ms. Alvarez. She can't leave."

"Excuse me," said Charo.

"My sister cannot leave this hospital," said Miranda.

"What are you talking about?" said Charo.

"She said she's leaving," said Coco.

"Nobody's leaving," said Charo. She glared at Coco. "Where is she now?"

Coco shrugged.

They fanned out, searching madly as if on Amber Alert. "Anyone seen Lucy?" they called, in the visitors' lounge, the nurses' station, the hallways, room after room. They opened bathroom doors, closet doors, poked their heads under couches, under beds, in places far too small for a grown woman to hide.

They found her sitting alone in the library, her sack of clothes on a metal chair.

"You are not leaving," said Miranda.

"I am," said Lucy.

"You are not leaving." Miranda could not think of anything else to say.

"I took a pill," said Lucy.

"I'm afraid there has been a misunderstanding," said Charo.

"You said I could leave if I took the pills. So I'm leaving. Aren't I?" Lucy glanced at Charo, then her sister. Coco sensed her friend was in real distress.

"You need to get better," said Miranda.

"You're upsetting her," said Coco.

"You're upsetting *me*," said Miranda. "She's not going anywhere."

It is impossible to inject logic into an irrational mind. Yet somehow, she could not stop trying.

"I took it," said Lucy. "Abilify . . . two times." She held up two fingers.

"Abilify? Why Abilify?"

"She agreed to it," said Charo. "Now, let's all calm down."

"Didn't you read my notes? Why are you giving her Abilify? She won't stay on it. It gives her migraines."

"She agreed to take it," said Charo. She folded her arms, in defense of her victory.

"Where the hell is the attending?" said Miranda. "I want to speak with him, *now*."

"This really isn't . . ."

A loud thud. Charo stumbled backward. Lucy Bok had hurled her sack of belongings at a bookshelf full of old encyclopedias. She dropped to the rug, her face in her hands, slim torso shuddering with weight.

"Oh, honey," said Charo. The girl was crying hysterically. She had never exhibited this kind of emotion before.

"It's okay," whispered Miranda. Instinctively, she extended a hand to smooth her sister's hair. Stopped. Carefully backed away.

"I'm sorry," said Charo.

"You've done it now," said Loco Coco. "Come on, baby." She reached down to remove Lucy's red rubber boots. Patted her roommate on the head.

༆

The smells permeated throughout the ward: savory, fried, pungent, sweet, meaty, spicy, irresistible. This was what she could do: offer diversion, supply food as truce. She could be of practical use. Miranda Bok had forgotten about the Golden Duck, until she discovered the old receipt crumpled in the corner of her purse.

Each of the twelve Styrofoam boxes was positioned exactly eleven inches from the next. To the left of each box sat a plastic spoon, to its right, a fork. The boxes ringed the entire perimeter of the ping-pong green. Paper plates, napkins, forks and wooden chopsticks were arranged neatly in the middle. Loco Coco clapped, satisfied. She had recruited one of the OCDs to set the table.

"Here we have shrimp with snow peas," she said, the perfect hostess. "And this is sesame chicken. Spicy eggplant. Ahhhh. . . . king crab legs."

"Enough for everyone," said Miranda.

Crote Six smacked their lips.

"Help yourself," said Lucy.

Hulk dumped the entire box of sesame chicken onto his plate.

"Pig." Loco Coco glared. "Didn't your mommy teach you to share?"

"Mmm," said Hulk, ignoring her. "Delicious."

They chowed down like prisoners, licked their lips, helped themselves to more rice and more shrimp and more king crab legs. Upon finishing, the patients emitted a collective groan. "Thank you, sister," they said. They adjourned to afternoon activities with their salty bellies. The staff hoped they would all take naps.

Coco went to her favorite armchair by the cluster of potted

plants, turned it to face the outside. She'd just gotten comfortable when Charo entered the lounge, waving a red purse in the air.

"Does anyone know about this?" said Charo.

It belonged to the mother of one of the new admits. Now minus a substantial sum of money.

"Does anyone know about this?" Charo repeated calmly.

"Sure," said Coco. She rotated her chair. Watched Big Juan's rear end swing from side to side as he chased the ping-pong ball. "He knows." She pointed a finger at Hulk.

"Liar," said Hulk.

"I am not, I saw him. He was looking for money."

"Why would I take anyone's money?" said Hulk.

"Drugs," said Loco Coco. "Everyone knows Hulk will do anything for his drugs."

"Quiet down," hissed Charo. She was not interested in confronting Hulk.

"He'll take a little girly-boy into the bathroom, lick his balls for money," said Coco.

Charo groaned. Hulk roared. He leapt to his feet, grabbed one end of a vinyl love seat, hurled it at the wall of windows.

Code Green.

Nurse Bob came running. Tall Paul rushed in. It took four staff members to restrain Hulk, two to restrain Coco, who kept kicking her feet, aiming for his groin.

Lucy Bok crawled on her hands and knees by the window, rescuing the battered plants. A few of the plastic yellow buckets had cracked, littering the floor with leaves and dirt.

"Are you okay, Lucy?" asked Tall Paul.

Lucy's hands trembled. She bit her lip. "No. I'm not okay."

"Did the meds make him like that?" asked Lucy. It was the next afternoon.

"No," said Nurse Bob.

"I saw him take his pills. Aren't they supposed to stabilize him? So why'd he do that?"

"I don't know," said Bob. It was a good question, with no good answer. "Each patient has to deal with his own issues."

"He threw a *couch* at the window."

"Yes, I know." It had shaken Bob, too, and everyone else in the ward. "Look, Lucy, the treatment team discussed your case this morning. You've been doing well." These last four days on Abilify, and already the girl's thoughts had become significantly more lucid. Her speech flowed. "How do you feel?"

"Throwing a couch at the window is an *issue*," said Lucy.

"Ms. Bok, let's focus."

"Everyone in this place is crazy, and they're all doped up on meds." Lucy pounded her fist on the table. "No more pills."

"I'd advise against that. You've been making excellent progress. Have you noticed a difference?"

"Schizophrenia doesn't define me. It's not who I am. We learned that in Group today, didn't you hear?"

Nurse Bob sighed. "Lucy. Wouldn't you like to get out of here, go . . ."

"Sorry, Bobby. My eyeballs hurt." She stood up, walked away.

Nurse Bob swallowed. He'd seen it before, the way these illnesses chipped away at a person's core. Lucy Bok wasn't one of those hopeless cases, trapped behind a wall of psychosis so thick a sledgehammer couldn't break through. But if she wouldn't help herself, what more could he do? Even with his decades of experience, this one hurt him somewhere inside.

"What about the court hearing?"

Charo looked down at her lap. "We didn't file for it when she started taking the medication."

"Christ," said Miranda. She had insisted. She'd insisted they give her the other drug and they hadn't listened. And now? Now what?

Charo braced herself for a barrage of verbal assaults, but it did not come.

"I'll speak with Dr. O'Hara," said Nurse Bob.

"The soonest we could file is next Monday," said Charo. "They only take applications on Mondays."

"Next Monday?" said Miranda. It was Tuesday. "We have to wait another week just to file? Are you kidding me?"

"And then probably another week for the hearing to be scheduled," said Nurse Bob. *Clusterfuck*. He said it aloud.

"So what do we do now?" said Miranda.

"We file. We keep trying to get through to her."

"This is ridiculous."

"It's difficult," said Bob. "We'll try again. I'll offer the Zyprexa. I know she doesn't like the weight gain, but it's worth a shot. Maybe she can switch to something else when she's out."

When she's out. When.

"What if I stuffed the pill in her tuna sandwich? Would I get arrested?"

Bob laughed, surprised by this candidness. "It's her choice," he said. "Court order or not, ultimately, it's her choice. You have to believe this. She has to take responsibility for her own life."

Charo felt a sudden pang of sympathy for Miranda Bok. She knew Bob's was the party line, but hadn't they all harbored similar thoughts at some point? And what about that baby? Was it her choice, to have a mother stuck in the nuthouse? Didn't she have a right to have her mother back, if a couple of pills would make things right?

"The boyfriend," said Charo. "I still think we should bring in the boyfriend. He's the most important connection to the baby."

"But the boyfriend . . ." Miranda sighed.

"You don't like him," said Bob.

"It's not that. I mean . . . no, it's not that."

Bob got it. Of course. Miranda Bok was afraid of scaring the boyfriend away. Terrified he'd abandon Lucy and the baby, and then what would happen when she ditched her meds the next time? Or the next?

"I've tried contacting Manuel several times at the house number," said Charo. "He's impossible to reach. Maybe you could get in touch with him? Or is there other family?"

"No," said Miranda. "No, I don't think so." She shook her head back and forth.

"We'll keep trying," said Bob.

Defeated. Miranda Bok looked defeated.

Following Hulk's incident, Lucy Bok decompensated. Her thoughts grew splintered, her speech slowed, she drifted toward a silent entropy. At patient evaluations, Nurse Bob noted the sluggish heaviness in the air. Even Charo, usually full of opinions, was quiet.

Tall Paul observed Lucy by the pay phone. Her sister must've loaded her up with quarters, because she punched in number after number, seven beeps in quick succession. "They've taken my baby. I need help." She rattled off a street address. Paul shook his head.

The days passed. Winter seemed to gradually wear itself out. Temperatures hovered just above freezing. Slush prevailed. Loco Coco complained she was hearing scary voices. "In which ear?" asked Bob. Coco tugged at her left lobe. The treatment team knew she was faking it—auditory hallucinations did not present in such a manner. Coco was a kook, but no longer required hospitalization. Charo's task was to find somewhere to discharge her—someplace other than the street.

At least the court finally confirmed a date for Lucy's medication over objection hearing.

"I have to warn you," said Nurse Bob. "Dr. O'Hara is skeptical." The doctor's inclination had been to move forward with discharge. Lucy's current presentation was far too calm.

"I'll handle it," said Miranda.

"This is a tough situation," said Bob.

"I know that."

"Even if she . . ."

"Once we get her back on her meds, she'll be fine," said Miranda. *I'll take care of her, Ma.*

"But Ms. Bok, you should know . . ." Nurse Bob paused. Each of these psychotic episodes was toxic to the brain, resulted in cognitive decline, and it was impossible to predict how much of a person might be irretrievably lost each time. It would be a long, long road. "Ms. Bok, what I mean is . . . you can't keep fighting your sister's illness all by yourself."

A baby bird, Jie. Look!

Where, Mei?

In the backyard, by the swing set.

It's a robin. But see, it can't move its wing.

It's hurt. We have to help him, Jie.

Let's bring it some water.

Water. Yeah! Can we keep him, Jie?

I don't think so.

Pleeeeeease?

We'll put it in a shoe box, let it rest.

A shoe box. Yeah! I'll keep him in my room.

Mei-mei, no. A bird is a wild animal. It doesn't belong in your room.
We'll keep it outside on the porch.

But I need to take care of him, Jie. He must be so scared!

It's okay, Mei. I promise, it will be okay.

Early the next morning, a tap on her shoulder.

Jie, wake up.

What is it, Lucia?

The BIRD.

What?

He's dead.

What?

The bird is dead. He's not moving. See?

He's probably resting.

He's not resting. See? Is he resting?

I don't know.

See? He's DEAD.

I'm sorry.

I told you I should've kept him in my room. I TOLD you.

I'm sorry, Lucia.

He's not fine. He's dead! You promised it would be okay AND NOW HE'S DEAD.

I'm sorry, Lucia.

He's dead, and it's all your fault.

They refused to speak for the rest of the day. That night, she curled up in a ball, faced the wall, shut her eyes to sleep. But she could see only the robin in its cardboard coffin, which they'd buried in the yard. She cried to herself. *I'm so sorry, little bird.*

"Jie?"

Again, that annoying tap.

"Jie? Are you crying?"

She did not respond.

Lucia's skinny arms wrapped around her neck. "It's okay, Jie. Guess what? I was crying, too."

Miranda was suddenly angry. She would not give in. Rustling the air in the back of her throat, she let out a convincing snore. But Lucia stayed draped across her back, in her nightgown and six-year-old stubbornness. Every now and then she patted Miranda's head and whispered, "It's okay now, Jie. I know it wasn't your fault."

When Miranda opened her eyes the next morning, every part of her body ached. She ordered chicken noodle soup from room service. It arrived, cold. She sipped three sips, pushed it away. She picked up the phone to call Charo. *I'm not feeling well. I won't be in today.*

A stomach virus, she told Stefan.

"Crap," he said.

"I'm like the undead," she said. "I can't move. Like when I try to walk, I fall down."

"*Schätzli.*" He sighed. "Go to the hospital, for God's sake. They have doctors there."

"But it's a virus. They can't do anything."

"Then come home, Miranda. Why don't you just come home?"

"I can't," she said. But she pictured the wicker rocker on their back porch, the foothills dotted with cows, the Stöcktalersee sparkling blue.

"Why not? You've done all you can there."

"I just can't, Stefan. I can't." Her words wobbled. The room was spinning. She coughed to regain control of her vocal cords. "Because if she's on her pills and she's sane and she loses her job or squanders her money or sleeps with some jackass and gets pregnant and has babies, well, then fine, okay, that's her choice, that's her life. But if a psychotic illness makes her think aliens talk to her through the TV and she can control people's thoughts and she needs to procreate to save the human race, and that's why she's losing her job or having babies . . . well, then, yes, I feel fucking responsible."

She paused, out of breath, yet somehow relieved to have articulated her moral distress.

"Sweetheart, come on. It's going to be okay."

"Stop." She snapped. "Stop telling me that, Stefan. You don't know that. This is not some fairy tale. Things don't turn out okay just because you want them to."

She couldn't bear it, the placid consolation, another rational reply. A cramp pricked her side.

But it was not his fault. Of course, she knew this.

She tried to soften her tone. "What about your day? How is Rafael doing?"

"Rafi's coming home this weekend. That will be nice. Sophie has a recital."

His enthusiasm, weaker than usual, not quite convincing.

"That will be nice," she echoed.

"I had to tell three patients they had cancer today."

"Oh God, Stefan. I'm sorry." The room, spinning again. She felt like a shit.

"It's been a long week."

"Yes."

In the silence, their mutual exhaustion.

"I miss you," he said.

"I miss you, too."

"Miranda, please get some rest."

"I will," she said.

She crawled out of bed, ran a long, hot bath. Steam blazed through her pores. She focused on the soft flicker of shadows, the wet warmth of water, that cavernous space in her expanding diaphragm. And then she was diving headfirst into her sister's dark, vacuous eyes, swimming behind the eyeballs, clawing with tiny, ineffectual fingernails that sprouted into giant pitchforks, burning red like the devil's, and she would stab, more violently, with her body in every blow, screaming, *Where are you? Where the fuck are you, Lucia?*

She returned to bed. Flipped on the television. The sound hurt her ears. She shut it off, shut her eyes. Tried to snuff out memories of her sister as a bucktoothed girl practicing flyaway dismounts from their old purple swing set, she standing below on a beat-up old mattress—*I gotcha, I gotcha*—arms outstretched, as Lucia sailed through the air.

An unlikely dream that night: Ba. In the doorway, but she could not see his face. From his pocket, he pulled out a lucky jade pendant on a long, gold chain. *For my best daughter in the world!* He helped hang it around her neck. *Look, Ma, isn't it pretty?* Ma, angry, her mouth moving fast. Miranda, with fumbling fingers, trying to undo the clasp.

She woke, sweat drenched, pillow salty with tears.

She lay in bed three more days. She sweated, shivered, sipped ginger ale. She could not recall ever feeling this physically ill. On the fourth day, housekeeping knocked and she couldn't decide whether or not they should go away. Paralyzed in bed, thoughts in slow motion, she heard the click of the lock, a woman's voice, then her own dizzy mumbles. *Yes, please. Yes.* She watched them bang around for a few minutes, pulled a pillow over her head and fell back asleep.

Jie, can we bake cookies today? Can we collect worms in my shoe? Make hot chocolate out of mud? Sing that song again, the one with the bones. I'm a skeleton. I'm a lion tamer! Let's go to the zoo. Can we play the word game again, Jie? How about this one: Shenandoah. That's a good one, Mei. Elixir. Ineffable. Gossamer. Defenestration. What's that? To throw someone out a window. No way. Yeah! Okay, this one's really good: E-phem-er-al. Jie, do you believe in happily ever after?

When her eyes opened, she found the room transformed. Her clothes folded, stacked neatly on top of the dresser; the trash cans emptied; the heap of damp towels on the floor, gone; boots lined up by the door. And the sheets! Tucked at the corners. Everywhere smooth and clean. The thought of all this happening while she lay unconscious—it bothered her. Though not enough to keep her from sinking back into her pillow, reveling in this small bit of comfort just a few moments more.

He was bulkier than she remembered, filled out in the chest, his jawline sharpened, less boy, more man. His hair was longer, shaggier, like a bedraggled rat, though admittedly she was unfamiliar with the current styles.

"Come in," he said.

"Is the baby sleeping?" she asked.

"No. Please, come. I'll show you."

She followed him through the kitchen. They entered a bedroom, not much larger than the mattress inside.

"Esperanza, *esta es tu tía.*"

The baby, so tiny, in her bassinet. She sucked in her breath.

"She's beautiful, Manny."

"Her name is Esperanza. It means hope."

She blinked back unexpected tears.

Esperanza was beautiful, truly. Exotic. Hard to categorize. Dark teardrop eyes, her father's brown complexion, her mother's delicate features, a headful of unruly curls.

"She keeps scratching herself," he explained, settling his daughter in his lap. Finger by finger, he clipped the tiny white crescents from her nails, brows furrowed in concentration. The baby wriggled, a miniature slide show of human emotions: bewilderment, curiosity, fright, discomfort, wonder, glee, fatigue (*yawn*). Finished, he inspected each of her fingers again, checked with his thumb to ensure nothing sharp was left.

"All done, Essy." He kissed her forehead, cradled her in one arm, like a football.

They headed back into the kitchen. The yellow linoleum floor looked dingy but clean. Pots hung from a rack above the sink. He filled a kettle with water, set it on the stove, wiped stray crumbs from the Formica table with a sponge.

"How is Lucia?" he asked.

She wondered where to begin.

"Have you heard of schizophrenia?" she said. "It's a brain disease. She has a chemical imbalance in her brain."

"You said. Over the phone. You mentioned it."

"If she takes her medicine, she's fine. But if she doesn't, well . . . that's why she was acting so strange."

He nodded, but did not look at her. Kept his focus on Essy, wiped a trail of drool from her chin with a dishcloth.

"Crazy," he said. "She was crazy. *Loca*. I was scared."

"What did she do?"

He shook his head.

"Please, it's important. I need to tell the doctors."

"She was sitting all day in her room like a zombie, wearing socks on her hands. When she talked, she didn't make any sense. She wouldn't let anyone watch the TV, kept turning it off, but then sometimes, she turned it on full blast. One time I came home, she'd burned her fingers. Another time I found Essy covered in shit."

She winced.

"She thought there were bugs everywhere." He paused. "But it turned out she was right about that."

He fetched two mugs, two tea bags. Tea. She was pleasantly surprised. "Would you like to hold her?" he asked. He held out the baby.

"Oh, no, that's okay."

Essy gurgled, smiled. Miranda smiled back.

"You see, she knows you are her auntie." He laughed.

"Oh. Well. Okay, I guess."

He placed her niece in her arms. The bundle, so light. The life, so new, so innocent. So beautiful.

Her insides ached, a tangle of want and pain.

Esperanza squirmed.

"Hi, baby," she whispered. "Shh. Hi there." Miranda touched the tiny hand to the tiny mouth. Essy sucked happily on her fist.

"You are good with babies," he said.

See, Ma, Mei-mei is smiling.

"Manny," she said. She was afraid to look up. Pinned her gaze to her niece's face. "Lucia is still not taking her medicine."

"What do you mean?" he said.

He was confused, of course. She felt achy, sick, exhausted all over again.

"I thought she is in the hospital."

"She is. But when she's sick, she doesn't understand why she needs her medication."

"But they are helping her there?"

"We're trying. We thought maybe you could visit her, talk to her." We. She and Charo, a "we." The two of them, in agreement. It had come to this.

"With the baby?" He was skeptical. "I don't like hospitals."

"No, not with the baby. But I could take you there."

She watched his struggle, the story on his face. He was considering, weighing, wrestling with it: whether or not to get involved. The kettle started to sputter on the stove.

"Lucia wants to see me?"

She stroked Essy's chin, pretended she hadn't heard. She wasn't sure anymore why she had come.

"The doctors, they help her there. She will be okay, right?"

He looked forlorn, lost, like an abandoned dog. She could not lie to him. "I'm sorry, Manny, but I don't know. No one knows what will happen. Lucia's illness, it isn't easy—I mean, it's really, really hard."

He nodded, grave.

"She needs help. And support. Someone responsible. Someone who understands her illness."

The words, so unwieldy. Unappetizing from the second they dribbled from her mouth. She should've brought the pamphlets, the brochures, the *25 Tips*. She didn't feel like explaining anymore.

"My situation, it's not easy either," he said.

Of course, she understood. "I can try to help," she said. "If you need anything, I can help, I promise."

His eyes had fallen again. He seemed not to hear. "I will pray," he said. "I will pray for her."

What does that mean? she wanted to yell. *Will you go or will you stay? Will you care for her? Will you take responsibility for her illness? Will you know what to do?*

But he was just a kid.

The kettle was screeching. She felt a lurch in her gut, a wrench of revulsion, a desperate desire to be transported away. She wanted to go home. To Switzerland. To her husband. To her life. To the wicker rocker on their back porch with the view of the Alps. She stood to leave, but in her arms lay a baby. Esperanza had fallen asleep.

༜

Is there other family? Friends? Anyone?

She dialed. Waited for the click at the other end of the line.

"Jie! Long time!" he said, with his usual exuberance, and she could picture him sitting on that rickety red bench in the East Village, his duck lips and gray eyes and his big, wide smile. "How is everything?" he asked.

She considered where to begin. Instead, she cried.

Lucy Bok lay on a couch by the window, soaking in sun like a tropical plant.

"Hi, my sweetie," he said.

She looked up, blinked, disoriented by this unexpected guest.

"How did you get here?" she said.

"I have legs," he said.

She blinked again, puzzled, as he toured the lounge as if inspecting an old friend's new pad. He touched the wide-screen TV, assessed Big Juan's technique at the Ping-Pong table, admired the wall of windows, the view, the potted plants.

"Is that *him*?" Charo elbowed Nurse Bob.

"I don't think so," said Bob.

"Then who is he?" said Charo.

Bob wasn't sure. Asked to sign in to the visitors' log, the man had penned an illegible scrawl. *Good morning. Hola. Bonjour.* He greeted all who passed. The staff smiled, charmed by the man's frankness, his big, crinkly eyes.

He knelt down to peek under each of the vinyl couches, peered behind a thick curtain.

"What are you doing?" asked Lucy.

He wiggled the tip of his nose. Frowned. "Where's the Ostrich?" he said.

"Ostrich?" said Lucy. Then suddenly, she laughed, lit up for a quick moment. "No ostrich," she said.

"No ostrich." He grinned.

They played chess. He kept correcting the way she moved her pieces, but she didn't seem to mind. Nurse Bob noted an ease in her face, the usual tension losing its grip.

"Uh-oh, here comes the sister," whispered Charo. Miranda Bok, waltzing in with her high-heeled boots, dropped her coat over a chair.

"Yonah!" she said. "You're really here!"

"Of course," he said.

An odd couple, thought Nurse Bob, but the embrace he observed seemed genuine. Bob noticed now, the man had a prosthetic left arm, though he seemed in no way impaired.

"How did you get here?" said Miranda.

"He has legs," snapped Lucy.

Yonah let out a deep, gut laugh. "We're playing chess," he said. "Lucy's gonna beat me again. Come, sit."

Charo inched closer, fascinated.

"Uh, nosy. Don't you have work to do?" said Bob. Yet he could not help but linger, too.

The guests stayed through lunch. Bob was in the break room microwaving a lasagna when Charo came rushing in.

"It's him," she said.

"Who?"

"*Him*," said Charo. "The boyfriend. He's here."

They found him sucking water from the fountain. Manuel Vargas was handsome, sexy, possessed a fitness of youth, but in his eyes a skittishness showed.

"You're here to see Lucy?" said Nurse Bob.

"Yes," he said. "Is it a good time now?"

They accompanied him to the visitors' lounge, where Lucy Bok's guests were just putting on their coats. Miranda spotted him first.

"Manny . . . ?" In her face, the rest—the surprise, the *what the fuck?*

Manuel's gaze swept the room, hovered at the Ping-Pong table before settling back on the sister, then Lucy, then the man beside her. A razor-sharp silence. Manuel, like stone. Then a scowl. Eyes narrowed. He hardened his stance, marked his ground. Territorial, like a wolf.

Bob stepped toward him, charged, tense. Charo, too, by instinct, as if responding to some internal alarm, a call to defuse the situation.

They were preempted by Yonah's outstretched hand.

"I'm Yonah. Nice to meet you."

Manuel's expression remained blunt, hostile. He stared at Yonah's hand. Did not raise his eyes. No one spoke. The air seemed sucked from the room.

"I have to go now," said Yonah. He turned to Lucy, wrapped her in a giant bear hug. "Be good, Lucy Goosey. Listen to the doctors, okay?"

She nodded. Waved. He blew kisses as he walked away.

"Manny," said Miranda. She stood there in her cream-colored coat, fiddling with her buttons. "It's nice of you to come."

She coughed, tugged at her hair, scratched the back of her neck. Bob had never seen the sister so uncomfortable. "I need to get going, too," she said. "But I'll come by the house again. Sometime soon."

She left without saying a real good-bye. Charo saw her hurry to catch up with Yonah by the elevators.

"Yonah. Yonah!"

He turned, smiled. "Jie. Don't worry. She's gonna be fine. Everything's gonna be okay."

And in his big embrace, Miranda could almost believe it, that he possessed some clairvoyance she did not.

"So, what's up?" said Manuel. He squeezed Lucy's shoulders, sat, stuck his hands in his jacket pockets. "This is a nice hospital."

Lucy studied him, as if startled by his size. "You," she said, finally. She went to the bookshelf, returned with a box, Connect Four. "Wanna play?"

Bob drifted closer. The boyfriend seemed relieved, more comfortable with this plastic barricade between them. She dropped in a red checker. He dropped in a yellow one. Stroked his chin, concentrated on the holes.

"Want some juice?" she said.

"Sure." He stood when she stood, as if fumbling for etiquette on a first date. "The food here is okay?"

"It's the pits," she said. She stuck out her tongue. "Rice. Can you bring me rice?"

Manuel's face softened. "Sure. We got rice."

"Yeah, rice. And beans."

They kept playing the game. He loaded up in the middle, she went heavier on the sides. With only two slots left, she won. Big Juan Lopez slapped her a high five.

"So what's new at the casa?" she said.

He didn't reply.

"What, I've been gone for weeks, and nothing's new?" Lucy's tone suddenly laced with aggression. She was like that these days, the next moment calm, back and forth.

"Essy is sitting up," he said.

Hearing her daughter's name, Lucy seemed to pale.

"Sitting up," she said, digesting this information. "What, she didn't sit up before?"

Manny shook his head.

"And Susi?"

No answer.

"Where is Susi?" She looked around. "I'm locked in jail, and no one comes to visit."

"Susi is gone," he said.

"Where'd she go? On vacation?" She let the checkers crash onto the table.

"I don't know."

"Where? Disney World?" She let out a shrill giggle.

He didn't laugh. He whispered. "Susi was taken away. Police came to the house, looking for the baby."

"Which baby?" said Lucy.

"Esperanza."

"Esperanza? Essy?" She giggled again. "Why would she have Essy?"

"She didn't," said Manny. "But the police took her away anyway."

"Must be on vacation," said Lucy, frowning. "When's she coming back?"

"I don't know." Droplets rolled over his cheek. He brushed them aside. "I don't know where she is."

"Probably in Arizona." Lucy dropped her voice. "The FBI. Bastards. But why would they want Susi?"

"I don't know," said Manny. "Mrs. Gutierrez, she said someone came to the house, looking for the baby. Susi, she didn't want to tell them where the baby was. She wouldn't cooperate."

Lucy closed her eyes. She sat quietly, tilting her head to one side. "When did she go?"

"A week ago, maybe."

"A week. One week. What day is it today?" Lucy called out to Nurse Bob.

"Friday," said Bob. "Today is Friday."

❧

Alone once more, Lucy Bok paced the halls, buffing the floor tiles with her paper slippers. Tall Paul said hello, attempted to catch her eye. She did not respond.

"What's wrong, baby?" said Loco Coco, shuffling beside her.

"I did it."

"Did what? You didn't do nothing, baby."

"I did," said Lucy. "I did it, and now she's gone."

"Who's gone?" said Coco. "You've been here this whole time. I know it, I'm your roommate, remember?"

Coco followed at Lucy's heels, lapping the unit until they reached their room, watched her climb into bed.

"Hey, guess what?"

"What," said Lucy.

"I'm getting out soon."

"Out?"

"Outta here."

Lucy frowned. "Where are you going?"

Coco didn't answer. She pictured her nephew's two-room apartment, its filthy kitchen, grease caked on the counters, sink overflowing with cloudy water. She'd sleep, cramped, on a twin futon couch infested with fleas, surrounded by old newspapers stacked to the ceiling (better than the floor—she'd tried that, too, the worn spot on the rug in front of the TV tuned to a sports channel, and she hated boxing, wrestling, ultimate fighting, and her nephew hated having her there). That show about the hoarders, about the woman found dead, partially devoured by her sixteen cats, it could happen to her in there. But if not there, where?

"Susi. Susi's gone." Lucy clutched a pillow to her chest.

"Your baby? She's all right. Didn't that boyfriend of yours say, just today, she's doing great?"

Coco could not extract any further information. Her roommate lay in bed for the rest of the day, buried under a sheet. Coco listened to her sniffle, cough, whisper, cry. When it had been quiet awhile, she wondered if Lucy had fallen asleep. She tiptoed over, poked at the lump. When it didn't move, she lifted the sheet.

"We need help," mumbled Lucy. Her forehead was sweaty, her eyes open wide. "Susi needs help," she said.

"Who is Susi?" asked Coco.

"My *hermanita*," said Lucy. "My friend."

"I thought *I* was your friend," said Coco, pissed. Visitors always messed up everything.

❧

Miranda curled into a ball on her flowery bedspread, stared out her motel window to the night on Route 9: speeding red and yellow dots, triangles of fluorescent white, snow falling sideways, until finally, the quiet dark. *Extremely high functioning, Your Honor. She has insight when she's well. We lost our mother to cancer. The stress, Your Honor, a trigger, no doubt. And she has a baby now. A beautiful baby girl, four months old. A baby deserves a proper mother, Your Honor. She can be a good mother when she's well. She speaks five languages. She plays the violin. She was always excellent at puzzles as a child. She's genuine, she's warm, she plays well with others. Can't you see? She doesn't deserve this, Your Honor. She's my sister, Your Honor. She's my family, Your Honor. I love her. I need her back.*

꩜

Who knows why they do it? You'd drive yourself crazy, trying to figure it out. If it was something you said, or the doctor said, or the social or the medical student or the janitor or God, or those gods muttering insults in their ears. Maybe it was the ex-husband, the boyfriend, the sister, the roommate, maybe it was the threat of court, maybe it was a tidbit seen on *Family Feud*, read in *Better Homes & Gardens*, heard at Group or overheard in the visitors' lounge. Or maybe, as Bob most often surmised, they just couldn't stand it anymore, being here. Whatever the reason: She did it. One morning Lucy Bok grabbed the white pill, opened her mouth, downed it with a thick gulp of water. She remained compliant thereafter.

Day by day, the staff observed her, her mind ever more present in her body. She seemed to unfurl, like a fern receiving water. She was pleasant, polite, communicative. She volunteered in Group. She played Ping-Pong, tended to the plants, helped organize the boxes in the self-care room. Manuel visited, brought her cartons full of rice and beans and garlicky stews. Charo was glad to see he seemed attentive, competent. She called a meeting in her office.

"I'm ready to leave," said Lucy.

"Yes, I believe you are," said Charo, smiling. The treatment team was already looking at discharge dates. "What do you think?"

"She's doing great on the Zyprexa," said Miranda.

The boyfriend nodded. He'd sat in shock the first time Charo briefed him on the illness, explained to him in careful Spanish that there was no cure, only management and vigilance. Relapses were likely. Routine was key. Sleep. Stress management. Of course, the medications. He was given pamphlets: *Treatment Options, FAQs 4 Caregivers, Bipolar Symptoms and Signs.* Miranda, engulfed by a torrent of sympathy, could not look at him. *I love my daughter* was what he had said. *My daughter needs her mother, so for my daughter, I will try.*

Nurse Bob agreed, it was a remarkable recovery. The girl had shown insight, which he hoped would continue to improve. And that sister, softening with relief in front of their very eyes.

Miranda patted Lucia's arm. Charo smiled again. No one said it: *I told you so.*

૭૦

Esperanza was a beautiful baby. Each staff member cooed when they saw her, shrieked when she cooed in return. "She's just gorgeous," they said, patting Manuel on the back. "And what a darling outfit that is." They pinched the toes of her duck-footed yellow pajamas, patted her pink fleece hooded jacket with ears. Charo nodded and smiled to each of them, as proud as if the baby were her own. Nothing was more wondrous than a baby, especially in a psychiatric ward.

She escorted Manuel to the nursery. This was what they called the small, windowless visiting room stocked with a few random soft toys, a rocking chair, a handful of children's books. It was private, secure. Lucy Bok sat, waiting.

"Essy," she said. "Oh God, Essy. You're here." Manuel carefully handed her the baby. She gazed at her daughter, stroked her forehead, her chin, her nose, her cheek, rosy from the cold outside. Then she rested the baby's torso across her chest, Essy's head on her shoulder. She patted her back, kissed her hair. "Essy, Essy, Essy." Lucy closed her eyes. And the baby smiled, content with the scent of her mother, occasionally turning her head as if to check that she was still there.

Charo found herself looking away, eyes blurry, cheeks wet. She left them alone, relieved.

On the day of her departure, Lucy spent the morning in the library, filling out discharge forms. By the time she finished it was almost lunchtime. The exit plan was in place. She had been assigned to the hospital's intensive day program, three days a week for twelve weeks. Following that, she would transition to outpatient care with a psychiatrist once a month. Psychotherapy, family counseling, and follow-up with a social worker were strongly recommended. Her prescriptions had been faxed to the pharmacy on Main Street.

Nurse Bob poked his head in as she was packing her things into a small duffel bag. "You all set?" he said.

"I think so," said Lucy. She glanced around the room. Noon rays bounced off the glossy white walls. The beds donned fresh white sheets.

She looked radiant. Alive. Swung her hips as she marched down Hallway B, dressed in a purple ski jacket, furry boots, hair bouncing on her shoulders.

Big Juan Lopez whistled. *"Oye, Mamacita!"* he called.

"Where's Coco?" said Lucy. "I need to say good-bye to Coco."

The armchair by the window sat empty. Outside the sun shone. Much of the snow had melted. Lucy walked over to examine the cluster of potted plants, fingered their leaves, prodded their soil. She nodded, satisfied.

"Has anyone seen Coco?" she said.

Charo touched her arm lightly. "Coco was transferred to a medical unit."

"But she was scheduled to leave today. Wasn't she?" Lucy blinked, confused. "She said she wanted to leave together."

"Stabbed herself in the eye with a chopstick," shouted Big Juan. "They don't call her Loco Coco for nothing."

To Nurse Bob and the treatment team, it had come as no great surprise, but he saw the shock on Lucy's face.

"Is it true?" she asked.

"This morning. I'm sorry. But she'll be all right."

She frowned, deep in thought, clearly saddened. *Patient exhibits appropriate emotional response.* He took it as a sign of her continuing recovery. Nurse Bob wondered if it would make a difference in her outcome, that the choice had ultimately been her own to take the pills.

"Could it have been . . ." Her eyes darted. "Something I said?"

Nurse Bob sighed. He shook his head. "No, doll, she did it to herself."

Manuel Vargas stood by the nurses' station, holding a colorful bouquet of flowers.

"You go on," said Bob. "God bless, Lucy, and good luck. I bet that baby girl of yours can't wait to see you again."

Lucy Bok spent a total of forty days in Crote Six. Bob knew the odds were against her, that she would most likely be back. But if anyone could beat the odds, she could.

4

Lucia

First thing I noticed about Manny, the mole on his left cheek, a perfect circle, the size of a dime, and smack middle like a doorbell.

A mole? you say. He has such lovely features: crinkly brown eyes, prominent brow ridges, a soft, fleshy philtrum above his soft, juicy lips. The mole was distracting. Not that it bothered him. He never touched it when nervous or favored the other side. We went to a Dominican bar and danced bachata and he pressed it into my forehead, just above my left eye, and it was big and round and black but not hairy or scary, and his breath was cinnamon gum. As the night wore on, I wanted to lick it. Taste it. Later, I mean *later*, snapped awake and sizzled electric, I was convinced it was a recording device, a secret camera, that it would activate with a correct fingerprint or retinal identification and officers from some central compound would descend like flying monkeys, gather me and take me away.

His essence? A dog. The coloring of a German shepherd, with on-guard ears and that sharp, wolflike masculinity bordering on feral, rabid, but I detected something gentle, even fragile, underneath. The way he stood in public, not quite raised to full height, hands in his pockets, downcast eyes, I knew he was an illegal. Skittish.

"You know what's sad?" he said, one of those first evenings we sat together in front of the Vargas house, under the summer moon, holding hands.

"What?" I said.

He pointed down the street, to a frail-looking elderly couple trying to maneuver an L-shaped couch into a U-Haul van. They kept banging it into the side of the door.

"Wait here," he said.

I knew he was decent. Kind. He could lift heavy weights. What I didn't know about Manny, I didn't know he would stick. Stick by me and my baby girl.

And is this a good thing?

This is me, at the p-doc's. He's tapping one big brown shoe, *short-long, short-short-long*; it must be a professional no-no, but he's oblivious.

"A good thing? Sure. I guess so."

He's new. A mandatory assignment, since I've finished with my twelve-week outpatient follow-up program at the hospital. Older, bland-blond face, side-part hair, an overall beigeness, though he's irregularly tall, thus also a bit grasshopper-like, uncomfortable when seated, like he's had to accordion his limbs to fit into some toddler's chair.

Not much interested in moles or surveillance or even balmy recollections of romance, he wants to know how I'm doing for *support*.

"Support?"

"Yes."

He's already run the standard battery of questions, checked the check boxes, computed the data: *hears voices = schizophrenic; too agitated = paranoid; too bright = manic; too moody = bipolar;* and of course everyone knows a depressive, a suicidal, and if you're all-around too unruly or obstructive or treatment resistant like a superbug, you get slapped with a personality disorder, too. In Crote Six, they said I "suffer" from schizoaffective disorder. That's like the sampler plate of diagnoses, Best of Everything.

But I don't want to suffer. I want to live.

I sit up straight. One hand on my lower back, the other on my belly, I take a deep inhale. *Control top pantyhose. Two lace-up corsets. Spanx. One traditional postpartum faja.*

Oh, *support*.

He doesn't smile. He is not mildly amused. My parents are dead and my sister lives in Switzerland. Time's up. The face, not a crack, ungiving as stone! *Aiya*. He sends me away with a prescription.

I go away. I run away! I get in my car. It's raining. My windshield wipers drag as they swipe, a raggedy sound, one small boys would erupt into giggles over because all they can think of is farts. All I can think is, it's not like the old days, when some stoical psychoanalyst would hear you out for hours and hours, withholding judgment while you lay on their sofa expelling your word-salad thoughts and florid delusions. Nowadays, it's about pharma, drugs, and it hardly matters that all those tangled thoughts originate from a sentient being—a real person. Not a lone frontal cortex with its wiring gone awry, though you could picture it, that renegade mass, all veiny and purplish and intestinal looking.

I drive to Cousin Delia's house. She's not really Manny's cousin, but it doesn't matter, Essy loves her and her two older girls.

Today, Essy's new trick: she crawls . . . backward. I sweep her up, press her cheek to my cheek. "Sweetie girl," I say. My *bao-bao*, my *hija*. The life in her body so buttery warm.

"Bah," she says. A finger in my eye. That beaming face. This is the best part about leaving her—to come back to this.

We go pick up Manny. This is the routine, twice a day, because Manny hates to drive. He works as a line cook at the Porky Pig, the twenty-four-hour diner where he started as a dishwasher. Despite its name, it's a local hot spot with a certain cachet, the kind of joint where you find mini-jukeboxes in each booth and ogre-size portions on heavy white plates (except for the orange juice, fresh-squeezed, that comes in single-gulp glasses). Manny claims celebrities go there all the time, but he hasn't spotted one yet, personally.

Today I bring Essy inside. There's a fried chicken special for us early birds, and Manny loves fried chicken.

"How was the doctor?" he asks.

"Starchy," I say.

"*Cómo* a potato?" He picks up a French fry, waves it in the air.

I pick up a French fry, wave it back. "Exactly," I say.

"Huh." Two fries later, a grin sneaks across his face. "*Riiico*, no?" He does a yum-yum tap on Essy's belly until she laughs.

This is Manny, on a good day. I kick him under the table.

"But you'll go back," he says.

It's a question or not a question, I can't tell, but he's Very Serious.

"I'm supposed to," I say.

It's an answer or not an answer, but he says, "Okay," reaches over and squeezes my hand. His is always a little bit clammy.

When Esperanza was born, a pair of serpents lived inside my head. Their job was to warn me of the dangers of motherhood, which boiled down to this:

If you touch your baby, she will die.

My body, commandeered, a vessel of evil, was leaking evil into my child.

The serpents spoke in opposite voices. If one was soft, the other was loud; if one politely reminded me to keep my hands to myself, the other said I deserved to have my arms lopped off for not listening. They scrutinized my every move. *She is removing the baby's diaper. She is wiping the baby's bum. The baby is crying. See, the baby is no good. Cheap. Defective. Don't touch baby like that! Chop it off! Return to the proper authorities for a refund.*

Twelve touches, they said. Twelve more touches. Then my baby, contaminated, would die.

I didn't tell anyone. First, it was a secret. Second, I was ashamed. Third, I couldn't stand to hear the human population's efforts to convince me it wasn't true—*you're sick! you're sick!*—that was all part of the plot. So I wore thin cotton socks over my hands, dressed my baby in layers, cocooned her in blankets, avoided her skin coming into contact with mine. If I did as I was told, I hoped they might spare her. But it was hard to be a good mother like that.

⚭

So this is me, with Essy, eight months old. In the basement of the First Unitarian Church. A circle of women, all new mothers, has turned its attention on us. The group facilitator starts each session with a question, and today's icebreaker is, *What were your first thoughts as you held your baby?* Standard answers seem to be "miracle" and "love," though one woman, a catlike Pakistani with glassy green eyes, has nerve enough to say, "Not much, truthfully." But I can't exactly tell the truth.

"Blessed," I say, taking in all the breasts around me, both free-flying and poking out of nursing bras. I've never seen so many breasts before—pointy, droopy, splotchy, smooth, jiggly, perky, flat, like the Seven Dwarfs. I imagine their cartoon voices. "I felt scared. But blessed."

The mothers bob their heads. I can tell this is an excellent answer. The woman to my left, cross-legged on the floor, makes googly eyes at Essy. This is a sign a mama likes you, if she genuinely tries to make your kid laugh. She has a greenish complexion, oblong breasts that splay apart, and when her son, in her lap, tilts his chin upward, he can reach her and suck away. Hands-free! Very impressive.

Eggplant. Definitely eggplant. And when this comes to me, something inside my stomach topples over. I think of my sister, Jie.

Okay, me. What am I?

Oh, Jie, that's easy. A porcupine!

For some reason, I'm remembering all of Jie's floors, the ones I slept on over the years. Three different dorm rooms in college, a shared studio in Chelsea (partitioned off with a world map shower curtain), a one-bedroom sublet in Gramercy Park (the only available spot, in the hallway, with a mangy dog), a loft space in Tribeca, the apartment she shared with her friend Tess in Washington Heights (where she had to smuggle me and my boyfriend in and out through the fire escape). Wherever she lived, whenever I visited—as her starry-eyed *mei-mei*, as a restless teen, as an itinerant college grad— she would blow up the air mattress, unroll her red Coleman sleeping bag. *Here you go, Lucia.*

It used to be simple, like that.

Now Jie mostly stays away, swoops in only to unleash her wrath upon whichever Person of Importance she deems most incompetent. She stuck around until I was sprung from the p-ward, then swooped back to Switzerland. I'd say I felt ninety-five percent relieved when she left, five percent like an abandoned cat. But, well, she would've gotten a kick out of these mamas, anyway.

After introductions, we go back around the circle to discuss the most challenging moments of our weeks. With the newborns, the gist of anxiety seems to be that they won't eat; for older babies it's that they'll never learn to sleep. I don't have much to say about it, because Essy is a good eater and sleeper, but I know I shouldn't say that, so I say, "Essy throws up in her car seat."

"Oh, no!" Some of the mamas cover their mouths in an oh-no way, some of them like it might be contagious.

"Regularly?" says Eggplant.

"Is it spit-up or vomit?"

"Does she have reflux?"

"Had she just eaten beforehand?"

"How much does she weigh?"

The mothers chime in, but I know spit-up from vomit and it only happens in the car, and Essy eats or drinks every few hours, so it's hard to say. I've talked to the pediatric nurse, who had me come into the office, but Dr. Vera Wang gave Essy only a cursory inspection, asked a few questions, then told me everything would be fine. "It's just a phase," she said. "It'll be okay. And *you*, are you doing okay?" The way she asked, in that raised-eyebrow way without actually raising her eyebrows, made me suspect that she knew, and I thought maybe I should just come out and say it: *Yes, I'm taking my meds.* But it isn't really any of her business.

"Sometimes the biggest challenge is just staying awake," I say.

The mothers laugh, bob in agreement, roll their knowing eyes. This makes me feel good somehow, to think I've broken some ice.

I go back to that group a few more times. It's an odd mix of people, lots of older, hand-wringing Westchester housewives, a few immigrant women, two teenagers, but it's sweet how everyone tries to get along. Faith (aka Eggplant) invites me on a coffee date, and Essy sleeps the whole time while her baby fusses and she has to keep lifting up this sunflower nursing cover that's like a giant apron and it's like sunflower, breast, sunflower, breast, and I get so distracted I can barely carry on a conversation. So she talks, mostly about her complicated pregnancy and how blessed she feels that her doula was able to help her follow her birthing plan and how she got through her natural labor in spite of the pushy OB who was all ready to go C-section. I admire Faith's ability to withstand pain, but all her words make me kind of tired.

The woman I like best is Nipa, the cat-eyed Pakistani, who confides to the group that she's a breast cancer survivor, two years in remission. After this, I notice some mamas try to sit closer, to absorb her strength, while others seem to shy away. "Isn't that, like, *irresponsible?*" I overhear one of the Westchester housewives say, and I kind of hate her forever right on the spot.

Nipa and I meet in town. A crisp fall day, perfect for strolling down Main Street. We wheel past Pizza Palace and the Korean grocery and the laundromat, where the door is propped open, and I'm comforted by the detergenty-fresh thuds and clangs.

"This is where I met Essy's dad," I say.

"No way. That's so romantic comedy," says Nipa, and I have to laugh.

We head to the waterfront, where the wind picks up and the river shimmers, all zigzagged, and yellow leaves start to fly. When we reach the playground, Nipa confides to me that her doctor thinks she's suffering from postpartum depression.

I'm floored. First, she is telling me. Second, she's wearing makeup and her hair is clean, and her Natey is perfectly cherubic with his rolls of chin fat and cream bun cheeks.

"It's weird," she says. "In all these years, no one's ever told me I *suffered* from cancer. I'm a fighter. A survivor, you know."

"That *is* strange," I say.

She doesn't seem sad, not like Jazz, the girl in Crote Six whose eyeballs were permanently glued to her feet. But Nipa says she's cried every day since her Natey was born. "It seems silly, right? To be crying when everything's fine?"

Well, why not, I figure, because if pain and tears were correlated, surely we would've all drowned by now.

"Or we'd be living on arks," says Nipa, and for a second I'm confused, until I realize I've spoken aloud. She sweeps up her hair, piles it on top of her head, and it stays there like a big brown donut.

"Do you feel hopeless?"

"Maybe. How do I tell? I feel so wishy-washy." She reaches down to pry a wood chip from Natey's mouth. I suggest we move closer to the swings, where the ground is that foamy rubber made from recycled tires, but she doesn't want to deprive the kids of their tactile exploration.

"It's really hard," I say. That's usually the best thing to say. It occurs to me that no condition covered in the DSM-IV is ever followed by the word "survivor," but I don't mention this.

"Are you seeing someone?" I ask.

She blinks, quizzical. "I'm married," she says, and I'm so embarrassed I have to lean forward to pretend-wipe Essy's face. *I meant, like, a shrink.*

She asks whether I'm working and I say I hope to again, soon. My last job I wrote features for a newspaper in Queens. Nipa taught high school math in the Bronx for twelve years, started the week after her college graduation, continued through her treatments, but quit when Natey was born.

"Now I feel stupid and useless," she says.

"Oh, I feel stupid and useless, too," I say, and her cat-eyes glow a little brighter.

I tell Nipa I used to cry all the time, too. She asks why, but I can't bring myself to say. Even the thought of it makes me feel ashamed.

The serpents invaded my head after Essy was born. I would sit in my bedroom, not moving for hours, terrified to wake them. Flanked by banana plants, oriented by the window, my knees pointed precisely to two o'clock. I needed to align my body with the earth's magnetic field, like a grazing cow or caribou—only this way could my innermost thoughts resist detection by the mind X-rays from Central Compound. Any sudden movement or breach in concentration, I was sure, could have cosmic consequences, like causing an Olympic figure skater to miss her triple Lutz, or a driver to plow onto a snowy sidewalk, or an airplane to fall out of the sky. But even within silence, the stimuli flourished: photons in the sunlight made my skin itch; tiny creatures stampeded in the walls; invisible rays from the light sockets leached vital qi from my meridians.

Sometimes, I heard babies.

"Can you hear that?" I'd ask Manny.

"What?"

"They're crying."

"Who?"

"The babies."

"No, Lucia," he said, pointing to the bassinet. "Essy is asleep."

The serpents, they mocked me—*stupid girl, made you look!* Then

I understood, all the crying babies were a recording played by Central, an evil trick to divert my attention from my child. I would outsmart them, ignore them—but I ended up ignoring Essy's cries, too. Finally, Manny got angry, threw his temper around, and when he insisted on having Susi's sister, Betty, watch Essy in her home, I gave in. Then I was consumed by guilt.

I kept the socks on my hands, like a scarlet letter, even when I was alone. One time, as punishment, I gulped down half a bottle of laxative, then crawled next door to Mrs. Gutierrez's garden and lay on her flower bed. The ground was frozen (it was middle of winter) but I was sure if I focused intensely enough, I could will a daffodil up from the earth. If this happened, I reasoned, it would be proof that my body had been cleansed of its poison. Three hours later, Mrs. Gutierrez found me prowling on my hands and knees. "I can't find them," I mumbled. "Find what?" she asked. My fingers and toes. They were numb.

She brought me inside. The warmth of her house smelled suspicious, like vitamins and beef broth and soap. "You need a doctor?" She peeled the socks from my hands, touched my fingers, frozen like grape Popsicles. "Maybe I need to take you to a doctor," she said. No way, I knew better. A doctor would send me to the lock-up hospital for sure. Mrs. G pressed hot washcloths to my face, wrapped my hands and feet in iron-warmed towels, brought me a bowl of hot soup. Two sips and I ran to the toilet, stayed bolted there for over an hour. The serpents hissed. One giggled, one cursed. Slowly, I regained sensation. It burned.

When the serpents were awake, my first instinct was to muzzle them by turning up the television. But electromagnetic waves were bad for the baby, and if Manny was home, he'd shut it off. I knew he worried, sensed his thoughts in distress, and I wanted desperately to tell him I'd find some way to care for our daughter. But by that point I found it hard to speak—my mouth moved, but to form the correct sounds seemed impossible. Well, words were a trick, too easily intercepted by Central, I'd need to devise a telepathic code. "Witness Protection Program" meant home, "bread" meant poison, "awake" meant scared, and Essy was "my pancake" or "pet" or "our bumblebee." Of course, this schema ended up being far too complicated. Just thinking about it left me exhausted, mute.

Some days I tried to seek refuge in the loudest place I could find, like Pizza Palace or the laundromat or a fitness class at the Y. But people were risky. Spies gossiped and conspired to wring out my thoughts like they wrung out their wet gym towels. They knew who I was, in spite of my disguise as a Sweet Asian Doll. *She's trying to hide. Why is she hiding? It's time to open her up. Expose her.*

The Chinese restaurant in Greenburgh turned out to be the most effective din, especially at lunch hour, when the serpents had to compete with the crowds. And when the noise thinned I clamped on my headphones and blasted Ella Fitzgerald, who mourned for me as I lay down my chopsticks and washed my fingers in tea. *She's lying on the floor. She's curled up like a ball. She's crying. Are her eyes made for crying? Cut them out! Stop her crying now!*

I stopped crying. My insides dried, cauterized. I had no tears left, but I wanted to die.

After I entered the hospital, the voices quieted, but it didn't take too many brain cells to figure out that Crote Six was an anagram for EXORCIST and only one *E* shy of EROTIC SEX. Central was broadcasting to China, to teach people there about safe sex and mental hygiene. And while I was trapped in their prison, the FBI schemed to steal my baby. I called the police, the fire department, three city council members who turned me away. *Help.* Finally, Child Protective Services said they'd send someone to check on the baby. This made me feel slightly less agitated.

I'd been in lockup before, I knew my rights: If I stayed calm, posed no immediate threat to myself or others, they'd have to let me go. I was the subject of a top-secret government experiment; a journalist working undercover on a sensational exposé; a finalist on a TV reality show—any day now they'd announce the results of the audience vote! The days passed. Little changed. My concerns faded in urgency as life became its new routine: mealtimes and groups and ping-pong with Big Juan, the drama of Hulk and Loco Coco and the other patients in the unit. Gradually bleached of purpose, I'd stand by the windows, projecting my reflection onto the winter. I was the snow and the fog and the wind and the cold. I was the blue scrub, accosted by other blue scrubs, illuminated by fluorescent white lights. But it was different this time, because of Essy. I had a baby now. They would never let me go.

The doctors say I have insight; I can talk about the past, recognize something was wrong. But the truth is, I'm still not sure how to tell what's real—because when you're inside it, it's your reality, and if your own perception of the world isn't valid, then what is? Here's what I do know: I spent a total of forty days in Crote Six. I missed my baby's first laugh, first solid foods, first tooth.

On the day I was finally released, Manny brought me flowers, a dozen Gerbera daisies, and drove the whole way home at exactly two miles under the speed limit. It felt fast, *wheeee!* And it was spring, with tulips and daffodils and blossoms exploding from every tree. I wanted to yell, *I'm free!* "Can I do that?" I asked Manny. "Oh, Jesus," he said. He rolled his eyes but I think he was really nervous. "Joking, geez." Doped up as I was, I still pinched his cheek, stuck my arm out the window and waved to everyone on Main Street.

We stopped at Cousin Delia's first. Essy sat on a plastic floor mat in the kitchen, scooping yogurt in the general direction of her mouth with her fingers. My baby. Sitting up. Feeding herself. I started to cry. I couldn't help it. When Manny had brought her into the p-ward she'd seemed like a borrowed doll, something I couldn't possibly keep. Now I kissed her yogurt-smeared face. I kissed Manny. I kissed Cousin Delia. I beamed the whole way home.

The house looked respectable. Some debris in the front yard, but a freshly swept stoop (Mrs. Gutierrez, no doubt), and only a few hardened food stains on the kitchen floor, a handful of dishes in the sink. Upstairs, I emptied my plastic bag full of personal belongings; clothes got tossed into the laundry heap, toiletries restowed in the bathroom. I brushed my teeth. Flossed. Filled a cup and watered my banana plants. I named them: Dusty, Dusty Two, and Parched. Lying back on the futon mattress, I studied their fronds, such lovely green veins, neat and parallel, in contrast with the wild, crisscross cracks on the ceiling. I sat back up. I pointed my knees to two o'clock. The room felt different. Once thick and seething, it now sat eerily still, as if it'd been depleted of some elemental particle.

The Vargas boys acted like I'd never been gone. "Everything is fine with your family?" said Carlos, and I said yes, and no one asked me anything more. I figured Manny had explained my absence in whatever way he thought best and I felt grateful to him for this. I knew the social had given him pamphlets and explained to him a lot of things, like how I had a Very Serious Lifelong Condition and how to best speak to me in a Supportive and Nonthreatening Manner, and how Very Important it was that I Take My Pills, even though they would make me tired and I'd need extra rest.

On the day of my own homecoming, I decided to bake Chinese almond cookies.

"The almonds are from China?" said Hector. He laughed at his own joke. Slid his stool closer to the small TV on the kitchen counter.

"They're usually for special occasions," I explained, but he was too absorbed in the news. We all know Hector is in love with Mindy Griffin, the reporter on channel 9 with the blond halo hair and spectacular cleavage.

The refrigerator hummed. The kettle boiled. Essy beat on a colander with a wooden spoon. Eventually, she whacked her finger. "Bad spoon. Bad, bad spoon," I said. I hugged her, kissed her, but she kicked and flailed and pushed me away, inconsolable for a good fifteen minutes. "Essy. *Hija*," I pleaded over and over. "Mama's here. Essy, Mama's here." Finally she pressed her wet face into my shoulder. When she fell asleep, I brought her upstairs, then returned to my mixing bowl. I strained my eardrums, now attuned to the frequencies of her doleful cries—but I heard no cries. Reports included a drunk driving accident on the Pelham Parkway, a house fire in White Plains, traffic on the Tappan Zee Bridge.

You did that, right?

"What?"

"You did that, right? Reporter. Manny said you used to do that, like on the news."

"Oh. Right." Hector! "I was a writer. I was on TV only once."

"Oh," he said. "I thought . . ." He pointed to the screen, started laughing, *kuh-kuh-kuh*. Hector has a great laugh, like how a penguin would laugh if penguins laughed, so then I had to laugh, too.

I beat together flour and butter and sugar and eggs. I watched Mindy Griffin. I waited. The screen flickered at me but there was nothing. Or rather, there was something, but it felt far away, no longer in my realm of concern. Maybe for the serpents it was like trying to talk in outer space, with no air to conduct the sound.

For the first few weeks, Manny went all domestic, made the bed, folded laundry, cooked me breakfasts with chorizo and eggs. The Vargas boys were on their best behavior, but I missed Susi, my sweet *hermanita*, with her denim jacket and miniskirts, who was always sprucing up the place with crepe paper streamers or vases of paper flowers or cakes with bright-colored frosting. She was taken away while I was stuck in the p-ward, and I'm convinced it was my fault;

when I went to find her sister in Pleasantville, it turned out Betty had gone, too, moved out of her apartment. "Where would she go?" I asked Manny. "Back to Ecuador?" He said he didn't know. These things happened, like with Jimmy Prieto. I could see it stressed him out to talk about it, so I didn't bring it up again.

Soon after I came home, Essy got sick. She coughed and cried, broke out into a rash one night. The pills knocked me out, I didn't hear her—Manny called Dr. Vera Wang and took care of everything. The cough lasted for weeks. I told Manny he should wake me, but the one time he did, I was completely disoriented, changed her without putting a fresh diaper on and in the morning she was covered with shit.

"Sorry," I said. "I'm so sorry." I washed her in the shower, scrubbed the bedsheets in the tub, sprayed the mattress with bleach and vinegar.

I didn't try to explain to Manny about the meds, how some days my head feels like it's been mulching underground for the duration of a New England winter, how they've tried me on twelve different drugs over the past five years. One made me gain thirty pounds, swell up like a balloon animal, all twisted and pinched and skin too tight for my body. Pop. The next pill caused headaches, the next diarrhea, the next shot me deep into a neuroleptic daze. They prescribed pills in combination. Added pills for the side effects, then pills for side effects of the pills for side effects. They kept upping my Xanax. I couldn't *feel*. Finally I said, No more pills.

I take only one kind of medication now. They adjust the dosage. Sometimes I still slosh around, dense and slushy like a watermelon; other times I'm flat, de-fizzed. And every night, Manny barges into the bathroom, hangs around until I finish brushing my teeth so he can watch me swallow the pills. After a few weeks of this I can't take it, I tell him it makes me nervous, like I'm back in Crote Six. I'm not a prisoner anymore, and I refuse to be treated like one.

This is me, at the p-doc's again. It's slow going with Beige, but he's meticulous at least, records everything in his notepad with his rollerball pen.

"How's the fogginess?" he says.

"A little better. Lighter. Less San Francisco, more L.A."

Fog: less San Francisco, more L.A. There must be a lot to parse in that statement because he's scribbling away for a full minute.

"I notice you've been rubbing your eyes."

"Spring," I say. "Because everything has to have side effects, I guess."

He doesn't smile. He jots again, asks if I'm familiar with tardive dyskinesia, and I say yes, I know, it's a nasty long-term side effect of the meds, where your tongue falls out of your mouth and you twitch and shake. He explains it anyway, neurological effects, et cetera et cetera. So we can be *mindful*. As if I'm not already terrified.

"How about the voices?"

I say they've gone away. Because the truth is, even if the whispers float around the edges, it's better than the zombie haze. Then he asks if there's anything particular on my mind today. Something I'm hoping to get out of the session. For the first time, he sounds like a therapist!

I tell him I'm looking for a job.

"Oh? What kind of job?"

"Local news reporter. Preferably a daily, but I'm looking into radio, maybe TV, too."

"I see," he says. His tone stays even but I catch the slip, the flinch, that arc of the brow, the subtle shift of weight.

"Well, I need a job. Now that I'm not stuck in group therapy sessions every day. And I studied journalism."

He nods, expressionless, rests his elbows on his knees, his chin on his loose-clasped hands. He's thinking awhile, sorting his words. Finally he says, "Did your last therapist speak with you about setting Attainable Short-Term Goals?"

Attainable Short-Term Goals? I picture an ice hockey rink, and he's wearing one of those creepy white masks with holes. Hannibal Lecter. I quickly blink him away.

"What I mean is," Beige continues, "don't you already have a very important job?"

Hannibal Lecter gone, my mind runs blank, so I scan the room with my eyes, the universal sign for, *Um, am I missing something?* Then he is smiling at me! Showing his teeth, yellowish, and this is a first, a landmark event, but still I find nothing to say.

"Aren't you . . . a mother?" Beige unclasps his hands.

"Oh." Hot embarrassment floods my body, though I'm not sure why. "Sure, I guess. I mean, yes. I am."

He nods and nods and smiles.

When I get in the car, I'm all fluttery. I sit on top of my hands. I say it out loud: *Fuck you.*

༄

"He said that?" says Nipa. "A *doctor* said that?"

"Yeah."

"That's so obnoxious. Fuck him."

༈

I keep on looking. I scour the ads, send out résumés. I try for news reporter, cultural editor, arts magazine proofreader, radio show fact-checker, Web content manager, ghostwriter. One day I'm with Essy at the laundromat, checking out the bulletin board while she's mesmerized by the dryers. I find an ad for "art assistant" at one of those Paint-Your-Own pottery studios. I apply for that, too, what the hell, I apply and apply and I wait. Whenever I get called for an interview, I sling on my favorite pair of heels, red suede Mary Janes, tamed with my most conservative skirt. I'm overqualified, underqualified, the position is filled, but everyone compliments my shoes.

To stay active, I assign myself projects, including a feature story on El Pollo Loco.

"El Pollo Loco?" says Manny. "Are you serious?"

But I get a good vibe from the chicken guy, in spite of the creepy rubber suit. And the suit, well, it's intriguing.

We meet at a coffee shop. He's punctual. He takes off his chicken head and he's early fifties maybe (he won't confirm), lean and Germanic, with chiseled features and pale gray eyes. Sweaty, intense, with an ants-in-the-pants energy too big to be confined indoors—so it's only mildly shocking to learn he's an ex–fighter pilot who flew in Iraq, with a daughter in her last year at Vassar. I ask the obvious question: *Why?* "I *am* El Pollo Loco," he explains, and when he puts on that suit every morning it's like climbing into his own skin. There's something reassuring about this fixed identity, instantly recognizable to everyone in the world, including himself. "Why so rubbery? So . . . dead looking?" "My insides turned out," he says.

He's also an artist, a sculptor. He invites me to his dilapidated garage-studio, where he's created hundreds of molds of human body parts using aluminum foil, glue, and Scotch tape. "Are the parts . . .

yours?" I ask. "Mostly," he says. Shiny, crinkly. Hands, feet, torsos, ears, elbows, toes, even teeth. On one wall hangs a series of faces ("all mine"), on another a series of penises ("not all mine"). It's fascinating in an overly intimate kind of way, kinky and very medieval. "I got more," he says. Art has saved him, because the only time he can stand still is when he's working. Then he confides, he's never shown his work to anyone except his dog, a rescue greyhound he calls Chum. Not even his daughter. "I don't really see her," he says. "Fucked up too many times." He gets into it, how she was born premature, how he was stationed overseas, how his wife left him for his best friend from college, and as he talks he bounces one knee, then the other, and his pupils recede like he's transported in time. When we say good-bye he shakes my hand, his hot and vigorous, and I feel honored, somehow, humbled.

The next time I run into El Pollo on Main Street, his eyes are all buggy and he's yelling at a parking meter. Pumped on amphetamines, probably bipolar, too, symptoms exacerbated by his PTSD—that doesn't make him any less interesting, but when I e-mail a couple of my old editors it turns out no one wants a story about another crazy vet. I write it up anyway.

A week later, I get called for Art Assistant!

The proprietor is a thin, purple-wearing lady, long gray hair in a ponytail, pale skin that looks easily bruised. Henlike, soft-spoken, she explains to me about her cats, how Austin has been puking up hair balls all morning, how Abby likes to nap under the easel.

She pores through my résumé, taps with her pencil on the linen-textured paper. *English. Tap. Journalism. Tap. World Teach. Tap.*

"And why did you spend so much time in . . . South America? When you are . . ." She waves her pencil in the air, that circular wave people resort to when they're blocked.

"Chinese-American."

"Chinese!" She taps again. "That's very far away from . . . Costa Rica." *Tap*. "Bolivia." *Tap*. "Colombia. Ecuador. Brazil." *Tap, tap, tap*.

I'm flustered, confused. For a second my brain feels like it's full of holes. She waits expectantly. But what would it be, I wonder, to conduct one's life as a Chinese life instead of just a life? I speak Chinese, I cook Chinese food, practice tai-chi on occasion and drink oolong tea, but to flaunt one's authenticity seems terribly gauche. I'm human first, aren't I? Aren't we all?

"Is there something special about . . . these countries?"

"Oh. Yes." The face, so open. Puzzled. "Yes. Well, in China the traditional music is played by the *erhu*, that one-string instrument that sounds like a dying cat. But in Latin American countries they play salsa and merengue and even the old people go to parties and dance." I know it sounds silly, simplistic, but it's the best I can do to convey it, the essence, these cultural differences captured in a nutshell.

Purple Lady frowns, Very Serious. "I'm afraid I'm not familiar," she says. She continues tap-tapping. Then, "Do you like working with people?"

"Oh, yes! I love people."

"Wonderful." The wrinkles on her forehead smooth themselves out. "And can you tell me why you'd like to work here?"

I blank again. But I tell the truth. News is high stakes, high stress all the time, deadline driven, and I don't know if I can take the all-nighters anymore. I mention I've been through a few rough patches lately, and outcomes for my "condition" improve with minimized stress. It's what the doctors always say.

"Oh." She nods.

She promises to get back to me in three or four days.

I get in my car. I hear her voice like an echo. *Oh*.

Purple Lady doesn't call. I call a week later. She says sorry, she's found a better fit.

I drive to pick up Manny from the Pig. I don't say anything. He pulls my head to his shoulder, rests his cheek on my forehead. That's when the little voice in my ear calls, *Mama*. Essy. My baby's first words! I whip around, but her eyes are already closed.

I don't tell Beige about Purple Lady. I don't tell him anything about the job situation, though he asks politely and seems contrite, as if he's gone back and read some professional manual and is now trying extra hard to contain his subconscious biases against people with my diagnosis. He's just a person, I suppose, not some robotic insect after all. Instead, we talk *history*. He asks about my first episode. "Insight is so important," he says.

First time it happened. "It," the *zing*. Freshman year of college. I was visiting the art museum, staring at Picasso's *Girl Before a Mirror*; the painting felt curiously bright. Ten minutes I stood there, you couldn't have pried off my eyes, and then came my reward: the colors bubbled like something alien, and the girl's body parts came to life! First her breasts jiggled, like ornaments dangling on a Christmas tree, then her stomach growled, then half her cubist face laughed openly at me while the other half distorted into a leer. *Oh, Picasso, what a trick!* I thought, enthralled by my own dreamlike state.

Well, the girl was me, of course. With one face for myself, one for everyone else, the People of the World. But no. That was wrong. There were the in-betweens: my mother, my sister, my roommates, my friends. And my boyfriends, never quite satisfying, though why relationships did or didn't work, I still couldn't figure—maybe I needed more faces, one for each person I knew, or maybe infinite, for each new person I was still to meet! And then it hit me. Oh, Great Master, revealing to me the ways of human nature, the ideal of the soul mate, why true love was so hard to find. *Zing!* The faces. We each had too many faces!

I took out my sketch pad. Crayons to paper, I drew furiously. Circles, squares, triangles, color-coded for physical, intellectual, emotional needs, sense of humor, artistic appreciation, sexual adeptness, musical tastes, compatibility for travel and confinement in small spaces . . . If I could capture it on paper, create an artistic representation of human relationships, then it would finally all make sense. I rushed to my dorm room. I skipped lunch and dinner. I sketched the whole night, in the dark, afraid that light would interfere with the synaptic conductions in my brain.

By the next afternoon, the electricity had subsided. I squinted at pages and pages of my multicolored scribbles, trying to reconjure the excitement—but the connections, they were gone. Later, ravenous, I went out for pizza with a group of dormmates, perfectly content to be one of the pack.

It wasn't obvious then that anything was wrong. But the serpents, maybe they were born that day. Every now and then I'd hear tiny cries or whispers, like when background music played at a coffee shop or when air rushed through the trees. Too porous to catch, they slipped in and out, but slowly I learned to divine their special messages—through the words on a billboard or a passing truck, in the patterns of traffic lights. *The Juice Is Loose! Share the Road. Red, red, red, red, green.* Maybe I started to court them. Seek them. I fantasized about my very own muse.

Summer after freshman year, I taught English abroad. Luck, or fate, put me in Quito, where I was thrown into communal life: giant shared house full of gringos and pool tables and no hot water, co-op-style dinners taken out on the front stoop at dusk, tacos or spaghetti or vegetarian stir fries, pineapple crushed ice late night. Ten weeks stretched forever, friendships on fast forward, forged on the morning walk to the bodega or a bumpy bus ride or a jungle hike, cemented by nightfall, sprouting into love affairs with students or taxi drivers or *salseros* or bullfighters. Oh, golden summer! Each day sharp and transformative, glowing and singular, each moment a glittery embrace. People think of home as a single fixed place, but when I went traveling, I found the community of extended family I'd never had. Later, I learned there's a Spanish word for this: *querencia*. It refers to that place in the ring where a bull feels strongest, safest, where it returns again and again to renew its strength. It's the place we're most comfortable, where we know who we are—where we feel our most authentic selves.

I headed back to Latin America after graduation, propelled by the breeze of twenties-hood. Each time I set foot in a new city or town or forgotten fishing village, I felt like I'd been recharged, remade. And the beautiful people smiled, or stared, or stopped to talk, welcomed me into their shops, their gardens, their huts, their shacks, introduced me to their children and sisters and *tías* and *abuelas*, fed me *llapingachos* and *fritatas* and *ceviches* and soups, and I swelled with bliss. Those days were forever, life pouring into me all thick and spicy and I was bottomless. It's like this, I think, to be happy.

But as time passed, I sensed tiny impulses like electric shocks, allusions to the next adventure. Somewhere, there was more. True Calling, ready for embarkation, True Love, waiting to be found! One day I woke and I knew it was done. After three years away, I returned to the States. I was convinced I had important work to do: to document the world.

I plowed through my journalism program, three internships, got hired by a weekly in Connecticut after graduation. I pitched a story to an editor who had visited our investigative journalism class, and to my amazement, she said yes. That summer, I spent six weeks in Vietnam, researching a story on mail-order brides. The scene was tense, seedy, grim—yet what work could be more exhilarating? I befriended a family with six homely daughters, five sold off to Taiwanese businessmen. The eldest had just committed suicide; the youngest, enlisted, awaited her fate. I staked out university cafés, karaoke *ôm*s, the *nhà nghi*s where rooms rented by the hour. True Calling, found: I would become a spy! Penetrate borders, bridge cultural divides, infiltrate the sleazy shadow worlds of Asia—Cambodia, Thailand, Laos, even North Korea. One day I decided I no longer needed a silly American disguise. I stopped eating, bathing, wore the same clothes for weeks. Exteriors didn't matter to the People of the World. I interviewed bouncers and garbagemen and prostitutes, the homeless who looked not too unlike myself after a while. My mission: to tell their stories, to become a Voice, their savior.

By the time it became obvious, I'd crossed the threshold, lost all capacity to distinguish what was real from what was not. The professional term for this, I learned much later, is "conversion," and suddenly everyone I knew spoke in worried whispers, and this alarmed me—I had to reassure them that they'd all be just fine! I lost my job in Connecticut, but told myself it had been too restrictive anyway. After all, the People were in every neighborhood in New York—even in Providence, where I lived on Jie's couch for a while. At times my burden felt so overwhelming, I physically froze. My brain emptied, and all my thoughts seemed to float into a comic strip bubble two feet above my head. Words felt sticky, gummy, like the old typewriter I used in the seventh grade. Soon I was convinced some Higher Authority had bugged my bedroom, tampered with my computer, my e-mail, forged handwritten notes with my name. I couldn't sleep. I didn't eat. And then the serpents came.

She is sitting in the middle of the street. Stupid girl, sitting in the street. Under the manhole cover she thinks there's a man.

It was a stern policewoman who found me, hands clamped over my ears, singing at the top of my lungs. I was brought to the emergency room. It was Jie who came, who physically restrained me from leaving the waiting area until I was seen and involuntarily committed.

That first hospital stay, I was a compliant patient, a Sweet Asian Doll, and for this I was branded with a Severe Lifelong Mental Illness. Later, I would be told I had a twenty percent chance of maintaining a full-time job, a twenty-five percent chance of living independently, a forty percent chance of attempting suicide, a ten percent chance of succeeding.

I was twenty-six years old.

⁓

This is life. One day, then the next. Essy's first birthday arrives. I get a package from Jie, picture books and dresses and four boxes of Swiss chocolates, along with a card that says, *Lucia, please give Esperanza a birthday kiss from her Auntie. Hope everyone is well. Please be sure to take good care of your health!*

My health? Well, I'm pretty sure that's Jie's code. It means: Lucia, take your pills.

I give the chocolates to Manny. He devours half a box. He's grilling steaks out on the front porch, freezing his ass off in a T-shirt and gloves. I've baked a cake, put up yellow and white streamers, a birthday banner, hung a donkey piñata above the kitchen sink. Susi would've approved. We light a candle. One! One year. Already one year. Only one year. It feels like my baby's been on this earth forever.

Christmas comes, sneaks down the chimney, New Year rings itself in while I sleep. Essy goes bipedal—she wobbles, she toddles, she's off to explore, I'm chasing after her. That winter is so crazy, one storm trailing into the next, and Mindy Griffin's interviewing traffic cops and plow drivers and power line technicians, and every meteorologist in the tristate area revels in the snowfall numbers like a rah-rah sport. Driving is slow. I shovel out the car, fight with neighbors over parking spots, which they claim with crates and cones and folding chairs, a toy wagon full of stuffed animals. Our neighbors, they can be fierce.

Manny takes on double shifts at the diner. He's stressed about money. Whenever his Mami calls he's broody for days and won't say why. When he works late, he drives himself home. One night he spins off an icy patch near the reservoir and skids into a ditch.

Luckily, it's before dawn, no other cars on the road. Luckily, it doesn't happen three hundred feet later, where he would've crashed through the guardrail into the water and ended up on the channel 9 news. Manny refuses to flag anyone for help, so he starts walking home, goes about half a mile when a police car pulls up alongside him. He's terrified. The officer asks if he needs assistance, and might he know whose car has been left back there? Poor Manny. Luckily, the cop isn't a dick. Luckily, Manny isn't hurt, but the car is totaled, and the accident freaks him out and he can't sleep for weeks. He stays up all night watching telenovelas, complains of stomach pains, and when he does sleep, he grinds his teeth so hard it's worse than a dental hygienist with a metal scaler.

"Are you okay?" I say. He just looks at me with his dog brown eyes. But he doesn't bring up what I think he's going to bring up— the papers. So I don't either. It's awkward, complicated, and the truth is, I don't want to get married again, not like this, anyway. But for Manny, well, it occurs to me that maybe there's one thing he's more scared of than getting deported—me. Maybe that's why we're both tiptoeing around.

"Fredy has been sick again. Mami's worried," he says. Fredy, his youngest brother, born slow, with the defective heart and coughs and constant chest infections, who is always running out of air. Poor Fredy. I go to the Chinese herbalist, who sells me six packages of herbs for weak pulse, diagnosed as qi deficiency. Mami will need a special clay pot to brew the tonic, so I find a pretty mustard yellow one with bamboo leaves painted on the side. I bundle it with three-for-five-dollar I HEART NY T-shirts and bubble wrap, along with detailed preparation instructions. Packages to Ecuador need to be sent via courier, but when I tell them it's medicine, they refuse to take it. I bring the herbs home, wrap them in tissue paper in a pretty red box, take it back another day. I tell them it's seasonings for soup.

"Thank you," says Manny.

"*De nada*," I say. I hope Fredy is okay, because no matter what kind of illness, being sick really sucks.

Deep February, I land an interview for my dream job, at last. Feature reporter for a regional daily!

The interviewer's name is *Dirk*.

"NYU. English major," he says, nodding. Tall and blond with a dimpled smile, curly bed-head hair just disheveled enough to redeem his unfortunate mint green shirt.

Turns out we graduated from NYU four years apart. He asks if I worked at the paper there. I never worked at the paper, but we play the name game and figure out we both had the same academic adviser.

"Not a bad guy. Brilliant writer."

"Decent lecturer. Kind of odd."

"A little awkward."

"In that turtle-like, professorial way," he says.

He's gracious. We bond over our shared lukewarm enthusiasm.

"What did you do in college?"

I tell the truth. "I pondered. A lot. Probably too much."

"I minored in ponderance," he says.

We discuss classes, dorms, graduate school, and then my internships, the paper, the job, the culture, the expectations.

"Your book is good," he says. He flips through my clips, pauses at my piece on Vietnamese brides.

"What'd you think of Hanoi?" he asks.

"Rich. Rich for the senses. For the soul." I gush, feeling stupid. But it turns out he's been there, he gets it. Dirk has seen so much of Asia it's intimidating.

He points to my piece on El Pollo Loco, never published, but I stuck it in anyway. "This one is good, too. Why haven't you worked at a daily before?"

"Just busy, I guess."

He glances at the bottom of my résumé, the part with the "additional information." Fluent in English, Spanish, Portuguese, Chinese. Some Hebrew. Violin. Electric bass. He raises his eyebrows. "Electric bass?"

I smile and he smiles, shows his celebrity teeth; he worked his way through college playing drums in wedding bands and somehow I'm not surprised. "This all looks very good," he says. "We'll do the standard reference checks, but it all looks good. I should be able to get back to you in a couple of days."

I shake his hand. It's warm and dry and firm.

That weekend, I'm buoyant, giddy, like a schoolgirl waiting to be asked to prom. Nipa calls. It's one of those warm, teaser days in early March and she's meeting some friends down at Ryder's Park. Sure, I'll join.

Essy walks, all twenty-two pounds of her tottering from side to side. She's like some mythical creature, freshly hatched, embodying awe and delight as she stomps through a mud puddle. *Stop that! It's dirty!* I hear the words in my head, but I don't let them out. I let her stomp away.

Natey is beautiful, cherubic as ever. Nipa glows, too. Something about her feels different now. Lighter. She's found a new job at an at-risk youth center in Harlem, which is something she's always wanted to do.

I tell her about the interview.

"Oh, that sounds perfect," she says. "And all those Points of Connectivity. It's perfect. You're going to get it for sure."

"You think so?"

"*You* think so," she says, all go-go girl. "That's what matters, right?"

On Monday I wait. On Tuesday I wait. When six days have passed, I send a polite e-mail. The reply pops up right away.

*Hi Lucia, I enjoyed speaking with you as well, but unfortunately, we
don't feel it's the right fit for our organization. Sorry for not getting back
to you sooner. I wish you the best of luck. D.*

I stare at my computer screen so long the letters start to wiggle.
I blink them back into shape. First, it's so abrupt. Second, it's so final. Third, *D*?

"We have jobs. Diner has jobs," says Manny. "Hostess job. Dishwasher. Place across the street has jobs."

I don't say anything.

"Next one, you'll get it," he says.

Next one. I lie on our futon mattress like a gutted fish. Stare up
at the ceiling, the paint peels, the crisscross cracks, the dome light
fixture, white and opaque, reminiscent of a silver-nippled breast.

*Aiya, Lucia, she wants to run wild. Cutting school, sneaking around
with boys, never thinking about future. You think this is fine?*

But Ma, Lucia is smart. She'll figure it out.

I trace the cracks back and forth with my eyeballs, I look for a
sign: If I find a path that traverses the ceiling without crashing into
the breast, it means I'll find a job by the end of the month. . . .

Manny gives Essy her bath, towels her dry, dresses her in her ducky
pajamas. She's had trouble sleeping since she grew out of the bassinet
and moved into our bed. When we leave the room she screams, *UP!*
"Maybe we should let her cry it out," I say. But he lies next to her, rubs
her back, hooks her fingers on his pinky until she calms. When he
sleeps, I touch the mole on his cheek. I ring it like a doorbell.

Lucia can do anything she wants.

I find my phone. I creep downstairs. Shaking, I impulse dial. I
hardly ever speak to Jie anymore. We e-mail, and it's sporadic. But
for this, she's the only one who will understand.

"They know."

"What are you talking about? What is it, Lucia? What's wrong?"

She sounds frantic. I forgot, it's the middle of the night over there. I tell her about the interview.

"They were about to hire me, and then they didn't. They must know."

"About what?"

"The hospital. My records."

"Oh, Lucia." Now she's yawning. "But how would they know?"

"I don't know."

"It's private."

"Maybe I'm blacklisted."

"Medical records are private. It would be discriminatory. Anyway, why would you think they know?"

I tell her about NYU and ponderance and Vietnam and bass. The Points of Connectivity. I know when a conversation feels right.

"Oh, Lucia." She sighs.

"What do I do?"

Make your bed.

"Do I call and ask him why?"

I can hear the whir of her professional brain, evaluating the situation.

"I guess . . . I don't think so."

Lie in it.

I can't help it, I start to cry.

"I'm sorry," she says. "I don't think there's anything you can do. But it's just one interview, Lucia. I'm sure you'll find something else."

"But you don't know. . . ."

"You're a really good writer. You'll find something. I know you will, Lucia, it will all work out. How is everything else? Is Esperanza okay? Did you get the package I sent?"

But I'm not in the mood.

I head back upstairs, lie next to Essy, listen to Manny's snores.

Why is Lucy crying?
Me? Who am I?
Schizophrenia does not define who I am.

That night I float back to my mother's house in New Jersey. The one with the purple swing set in the backyard, green shag carpets, basketball hoop in the driveway.

Ma has cancer.
What?
Cancer. Lung cancer.
Oh my God, Jie. What do we do?

Spring of my junior year at NYU. Jie at that behemoth consulting firm, working with some telecommunications client (she was miserable). She took charge of everything—the appointments, the follow-ups, the endless research. I was the one living at home in New Jersey that summer, working as a temp (the only summer I didn't go abroad), but Jie was always buzzing around. That was the summer Ma was too weak to move, knocked out by infusions, hospitalized with infections, waiting for transfusions, or, at best, resting in her favorite green suede recliner, listening to her Pavarotti. Sometimes I'd take out my tall spiral notebook. *Ma, tell me a story.* Or, if she was too tired for a story, *Ma, teach me how to make Mapo tofu.* It was the summer I learned how to cook, and I jotted down every recipe Ma could remember—spare ribs with garlic and honey and five-spice powder, lion's head meatballs, almond cookies, *char siu* and shrimp fried rice. *Use day-old rice, right, Ma? Yes, day-old is best. Set the shrimp on a paper towel in front of a fan. To cook up crisp, they must first be dry.* On Christmas Eve, she was declared in remission. We celebrated by roasting a duck, Peking-style. *To health,* said Jie. *To life,* said Ma, and I nearly dropped my cup of *baijiu.* To be honest, I'd never allowed myself to think she wouldn't survive.

The only p-doc I ever liked was my first, Dr. Hassan, a young Iranian woman with a British accent. "Stress," she said. "Stress and drugs are the riskiest triggers. You should learn to watch for the signs." *Signs?* "Prodromal symptoms. The ones that forecast a break."

She focused on wellness: daily routines, proper nutrition, exercise, sleep and self-care. I never got to bed early, but I ate mostly organic, took brisk walks, practiced yoga and tai-chi. And then I met Yonah and fell in love.

His essence? Something big. Bulletproof, with the presence of a rhinoceros, yet still unassuming, slightly comical, like a duck.

"Hey you," he said, that first time we met. "I am owner of this store. I give you present, you stop eating from my bulk food aisle." He handed me a small, hexagonal-shaped box tied clumsily with red ribbon. It was filled with macadamias.

"For one week I see you sampling my nuts. You are embarrassed now?" he said, but he said it laughing, because Yoni, only his heart is bigger than his mouth. We played chess, drank wine. I barely even noticed his injured arm; the rest of him was too alive.

Shortly after we met, my mother died. That day at her funeral, he stood beside me, I knew he was my angel. "Why are you crying?" I said, watching him wipe his eyes. "Why you are not crying?" he said. "Your mother is dead. You are daughter with no mother. I love you. Of course I cry."

We got married. Divinely blessed, my thoughts popped like fire-crackers, my heart swelled with happiness, my body exuded a mag-netic energy. I was an aura of love, a goddess in heat, and people sought out my company to tell me their stories, even virtual strang-ers: Mrs. Sato, the quiet divorcée (who carried a gun as well as a Pomeranian in her handbag), preferred Indian men and anal sex; Juan Carlos, the Colombian guitarist who rehearsed in the basement, had lymphoma, but refused to let his bandmates know; Mr. Taka-hara, the multimillionaire developer, invited me to his private island in the Bahamas (an impulse purchase he'd made the previous winter) to ghostwrite his autobiography. I was the hub of the neighborhood.

"*Hypomania,*" said Dr. Hassan, "is characterized by a pervasive elevated state, euphoria, increased creativity and productivity." Well, what person in their right mind would want to switch that off? I had every intention of staying that way forever.

I didn't catch it in time.

The glossy sheen faded. One night I became convinced Yonah was broadcasting my life to Israel via the security monitors in our bedroom. I felt devastated, betrayed, and the world's troubles draped over me like a heavy tarp. Mr. Takahara was falling into bankruptcy. Juan Carlos needed me to cleanse his body's qi. Mrs. Sato beckoned to me with each tilt of her chin—I was a geisha girl, to join in her multicultural orgies. I retreated. Suspicious, irritable, overwhelmed.

"What's wrong?" asked Yonah.

I couldn't say. The words had fallen out again. And in a rush, the voices came.

The serpents whispered: *Her ovaries are shrinking. Her eggs are dying. The baby needs to be born.*

A baby, trapped inside my ovaries—an actual, teeny-tiny human, fully formed! She was crying. She needed me.

I watched Chaka and Noemie in the store, enthralled by their baby boy. How he slept, how he nursed, how he cried to be understood but never judged or demanded explanations. I could learn. I could love. Like the rest of humankind. I only needed to hold my baby in my arms.

Of all the thoughts I was experiencing in those days, these turned out to be the most reasonable, sane.

I pretended along in the hospital that time, stayed quiet, played nice. Within a few days I was released.

Sometime later, I said good-bye to Yonah. I left Manhattan. I didn't hesitate. Here's the thing: When the serpents come, they seize control via the heart, erase all self-doubt, and life exists only day to day. In those moments, it makes perfect sense to succumb to them and their unwavering conviction.

Sometime later, I found myself in another p-ward up north.

But when I got pregnant, that tiny being inside me would become my angel. I ditched the pills. I lived my life. Forty weeks' truce—peace, the serpents in hibernation. Then my baby left my body. My *bao-bao*, my *hija*. Esperanza, my love. The serpents returned, with a vengeance.

༄

Last day of April, I'm offered part-time work. Copywriter for an online vitamin retailer. It's cracker dry, but I learn to extol the benefits of melatonin and colonic cleanses and raspberry ketones. I make them sound irresistible.

"Should we celebrate?" says Manny.

"Why not?" I say.

His favorite spot is the Ecuadorian buffet, but it's so warm that weekend I'm in the mood for the beach. So we decide on Croton Point, on the Hudson, not far away, and that morning I hear from Nipa, who I haven't seen in two months, so I invite her to meet us there, too.

It's crowded. A perfect, glorious day, and apparently everyone's had the same idea. We pick a spot, unfurl our blanket. Manny has packed a picnic lunch in a real basket, with peanut butter and jelly sandwiches and carrot sticks and cut-up fruit—it's sweet, especially since he doesn't usually like peanut butter, or sandwiches, which I say makes him un-American. It's a joke.

We watch the kids race up to the water's edge, squeal as it touches their toes. We flick off Essy's shoes, let her run in the sand. A second later, she shoves a wet fistful into her mouth.

"No, no," Manny yells.

"Let her be," I say, laughing. "How else will she learn?"

Seagulls, bold as rats, fat as rabbits, squabble on the shore. As Essy gives chase, their tiny feet patter this way and that, the flock like an organism, a spill of water, magically changing shape.

Manny runs after Essy. He's showing her how to skip stones in the water when Nipa arrives, elbows linked with a big beefy white guy with a bushy beard who's walking bowlegged like a country singer.

We hug. "This is my husband, Winston," she says.

"Nice to finally meet you," I say. Winston slogs after Natey, who has headed straight for the water.

"Is that your husband over there?" Nipa points to Manny, feet submerged in lapping waves.

"That's Manny," I say.

"I have news." She's beaming. She pats her belly.

"Are you *pregnant*?"

"Twelve weeks. I've been dying to tell someone."

"Wow! Congratulations!" I say. And then I can't help it, I'm picturing Nipa's skinny frame being pounded by Winston, the great woolly mammoth. "How are you feeling?"

"Exhausted," she says. "But getting better. Second trimester is so much more tolerable, right?"

"Right," I say, though I can't really remember. Pregnancy feels so deep in my own past, and I haven't been able to think of it as a repeat event. Not with all that happened after Essy's birth.

"Hey, what happened with that news job? The one you interviewed for?"

"Oh, that." I extol the benefits of writing about melatonin and colonic cleanses and raspberry ketones. Make it sound irresistible.

And then I hear it:

Is that you?

Lucy, is that you?

The voice, low and froggy, wafts in the air, but from the surprise on Nipa's face I know it's real. I whip around to a shock of pink hair, tough, weathered skin, face too small for its buggy eyes. A bull, I think, or a bronco at the gate, or maybe a slab of beef jerky.

Coco. Loco Coco. I haven't seen Coco since the day before I left Crote Six, but it's her all right, in a white V-neck undershirt and orange tights, still grinding away on her wad of gum.

"Lucy! Knew it was you, baby." Her rough cheek against mine as she hugs me tight. "This your friend? You got such nice-looking friends, baby. And where's your little girl? Is that her? Oh my God, you're not kidding, she is too gorgeous. Lord, how time flies. What's it been? A year?"

It comforts me somehow, to see she's still the same Loco Coco with her pinball energy, all flashing lights and snapping rubber bands. Her eye. I remember. She stabbed herself in the eye with a chopstick the morning she was supposed to leave the p-ward.

"How is everything?" I say.

"Grand. Just grand, baby. Beach on a day like this? I've been living with my nephew real close by, just for temporary. You been back to the Holiday Inn lately, baby?" She winks.

I shake my head.

"Big Juan's got a crush on you. Hell, they all do. Who wouldn't,

right?" She's asking Nipa, who nods emphatically. I'm reeling from
the dissonance.

"Nipa, this is . . ."

Coco's over by the waves, squatting near the kids. Natey shies
away. "Hey, pretty thing. Me, Coco." She puts out her hand. Essy
returns the high five.

"Too gorgeous! Just like her mama." Coco is back, pinches my
arm, flashes Nipa her toothy smile. "Me and this one go way back,
she's got a heart of gold. I don't want to keep you, baby. But you
gonna take me to that Chinese joint sometime, right? King crab
legs. Buffet style. Remember, baby?"

"Sure, Coco. All you can eat."

"I'll give you my number. Got a pen?"

She scribbles on a napkin. "I'm right up there." She points to the
sky, though maybe she's referring to one of the towns across the
river. "Rents outta control, right? Ta-ta, baby, I gotta run. You call
me. So nice to meet." She waves, Very Royal, takes a quick bow. And
then she's gone, and the air is still.

"A character," says Nipa.

"Yep. A character," I say.

She doesn't ask any more, but it's Winston who lumbers over, all
pink and out of breath, huffing, "Who was that crazy lady?"

"Lucia used to play in a band," says Nipa. As if this should account
for such bizarre behaviors, and I'm grateful. Nipa and I talk kids, but
personal stuff we still mostly hide away.

"Nice friend," says Manny, after they've gone, and I explain how
Nipa and I met in the basement of the Unitarian church. I'm sure I
told him before, about all the different-shaped breasts, but he must
not have been listening because what man wouldn't remember that?

"Her and that big dude are one funny couple though," he says,
and I have to laugh. Sometimes Manny and I get each other like
that. "So what do you think?" he says. He sprawls out on the blanket,

all fidgety, scrapes crusted sand off the bottoms of his feet, pops a grape into his mouth. "Maybe it's time to get married, no?"

I blink. I look up, as if words are falling out of the clouds. He's not looking at me. He's chewing a grape. So I run to the water. I run in all the way up to my waist.

Days pass. Weeks pass. He doesn't say anything, but I feel it in the air sometimes. About what he said, I'm not sure anymore, what the words were exactly. Maybe we should get married? Should we get married sometime? Is it time to get married? It might be good to get married? One thing I know it was not: "Will you marry me?"

༄

Ma, what happened to Ba?

Your father died in an accident.

What kind of accident?

A car accident.

What was he like? How did you meet?

I was arranged to marry another man. But then I fell in love with your father.

That's so romantic!

He was smart. Very smart. A brilliant scientist. He could charm a snake with his sweet talk, make a bullfrog laugh. He swept me off my feet, as they say.

But Gong-gong Po-po didn't like him.

That's right.

Why not?

Aiya, Xiao-mei. Very complicated. Family matters.

But we don't have family, Ma.

We have three of us, Xiao-mei. Easier this way.

Ma, from a prominent family. Gong-gong Po-po suspicious of Ba, who came from a tiny village in the countryside. But they'd married, had a child, and Ma's family had grown fond of their new son-in-law (*I tell you, with his mouth, no one can resist your Ba*).

In the end, it was about money.

Gong-gong Po-po loaned your Ba money. Lot of money, some belonging to government. He lost it all. Big shame, big dishonor on family. Big disaster for your Gong-gong Po-po. They kick us out. This is hard, hard time. Everything wrong. Your Jie, probably too young to remember.

You stayed with him.

Yes. A waxy glaze settles over her eyes. *I stayed with him. I gave up my family. I thought it was right.*

But were you happy?

Happy? Aiya, Xiao-mei, you want too much, don't be greedy. This is too much American.

But you came here to be an American, Ma. You came all alone. Tell me about the airplane.

Aiya, the airplane again!

As a child, I ask for this story all the time. Shanghai to Hong Kong to Honolulu to San Francisco. A turbulent ride. The fat *gweilo* beside her vomiting into a paper bag. Not once, not twice. Seven times.

And the lady behind us offers roast pork bun to your Jie. Can you imagine? That fei gung like that, and all Chinese can think of is food.

I was in your belly.

Of course you were. Months you were in there, making me sick. I kept thinking, I'm going to be sick. But you kick me. You say, keep on going.

Were you scared?

No time to be scared! You were waiting to be born.

I was born in Tennessee. Full of golden-hairs.

How many thousand miles I travel to give birth to my bao-bao in this foreign land. I think I am in a dream. No husband. No family. Only Third Uncle who agreed to sponsor my visa, and he is not even blood uncle, he is uncle married in from your Ba's side, who owns a shoe-repair shop and speaks Taishanese. A dialect Ma can barely understand.

Were you lonely?

I was free. In China, never free. Your Ba says to be free we have to go to America. We make plans. But then . . .

At this point, her lips draw into a thin, red line. She pinches my cheeks, braids my hair, scraping my scalp with bobby pins.

When can I go on an adventure, Ma?

Aiya, Xiao-mei, you are here, in America. We have house. With yard. And swing set! Good life. I tell you, it's hard to believe.

I have no memories of Tennessee. Only memories of the way I pictured Ma there: as a fearless pioneer.

I try to imagine it, Manny and me holding hands before a crusty magistrate. What I see is this: black and white floor tiles, dingy lights, Yoni and me down at City Hall, Jie as our only witness.

What was marriage, then, but a piece of white paper packed with tiny type, signed by a city clerk? A convention, a formality, hardly relevant, because true love is the only tie that binds! It's what I thought at the time. But now, at night, in the dark, flanked by two sets of breaths, four arms, four legs, a click of teeth—well, I'm tethered to a different life. But I'm still not sure I want a piece of paper to dictate what it is.

I focus on Essy. We'll take a special trip, just the two of us.

"T-r-a-i-n. We're taking the t-r-a-i-n. We're taking the t-r-a-i-n to the Big Apple today."

We stroll down Main Street and everyone smiles as she waves her baby-wave, opening and closing her little fist.

"Ap-ple," she says. *"Manzana."*

"Big Apple," I say.

"Manzana grande!"

She's smart. Holy shit, my baby is smart. I want to flag down a passerby, this man, a biker, another parent with child. *Manzana grande! Did you hear that? Seventeen months old. Manzana grande! My baby is smart!*

We go to Central Park, to the zoo. Jie brought me here as a kid sometimes; we'd buy two bags of nuts from the street vendor and imagine all the animals were our relatives. *Auntie Emu from Australia is grumpy again. African pygmy snake is too shy to say hello. Where will you live when you grow up, Jie? Mmm, maybe here in New York? Well, I'm going to live in the whole wide world!*

I take Essy to see the gorilla. I beat my chest, and the gorilla presses her nostrils against the window, fogs up the thick wall of glass. Those wary eyes, the leathery black palms. I press my hand to hers. Essy slaps her pink fingers on the window, too, until a nervous volunteer tells us to stop.

Twelve more touches.

We pass the bats and frogs, penguins and sea lions, a sloth, a banded mongoose, two polar bears. Our last stop is the petting barn, where goats and sheep and potbellied pigs chomp pellets from Essy's hands. The chickens intrigue her; she chases them and they cluck away, and we're there for half an hour playing this game. "Come on, *hija*. We have to go now." "Aww," she says. But suddenly I'm sad to say good-bye, too, knowing the animals will stay, day after day, confined to their pens and cages.

Essy likes the carousel best of all.

Then she falls asleep in her stroller and I walk downtown, down, down, all the way to Chinatown, where I buy a taro milk tea and six pineapple buns. I pass the congee shop, the egg tart man, the beauty parlor where Jie and I used to go together for our haircuts and five-dollar pedicures. It's not a conscious plan, my feet taking me up Bowery, Grand, but then I'm crossing Delancey, greeted by pizzas and knishes and halal meats, the wholesale luggage stores lining Orchard Street, where bearded men with turbans wolf whistle before they yell, "Suitcase for fifteen dollar! Okay, ten dollar!"

I keep walking north, cross Houston Street.

We'll surprise him.

Essy, look! This is where Mama used to live! But my baby is still asleep. From a block away I can see a new lemon yellow awning, and a frozen yogurt shop where the old Polish diner used to be. But there's the same chalkboard easel with loopy handwriting out front: *Acai bowls. Wheatgrass shots. Green Power smoothies. Come Inside!* The same rickety red bench, host to musicians and tattoo artists and bartenders and iguana owners and posers who drag long and hard on their rollies. But when I step inside, I find neon signs on the exposed brick walls, shiny chrome tables instead of the wood ones with uneven legs. The bulk nut bins are gone. I don't spot Chaka or Jonny or any of the old crew, just an ultrahipster Japanese guy working the juice bar, who whistles through his teeth.

"Is Yonah here?"

"Who?"

"Does Yonah still own this place?"

"Oh. I don't know. Sorry. You should talk to her."

He points to a woman sitting by herself at a café table, parked behind a laptop screen. She wears red-rimmed sunglasses and a cap-sleeved pink T-shirt. Noemie!

"Oh my God, Lucy, is that you? Is that your baby? Oh my God, congratulations!"

She jumps up. We hug, kiss on both cheeks. Noemie is the manager now, in charge of ordering and scheduling and keeping the books. I remember her as a flirty teenager, and now here she is, all mature and responsible.

"Is Yonah here?"

She frowns. "Oh, no. He doesn't work here anymore."

"They sold the store?" I blink.

"Oh. I don't think so." She frowns again. "But he was sick of it. Yonah went back to Israel right before the new year. He said he'll stay there for a while. You didn't know?"

No, I didn't know.

The hurt catches me off guard. I'm twisted up, like a kite in a gale. I'm not sure why I'd expected to be informed—I left him and he let me go. *Friends, we always gonna be friends*, he'd said, because Yoni is like that. But don't friends tell each other things like this, like moving an ocean away?

That night, like every night, the three of us lie in our futon bed. Manny's zonked, flat on his back, arms by his sides like a mummy. I read to Essy. Then I sing to her. Then we talk about her day: *Did you like the zoo? What animals did we see? What did the sheep say? What did the gorilla do?*

"Lilla."

"Did you like the gorilla?"

"No."

"No? But didn't Essy wave to the cute gorilla?"

She shakes her head, Very Solemn. "Scary."

"Oh, no, Essy! You don't have to be scared of gorilla." I look into her enormous eyes.

"Lilla hurt."

"Oh, sweetie." My body tenses, with animal instinct. "The gorilla won't hurt you. No one's going to hurt you."

She pokes me with her finger. "Lilla hurt Mama."

Lilla hurt Mama. My baby, using three-word sentences, my baby, exhibiting empathy for the very first time! "Oh, no, Essy. Gorilla's not going to hurt Mama. No one's going to hurt Mama. I promise."

"Hurt Papi."

"No. Oh, no." I pat Manny's back. He's grinding his teeth, a hint of cinnamon on his breath. "No one will hurt Papi either. I promise."

She falls asleep. I close my eyes, curl up beside her, her smooth cheek warm on mine. I see the lemon yellow awning, the lustrous chrome tables, Noemie in her pink T-shirt. *Yonah went back to Israel.* Israel! An ocean away. Israel. Another world, another life. Just like that.

Two weeks later it's Manny's birthday. I cook Chinese duck. First I steam it, then I roast it in the oven until the skin is brown and crisp.

I serve it Peking-style, sliced thin, fanned out, with flour tortillas and scallions and plum sauce. The Vargas boys devour everything. "*Delicioso*," says Carlos. "Quack, quack," says Essy. She can yum-yum tap her own belly now.

We put twenty-seven candles on Manny's birthday cake, just for the hell of it.

After Essy is in bed, Manny and I sit outside on the steps of the front stoop, licking frosting from our fingers.

"Happy birthday," I say.

"Thanks," he says. We clink our beers.

It's a perfect June night. The smell of hot pavement gently subsides. Gnats come to fill the air. Mrs. Gutierrez emerges to sweep her stoop, then disappears back inside; minutes later, we hear her snores. This modest piece of local calm, sitting on a stoop after a family meal, I'm gripped with a strong déjà vu. Those years I traveled abroad, moments like these felt commonplace, but this one feels impossibly rare.

There's a word for this in Portuguese: *saudade*. It's not exactly nostalgia, there's more of a longing in it, for a feeling or way of life that may be impossible to recapture—that may or may not have even existed in the first place. "An indolent dreaming wistfulness" is how I've seen one writer describe it. Now *that's* a great word.

"Hey, Lucia," says Manny.

"Hey, Manny," I say.

"I've been thinking about something."

"Yeah, what?"

"You know, that . . ."

I know. I know. I know what he's going to say. And I know he doesn't really want to say it because he's fidgeting again, all awkward, trying to hide behind his machismo, just like that day at the beach.

But here's the thing about Manny: He'd do anything for his Mami. It's like she's built into his skeleton.

And that's when it comes to me, at that very moment, like one of those cartoon lightbulbs—*DING.* "Manny," I say. "Manny, I have an idea." I grab his leg. And it's so obvious, I could burst!

"Yeah? What?" he says.

"We should move to Ecuador."

࿓

Move to Ecuador?

"It makes sense, right?"

"You tell me," says Beige.

It's been a while since I've seen him. I tell him about the day at the beach.

"Marriage?"

That flinch of the eyebrow, the tap of the foot. But Beige, he shows restraint.

"So what are your thoughts? Are you interested in getting married?"

"It's not exactly an interest, like watching cooking shows or following European politics. . . ."

Beige frowns. Well, by now he knows when I'm joking.

"I don't want to get married again. I just don't. I don't think either of us do." This is the truth. And to my surprise, he nods, without judging me like I'm some heartless beast.

"What does Manny say?"

"He's thinking about it."

"Marriage?"

"No, moving."

Because marriage is a piece of paper signed by a city clerk. But moving, it solves everything!

Manny lives in fear. I worry. Whether he'll come home safely after his double shifts, whether he'll crash our newly leased Ford Taurus, whether he'll get into some stupid fight playing soccer and get himself hauled away. Mrs. Gutierrez says it doesn't matter where you're from, they dump you in Mexico; illegals are always getting busted on the news. And it's expensive here, even rents in the immigrant neighborhoods keep going up. I have savings, left by my mother, which Jie helps me invest, but at this rate it won't last.

"And Manny, he'd like to go back?"

"He loves his family. He misses them. He isn't an orphan or a political refugee or escaped from abject poverty, if that's what you mean."

Beige uncrosses his legs. Crosses them the other way. "And your sister?"

"She's in Switzerland."

"Have you told her?"

"Not yet." Jie's not my keeper. I'm annoyed.

"And your job?"

"Vitamins."

I've been thinking about something else, too, a new project. One night as I replayed that dream job interview in my head ("D" browsing through my clips, *This one's really good, why haven't you worked at a daily?* rewind, rewind), it came to me: the book. The one I'd always meant to write. My cheeks flush as the words tumble out, but I don't care what Beige says about Attainable Short-Term Goals.

"A compilation. Stories. Profiles of street people. *Unheard Voices.*"

Beige nods. He smiles! An honest smile. I guess we've come a long way.

So I surprise myself. I *share.* I tell him, when I was a little kid, I made believe I had seven grandmothers.

"I didn't know," he says. "You never brought it up."

One on each continent. And later, when I learned Antarctica was just ice, I assigned myself an extra in North America—Grandma Daisy in Florida, who I'd visit on school vacations like Anna and Missy Bachman always did, with their freckles and sunburns and peeling brown noses, and then Grandma Beth, who wore spectacles and knitted sweaters and scarves and lived in a secret hideaway over the river and through the woods, accessible only by sleigh, who I'd see every single holiday and who would cook us big fat juicy turkeys.

"Family," he says, nodding.

"Family. For Essy. A real home."

Home. The word itself, round and comforting. Home. With multigenerations of *abuelas* and *abuelos* and *tías* and *tíos* and cousins who will fuss over Essy at family parties. *Qué linda! How beautiful and clever she is!*

Besides, we all hate the cold.

"It would be a big move," he says.

"It's beautiful there. It's a simpler life."

"Simpler?"

Querencia.

I'm not sure how to explain, to his sage green walls, his framed diplomas, his wall shelf packed with psychiatry tomes and cacti and knickknacks from exotic places, his aspirational calendar featuring sturdy rowers at sunrise.

"Less pretending, maybe. Do you ever get tired of pretending?"

He jots in his notepad.

"It's a big decision," he says.

Sure it is. And, it's a clean slate.

Fall approaches. I'm stuck on it. Think about it every day, pros and cons, but the arguments in my head are for Manny's benefit, my heart is ninety-nine percent set. Nipa has put Natey in a preschool. I show the price sheets to Manny, explain that these programs tout their *play-based curriculums*. "What?" he says. "This is as much as rent. We pay this so she can play?" I don't have much to say about it, because Essy should play in fields and dirt and ponds and streams, in shady woods and lush countryside with wide green spaces. I say, "In Ecuador, money goes a long way." We'll buy a house of our own. A modest bungalow, not too far from town, but with acres and acres of land. We'll plant fruit trees and vegetables, raise goats and pigs and free-roaming chickens, collect milk and gather eggs. We'll have family nearby, always in and out, inviting each other over for dinners. Essy will be loved. I can tutor or teach English or write travel guides or we'll open a café or a bed-and-breakfast or start a tour company or build eco-lodges—we'll be self-starting entrepreneurs, why not? Anything is possible in a country where costs of living are low and regulations are lax. We'll be like pioneers. Like Ma.

One day Jie calls me out of the blue. She's "checking in." I can't help it, I'm excited, I tell her my plan, but when she goes all quiet, it's her skepticism that's loud and clear.

"What," I say, though I can't see how it matters. She's in Switzerland.

"Well . . ."

"Well, what?"

"It's a big decision, Lucia." But then she adds, softly, in her big-sisterly way, "It sounds exciting," and I drop my guard a little.

"Yeah. If I can convince Manny."

I ask her what's up with the Elk and she says he's been out of town, traveling again for work, and now his son is having a rough time and wants to drop out of boarding school.

"Teenagers," I say, though they're aliens to me, too.

"Stefan wants Rafi to come live with us, but his ex won't allow it."

"Oof. Well, what about you?"

"Oh, I don't know," she says. "It's not my decision." But she sounds kind of stressed. "He's decided he's a *vegan*, Lucia."

"A vegan?"

"What on earth would I cook?"

"Bye-bye, spare ribs," I say.

I get her to laugh. But I feel kind of bad. I always thought Jie had a perfect life.

One day in November, I go to the Pig. There's Manny, bundled in his puffy down coat, huddled on a curb in the parking lot. He's been demoted. He's had to bus tables all day.

"What?" I say.

One of the other line cooks has accused him of stealing from the pantry.

"Christ. What did you say?"

"I said I didn't do it. Boss believes him. What else can I say?"

He's droopy. I'm mad. What the hell, suddenly I'm just so cock-fighting mad. "Stealing what?"

"Ham."

"You mean, like, a slice of ham?"

He sighs. "A big ham. A big whole ham. *Jamón*."

"*Jamón?*" I picture it, Manny cradling a big whole ham like a football. I can't help it, I start to laugh.

"Why are you laughing?" he says.

I'm laughing so hard I can't answer.

"Fuck it," he says.

And that's how it's decided.

We tough out the rest of winter, knowing we won't face another. We set a departure date.

"An exciting adventure!" I say to Essy. "We're going on an exciting adventure!"

She believes it. I believe it. "There will be animals," I say. "Horses and cows and sheep and chickens."

"Chickens?" says Essy.

"Chickens, free-range organic chickens!"

"With eggs?"

"Fresh eggs every day!"

"Hard-boiled."

"Sure. Hard-boiled, *hija*."

The floodgate's opened. The possibilities! But whenever I spring the news to people, it's the same refrain: *For good? Forever?* "I'll come back to visit," I say.

I gather documents, file paperwork with the American embassy. I sell our possessions or give them away. Time zips by when there's so much to do.

One night I dream of my mother. I'm on a big ship. She's standing on the shore. *We're the same, Ma!* I yell. *Don't you see? We're the same. We're not afraid.* She doesn't say anything, but she waves.

On my last day of work, my coworkers from the vitamin job take me out for dinner. We go to a Mexican restaurant, get happy on margaritas and everyone's all gung ho about my big adventure. When I get home, it's after midnight, and the house is dark except for the blue glow from the television in our room. Manny is still up, watching a Mexican telenovela. I sit next to him. He switches it off.

"You don't have to do that," I say. "I'll be asleep in a minute."

"Your sister called me today," he says. Very Serious.

"My sister? Miranda? From Switzerland?"

He nods. Something inside my stomach topples over. It starts to churn.

"She is worried," he says quietly, and I understand. The truth comes out, of course.

Jie always used to be on my side, but now all she sees is my illness.

I brace myself for the lecture. I'm sick, I'm reckless, I'm irresponsible. But to hear Jie's words come from Manny's mouth, I can't help it, the tears spill out of my eyes.

"It's okay," he says. He pulls my head to his shoulder. "I told her it will be okay. I said in Ecuador we can have a good life."

I hug him. I cry. I curl up beside him, my rounded back pressed into his chest.

"We can open our own business," I say.

"No boss," he says.

"No boss! No more working for the man."

"No man. Only me." He grins.

"An Internet café. Or a store."

"A hardware store. A paint store."

"A restaurant. An ecotourist lodge!"

"Motorcycle rentals."

"You can build the huts."

"Hut rentals."

"Hut rentals!"

"You spray the bugs. I sit on my ass and collect rent, like landlord Harry." He laughs.

We watch the telenovela, trying to make sense of which of the maid's triplet daughters gave birth to the drug kingpin's son. Manny holds my hand. He doesn't say any more, but I find out later he called his Tío Remy, whose daughter works as a nurse in Quito, to make sure they stock my pills.

Bye-bye Vargas house. Bye-bye Mrs. Gutierrez. Bye-bye Coco. Bye-bye Beige. Bye-bye playground. Bye-bye Hudson. Bye-bye Nipa. Bye-bye Natey. Bye-bye Pig. Bye-bye laundromat. Bye-bye Ecuadorian buffet. Bye-bye Main Street. Bye-bye El Pollo Loco. It turns out Essy has no problem saying good-bye.

The last item left in our room is an old bathroom scale. The rest of our belongings I've squeezed into three brand-new suitcases, giant red plaid, the ugliest I could find down on Orchard Street. Each weighs in at just under seventy pounds, and we heave them into the trunk of our yellow cab, all two hundred and ten pounds of our lives. As we drive away, I say to Essy, "Wave, bye-bye house!" And then as our airplane lifts into the sky she says, "Mama, wave again!" Bye-bye Westchester. Bye-bye Manhattan. Bye-bye New York. Bye-bye America.

Part Two

❦

5

Lucia

The cabin door opens and she's enveloped by warm, tropical air. It's dense. Moist. It slicks down her throat, shuttles through her lungs, her veins, to her heart. This is the oxygen, more potent, the well, more pure, this is the new breath, new earth, new air, new life—she is coated with newness inside and out!

It takes two bus rides to reach the city of Cuenca, a third, slow and bumpy, to reach a tiny town called Martez. Hardly a town, maybe a village, it's a single road lined with low, boxlike buildings, where women in traditional shawls squat next to buckets, hawking their vegetables. Six eggplants here, six cabbages there, ten avocados, thirty potatoes, a handful of peppers, three watermelons cut from the vine that morning. Freshly harvested, to be eaten the same day, so she pays twenty cents for six guayabas and the *abuela* hacks one open with a small, rusty hatchet and she sucks sweet pulp to quench her thirst. "Essy, want to try?" Wide-eyed children swarm to greet them, waving plastic bags full of gummies, candy corns, lemon and lime sour balls. "Essy, try this! It's better than candy." Manny swats the *niños* away.

His Papi arrives in a pickup truck, a battered red Toyota with scratches and dents like it's been mauled by some foamy-mouthed carnivore. Fredy's in back, curls big and tangled from the dusty wind, grin so wide it splits his face. He's got the characteristic look of a Down's kid: up-slanted eyes, flattened profile, tongue hung like a weary dog. But the way he lights up, leaps out of that truck when he sees his brother, it's *enough*. The joy, the love! They must've told him so many great things about Manny, the *hermano* who went to Nueva York like a legend.

Papi is a plow of a man, solid, tireless, rooted in the earth. Dressed in sleeveless white undershirt, cutoff denim shorts, he's a darker, heftier, more leathery version of Manny—handsome, with the same boxy face, prominent brow ridges. They shake hands before embracing in that awkward man-to-man way, high up around the shoulders instead of chest to chest.

"Did you have a good trip?" he asks.

"A beautiful trip," she says.

Fredy offers a green lollipop to Essy, helps unravel the wrapper. Essy can't take her eyes off him. She points to his belly button, blooping out from under his Teenage Mutant Ninja Turtles T-shirt. "Gordito," she says, and back home Lucia would've had to shush and whisk her daughter aside, glance around apologetically, hoping no one overheard. But here Papi and Manny just laugh. Fredy is flabby, porky, obese, for a boy of twelve. Gordito. It's the truth.

Papi slings their red plaid suitcases onto the back of the truck, stacks them in a pyramid.

"You and *niña* sit in front," he says, gesturing to the cab. "The boys in the back."

She reaches for Essy's hand.

"No, Mama! I want to sit in the back!" Her daughter tugs away, waves her lollipop in the air like it's a magic wand, slows to aim it straight at Fredy. "With that one."

Lucia frowns. Maybe she's skeptical for a minute, but Manny and Papi don't bat an eye. So Essy clambers aboard, plops herself in Manny's lap, and Fredy reclines on the mountain of luggage like it's a comfy beach chair, points to puffs of clouds in the sky. "Mama, look at me!" says Essy, waving, and Lucia, up front next to Papi, twists and cranes to watch them through the mud-caked window. When they peel out of town, Essy unleashes a scream of joy: "Eeeee-ha!" She screams all the way to Papi's farm.

This is her just-turned three-year-old daughter: unbuckled, unharnessed, hurtling down a dirt road on the back of a pickup truck. Her long dark hair flies free in the wind, lashes at her beaming face. Oh, if the mamas from Group could see them now!

Mami greets them at the farm. *"Bienvenido a casa! Un abrazo, Lucy."* She's short, wide-hipped, with a low center of gravity, formidable for her size (unmistakably, a bear). She draws Lucia into her bosom, a cocoon of warmth, a true womanly embrace. "And you, you must be Esperanza." She drops to her knees. Essy burrows her face into her mother's legs, until Mami coaxes her out with a piece of honey cake. Mami's kitchen is spotless; colorful woven baskets hold everything from bread to knives to straws to eggs. On the wall hangs a silver plaque of Madonna and Child next to a Statue of Liberty calendar, days marked off with sturdy red X's. "Where are Juan and Ricky?" asks Manny. "They'll come home for lunch," says Mami, and when they come, they come running, panting with excitement— dashing teens in school uniforms, starched white shirts and long brown trousers. "You're an old man!" they yell, throwing punches at Manny, who punches them back, and it's like he's never been away.

They are shown to a small bedroom with bright orange walls. The bed, covered with a lacy bedspread, something handmade (knitted or crocheted, she can never tell the difference), the mattress soft but comfortable. She tells Manny she'll rest her eyes for a minute. It ends up being all night.

She wakes to the smell of dew, calls of birds, high-pitched hums and chirps of busy insects. No cars, no buses, no screeching sirens, just the clacking throttle of a tractor at work in a distant neighbor's field. Manny and Essy are both snoring, so she climbs out of bed, drapes Manny's arm across Essy's back in case she starts to roll. She slips into a sundress—no more bulky sweaters, no more heavy coats, no more boots! Everyone in the house is still asleep, so she heads outside for a walk. It's a glorious new day. Everywhere she turns, only big uninterrupted sky, lush green terraces rolling up the hillsides, peaks gently bumping the horizon. She follows a trail through tall grass and is delivered out onto a pasture, freshly cleared, drenched with ripeness, cows and hay. Nature is perennially in bloom in Ecuador, and she feels at ease in its presence; even the traces of smoke and sawdust in the air feel familiar on her skin. In this part of the world, someone is inevitably burning or building something somewhere nearby. She stretches her arms, starts to spin like a child, faster and faster, until the world becomes a kaleidoscopic blur, until she gets so dizzy she must sit down. And then she lies on her back and watches the sky untwist, the clouds unwind, around and around and around.

Maybe she falls asleep for a minute. Next she's rubbing her eyes like a fairy-tale princess, biting on her thumb to make sure this isn't a dream. Trekking back to the house, she smells frying meat. Mami has cooked breakfast—chorizo, eggs and rice with cilantro, guanabana juice, all neatly arranged on the wooden picnic tables outside.

"You like?" asks Mami. Gestures from the food to the fields to the distant mountains and blue-gray sky.

"Yes," she says. *"Es muy bonita."*

"Paradiso." Mami nods proudly.

Paradiso. She agrees.

Querencia.

That weekend, Manny's parents host a welcome home party. With Mami's six sisters and Papi's three brothers and *tíos* and *tías* and cousins and a slew of neighbors, too, it feels like more people than she's known her entire life! They roast a pig, four chickens, half a dozen guinea pigs (*cuy,* Ecuadorian specialty!), set out soups and tamales and empanadas and *llapingachos,* four pots of beans and rice. Mami has even baked a belated birthday cake for Essy, decorated with jelly beans and Jell-O and mini-marshmallows. And when they sing, *feliz cumpleaños,* it's like a full-on chorus and Essy's eyes grow round as marbles as she basks in the attention, puffs her cheeks, blows out three candles. Then she's off with the pack, babies to teenagers, tearing through the house, into the fields, chasing animals, wielding sticks, playing ball games and hide-and-seek. No one worries about bedtime. The moon comes out. Lightning bugs flicker. As the night wears on, men slam shots of *aguardiente.* The older generation favors plaid button-down shirts, the younger sports neon tracksuits. Drunker and drunker, bolder and sloppier on the dance floor, and Manny mops his forehead as he loosens his hips, passes from *tías* to cousins to *chicas* with tight strappy tops and wedge heels and miniskirts. He is a smooth dancer, with an easy lead, hand in the small of the woman's back. Lucia dances with the neighbor, Roberto, who sprays saliva into her ear as he sings, and then Tío Remy, who asks questions as he spins her around. *Te gusta el campo? Te gusta nuestro país?* Does she like Chinese food? When he lived in Quito he had a lady friend who was Chinese, an excellent cook who had very soft hands.

She is winded. The air is thin and her red blood cells haven't adjusted to the new oxygen levels yet, so she breaks away to mingle with the older women, who shout to be heard above the deep thuds of reggaeton and tecnocumbia. "I am Sylvia's cousin," they all seem to say, and it's as Manny once said: he has enough *tíos* and *tías* and cousins to populate an entire village. *Is that Esperanza? Qué linda! Will you have more? You must have more.* They pat their bellies. She knows they're not referring to a second helping of flan.

Next morning, she and Essy are the first to wake. She is disoriented; the kitchen has been left in complete disarray. She washes dishes, pots, wipes down the table. Then she boils water in Mami's stainless steel kettle, brews herself a cup of hot tea. Soon Mami appears in pink bathrobe and clear plastic slippers. *"Buenos días,"* she says, and Essy giggles, points to the rollers in Abuela's hair. Mami shoos them out of the kitchen; party or no party, it's time to prepare the next meal.

They eat breakfast outside. Scrambled eggs, fried potatoes, naranjillas and plantains. When they're finished, Papi stands at the head of the table, broad gummy smile stretching from ear to ear, parenthetical grooves carved into his face. She sees that smile in Manny and his three brothers, an unmistakable family inheritance. She sees it in Essy, too.

"We have something," he announces. He nods to her. "For you."

"Me?"

"For welcome," he says.

Caught off guard, she glances at Manny, who's looking away. Papi leads, they follow. Through the campo, past Mami's vegetable garden, an old barn, a field of lazy goats, past a meadow, a trickling brook, down a steep hill of wildflowers, up a winding dirt path. They walk for ten minutes, maybe more, Essy perched atop Manny's shoulders. At the end of the dirt path, a flat clearing, and behind it rises a lush, green mountain. They stop.

Mami's crinkly eyes, smiling. Papi, all teeth, like the Cheshire cat.

"What is it?" she says.

It's a small casita. A house shaped exactly the way a young child draws a house: a triangle on top of a rectangle, inside the rectangle, two squares. Built from chalky wood beams, tin sheets for a roof, packed dirt for floors. In the kitchen area, a sink, a double-burner stove, a metal table with three folding chairs. On the wall hangs a calendar supplied by a local gas company, next to a gold-framed picture of Jesus Christ. In the bedroom, a queen-size bed with another lacy bedspread, a wooden desk, wire shelves, a high-backed rocking chair. Mami has sewn curtains, flowery pink with three tiers of ruffles like a young girl's dress, which artfully adorn the gaping window holes.

"It's simple," says Mami.

"There is no toilet yet," Papi apologizes. He hasn't had time to build an outhouse, but he will get to it soon.

"For now you can come to the house," says Mami. "Or . . ." She gestures toward the trees.

"You like it?" says Papi.

All eyes on her. Her palms sweat. She doesn't know what to say. It takes several moments before she fully comprehends that this house is for *her*, for them, for their little family. They are to live here, on this land, in this spot, at the foot of this mountain. For now. For how long. Forever? She swallows, unsure of what this means.

She has traveled in this country before, seen the shanties where families live in cardboard shacks and piss in buckets. With a parcel of arable land, a water source, Manny's family is not poor like this, but she is certain they are far from rich.

She says, "This is so generous. Thank you."

Mami beams.

They move into their new home later that day. She unpacks their red plaid suitcases.

"What do you think?" says Manny, in bed that night, their daughter asleep between them. And she surveys the lacy bedspread by their feet, the neat stacks of clothing she has organized onto their wire shelves (His. Hers. Essy's), the pink ruffled curtains now drawn closed.

"It's beautiful," she says.

"Temporary," he says. "I will build us a house, a good one. I promise." He reaches over to caress her breasts.

Early the next morning, he goes with Papi to buy tools. They need to cut trees, clear brush behind the casita. She sets off with Essy to visit the main house again. The child runs ahead, her ability to find her way as instinctual as her easy, graceful gait. Gifts. Her daughter, with so many gifts! As they approach, she sees Mama and Tía Camila through the kitchen window. Camila is Mami's oldest sister, the same stocky shape. Mami waves. Fredy is in the garden, feeding the chickens. Essy runs to join him.

She's offered coffee, mango, a slice of honey cake. The women mix masa, shred cheese, pound plantains. They demonstrate how to wrap tamales, laying out the leaves, flattening them with a fist. Like this. No, like this! Not like that. Like that is too slow. They laugh. They gossip. She basks in their warmth. She remembers when she and Jie used to be like this. Close.

She sits on a low stool by the open door. Fredy is by the pigs, crawling on all fours. Essy vaults onto his back, wriggles up to his shoulders. He bucks like a mule, braying dramatically, tosses her into the dirt. *Again! Again!*

"*Cuidado!*" calls out Tía Camila.

"Fredy is such a sweet boy," she says.

"All my sons." Mami strikes her chest with her fist. "Big hearts. Good boys."

"He's strong," she says.

Tía Camila shakes her head. "Not so strong, this one. Born this way. He needs to be careful."

Mami sighs.

"Doctors say it won't last, his heart," says Tía Camila.

Lucia remembers the herbs, wrapped in the pretty red box, and the clay pot she picked out, mustard yellow with bamboo leaves painted on the side. She could ask, but Mami's eyes have sprung tears. Quickly, they are wiped away, and Mami brushes herself off like she's clearing crumbs off a table. "You see what it is like to be a mother," she says. Lucia nods.

"When will you and Manny have another?" says Tía Camila. "One is so lonely. Surely Esperanza would like a baby brother or sister."

"My granddaughter is a beautiful child," says Mami. "It would be a shame not to have another."

"A woman cannot waste too much time," says Tía Camila. "Sylvia knows."

"Oh, Camila," says Mami.

This. Of course, this. Among women, always this.

Twelve more touches.

She manages a gracious smile. "What will you do after you prepare lunch, Mami?" she asks.

"I will prepare dinner," says Mami, laughing. And she takes her time—soaks the beans, cleans dirt off the carrots plucked from the garden, peels the potatoes carefully with a paring knife. These are her days: cooking, cleaning, harvesting fruits and vegetables from the earth. She has nowhere else to be, nothing else to achieve, only chore after chore after chore.

∽

This is how she falls into routine. It doesn't take long to figure out how to parcel out twenty-four hours. Every morning there's breakfast to prepare: tea, eggs, potatoes, rice. Manny heads off to cut terraces in the hillside, weed and water and repair the endless roster of items in disrepair: the truck, the tractor, the gate, the trough, the pipes, the roof, the fences around the property. And there is still the outhouse to build. Papi has helped set up an irrigation system for the land behind their casita, involving a complicated system of hoses and sprinklers that must be moved by hand every six hours. If it works, they'll plant crops—cacao, papaya, passion fruit, plantains, a grazing area for animals.

After breakfast she washes dishes. Then she sprays water on the dirt floor, quickly sweeps crumbs with a broom onto a newspaper. Sometimes she and Essy visit the market in town to buy rice or vinegar or household detergents, the few items they don't produce themselves. Sometimes she weeds, tends to the small garden where she's planted cucumbers, radishes, peppers, herbs. Soon it's time to prepare lunch. Manny returns. They eat together. These days, he's always hungry.

After lunch she washes dishes. Then she washes clothes. At first she tries to do it outside in a plastic basin. Later she learns to head down to a wide section of the river where the local women gather with children in tow. The river bubbles, rich and earthy like chocolate, with a faintly metallic smell. In the beginning Essy shies away, clings to her legs, must be forcibly pried off and set down on the muddy bank. The women pretend not to notice. They scrub their clothes against a flat rock, rinse in the stream, lay the garments on the grass to dry. She has washed her clothes in kitchen sinks and bathtubs and large metal pots, in coin-operated machines in hot, musty basements where she's had to pluck out lint and gum and strangers' hair and stand by counting down minutes. Here, only the power of the river and sun. She stands knee-deep, scrubs a pair of blue jeans, imagines tiny specks of dirt released from the fabric's pores, the river carrying away the filth. A bird flies overhead. Oh, how lucky to enjoy this lovely view!

Eventually Essy tires of her own tantrums. She joins the other children, splashing and digging, throwing sand, skipping rocks, chasing after tiny fish. An afternoon in the sun and the child is tired, whines and begs for a piggyback ride or simply falls asleep. Either way, she must be carried home. With Essy in tow, even the simplest chore can stretch into a daylong affair.

Evenings, she takes out her laptop computer, opens her files, but the glare of white light always feels too harsh, unharmonious with her surroundings, so she shuts it off, sits cross-legged in the high-backed wooden rocking chair, turns her attention to her notebook filled with outlines, lists, interview ideas. "What are you doing?" asks Manny. "Work," she says. She jots a few notes until her chin starts to drop, then crawls into bed (Essy asleep, Manny awake), watches the small television sitting on top of the desk, though the reception is poor, with only two grainy channels, but they like to listen to the Colombian telenovelas. There is no local news.

At night she dreams of the river, all bubbles and suds. Her back is sore. Her skin is brown. Rough and cracked, her knuckles bleed, fingers turn chalky white. She can hear Ma's voice, hoarse and appalled: *My daughter, with the hands of a servant, aiya!*

⁂

One night they're watching television and the picture cuts out, all that's left is static. They sit at the kitchen table, play cards, rummy or *cuarenta* or crazy eights.

"What do you think about moving into town?" she says.

"What?" says Manny.

"Town," she says, setting down three queens.

"What town?"

"Martez." Hardly a town, barely a village. Twenty minutes away via Papi's truck.

"Why?"

"We could open some kind of business. You know, a store, or a restaurant, or an Internet café."

"In Martez?" he says, laughing.

"Maybe a laundry business."

He raises one eyebrow. "Why would we do that?"

"Well, it'd be a great business. Remember, didn't we talk about starting some kind of business once we moved here? And do you have any idea how much time I spend washing clothes?"

He shakes his head, but not a simple "I don't know," more tinged with invisible eye-rolling, though his glance does not waver from his cards.

"Imagine how much time we'd save all the women around here if we provided a laundry service once a week—you could do pickup and delivery, I'd do wash, dry, and fold."

"But then what would the women do?" he asks.

He is looking straight at her, but there's no wink, no grin, no hint of humor on his face. She swerves her gaze to the floor.

Something in Manny has shifted, she can tell. He's confident in a way she has never seen before—the way his shoulders sit back, how he walks with a slight swagger, and for a while, this renews her sexual appetite and they make love in places where Essy is not: on the kitchen table or in a chair or on the hammock outside the casita, mosquitoes sucking at her legs. He smokes with his cousins, plays *futbol* with his old schoolmates, and she can see the *chicas* appreciate his good looks. The campo suits him. Essy senses a change in him, too; whenever she hears the heavy plod of his boots, she runs to him like a puppy, paws and begs until he picks her up, swings her around (*higher, Papi! higher!*), sets her on his shoulders. They march into the house. He asks, "What's for dinner?" And if he doesn't like what she has prepared, the way it looks or smells, he marches across the fields to his Mami's kitchen.

Now she wonders: *Who is this man?* It's the first time she's thought of him simply as a full-grown man, not a guy, a *novio*, one of the Vargas boys.

"What would the women do?" She repeats his words.

"Yeah. What would the women do, if you were doing their laundry?" He sets down three aces.

Her face feels hot. Her chest tight. Something squirms in her temples. She can find no words with which to retaliate.

She knows he is watching. She knows he knows that she hates it when he watches, that it makes her feel small and deficient, like a parolee or a zoo animal or an erratic child. And so each night—after she washes her face and brushes her teeth and spits into the basin in the kitchen, all the while sensing him slink out of bed, sneak to the doorway to watch, proctor, spy, as she pours another cup of boiled water from the plastic jug kept on a low shelf next to the rice, retrieves from a high shelf the small orange bottle masquerading as a spice—she carefully, deliberately, turns her back to him, facing instead the gas company calendar or the gold-framed picture of Jesus Christ, though he does not know it's deliberate because he doesn't know she knows he is watching, but she has always known, and this is the way she saves some fragment of herself, her center, her dignity, as she throws back the small white pills. So one day when he says, *Let's take a trip to Cuenca,* and she says, *Why?* and he mumbles something about buying new boots and tools and maybe some fabric for Mami and maybe some shoes for Essy and then finally says, *By the way, I think you may need more pills,* she is not surprised. But it feels like a violation, even though she knows he watches. An unspoken breach of trust.

But there is only one *farmacia* in Martez. It's dirty and understocked and unreliable. So one Saturday Papi unloads them from his banged-up pickup truck and they wait and wait on the main *calle*, chitchatting with Vera and Isabel and Luz and their bucketfuls of potatoes. Vera's brother, a paraplegic, has married a Taiwanese nurse and now lives in Taipei; Isabel's youngest son is mute; Luz, Vera's daughter, dreams of raising roosters for cockfights in Guayaquil. The stories! She digs out her notebook. A handful of children come by waving bags of candy. Only the transients still mistake her for a tourist.

Finally, they board a chicken bus, one of the old yellow school buses from the States that has been granted an illustrious afterlife, spray-painted with neon colors and flamboyant designs. The bus stops and starts. One woman sits with a crate full of guinea pigs in her lap. Another boards with three chickens. Essy's eyes grow wide. "Chickens can ride the bus?" She laughs like it's the funniest thing she's ever seen in her three-year-old life.

After the quiet of the campo, the city shocks the senses. Salsa and merengue blare from the shops, taxis blast their horns, buses barrel around corners spouting blue diesel fumes. But she savors it—the people, the bustle, energy in motion. She imbibes the sounds, the smells, the colonial grandeur, the archways and ironwork and domed cathedrals, cobblestone pavements and red tile roofs. Pretty, but not pristine. And everywhere, everything in bloom.

They decide to shop at the biggest mall in Cuenca, all white lights and flashy signs and floors gleaming like mirrors. Her daughter's mouth forms a perfect O. It's been a long time since they've seen so many *things*.

"This one, Mama." Essy holds up a pink sequined flip-flop with plastic daisies.

"How about this one," says Manny. He pulls out a boy's sandal, blue with double Velcro straps, appropriate for tromps through water and mud.

"That's ugly," says Essy.

"She's kind of right."

"That one, it scratches her feet, it breaks in five minutes."

"Please, Papi! *Gracias*, Papi! Please, Papi! Hooray, Papi!" Essy jumps up and down, pumps her fists as though she has already won. It's an effective technique; he can't resist. He scoops her in his arms, dangles her upside down by her ankles as she squeals in mock protest. In the end, they buy both pairs, a fuzzy pink purse and sunglasses, too.

Another store sells only traditional fedora hats. Another sells only yarn, another only embroidered towels, another only kitchen items. She spends twenty minutes choosing a bright yellow enamel pot with a thick bottom, ample enough to accommodate soups and stews. Ten minutes in search of the perfect nonstick frying pan. "Just big enough to hold two fried eggs without touching," she explains, and the *vendedora* finds for her one the exact right size. *Muchas gracias!* They exchange high fives.

For lunch they stop at an *almuerzo*, order chicken cutlets, French fries, cabbage salad, plantains. Outside, the drizzle has stopped, the clouds drift apart, the mountains surrounding the city snap into focus. Essy's stroller serves as a convenient shopping cart, piled high with boxes and bags. She wears her new pink flip-flops proudly, kicks her feet from atop her Papi's shoulders.

That afternoon, Manny takes Essy to a park, a playground, a candy store. Lucia heads to El Centro, but first winds her way through a pretty neighborhood lined with blossoming trees. Maybe it's one of those new gringo enclaves—each house with ornate wrought iron bars on the windows, fronted by a security wall of concrete or brick, with shards of broken glass embedded up top. In El Centro she finds a respectable-looking pharmacy on one of the main *calles*. The *farmacéutica*'s doughy body feels at odds with her alien-like face. Lucia passes her the empty vial. It is only when she glances up to see if the woman is raising her eyebrows, casting judgment, that she realizes—the woman has no eyebrows. No wonder she looks so strange!

Next, she finds a trendy Internet café, complete with two pet iguanas roaming the premises. How long has it been? Three months off the grid, unplugged. Time, enjoyed as a lazy blur. Now her in-box full of junk, except for a few messages from her old boss in Westchester, one note from Nipa, three from Jie, each spaced about a month apart. She clicks. The connection, painfully slow.

Hi Lucia, Hope you arrived safely and that everything is beauuuuu-tiful. Heard about the blizzard in New York. Bet you are glad you're not there. Shoot me an email and let me know the best way to reach you. Ok? Love, Jie

Hi Lucia, haven't heard from you. Do you have email access? What's the name of your town? What's your address? Should I send you some chocolates, or anything else? Hope all's well. Love, Jie

Lucia, everything ok? Please let me know. Take care of yourself. Jie

Jie. No news, lots of worry.

Hi Porcupine,
I'm here, and I'm fine. We're living in the campo, no internet, so I only check email when I come into Cuenca (~1.5 hours by bus). We went shopping today. I got a perfect pot and a perfect frying pan. What's up in Switzerland? I didn't hear about New York—we're in our own world down here. Manny's family threw a gigantic party for us, roasted a whole pig on a spit. Everything here is beautiful.
Lucia

Hi Funky Girl! We were down at Ryder's playground, thought of you. How is your Big Adventure going? Natey is . . . potty-trained! Can you believe it?! And Jasmine just turned one! I will be back to work in a week, at a new teaching job in White Plains. Much more convenient than the city. By the way, some bad news. Winston and I are splitting up. It was his decision and it feels sudden, but in a way we have been disconnected for a long time. It's been civil enough and I'll be fine, but of course poor Natey doesn't understand. I keep telling him, Daddy will still be Daddy, just in a different house. Our therapist says it's for the best, this happening while the kids are young. Take care down there, and come back to visit, ok? Miss you! Nipa.

Oh, Nipa. Poor Nipa! She misses her, too. How long ago was it, that day they first met at the mamas' group? She'd cried all the time. She sounds so healthy now, in spite of everything.

Hi Nipa, it's so great to hear from you! It's beautiful here, spring all the time, lush and leafy, the air like flowers. We live in the boonies, on a farm with Manny's parents, and I'm growing so many vegetables. Backyard organic! Wish I could zap you my tomatoes, I bet you could sell them at the farmer's market for three bucks apiece, but here I get only ten cents a pound. Everyone is well. Essy loves it here. I'm so sorry to hear about your breakup. Hope you're ok. Channeling blessed thoughts. As they say, everything happens for a reason. Lucia

She hopes her words are true.

Finished, she steps in line to pay the cashier. The girl, dressed in a denim jacket over a denim miniskirt, twirls a finger in her frizzy brown hair. Something about her feels slightly familiar. Susi. Susi! But no, it is not Susi. A quick stab of guilt, and then tears stream down her cheek and that silly children's song is stuck in her head:

Where, oh where, oh where is Susi?
Where, oh where, oh where is Susi?
Where, oh where, oh where is Susi?
Way down yonder in the paw-paw patch.

Come along, kids, let's go find her
Come along, kids, let's go find her
Come along, kids, let's go find her
Way down yonder in the paw-paw patch.

On the bus ride home, she asks Manny, "What do you think happened to Susi?"

He shakes his head, does not meet her eyes.

"Where was her family? Do you think maybe she didn't really get deported? Maybe the government figured out it was all a big mix-up. Maybe she was just away for a little while." Brightening at this thought, she pictures Susi in that kitchen with its yellow linoleum floor. Susi, hanging colorful streamers. Susi, baking a cake, decorating it with pink frosting flowers. Susi, cleaning the dirty dishes left in the sink by the Vargas boys. Susi, *hermanita*, whose presence she recalls as her sole comfort during those dark, muddled days. Susi, whose kindness remained free of judgment.

Essy. She has Essy. Here, sprawled across their laps, asleep, contentment on her face.

"Do you think she should go to school?" she says. She slides a finger down her daughter's nose. The skin, smooth and supple. Those eyelashes. Every part of her small being a miracle.

"School? Why?"

"Just for something to do. It might be good for her."

Manny shrugs. "My *hija*, she is beautiful." He strokes Essy's hair.

"Angelic."

"Amazing."

"Perfect," she whispers. She pats Essy's head.

"But especially when she's sleeping," adds Manny.

She laughs. On this, at least, they will always agree.

One morning she wakes and the air feels different. Thicker, heavier, with an earthy fecundity, it adheres to her tonsils and must be forcibly gulped. Her eyes water. Her legs itch. Essy is crying. She says her head hurts, and she has been bitten, too—scratched at the raised red bumps on her ankles, drawn blood, which now dots the floral sheets. The wet season has come. Each day's heat grows more dense. By noontime, animals flop in the shade; only their tails twitch to swat the flies. In the afternoons the clouds let out rain like a rage. The river swells, fat and turbid. Water bubbles in through the seams of the casita, turns dirt to mud; they place flattened cardboard boxes over the sludgy floor. At dusk, the rains cease. Swarms of gnats emerge to hang in the air. The mosquitoes return. She lights a citronella candle in their bedroom. Her thighs glue together when she sleeps. When she wakes, her forehead is damp, her hair matted. She whiffs a blend of excrement and burning rubber.

She hangs a mosquito net over the bed, a cascade of nylon mesh. "Seriously?" says Manny. He hates that they can no longer lie around and watch TV, just as he has rigged up a small satellite dish. Essy is happy. She's a princess! With her stuffed animal bunny as her knight, the bed their impenetrable castle, veiled in tulle, secured by moat. Dragons, keep out! We have swords! We're having a birthday party! The television is moved into the kitchen.

"Do you hear her in there? Talking to herself?"

"She always does that," he says.

"Maybe she should go to school. It'd be nice for her to have some friends her own age."

He dips his head, neither in assent or dissent, only to signal that he's heard. She doesn't bring it up again until one day they return from helping Papi dig out the rear axle of his truck from a ditch, and find the mosquito net in shreds. Essy has torn it down, ripped it apart, attempted to craft it into a pair of wings.

It is a village-run day care, with twenty-five kids, ranging from babies up to age six. An airy, cabana-like space with wooden posts, a thatched roof, unvarnished plank floors, attended to by four crinkly-eyed women dressed in traditional ponchos, all shaped like pears. They sing songs, play games, cook simple meals eaten on low rectangular tables. The older ones teach the younger how to wash hands, clean up, weave straw baskets or tend to the vegetable patch where they grow pump-kins and potatoes and squash. The children are dark and speak mostly Quichua, the indigenous language, which Essy does not understand. At first she protests. Cries. Clings stubbornly to her mother's legs. For two weeks, she cries every day, despite the coaxing and begging, reas-surances and threats, the candy Manny sneaks to her each morning as a bribe. Then one day, without warning, as they approach the front steps, she lets go of her mother's hand. Two girls, sisters, each with spindly brown arms, are dressing their dolls in the corner. Essy squats beside them. They examine her, curious. Lucia holds her breath.

After this day, her daughter rarely looks back, not even to wave when she calls out *Besitos! Good-bye!* and when she arrives in the afternoon by foot or burro or motorbike to retrieve her, Essy is always setting up a picnic or a birthday party with the other *niños*, and is never ready to leave.

Without Essy, the usual chores are completed in a fraction of the usual time. She feeds the chickens and pigs, makes yogurt and cheese with the goats' milk, adds dandelion, milk thistle, gingerroot to her garden. She can't remember when she last felt this efficient, like a fully autonomous being! Sometimes she takes out her narrow-ruled notebook, powers on her laptop computer, starts to type. Sometimes she walks to the main house to visit with Mami and Tía Camila, but they are usually talking about this woman or that woman who is now with this man or that man and she finds she doesn't really care. She weeds, forehead dripping, knees permanently brown with dirt. The steep hillside behind the casita is terraced and planted, rises up like a verdant green quilt. With that project complete, she decides she will bring up the outhouse again, the one Papi promised to build—but she can't ask Papi, she doesn't want to seem rude.

"What?" says Manny.

"The outhouse. Will you be able to start on it now?"

Essy hates to squat outside. Each time, it's *Mamaaaaa!* Terrible wails, and the child refuses to let go of her hand, totters back and forth, and the inevitable result: pissing her own calves or ankles, soiling her leggings or shoes, and then she screams again and must be sprayed down with the hose. Lately, the protest: *NO, NO, I don't have to go!* and she finds herself scraping shit off another pair of underwear with a plastic spoon.

"She'll get over it," says Manny. It's harvest season, the busiest time of the year. He and Papi have a lot to do.

"Then when?"

"Soon. I promise, soon."

That day he shows her how to kill a chicken by slitting its throat. His hands are quick, assured, and as she watches the creature jerk and twitch and bleed out into a plastic bucket, she finds she feels no tinge of remorse. It disturbs her. She cannot tell whether it is her closeness to the earth that allows her to accept the brutality of this act so calmly now, as part of the natural order, or whether she has been blunted and dulled by her pills. She douses the carcass in boiling water, plucks off the feathers, begins to remove the bloody viscera.

> *Shin bone connected to the knee bone*
> *Knee bone connected to the thigh bone*
> *Thigh bone connected to the hip bone*
> *Hip bone connected to the back bone*

It is one of her earliest memories as a child: Jie, singing. Jie, standing on a plastic lawn chair, that white one with the cracked seat, one of two handed down from a neighbor, which Ma had wiped clean with wet paper towels. "H-e-a-d bone, see?" said Jie, patting her head. "N-e-c-k bone. S-h-o-u-l-d-e-r bone." Pointing to each bone, she enunciated in her best English, made Lucia repeat and repeat until she was tired and cried. But that evening, when their mother came home, the two of them stood tall in their uncle's basement on their plastic chairs, shoulders rolled back, with ruler-straight spines, and they sang loudly and proudly as if they performed often on the grandest of stages. The swell of admiration she'd felt for her sister then! The love, the adoration. And her three-year-old body, full of bones inside, ready to burst with pride. Ma had smiled and smiled!

She misses her sister, the one of her youth. Is Jie painting pictures of flowers, listening to the Beatles or Pavarotti or NPR? Watching *Sex and the City*? Buried in the Sunday crossword? She cooks lion's head meatballs in her bright yellow pot, bakes almond cookies for dessert.

One day, Mami offers her an old sewing machine, a black and gold Singer with a manual foot pedal. She is touched. Clothing is expensive, especially with a child who outgrows things in a matter of months. She starts by sewing a pink apron for Essy. A matching one for herself. Then she finds a simple pattern to sew a dress from a pillowcase. On her first try, the elastic thread puckers, pulls at the neckline, and the sleeves are much too tight. She rips it out. Tries again, and again. Finally she sews on an orange ruffle, trims the hem with pink satin, attaches a sash. It looks like a real dress you'd buy in a store.

"See, *hija*," she says, triumphant as she holds it up.

"No, Mama, I don't like it." Essy sticks out her tongue, wrinkles her nose. New behaviors she has picked up at school. "I like my old clothes."

"You can wear it to your cousin's birthday party tomorrow night, okay?"

Essy shakes her head.

"Tomorrow. Not now," she says.

The next morning she brings it out with a smile. "See, it's a new dress." The cotton in her hands, so soft, smoothed from repeated washes. She lays the dress out on the kitchen table, fingers the pink satin piping sewn to the hem. She can hardly believe she has made this. From an old pillowcase! It's pretty. Really pretty. And recycled, no less! The mamas from Group would be impressed.

"Essy!" she calls.

Her daughter is outside, hopping from mud puddle to mud puddle, splattering their two new pigs, who she has named Princess and Pea. She will need to be sprayed down with the hose.

Manny emerges from the bedroom. Rubs his eyes. "What's going on?" he says.

"Come, Essy! It's a pretty dress. Look, orange and pink!" Her daughter's favorite colors. That pink satin piping on the hem, such a fine detail. "Look how shiny. Come, try it on."

"But I don't want to wear it, Mama."

"For the party."

Essy shakes her head.

"But look, it's beautiful." A desperation in her voice she cannot explain.

"No, I don't like it!"

"She doesn't want to wear it," says Manny, with a yawn.

Essy grabs the dress, darts back outside, throws it in the dirt.

"Essy!" She is seething. Calls out again. But Essy has disappeared into the campo.

"I'll get her," says Manny. He heads out and she waits, but they do not return. The girl will play all day with Fredy, pop in occasionally at the main house to take refuge with Mami, return in the evening with her hair full of burrs.

༖

Hi Farmer Girl, Your big adventure sounds like paradise. Things are ok here. The job is good. Winston moved out. My lawyer got me a pretty good settlement so I can pay for a nanny. I feel horribly guilty, but I need the help. Natey hates having someone else in the house, he's been acting out, tantrums and potty regression. Pooped in his pants three times this week—right when I got home. Joy! But in the grand scheme of things, I still think we're moving in the right direction. Like they say, happy mama = happy children, right? Nipa.

She has traveled to the city on her own today. Stopped in at the bakery, the flower market, the *farmacia*, where she smiles at the eyebrow-less woman, who smiles back. Last time, they exchanged pleasantries. This time, their names. Ana Maria. This is how she chisels her way into a tight-knit community. Her face is easily recognized, and in time, everyone in town seems to know who she is. *Lucia. The Chinita. But she is an Americana, no? From New York. A*

Chinita Americana? Verdad! It's common there. She lives in the campo.
With a daughter. The campo? If she lives in the campo, then why is she
always here?

Now she sips tea from a paper cup, watches the blip of the cursor,
taps her fingers on the mouse. A Sunday morning. The Internet café
is empty, everyone at church, though the music blares like a disco-
theque past midnight.

> Hi Nipa! Essy has poop issues too!!

She likes this sentence. She has to laugh.

> Sorry about Natey's tantrums. You sound awfully composed. Man-
> ny's been promising to build an outhouse for months, but somehow
> he's always "too busy." Not too busy to play futbol, of course, but

She rests her chin in her hands, stares at the blink of the cursor.
Lucy Bok?

The voice, a man's. An American. She looks up. He's handsome,
roguish. An acquaintance from her youth she can't quite place.

"Quito," he says. "Before your sophomore year."

Yes, of course, that first summer she lived in Quito! When they
lived in that gigantic shared house full of gringos and no hot water,
ate communal dinners every night on the front stoop.

"Jonesy! Have you been here all these years?"

He loves the expatriate life. Could never go back. He introduces
his girlfriend, a redhead from Indiana who can't be more than
twenty-one. Jonesy, always slick and smooth as a race car.

"Lucy and I taught English through the same program, a long
time ago," he says.

"That's amazing!" gushes the redhead. "And are you teaching
somewhere now?"

"It *was* amazing," Lucia says, smiling. She explains that she is trying to become a farmer. It isn't going so well. It's a joke, except not really.

A farmer? A Chinese girl born and raised in America wants to labor on a farm?

"Did you do that back home?" asks the redhead.

It's comforting the way she says it, as if home means the same thing to all of them, as if Indiana sits next door to New York. "Oh, no. Back home I was a news reporter. A writer."

"Oh, wow! No way!"

"I have a buddy here who runs the gringo paper," says Jonesy. "They're always looking for writers. I could put you in touch with him. I mean, if you want a job."

A job? you say.

No, it's impossible, a job in Cuenca, it's too far away. The bus ride this morning, relatively uneventful, still took over an hour. But Lucia takes down the friend's name and number on a napkin.

Later that day, she considers it. Running into Jonesy after all these years! A job opening at the English paper! She recalls the résumés, the phone calls, the failed interviews back in New York. And Beige, tap-tap-tapping his foot. But now, a fresh start. A reboot, right here in Cuenca. The coincidences, the signs, surely they cannot be ignored?

⁂

"Cuenca?"

"Yes, Cuenca."

"Why would you want to do that?"

They're sitting outside, playing backgammon. A single lightbulb dangles above them, exposed to the night, enticing bugs. She swats away a crane fly.

"It's a job, Manny. A paid news job! They offered it to me." The interview had been easy, relaxed. And just like that, on the spot! "They might even let me work part time."

"But in Cuenca. It's ridiculous."

"What, it's no worse than commuting from Manhattan to New Jersey or Connecticut. I used to do that all the time."

He rolls the dice, doesn't bother to look up. She hates it when he doesn't take her seriously.

"I *like* working."

He shakes his head. "There is plenty to do here. Plenty of work."

"It's not the same. This is a good job." The tinge of vehemence, unexpected. *I'll bring it up*, she'd told herself. *Just to see what he says.* But if she was unsure before, now it begins to feel like the best damn idea she's ever had.

"You need money?" he says.

"Everyone needs money," she says. "But it's not just that."

"What?"

She is on the verge of tears. Angry tears. Why should she have to defend herself? Why should she have to explain to him, when he will never understand?

"Writing is part of who I am," she says. In her voice, thin and sharp, a portent of danger, like a hairline crack in a glass.

He looks up, finally. Frowns, perplexed. Then again, those dog brown eyes.

"It's important," she says. "I need to work. Writing is good for me. It's good for my health." She knows, with those dog eyes, he does not want a fight.

"Lucia," he says. He inhales, sighs. "You do what you have to do."

You could say: This is the way two people drift apart.

She rides the chicken buses three days a week. The buses, unreliable, show up, or they don't. Sometimes they stop on the roadside to wait for a herd of sheep to cross, or the driver's grandmother to deliver a bag of laundry, or his sixteen cousins to roll in. In the height of wet season, small roads flood, or simply wash away. The rain hitting the roof sounds like an army of hammers. A bus can get stuck in the mud for days.

But she loves the job at the newspaper. She is relieved to be writing again, shaping ideas into words. Most of the articles deal with expat life—navigating the housing market, finding a doctor, the best hair salons and masseuses and gringo cafés. She discovers a tiny bodega owned by a Chinese man. Mr. Lo stocks chili oil, oyster sauce, glutinous rice, even chicken feet, chicken necks and heads (*very popular with the locals!*). Mr. Lo's father shuffles up and down the aisles with his walker anchored in ratty tennis balls. And Mr. Lo's wife, a former beauty queen from Shanghai, offers to cut her hair. How quickly the city shrinks to the size of a neighborhood—the paper is young; in time she'll tackle more substantive subjects. For now, she's content to flow at this slower pace, though her own life hardly resembles those of her audience, mostly retirees or recent college grads. On the rare occasions when she meets women her own age, they are single and childless and hypochondriacs, preoccupied with discovering their artistic sides.

Her boss is geeky, young, entrepreneurial. She soaks up the energy of the five teenage interns, who imbue the gray-walled office with joyful energy. Everything is the best! Or the worst! Oh, young lives yearning for drama, while nothing much is at stake! Their laughs make her laugh, she echoes their groans, appreciates their teasing and jokes. They listen to American rap, watch bygone American TV shows dubbed over by melodramatic Spanish actors. They ask all the time about America.

New York, is it very dangerous?

Did you meet celebrities in Hollywood?

She explains that New York and Hollywood are three thousand miles apart, but this concept never quite registers.

Do you drive a convertible?

Do you know Will Smith?

Do you have friends? Like Friends? In a coffee shop?

Sometimes they go out after work for *pollo con fritas* and colas. Surely she is closer in age to their mothers, but they don't seem to mind.

After one month of heavy commutes, she is tired. Despite her dozes on the chicken buses her head is fogged, her body fatigued. The pills drain her energy; always she has had to compensate. Now she lacks the stamina. Her eyelids droop. When Manny remarks on it, she snaps at him. It's the pills. She hates the pills.

One of Jonesy's friends offers her a studio apartment situated above an Italian café—a late-night hot spot for expats and backpackers alike, located on one of the busy *calles* in El Centro. No, she couldn't. But she'll take a look. The room comes furnished with a twin mattress on a metal frame, a metal dresser, an old hutch sink with a pink marble top, a heavy antique brass lamp; just that much is tight. But the dramatic French doors; the Juliet balcony overlooking the café tables on the street; the city an airy extension of her personal space—oh, she loves it! And the walk to work: three minutes.

Like they say, happy mama = happy children, right?

And when she approaches him this time—*This way I'll be less tired when I'm home*, and he doesn't even put up a fight, she finds herself both relieved and slightly disappointed.

On the eve of her first night away, she paces back and forth in the kitchen. She cooks vegetable soup, enough to last for several days. Sets it on the stove in the bright yellow enamel pot. Then she boils a pot of rice, picks three ripe mangoes and a perfect papaya from the garden. She cuts the fruit into bite-size chunks, carefully apportions the chunks into three bowls.

"I'll be back on Wednesday. That's three days. Just three. Is three a lot, sweetheart?"

Essy shakes her head.

"No. No, three is not a lot. Today is Sunday. Tomorrow Abuela will bring you to school. Papi will pick you up. It'll be Wednesday before you know it." She kisses her daughter's forehead, hugs her tight, finds herself teary as she packs a small duffel bag. She has never been away from them, not even for one night. Not since her time in the p-ward.

When she returns three days later, late afternoon, her hands are full of boxes and bags. A pair of shoes for Manny. A new lunch box for Essy with kittens stitched to the front.

Essy is playing with Fredy in the fields by the main house. "Mama!" She comes running.

Bao-bao. Hija. "Essy!" At first glance, so much tinier than she remembered. This girl, her child! It has taken three days away to regain this perspective, this awe, this appreciation for the newness of her daughter's life, so luminous and close to its beginning. But it will take only one day for Esperanza to resume shape as a singular individual: small, young, untrained and inexperienced, a fraction of an adult in size and years—yet certainly no less of a whole being. Lucia understands this now, as a mother. She folds Essy into her arms, burrows her face in her hair.

"Look, *hija*, I brought this for you."

Essy tears open her present. *"Gracias!* It's beautiful! Thank you, Mama!"

How did she not know, or had she merely forgotten, that she had such a wonderfully polite child?

"Mama, we're playing hide-and-seek. It's my turn to look. Play with us, Mama."

She needs to wash up, change her clothes. "You play. I'll come back in a few minutes," she says.

She heads past the old barn, the fields, the meadow, the brook, down the steep hill of wildflowers, up the winding dirt path. As she approaches the casita, she notices, first, the watermelon rinds. Then the seeds and pits, dumps of coffee grinds, chicken bones littering the ground. She can sense the odor before it hits her nostrils. Fetid. The casita is a sty. Dishes and mugs piled in the kitchen sink, the crusty pot of rice on the floor, next to a heap of Manny's clothes. The bright yellow enamel pot of soup still sits on the stove. She lifts its lid. It's full.

She cleans. She neatens. She washes. She sweeps. She heats the soup, forces herself to swallow down two large bowls. Dumps the rest out for the pigs.

The house zipped up, tidy again, she retrieves Essy. Together they lie in bed, surrounded by swaths of mosquito netting. They read a book. She sings softly in Chinese.

"No, Mama. Something else. The bones."

Back bone connected to the shoulder bone
Shoulder bone connected to the neck bone
Neck bone connected to the head bone
Now hear the word of the Lord

At the sound of heavy footsteps, her daughter calls out, "Look, Papi! Mama is home! She's here!"

"Here she is," says Manny. He lifts one corner of mosquito netting. Brushes her cheek with his cheek. He does not comment on the house or the yard or the clothes, neatly folded. "Welcome home," he says.

"Yep," she says. "Here I am. Home." She does not look at him.

The next week, she cooks vegetable curry in the yellow pot. The next, beef stew. The next, *sopa de pollo* with cilantro. Still, the same. And then one evening she returns from the city and it is humid and buggy as she trudges up the path to the casita. But this time she notices no trash, no seeds, no rinds. No offensive smells. She pokes her head in. The kitchen is tidy. Dishes stacked on the shelves. The bright yellow pot sits on the stove, empty.

"Hello?" she says.

In the bedroom, clothes are folded, stacked in three neat piles. Now she is suspicious. She walks outside. The fireflies just beginning to light. She sees Manny winding up the dirt path, Essy on his shoulders.

Her daughter slides down his back, runs to her. "Mama!" she says, throwing her arms around her neck. She pops inside, emerges with her stuffed bunny rabbit. Then, "Mama, where is Yasmin?"

"Who?"

Yasmin is Tía Camila's youngest daughter, Manny's cousin. She has been sent over by the women to help with daily chores.

༚

She is not resentful by nature. She does not complain. She has never complained. Not about the cold or the heat or the leaks or the mud or the flattened cardboard they must lay on the floor of the casita when it rains too hard, or the fleas or ticks or midges that inhabit their bed, which no configuration of netting can keep at bay, which choose her sweet blood as their feast and inflict painful red welts on her belly and legs.

She does not complain about the trash—the endless stream of plastic bags or bottles or wrappers or scraps or bones or toilet paper or glass or string or corroded metal parts that litter the towns, the roads, the riverbanks, the hillsides, that collects in renegade dumps around the campo, drawing stray dogs to mark it with their spray.

She does not complain about the men who hiss like snakes as she walks down the street, or the ones who call out *China, China*, or *Chiquita Chinita*, or the ones who leer openly, stare at her breasts or try to touch her hair or rub themselves against her on a crowded bus, or the ones who urinate on the sides of city buildings, or the children who do the same.

She does not complain at work about the painfully slow Internet connection, the intermittent phone service, or when rolling blackouts cause the electricity to zap out for half the day.

She does not complain when Tía Camila or Tía Alba or Tía Paula poke and prod with the same questions about her personal life—*when will you and Manny have another baby?*—or when they wrinkle their noses at her sweet rice desserts, or when Tío Remy tells her once again about his lady friend in Quito who cooks Chinese food and is highly skilled with her hands.

And so she does not complain about this girl, Yasmin, who is nineteen and chatty with small, perky breasts, who wears tube tops as she cleans the house and feeds the pigs and launders their clothes in the river and who quickly manages to scorch the bottom of her yellow enamel pot. Why should she complain? The dishes are washed. The clothes neatly folded, placed on the wire shelves. Everything is in order.

She focuses on Essy. Her daughter is four years old now. She blooms, like the wildflowers of the campo. She has recently befriended a pair of shepherd girls, eight and ten, who live on the other side of the hill. They roam everywhere with their dirty sheep and forlorn faces, and Essy follows them like a puppy dog. When the sun lowers itself behind the hills, Lucia walks outside with a whistle. Three whistles means it's time to come home. Essy mostly cooperates. Though the child refuses to wear shoes and whines and begs for candy all the time (and Manny indulges her, and then she complains about headaches).

One day Mami asks: "Why do you go?" They are preparing tamales. Tía Camila and Tía Alba mix masa with their hands. "Why do you go, to be away from your family, your child?"

She is caught off guard by the question. Her mind blanks, though she detects no rebuke in Mami's voice. She bites her lip, searches for words, tries to formulate an answer that is not a defense.

"It's what I did back in America," she says. "I was a news reporter. A writer. I studied journalism after college."

"*Una periodista?*" says Mami. Her face, still puzzled.

"I guess it's something I've always done. And I like it. A lot." How to explain? "It's hard to just stop."

"But this is not America," says Tía Camila.

"Esperanza must miss you," says Tía Alba.

She swallows. Nods. Tía Camila purses her lips.

She loves her daughter. She could leave her job in the city, return to the campo. Now their own crops are growing, there is much to be done. But with Ricky and Juan out of school, and Yasmin around, it seems to get done just fine without her. And on the days she's home in the campo she finds herself on edge, irritable, exhausted by evening. She can't say exactly why, but she finds her brain struggling to send words to her mouth, and when the words come, often she must swallow them down to avoid confrontation. Her favorite time becomes the rides in the chicken buses, those long hours back and forth.

One day she stops to observe a small day care on the main *calle*, two blocks from her office in the city. An idyllic array of children sit in a circle, white and brown and all in-between shades. The facility prepares three hot meals a day. The next day she requests to observe again. Rice and chicken and fresh vegetables.

"The food is super healthy. It's really nice," she says.

"You want to bring her to the city?" says Manny.

"I think she'd like it."

"To put her in a day care?"

She nods.

His jaw, open, his forehead scrunched. "No, Lucia. This is her home. My daughter lives in her home, with her family. Not in some dump in the city."

Some dump in the city.

The tone. It catches her by surprise. That mole on his left cheek, like an alien object. She could scrub it off his face.

"She's happy here," he says. "With Mami, with Fredy, with the *escuela* you found for her. She loves the campo. She's free. Isn't this everything you wanted for her?"

She swallows. Nods. Yes, she supposes, on this matter he is right.

Hi Lucia, Just wanted to give you a heads up, I'm sending a package for Essy to your city address. We were back in NYC last week. Stefan brought Rafael, so I played tour guide. Empire State Building, Statue of Liberty, Central Park, the museums, all of it! We even went to a hardcore punk show at an art space on Rivington Street, which ended up being mortifying for Rafi, dad and stepmom in tow (equally mortifying for us—well, he is into that kind of music and too young for CBGB's!). But you know the one thing he actually did like? Chinatown. Kosher vegetarian mock-meat dim sum! Only in New York!

Anyway, we were in the East Village, even stopped into Yonah's store. It looks different now, but Chaka and Noemie were there. They have three boys now! And I found this sundress for Essy at one of those cute new boutiques. Couldn't resist. I do miss New York. "Querencia," is that the word? Or "saudade?"

Are you all right? Please take care of yourself. Your health is very important! :-) Jie

Hardcore punk show? CBGB's? Jie? She finds herself irritated by this message, something in it forced, desperate. The sight of

Yonah's name irks her, too, weighs her down, like a lump of meat sitting undigested in her belly. She cannot indulge in a trip down memory lane right now.

She bangs out a reply:

> Dear Jie, I'll watch for the package. Thanks. I'm fine. L.

> Hi LuluBird, How's your crazy commute? Sorry can't really write, have papers to grade and kids have been waking up 2x every night. Natey screams his head off even if I bring him into my mind. Ha ha, did I just say mind?? I meant bed. Miss you crazy eights. When you coming for a visit? Nipa.

> Hi Nipa, I've actually rented a room in the city now, on top of a café where all the expats hang out. It's like part action, part cave.

She taps her fingers distractedly on the table.

> Miss you. Hard to believe it's been almost a year and a half. Can that be right? Feels like forever but also no time at all. L.

She is neither this nor that. Here nor there.

Here, she socializes with teenagers half her age. In the campo, it's his. His land, his house, his family. If he is in a generous mood, he might say it's theirs. But nothing is really hers. Even their casita is marked, with Mami's flowery ruffle curtains, with the perfume of another girl. Only this small room in Cuenca, where she has deliberately selected solid blue sheets and a dark green bedspread, can she call her own, and on the wall above the bed she has started to decorate, taped up photos and pictures snipped from magazines, all the most beautiful things: a glass flower, a mountain vista, hazy fog over London, a pair of Venezuelan waterfalls. In the density of the city, she feels alone. In the open space of the campo, she feels constricted, the eyes of his family ever upon her.

There is always another party, another birthday, another *quince*, another engagement, another celebration of another saint. And the music louder, the men drunker, the women nosier: *What's this, I hear, about Lucia living in Cuenca? Cuenca? But isn't Lucia standing over there by the Jell-O? She lives in Cuenca? No, no, she travels to Cuenca. By bus. For work. For work? She works for some gringo newspaper. In Cuenca? For this a woman travels alone?* Cuenca, it could be Mars.

She is not resentful by nature. She dances bachata with the *tíos*, sits politely with the women, doles out cake and Jell-O to the neighbors. She is not resentful by nature. But about Manny, this is where she starts to fray.

At night, when she feels his eyes upon her as she brushes her teeth and rinses and spits and thinks back to their conversations about the business they once said they would start together, the house they said they would build, and in the mornings when she is gardening and glimpses the exterior of their casita which he and Essy have taken on as a project, painstakingly painting a white rabbit on one side, clouds, a blue sky, and in the afternoons when he is watching *futbol* with his cousins or talking *futbol* with his cousins or playing *futbol* with his cousins, and in the evenings when he is watching telenovelas in the kitchen, she finds herself wondering: *How is it he finds time for such things but never has the time to build an outhouse, and meanwhile, she still must shit in the woods?*

She has asked, repeatedly, and then she stopped asking, and then she started asking again, and always the same answer, over the course of the year. *I'll get to it.* About this particular detail, the outhouse, is where she starts to fray.

One evening she storms outside, grabs a shovel from the garden, starts throwing dirt. She can dig. She need not wait for a man. If he will not do it, she will do it herself.

He comes after her.

"Are you all right?" he says.

"I'm fine," she says. "I'm working. See?"

He narrows his eyes. "Lucia," he says. Slow and steady as pavement. "You need to take care of yourself."

Jie's words. Always Jie. Like a shadow.

"Shut up," she says sharply.

"We don't have the same kinds of hospitals here. You get sick here, I don't know how to help you. You get sick here, you stay loco for the rest of your life."

Her blood, electric. She throws down her shovel. Bites her lip, walks away.

The next day she is back in the city again, and in the evening she does not go for *pollo con fritas* and colas with the interns though they beg her to join. She returns to her small bed in her small room, looks up through her dramatic French doors, to the night sky too cloudy for stars. She is hot. Itchy. Fresh mosquito bites have risen on her ankles, she digs in her nails with little relief. Heavy trucks roar by, axles shake her bones, smells of grease and salt mixed with cigar smoke roil her belly. It is so overwhelming she wants to shut the French doors. But then she'd be locked in a cave. So she lies next to her window, allowing the diesel fumes of the city buses to assault her nose, clog and contaminate her lungs. She coughs. Reaches between her legs, fingers deft, brings herself to orgasm. Still, she feels unsatisfied, strangely aroused, so again and again, and then lulled to sleep by the raspy sounds of German and tireless American twang: *"Well, in America, we ___ ."* When she wakes, she feels something inside her like a venom, a flare in her chest, a burning sensation just beneath her skin. The serpents. A thought flickers. She extinguishes it. When she slows her breath to listen, the air is quiet. It is only her.

But back in the campo, new frictions, even as Manny finally builds the outhouse (which he and Essy paint a bright purple).

There's the volume of the television. Muddy boots. A rake left in the garden that gets stolen overnight. And then money—how much they should contribute for all the meals they now take at Mami's when Lucia is away. He accuses her of neglect, missing his second cousin's *quince*. He says she doesn't appreciate his family, his mother. She is shocked. She loves Mami. She has always tried to be polite.

"You don't even cook anymore," he says.

"What?"

It's true. Because he never wants to eat her food. All those Sunday soups and stews she finds three days later, sitting untouched on the stovetop. It's a woman's humiliation.

"You could help Mami with the cooking," he says, coldly. "At least when you're around."

Her face grows hot. She feels stupid, ashamed.

One night, she dreams she is a clog, a tangle of lint and dirt and hair jammed in the curve of a drainpipe. One night, she dreams she is a black and tan puppy, lost in a bullring, begging for directions to the East Village.

I must do something.

She, Lucia Bok, is a doer of things. Like Ma.

It comes to her through a series of coincidences. Signs, you could say.

One night she is lying in her small bed in her small room, staring up at the night sky. From the café tables below, bits and tangles of conversation drift and rise. *A shaman cleansed my soul. Have you tried it?*

The next day it happens at the office. One of the interns asks if she knows anything about the plant medicine retreats in the jungle. The ones run by shamans. No, but she overheard some tourists talking. Why do you ask? she says. I thought it might make a good article, he says, so earnest.

It happens the third time at the *farmacia*, when she stops in to buy vitamins. Ana Maria smiles, they exchange pleasantries—*cómo está?*—and she mentions nothing of the itch under her skin or the burn in her chest, but today, quietly, respectfully, Ana Maria asks if, not to intrude or anything, but only as a suggestion, a matter of curiosity, if she is interested, she would like to visit a *curandero*.

No, not a shaman, not the ones in the jungle. A *curandero*. A traditional medicine man, a healer. Here in Cuenca. She could refer her to such a person.

Three coincidences. This adds up to a sign. She feels grateful, blessed, calm once more, as the recipient of the universe's guidance.

The *consultorio* is located on a quiet side street in an inconspicuous, unmarked house. In the waiting room, a shrine to the Virgin Mary, a glass case displaying foreign perfumes (Jōvan, Lancôme, Chanel), another with packages of vitamins and other Western medicines. The *curandero* must be close to her in age, but the skin of his face is loose, jowly, his nose and chin protrude with a shine. A witch. No, a gnome. But wearing a crown of red feathers and a white button-down shirt with decorative stitching, a bit pirate-like, stained with sweat at the armpits. Yet there is something about this man she instinctively trusts, some spark of kindness. He greets her in his office.

"I am Don Gonzalo. What brings you here?" he asks.

He asks many questions. About her habits and routines, her sleep and meals and bowel movements, her dreams and daily stresses. He observes her carefully—her eyes, her neck, her hands, her feet, as if he knows it is too easy to lie with words.

"*Debilidad*," he says. A general weakness due to spiritual intrusions. He will perform a ritual cleansing, a *limpieza*.

She sits on a low stool, close to the floor. He fetches a large sprig of dried herbs, bound together like a feather duster. She closes her eyes, hears the rustle of leaves, the flurry of air as he fans and beats it over her head while emitting high-pitched chirps. He spits into his hands. Touches her hair. Then he passes two eggs over her body and chants. To expel the malevolent spirits from her body, he later explains. He lights a tall candle. Rings a bell, inhales a puff of cigarette, blows the smoke into her mouth. Then he swigs from a bottle of spirits. One minute she smells the alcohol, the next she feels a spray on her face. For a moment she hovers outside herself, envisions the scene through her daughter's eyes. *Mama, why is that man dusting you?* He wraps her head with a towel. Swigs. Blows flame. *Like a dragon, Mama!* Her eyes clench shut instinctively. Heat roars up her back. But there is no fear. No doubt. Only faith.

When the ceremony is over, he presses a small crystal into her hand, a talisman for strength, and prescribes her a tonic, seven drops to be taken in a glass of water twice a day.

As she walks back toward the café, she feels emptied, restored. She marvels at the patterns in the cobblestone sidewalk, admires the large, colorful houses, their stalwart gates. Even the shards of glass on top of the security walls seem to radiate a friendly glint.

She returns to him.

The next time, she asks about his family. He has five children. The youngest, a boy of sixteen, studies the traditional ways. And the others? she asks. The others go their own ways, he says.

The next time, she asks if she may ask him more questions. She works for the gringo newspaper, she explains.

He is a modest, private man. Not exciting for the gringos. The tourists, they want to know about the exotic, the mystical, not what he sees with his eyes.

What does he see with his eyes? she asks.

The bluntness of his answer surprises her.

"You are unhappy," he says. "You keep things inside. You cannot find peace with all these things trapped inside, like a poison. Like this, you will not find the correct path."

Trapped? Poison?

She is annoyed, practically offended, by these words she finds both trite and vague. But she presses him. What, then, is the correct path? she asks.

"*Ay, Chinita,*" he says, smiling. "You are not ready. When you are ready, you will let go, find the ties that bind. Only then can you find the path."

Ready?

She has moved across an ocean to find the path. The new path. The new air. The new life, untethered to the complications of her past. The life of her own creation.

She returns to her daughter, whose skinny brown arms encircle her neck, who laughs and shouts and screams and cries. Wild and free, Essy is full of joy. She disappears again with the shepherd girls into the campo.

This is happiness.

That afternoon, she and Manny sit together quietly on the stoop outside the casita.

"Where does she go?" she asks.

"She has friends," he says.

She lets out a sigh.

He echoes it. Spits out a mouthful of watermelon seeds, turns to go inside.

At night, they lie under the mosquito net, Essy asleep between them. She reaches over, puts her hand on his chest. He grunts, turns away.

In the city, she lies in her small bed in her small room, mulling over the *curandero*'s words. Unhappy. Trapped inside. The ties that bind.

Ma, what happened to Ba?
Your father died in an accident.
What kind of accident?

A car accident.
But you loved him, you really loved him. Didn't you, Ma?
I did, Xiao-mei. Once, I did.

And then she thinks: I don't love him. I have never loved him. And love is everything. It is as simple as this, and she cannot think why it seemed so complicated before. *The ties that bind.* There is only one man she has ever loved.

She can hardly remember what it looked like, that shabby apartment in the East Village. Twin mattress on the floor of the living room, security monitors where she watched the store. Why did she leave him in the first place?

Then it comes to her. *I gave up love for a baby, traded my soul mate for a child.* She is shocked, ashamed that she has put this into words. These words. Bad words. Hurtful, like racial slurs, words that should not be thought at all and certainly never voiced. A mother loves her child unconditionally, without regret. But now encapsulated in words, that tinge of resentment ignites a physical pain, like something in her gut has caught fire. It rises, shoots up to inflame her esophagus, throat, coat her tongue, so she rolls it into a bolus and shoves it back but it lodges in her tonsils and she hacks and hacks until it pops back up and again she must swallow it down. For a few hours she clutches her belly, lies prone in her bed. It gets worse, it gets better, it gets worse. Perhaps it has been weeks, months, years, she has been swallowing it down and her throat, her esophagus, her mouth, even her teeth, now hurt from the effort. The *curandero*, he is right.

She yearns to hear his voice. But she doesn't know where he is. Somewhere in Israel. She has his old cell phone number and sometimes when she's at the office she dials it discreetly and it rings but then an automated voice clicks on. Sometimes it informs her there are technical issues with the number. Temporarily out of service. Other days it says the mailbox is full. Sometimes it rings and rings. It makes no sense at all.

There must be some way to find him. Of course there is. She has always been resourceful, she can track him down, even if he is in Israel. But if she has to try too hard, perhaps it's the universe's way of telling her this isn't to be. She doesn't believe in God, but she believes in a natural order, a higher directive, to be gleaned and mulled and acted upon. In this way, she and Manny differ. His desires remain inert, stuck in his heart. There is a word for this, a beautiful word that unfurls from the tongue: *velleity. The weakest form of volition. A mere wish, unaccompanied by an effort to obtain it.* This has never been her way. But the time must be right. Needs must be aligned. Perhaps they were misaligned in the past, perhaps that was why their relationship fell apart. This time, she is determined, it will not fail.

The days billow in and out. Every afternoon the clouds circle in from the mountains, hunker down over Cuenca, drop their rains before whisking away. The sun reappears, the pavement dries in patches. From her office window she looks out on the neighboring rooftops, where puddles disappear before her eyes. Week after week she watches the rains, each drop a flash of light as it touches down, blip, blip-blip, each blip like the blink of the cursor on her computer screen, and she is mesmerized, the patterns like a code, and then the puddles dry up before her eyes.

And then once more it's Essy's birthday, and there is a party with five candles and she and Manny take turns swelling with pride. How can it be that she loves her daughter even more now than a year ago, when she had already loved her then? But Manny dwindles away, preoccupied. And herself, each time she looks in the mirror a gray hair sprouts, and her body is tired like from treading water.

"So restless," says Tía Alba.

"And where is there to go?" says Tía Camila. "Even when Sylvia sends her sons away, they come back, you see?" She pats Mami's shoulder.

Tía Camila has never left the campo.

But Ma. She and Ma are the same. Doers of things. Ma, who gave up her family for true love. Ma, who came to America with one daughter's hand in her hand and the other safe in her belly. Ma, who worked her way from typist to bookkeeper to actuary, from Third Uncle's basement into the life of her own choosing. But when Ma appears in her dreams, this is what she says: *Xiao-mei, be careful. You are too much American.*

And then one day, at the end of the wet season, it happens.

She dials from the office and the connection is crackly, but it is his energy she feels, trickling into her ear. He is there, even before his voice surges through.

"Where are you?" she says.

"New Jersey," he says.

"New Jersey?" *New Jersey!* Not Israel.

"Close to beach. It's beautiful. Everything is good there?"

She stretches for words. Truthful words. "It's beautiful here, too."

"What?"

"It's beautiful here, too," she says, but so loudly the words lose their shape.

"Yes. It's night there now?"

"Yoni, are you there?"

"Yeah."

"I'm thinking of coming to the States." She has rehearsed this line to quell any sense of urgency. She tosses it, gently: "Maybe I'll come for a visit."

As if he were still down at the store, and she a quick train ride away. As if it were a week ago they saw each other last, instead of almost four years.

She tosses it. She waits for it to land.

"Yeah?"

"Maybe I'll come for a visit. Yoni, can you hear me?"

A click. A pause. No, no, he can't be gone—she shakes the phone up and down, taps it with two fingers, caresses it, coaxes it—please, come back. And then, he is back again.

"Oh, sure," he says. "But I'm gonna take a trip soon to Israel. Then maybe someplace out west, Arizona or Montana or Minnesota or something, someplace beautiful. Maybe I'm gonna buy some land, build a house. Then you come visit, I have a big house instead of a little shack!" He laughs, his bighearted laugh.

You come visit, I have a big house. Oh beautiful words! Everything in these words: Come. Big. Big enough for her. Big enough for Essy. I have. You come. An offering. She can see it, a big white house with a big green yard, a fence, a dog! You come visit. An invitation. A welcome. They had a dog once, a long-haired mutt with a black and tan face. Yoni got it from a shelter on the Upper West Side.

She tells herself it is for the greater good. She believes this is true. If she's gone, Manny will find someone else. A younger woman, perhaps, who will love him truly, and he deserves this kind of love, just as she does, and it will be easier if she is gone. Essy is young, she will forget quickly. Better now than later, like Nipa said. So she will tell him one night after their daughter is in bed and he is sitting in the kitchen, relaxed, shelling peanuts and watching television. Side by side with a Colombian telenovela, nothing feels like drama. She will say it bluntly. *It's not working out.* They fight and bicker all the time, such negative energy in a household is not good for a child. They will discuss like civil adults. He will agree. She can go. She should go. It's for the best. She will bring Essy to visit, of course. Summers. Holidays. School vacations. She will miss Mami and Fredy. Ricky and Juan and Papi, too, though perhaps not the others. The others are not so kind.

And with that, it is decided. She will go to Yoni. She will take Essy and they will go to him.

But when she arrives at the casita, the two of them are painting again, adding blue and purple polka dots to the white rabbit on the north-facing side. "Look what Papi did!" her daughter squeals.

No. Oh, no. This, in plain sight: He will not give up the child. He loves the child.

The Vargas house. The clay pot with the curved handle, shattered into a thousand pieces. His breath on her face like a wildfire. His unsteady hands, fumbling with the too-small, too-many snaps of a yellow ducky pajama, the determination in his eyes.

No. No. No. It will not work. Of course she cannot ask to take their daughter. He would never let Essy go. She will have to go alone. If she goes to Yonah, she will go alone.

And then she will visit, of course. Commute. She will make it work. She will see her daughter often. Summers and holidays, months at a time. And Essy will come to Arizona or Montana or Minnesota. Her daughter, a world traveler. She will love America. She will live the best of two lives.

Back in her small bed in her small room above the gringo café, she stares up at the wall, plastered with all her beautiful things. A pink coffee cup. Dewdrops on a morning glory. A pair of Venezuelan waterfalls. Well, she could jump on an airplane. This very minute. She could go see those waterfalls. Or someday, she could see them with Yonah.

But the next morning she is once again mired in ambivalence. The heat in her nerves like live wires. She must shake this off. She must go to him. She'll figure out the rest somehow.

Back in the campo, her daughter, down by the river, hurling mud pies with Fredy, or barefoot, screeching, catching fish with a net. Headstrong, independent, fearless, free. At dinner, sweet, helping Mami set out the dishes. Essy, at age five, already starting to read. She turns away, bites her lip.

I will go and come back. It won't be long, hija.

Her daughter is smart. And blissfully happy in the campo.

She sits with her thoughts on the chicken bus. She knows the drivers by now, the mud, the potholes, the stretches of road where she must hang on tight. She knows how to pack light—her notebook, a pen, raincoat rolled into a little ball—to keep her canvas backpack in her lap at all times, attached to her belt loop by a silver carabiner. She knows to carry her identification separately, in a flat pouch safety-pinned to the inside of her pants, to sit in the front, as close as possible to the driver, to keep a small amount of cash on hand—for candy, for fruit, enough to appease a lazy hoodlum. Three times in her life she has been pickpocketed—in a nightclub in Panama, a bus in Peru, on the A train to Queens during rush hour. Twice she has been mugged—a thin gold chain wrenched from her neck at the West Fourth subway station, a purse snatched off her shoulder at a noodle stall in Hanoi.

She has learned to be cautious, but it is not true to her nature.

So it is unexpected, when she is jarred awake from a gentle doze to find the point of a butcher's knife six inches from her face.

Blood, pooled to her feet. Stomach dropped like a sack to the floor. She feels cold. Freezing cold. Muscles in shock, useless. She controls her bladder, mostly.

Only her head feels light. Hollow. Emptied, with the exception of a single thought rising up toward the ceiling: *No, no. Please, I have a young daughter.*

She gives up her belongings. Her canvas backpack, a small sum of cash. A brown paper lunch bag with a Tupperware of beef stew, which is violently chucked to the ground.

The masked men move on, methodically working their way down the aisle like a pair of flight attendants collecting trash. Then they hop off the bus, gone.

"My notebook . . ." she says.

From the bus station her feet carry her straight to the office, where she huddles in the safety of familiar faces, where the interns rush to her side, all sympathy and indignation.

"Oh my God."

"Are you all right?"

"Have you gone to the police?"

"What did the bastards look like?"

She can't remember. All she can remember is the knife: dull gray metal, ten inches or so, with a slender, curved blade, a vicious point. Something wicked from a common kitchen.

She is shaken, disturbed. Her head feels weightless, detached from her body. Two of the interns volunteer to walk her home.

She lies in her small bed in her small room in the city. Today, of all days. That ride, of all rides. And how did she miss it, when those men came aboard, dark and suspicious, shifty-eyed. The wrong place at the wrong time. Unlucky. A coincidence. Or perhaps, inevitable.

She shuts her eyes. A siren's wail. The screech of tires. Dutch. German. Fumes, cigar smoke, thick in her lungs, a burning on her skin, real or imagined, she doesn't know. She yearns to speak with Essy, hear her daughter's voice, but the casita still has no phone. She could call the main house. But then Mami would answer. Or Tía Camila. And then everyone would know.

A woman, running around alone like that. What does she expect?

She crawls out of bed to escape the voices. Creeps downstairs. Steps outside, where two older couples, retired American expats, beckon to her. "Lucia! Come join us." She sits for a few minutes in the wrought iron chair with the heart-shaped back, sips 7-Up through a straw. But their words float, each syllable headed in its own direction, and she cannot follow their meaning. She could be a hologram, her solid self still embedded upstairs.

She excuses herself, returns to her room. Locks the door, shivering. She opens the bottom drawer of the metal dresser, where she keeps her hair dryer and rubber bands, the bitter-tasting tonic from the *curandero*, her ample collection of pills. Blue pills, white pills,

pink pills, red pills. The white pill now. The blue one, too. The blue
ones she hasn't touched in several years, but now anything to help
her relax. And seven drops of the tonic in a cup of water, for her
debilidad. She throws it down her throat.

She climbs onto her bed, pulls closed the shutters, banishes the
outside world.

She sleeps. She wakes. She checks her clock. It makes no sense.
One moment, groggy, like she has slept for days, yet only fifteen
minutes have passed, the next moment it is three hours later. Eyes
adjust to darkness. Her stomach growls. She cracks open the shutters. Adjusts her eyes again. The café tables below are empty. The
calle is empty. She falls asleep, and the next time she wakes, she feels
refreshed, throws open the shutters, but it is eerily still outside. The
moon is out, perfect and round. But the clock says six o'clock. She is
puzzled. It must've stopped. Time, stopped! For some reason, this
amuses her, and if only it were true, that she could pause the time,
go elsewhere for a while. She would visit Yonah. They'd sit on the
bench, chat with the smokers. But no, he is in Israel. They would
float in the Dead Sea, reading a newspaper. But no, he is in New
Jersey, by the ocean, and they will go for long walks, and Loco Coco
will offer to braid her hair.

But no. The incident on the bus. It's a sign. She must read the
signs, and now she sees, it has been distilled for her in the clearest
way possible. Her directive. Her role. Her identity. The words,
placed inside her emptied-out head: *Please, I have a young daughter.*

For a mother to leave her child, it's impossible.

She cannot leave Essy behind.

They will go in stealth. Disappear without notice. There can be no
other way. She will write him a letter. Apologize. Offer to bring
Essy for the summers, holidays, school vacations. Like joint custody.
Since he cannot set foot in America. But he is a man. He can have

more children. He can have twenty more children from twenty different *chicas*. She. She is too old.

She will go to the travel agency in Cuenca, her pockets full of cash. She will purchase two one-way tickets.

But no. In every plan, a hitch. Always, one must overcome unforeseen obstacles.

"You'll need to have her exit papers," says the travel agent.

"Exit papers?"

"Signed by her father."

"But I'm her mother."

The agent shakes his head. "No child allowed to leave the country without permission of both parents. Child abduction protections. It's the law."

But I'm her mother.

She stares at him in disbelief, this man in his cheap blue suit and blue tie. She bites hard on her lip. She will not cry. She shifts her stare to the wall, to the ceiling, to the floor.

"*Señora*, is there a problem? Do you still wish to purchase the tickets?"

The ceiling, descending, hovers just inches away from the top of her head. She pushes a packet of cash into his hand. "*Sí, por favor.*"

She is dizzy, trembling. Plunging toward entropy, and as she steps out to the street, each of her body's limbs seems to have its own mind. She needs a plan. A scheme. She sees how it is, this scheme against women, to make a woman ask a man for permission to go somewhere with her own blood-child. For nine months, she grew the child in her belly, and who has the right to say what she can or cannot do with her child?

She can forge it. His signature. A simple illegible scribble, a roll of the pen. But the thought makes her anxious. Her tank top sopping with sweat, she tries to breathe, relax. Breathe. Relax. She can't. If she gets caught, then what? Then she will be arrested. Then

Manny will know. He will know what she has tried to do and he will let her rot in some Ecuadorian jail to be devoured by rodents and forbid her from ever seeing her daughter again. And then what. All this, for what?

She cannot sleep. Eyes squeezed shut, she lies awake. She must align her thoughts. Make them straight. Fling them like an arrow. Abracadabra. Then, a flutter of wings. Opening one eye, she sees a pigeon has landed on the balcony. Dirty, limping, with a pecked-bald head, it must've just been in a fight. Poor bird. Pretty birdy. She'll fetch it a cup of water, but when she returns it is gone. Poor pretty bird, where could it go?

Abracadabra. She knows. She knows!

She will tell Manny she wants to bring Essy to visit her sister in Switzerland. It makes perfect sense. In all the years Jie has lived there, they have never visited, and that is unacceptable! Of course they want to go to Switzerland, to visit, to see the sights. The Matterhorn. Heidi. *Sound of Music!* Not once did she ever resent him for not being able to travel back when they lived in New York; it was a simple fact of their lives. But this time—this time she will say she would like to go to Switzerland, and she will invite him to come, because he'll say no, of course, because he dislikes change, he is a boulder of inertia, and he doesn't like Jie and Jie has never liked him. Well, they don't have a single thing in common, do they!

"For how long?" Manny asks, frowning.

"Four weeks," she says. Essy should learn something about the other side of her family, what little there is—this is true. This is true. This is the truth.

"It's a long time."

"It's expensive. Doesn't make sense to go all that way for a week."

He scratches his chin. She tries to sense his thoughts. Waits, hyperaware of her shallow breaths, jumpy and frantic inside. Surely he can see the guilt, thick as sludge as it oozes through her pores. She forces out a smile.

"You could come, too," she says. The words, a dribble, her lungs choked up, a rock in her throat as surprise rolls across his face. *What a great idea. A family trip!*

"No."

"No?"

He shakes his head. "No, I wouldn't go."

"Then I'll get two tickets." The two tickets to Newark, connecting through Atlanta, tucked behind her underwear in the top drawer of her metal dresser in the city.

He frowns. "It's a long time."

"It'll be wet season."

Wet season. It can be unpleasant. All the rain, the floods, seeping into the casita, turning the floor to mud, and they must lay down flattened cardboard and wear rain boots. Essy hates the mud.

"Mud," she says. She can hear it now, Essy wailing about the mud. Surely, he can hear it, too.

And then he nods, and she must suppress a shout. A nod. A slow nod. It's enough.

She is efficient. When she returns from the city the following week, she brings the exit papers, and when she leaves the campo again, they are signed by his hand.

She is buoyant. Giddy. All the world bright and beautiful again. She will miss the trees, the river, the winding dirt roads, the women squatting beside their buckets of potatoes, Vera and Isabel and Luz (Vera's brother's Taiwanese wife with a miscarriage, Isabel's youngest son starting school, and Luz, dear Luz, still dreaming about her cockfights!). She will miss the chicken buses. And Mami. And Fredy. But no, she cannot think about this.

The days pass, a blur. In the campo, she tries to tuck herself in a

corner, flatten into a shadow, remain quiet, inconspicuous, forget-
table. At the office, the interns amplify her excitement. Switzerland.
They've never met anyone who has gone to Switzerland! She almost
believes her own story to be true. *What will you do there?* Oh, her
sister will have plans, so many plans, all kinds of touristy things. She
tells no one—not the interns, not her boss, not Mr. Lo at the
Chinese bodega or the kindhearted *curandero*—that she does not
plan to return. She will work things out! She and Essy will stay with
Nipa while she works things out.

On her final day in Cuenca, she takes a circuitous walk before
heading into the office. Everything feels new once more. Bye-bye
red-tile roofs. Bye-bye cobblestone sidewalks, bye-bye colonial
archways and ornate railings and rows of Juliet balconies above.
Bye-bye palm trees and cathedrals and pigeons squabbling in the
square, bye-bye *almuerzo*, bookstore, post office, Internet café. Her
limbs feel light, as if injected with helium, her head floats over her
shoulders, even her eyebrows, her eyes, the creases in her forehead,
lured upward by some antigravitational force.

That evening, she does not go out for *pollo con fritas* and colas
with the interns. The next morning, she must catch an early bus
back to Martez. That weekend, she and Essy will make the long
journey from the campo to the airport in Quito. She still has to
pack, she explains.

That evening, she sits, goose bumps flaring on her legs as she
makes contact with the cold tile floor in her room above the café. She
has never, not once, sat on this floor, and now as she peeks under the
metal bedsprings which have supported her for over a year, she notices the candy wrappers and stray coins floating among the lint and
cobwebs and dust bunnies and hair. Her own dark strands of hair.

She notices a spider's web, a mesh of fine wires, tucked in the
corner of the room. Now that she is low, near the ground, she sees
the silky fibers glisten in the light like something wet and metallic.

She crawls over to examine it. There it is: a small black spider, no bigger than a dime. It has not yet completed its task. The web has only radial strands, like a wheel. She bends down, breath so close the strands waver and dance. She watches as Spider hops counterclockwise from spoke to spoke, dragging its thread. It fascinates her, to see a creature so busy in an act of creation.

She remembers learning once how a spider spins its web. About the nonsticky strands on which it sits while it constructs its sticky trap. She remembers reading about scientists who conducted experiments where they fed spiders the blood of severely ill mental patients, and the spiders spun cockeyed webs. This spider's web is a marvel of nature, perfectly symmetric.

She pricks her left index finger. A red droplet forms. She offers it, but Spider does not seem interested. It is still too busy, spinning, hopping, pinning its thread at each spoke like a housewife pegging laundry. She digs out a silver centavo from her pocket. With her right thumb, she presses the injured finger, squeezes a bubble of blood onto the coin. She watches the bubble jiggle, a delicate half dome. She places the coin on the floor.

The voices from the café are louder now, rough and German. She wishes they would stop. She dislikes German, its angry nature, its hard sounds, even worse than Hebrew. She keeps picturing herself at the door of Yonah's cozy beach house. A clapping screen door. A welcome mat to wipe off their shoes. Shoes! Neither she nor Essy have appropriate shoes for winter in New Jersey. Only a pair of tall rubber rain boots for mud. She looks at the piles of clothes she has folded, laid out on the bed. She has accumulated a few new items since she arrived, but nothing right for winter.

She is hot. Scorching hot. Burning hot. She will go for a walk. She needs air.

She heads downstairs. The Germans are still outside, their table crowded with frothy steins.

The *calle* is empty. Street lamps cast tall, looming shadows. Geometric patterns pop out from the cobbled pavement, the iron fences, the shards of broken glass on the walls. The walls, gray and ominous. Like the dull blade of the butcher's knife. A woman should not walk by herself at this hour. She cannot risk it, not now, getting mugged or abducted or robbed or raped. Not now. She must return to her room. She cannot let anything happen to her now.

She returns. She locks the door. She will pack quickly. Go to sleep. Let the morning come and gather her.

The spider has finished its work. The web hangs perfectly in the still of the room, waiting to snare its prey. Spider is nowhere to be seen.

She hears a sound. Wood on wood. A knock. Though it could be her imagination. No one ever knocks. No one knows she lives here, except her coworkers, and Jonesy. She wonders if he has come to wish her well. More likely, it's one of the drunk Germans wandering upstairs looking for *el baño*. Occasionally a patron does that.

This time it comes firmer. Knock-knock, knock-knock. Suddenly she is feverish with fear. An intruder. A burglar. The masked hoodlums from the chicken bus. She swings around, panting. Does she even own a knife? Is it better to yell out, confirm her presence, will this scare him away? A rapist. But she will scream out the window and everyone below will hear, and if they don't then she will hurl an object down to get their attention. Her eyes dart, lock on the antique brass lamp on the dresser. She can block the door with the dresser, tie a sheet to the bed frame, drop out the window. No. She is indulging in childish games, hide-and-go-seek, chase, planning routes of escape.

"*Quién-es?*" she says, deepening her voice.

There is no peephole, no chain, so she grabs the antique desk lamp, throws the weight of her body against the door. If she opens it and the stranger forces his way in, she will slam this object on his head, run to the window and scream for help.

"*Quién-es?*" She cracks it open an inch, then another inch more.

"Lucia?" says the voice.

A woman's voice! All at once her body relaxes. Why did it not occur to her, silly, that it could be a woman at the door?

"Lucia, open up."

It is Miranda. Her sister. *Jie.*

❦

She recalls what happens next as a jumbled dream: the figure pushing at the door, crowding into her room, all mouth: *You. You. You.* Commands and accusations. The crescendoing voice, buzzing of mosquitoes, everything too loud, too many words, and she covers her ears to stem the drain of energy from her head, because this is what they want: to drain her, to muzzle her, to take away her power, her feelings, her desires, her will, to shut her up and stuff her into a shoe box and stick it on a high shelf, where she will sit and sit and gather dust quietly like the mental patients of yore. *What the fuck are you doing? He's her father, Lucia.* You cannot. Thou shalt not. Like Moses and his ten commandments. And then her face under the spell of the figure's hot breath, frantic wetness spilling down her cheek. The spider. Where is the spider? *Where are the pills?* Pills, pills, pills. Always the pills. The pills like a leash around her neck and everyone with a hand to pull. *It's wrong, Lucia.* Too loud, too electric, she lashes out, all arms and fists. You want pills, here are the pills, and she rushes forward, thrusting the pills in the monster's face as it gags and spits. *I will tell him, Lucia. I will tell him what you've tried to do.* And then she hears her daughter's name and she goes blind with rage, GET OUT, yes, goddammit, yes, I am taking the goddamn pills. Four white pills in her palm, straight down her throat, and she pitches the open bottle out the window. There are your fucking pills. A shower of hail hits the pavement. *Lucia.* She jerks away, flings open the red plaid suitcase, grabs a tank top, hurls it to the floor—and then all the neatly packed items, the jeans, the bras, the books, the shoes, the hair dryer, at the window, at the bed, at the dresser, at the wall, and then the antique brass lamp at the monster by the door. It strikes, on the forehead, and then there is red, red, red. Blood, and the red-streaked too-loud figure a blur. *Stop, Lucia.* She covers her ears, musters every drop of air in her tightening lungs. YOU. GET OUT. GET OUT OF MY FUCK-ING LIFE.

She retreats into the corner, nose to knees, rocks back and forth. A thunder on the stairs. The Germans are coming, big men with rough voices. Her skin goes cold. *Please, no, don't let them lock me up. Please don't take me away.*

6

Manuel

She started acting different a few months ago. Not crazy, like loco, not the way she'd acted after Essy was born. But she kept secrets, and got mad if he asked too many questions. Though it was not his way, to ask many questions, and he often wondered if he should ask more. What of all those evenings she spent apart from him, in Cuenca? Did she have friends there? Were they *Americanos*? Were they young or old? Did she go straight home after work, make herself a bowl of noodles? Or did she loiter at the office, gossiping, go for drinks with her colleagues until the bars and restaurants closed? Sometimes when they were together she would stay up late, sit in the uncomfortable high-backed rocking chair in the corner of their bedroom, scribbling away in her notebook. "What are you doing?" he asked. "Work," she said. "What kind of work?" She shrugged, eyes tight on her page, and if he pressed she'd sigh, followed by a bloated exhale, and this meant she had nothing more to say. These past few months, she'd seemed extra impatient, exhaling often, as if she did not want to expend extra energy funneling her thoughts through her mouth, as if she'd rather expect him to read her mind.

But she was patient with Essy. As patient as one could hope to be with

264 Mira T. Lee

a child her age. She cooked her favorite foods, oatmeal not too thin, not too lumpy, chicken soup with the bones strained out, fried rice with green onion and gravy. She peeled her apples, halved her grapes, quartered her strawberries, adding a teaspoon of sugar if the fruit was underripe. She chided her: to clean up, to get dressed, to go potty, to go to bed, but she rarely raised her voice. He had his own challenges with his daughter, who seemed gifted with a limitless energy, who talked too much and too loudly, who dashed and jumped and punched the air, chased animals with sticks and climbed trees like a boy. "Why can't she sit still?" he asked. "What about tea parties and dolls?" He spoke of little girls as if he knew, but he was acquainted with few, only his cousins' daughters who played makeup and beauty pageant and pranced around at family parties dressed in leotards and tiaras and their mothers' scarves. On second thought, he was glad his daughter was not like that.

He was back in his country, with his family. The work was hard but predictable. Air seemed to circulate more smoothly through his body, in one continuous loop, without getting stuck, or sucked in, or expelled in frantic bursts. The days stretched before him like miles of empty space. He tried not to think of it as dull, or view himself as defeated; on the contrary, he'd seen more of the world than anyone else in this countryside, and now he reaped the rewards of his return, puffing up as he recounted stories of Nueva York. Now he walked with his shoulders thrown back, looked people in the eye for the hell of it, because for too long he had looked down or away. The girls, too. Sure, the girls!

And then when Lucia decided to take that job in Cuenca, she was gone three days a week. His *tías* tittered, but he tried not to care. And though it wasn't what he wanted, it was what she wanted, what she *needed*. He wanted to believe it: that she was cured. He made the best of things.

At Mami's request, Tía Camila sent over her youngest daughter, his cousin Yasmin, to help with assorted daily household chores.

Yasmin was nineteen, not particularly prompt or attractive or thor-
ough in her cleaning, but she was chatty and had many friends.
Luna, with the short legs; Guadalupe, with the stubbly *pepa*; Fabiana, who clawed her nails into his scalp and screamed for Holy Jesus
the Savior as he went down on her (that shit was hard to take).

Mami liked Lucia, even if she was as confounded as the rest of
them as to why Lucia felt it necessary to take work so far away. They
assumed it to be some kind of crass cultural difference, like chewing
gum or wearing shorts to church. The younger girls, teenagers,
liked Lucia, too—joked with her at parties, gossiped about boys,
took her into their confidences. She seemed to occupy that rare
niche between themselves and their mothers, though they could feel
she was constitutionally different somehow. He knew it, too, but it
had not mattered to him. In this way, he and Lucia were alike—
concerning themselves only with people as they are now, rather than
who they were in the past.

He helped Papi on the farm. The animals needed to be fed and
groomed and milked and herded. The sprinklers needed to be rotated, the fences mended, the grasses cut. When something broke, he
fixed it. When their tools were stolen one night because he'd left them
in the fields, he built a small storage bin. He could take care of these
matters that stood squarely in his field of vision. And he had learned
a thing or two in America, tearing down buildings with Maurice. He
could install proper windows, frame a door, patch a rusty tin roof for
a neighbor. He lagged on the outhouse, because soon enough he
would build a brand-new casa, from scratch—when things were a bit
more settled, when he had more time. A big house with a proper toilet
and bathtub and shower, a kitchen with proper cabinets and porcelain
tiles. And after he was done, he told Essy, they would paint it.

"Pink?" she said.

"Sure, pink." He laughed, picturing it. "And purple. And orange
and blue and all the other colors."

"How about stripes?"

"Yes, stripes."

"And dots. Polka dots?"

He laughed again.

"With a face? And a moon?"

"Sure. How about rabbits? You like rabbits?"

She nodded. "But Papi." They were sitting outside, feeding left-over coconut shreds to their two pigs, Princess and Pea. "Papi, I want to paint our house *now*."

This was the thing about children, they couldn't wait—anything worth doing had to be done right away. He thought for a minute, knock-knocking his fist on the splintered wood panels, weathered dull and gray. "Sure, *hija*. We can paint it now."

They hopped on the motorbike. Essy clung to him as they puttered into the village, but the general store was closed. Directed by the *carnicero* to venture seven kilometers south, he found a neighbor who kept a few gallons of white. "But I don't like white!" cried Essy. "It will have to do," he said. He placed the cans on the floor of the bike, puttered back to the casita. He thought they could start with the north-facing wall. He sprayed it down with the hose, showed her how to buff and sand and smooth the surface with a brick wrapped in sandpaper. The dry wood kept splintering. She grew impatient. He handed her a brush, hoisted her onto his shoulders so she could paint a cloud. "On the wall, *mi amor*," he said. "On the wall." Splatters of paint stuck in his hair.

That afternoon, they sat on the front stoop, awaiting Lucia's return from Cuenca. As she walked up the winding dirt path, Essy ran to her.

"Mama, look!" she cried.

"What is this?" said Lucia. Her eyes grew wide, her jaw dropped, her mouth formed a perfect O.

He was afraid her brows would knit together, her lips draw into a line.

"A cloud! A cloud shaped like a rabbit!" Lucia said. She giggled with delight.

She was unpredictable. She had always been a bit impulsive but now she complained: She felt fat, or tired, or too fuzzy and mushy like a rotten peach. He checked his temper, but it rattled his brain, caused him to tug at the hair on the back of his neck with his fingers, grind his teeth late at night. Side effects, she said. No, he said. It was the travel that made her tired, the long bus rides, the job, the noise and fumes of the city. "Take a nap," he said. He sent Essy away to play with Fredy. She slept on the hammock outside.

That night, like most nights, he listened to the sound of her brushing her teeth, and when it stopped he hopped out of bed to spy on her in the kitchen, careful not to be seen. He waited until he saw the tap—the small round object falling into her hand—before he returned to bed, quickly pulling up the sheet.

Each month or so, he would root through the tall shelf, hunt among the spices to retrieve the small orange bottle. At first, he'd simply inspected it to see if she was running low, and then, when she was, he'd sweat for days over how to bring up the matter. As casually as possible. But it never went well, and soon afterward he'd taken it upon himself to bring the bottle to the local *farmacia*, where he'd specifically requested they import this medication from Quito, but nonetheless, it was often unstocked, so he always felt victorious if he came out with it full. Back at the casita, he carefully dispensed one third of the contents into an old tin he kept hidden in the bedroom, inside a storage trunk. The orange bottle never went empty, but was also never more than two-thirds filled. She knew, of course, but she didn't question him. In this way they were like an old married couple, who preferred to pretend certain parts of themselves were invisible.

But she was unpredictable. One evening she ran outside, grabbed a shovel from the garden, began to dig a hole. "Lucia, it's getting dark," he said. "So what?" she said. "I have eyes." Her tone flippant, loud, with a bitterness that frightened him. And he did not say the word, the one that rang in his mind, the one the sister had repeated over and over again, the one Lucia despised: pills.

"Are you all right?" he said.

She kept digging, furiously hurling dirt.

"Are you all right?" he repeated.

"I can take care of myself," she said. She fell silent then, but he sensed a disdain, as if she knew he was hiding his fear.

He bit the inside of his cheek. He would not let it go. This he had promised Lucia's sister, before they'd left America: that he would never let this go. And though he did not owe the sister anything, he owed it to his daughter, he knew.

"We don't have the same kinds of hospitals here," he said, quietly. "You get sick here, I don't know how to help you. You get sick here, you stay loco for the rest of your life."

She stormed off into the woods.

The next morning she left for Cuenca and it crossed his mind: He never should've allowed her to take that job. But, no, that was his *tías'* way of thinking. Wasn't it? He knew Lucia, they didn't.

He went to see Guadalupe. She wasn't home. The next day he tried Luna. Her mother was there. Eventually he found Fabiana, and when she screamed for Holy Jesus the Savior, he clamped a hand over her mouth, plunged harder and harder, and when she clawed her nails into his scalp, he focused on the pain. Then by accident, he glimpsed his reflection in an oval hand mirror next to the bed, and for a split second, he thought he was looking at his daughter. He yanked on his jeans, returned quickly to the casita.

They were in the kitchen, beating together butter, sugar, eggs, wearing their matching pink aprons. "Papi, we're making cookies!" said Essy. He peered into the bowl. "Mmm," he said, yum-yum tapping his belly. His daughter beamed. She looked so much like her mother.

For Essy, he would try. For Essy.

And then one day he'd gone to Cuenca to open a bank account, ducked into an Internet café as it started to rain. By chance, he saw the girl in front of the vending machine, her reflection in the fluorescent white glare. She wore a denim jacket over a pink miniskirt, and when she moved, there was something familiar about the way her head and neck thrust ahead, the rest of her body in pursuit. *Giraffe*. Susi.

The memories flooded in. Imprinted upon him, the darkness of those days, inseparable from the chaos, the joy, the tender hysteria surrounding Esperanza's birth—back when his baby's eyes rarely opened and he was terrified he would drop her or smother her or crush her or starve her or that her nascent breath would simply stop. Only a handful of events (his infant brother Alamar's burial at sea, his departure from the campo, his arrival in America) were branded into his being in such visceral detail. And if he lay in the dark, he could hear it still, the skittering in the walls, the incessant clang of the radiators, low muffle of the television in the kitchen, tuned to channel 9. Whenever the sirens wailed, he smelled smoke, but it was always his imagination. The bedroom temperature oscillated, hot and cold, hot and cold, a delicate film of ice coated the inner panes of the windows and he'd scrape at it with his fingernails while the baby slept beside him and Lucia floated two floors above. He tried to banish them from his thoughts—the baby, Lucia—free himself for a minute or two, but the band of fear would stretch from his groin to his throat, a tension rod jammed in his chest. So he listened for the clip of Susi's footsteps, let the sheets absorb the tang of sweat and sex and rancid deep-fry oil and plaster dust and rose-scented perfume, and he pulled her on top of him and Susi would ride and ride until he exploded or until the baby woke and cried. No other lovemaking, before or after, ever came close to the rabid urgency of those nights. And then he and Susi would take turns bouncing Essy on the big green exercise ball that was not quite fully inflated, and with each bounce it sagged into the carpet with a hefty puff, as if bored by this repeated expulsion, and Susi would giggle, though he himself always worried the ball would burst under his weight. Such were the sharpened senses of those times, each day punctuated with shots of fear and doubt and adrenaline.

On closer inspection, this girl was shorter, wider, paler, with thicker calves, but the exact same moon face and too-small eyes. Probably no older than eighteen.

"Susi?" he said, even though he knew it was not Susi.

The girl shook her head.

"*Lo siento*," he said. He unfurled a shy grin. Continued to play the game. "You look so much like someone I know."

The girl angled her body away from him, skittish, like the squirrels he used to feed in New York.

"Susi Hernandez," he said.

A flinch of recognition. Then she stared at him and he thought she seemed a bit stupid. Or perhaps he had it all wrong.

"I know Susi from America," he said, casually. "We were friends in Nueva York."

The girl blushed, startled, but her face brightened. "I am Nele," she said. "Nele Hernandez. Susi is my sister."

The odds! The coincidence! he could hear Lucia say.

His heart pounded. Power surged up his legs. "I moved back awhile ago. We haven't really kept in touch. She is well, I hope?"

The girl reddened. He noted a trace of dimple. If only she'd release that smile. "Susi is in Esmeraldas now," she said, softly. "Outside of the city."

"Esmeraldas?"

"Yes. You know, in the north."

"Esmeraldas," he repeated. In the north.

"Outside the city." The girl named the barrio.

How did she get there? How long has she lived there? What is she doing now?

"She's . . . fine?" he said.

The girl's too-small eyes, squinting. Bizarre, how much she looked like Susi, every feature the same, yet he found her overwhelmingly unattractive. Her skin had no sheen, her chin moved sideways like a cow chewing cud.

"Yes," she said, finally.

"That's great. Esmeraldas. That's great." He repeated it, *qué bueno, qué bueno*, and now he was the stupid one.

He should've asked for a phone number, or an address, or to convey a message. But what would he have said? *Qué bueno, qué bueno*, he kept mumbling, and then she'd turned away and run off like the squirrels. He couldn't remember if he'd told her his name.

He should tell Lucia. Of course, she would want to know. She had been fond of Susi, the little sister she'd never had, crushed to learn of her disappearance. But a part of him wanted this new information all for himself. As if this knowledge of Susi's whereabouts, kept secret, could be stowed alongside those other memories, prolong their intimacy somehow.

He would let it go. Susi had been found. She was safe in Esmeraldas. There was no need to complicate things further.

And then one day Lucia came to him. She had an idea, she said. She wanted to take a trip, with Essy. She wanted to visit her sister in Switzerland.

It caught him off guard. He couldn't recall the last time she'd mentioned her sister. The name, once popping up at regular intervals, had all but disappeared. Lucia asking permission, this surprised him, too—if he said no, would she actually listen? But he couldn't think of any reason why she shouldn't go. And then seeing how happy she was when he consented, he found it reasonable that she'd miss what little family she had. She went from withdrawn and moody to ecstatic, giddy, floating over the moon. She sang *hey diddle diddle the cat in the fiddle*, every night before bedtime, and that song about the bones, which Essy adored. They were going on a trip! They would fly high in the sky on an airplane! They would see snow—snow! They would build snow forts and climb mountains and sit on the tippy-top, drink hot chocolate with marshmallows and eat cheese with holes. It sounded silly, such promises, but when he said so, jokingly, she snapped at him. "What would you know?" she said.

She was unpredictable. He was tense, unnerved. So one afternoon he found himself by the *teléfono cabinica* in town and he walked into a booth and called Lucia's sister in Switzerland. A whim. Because if he admitted he'd planned it, he would've been far too nervous. They had not spoken in years—not since he'd left America.

"Hello. This is Manny."

She asked immediately, "Is something wrong?"

"No," he said. He did not want to raise alarm. He told her about Lucia's job in Cuenca, of which Miranda was already aware, and about how happy Essy was at her school.

There was no reply on the other end and he was afraid the call had been disconnected, that Miranda Bok had been left hanging, annoyed. He was being evasive, he knew, and he knew she knew, and in the silence, he sensed her apprehension.

"Hello? Manny?"

He exhaled. "Have you spoken with her much?"

"Not really," said Miranda. "A few e-mails. What's going on?"

Then he tried to reassure her, but by the very fact that he was calling, it was impossible to sound convincing. He reassured himself instead. "She's excited to visit you in Switzerland, and Essy, too. Before, I was worried. She seemed sad, not saying much, that's all." The line cracked with static, but he continued to talk. "It will be good for her, some time away, a vacation with you and Essy. It'll be nice for her to relax." *Relajarse.* It was not a word often spoken in these parts, but it was a word emphasized by that social worker in that hospital. "It's hard, all the travel, back and forth to the city every week. I worry it's not good for her."

More crackling on the line. Like nerves, buzzing.

"Is she taking her pills?"

This was, essentially, the only question that mattered in their conversations. At times he felt its answer was more important to Miranda Bok than her sister's actual well-being.

"Yes," he said. "I think so." Though now he couldn't be sure, certainly not on the nights she stayed in the city, how did he know what she did then? And even in the kitchen of their casita, in front of the sink, he never spied long enough to see the pills go down her throat. He grew panicked. But no. Her behavior was not anything like after Essy had been born. She had been crazy, crazy loco, then. She was not like that. She was different, but not like that.

And then, as if she sensed his confusion: "Are you sure?"

"I think so. But I'm not sure." He felt a rush of relief, to share this burden with her. He had never told anyone about Lucia's illness, not even Mami.

"If she's not right, you can tell."

He nodded into the phone, but he wasn't sure, and he felt stupid, as he often did, speaking to Lucia's sister.

Only later, much later, would he understand. Later, in hindsight, they would come together on this: to wonder when it had become impossible to distinguish which parts of Lucia fell under her own jurisdiction and which belonged to her illness.

"Is she seeing a doctor?"

"In the city, maybe. She doesn't like to talk about it."

"If she isn't right, she needs to see a doctor. Do you have psychiatrists there?"

He felt suddenly heavy. Tired. He set down the phone quickly. He wished he had not made the call. It stirred up worry, that was all.

He tried not to think about the conversation as he walked through town. He bought soup bones from the *carnicero*, a bag of candy corn. Lucia would be leaving soon. They would have a break, it would be good for him. He could call on Fabiana or Luna or Guadalupe. Or see if a couple of his *primos* would be interested in taking a trip. He'd enjoy a couple of days on the beach. They could hit the bars and discos, go fishing, check out the tourists on the *malecón*. He enjoyed losing himself in all he might do, all the freedoms a man might take while his wife and child were away. Though they were never officially married, and this bothered no one but Mami; it no longer occurred to him to have that conversation.

Or, he thought, suddenly—he could try to find Susi in Esmeraldas. Susi Hernandez, who had disappeared one day from the Vargas house, that cold rainy afternoon he could still see so clearly in his mind. The sleet, the ice, the traffic on Main Street, the policeman shining a flashlight in his eyes. And then Mrs. Gutierrez waving her broom, dressed in robe and sunglasses as she called from her stoop: *Susi, taken by migras.*

Following the news, he had lived in a stupor for days, maybe weeks. It dawned on him: Susi had been his sole ally. She had shared his burden, knowing the truth. And one night the sirens screamed down the street and without thinking, he'd grabbed Esperanza and run out into the cold. His legs carried him to Main Street, past the familiar shops and restaurants, until he found himself sitting on the steps of the town's police station. He knew only that he was cold, and tired, and that he was sick of being so cold and tired and afraid all the time, and he wanted it to end. So he'd risen to his feet, reached for the metal door handle with his near-frozen hand. And that's when Susi's phone—which he'd carried in his pocket every day since she'd disappeared—had buzzed. As if on cue. Lucia's sister. "Lucia is still in the hospital," she said. "I'd like to come by to speak with you." He'd hunched back down on those icy steps, head hot and spinning, baby strapped to his chest. It had been weeks since the sister had promised to call him with news. He'd assumed Lucia was gone. Like the *Mexicano* Jimmy Prieto. Like Susi. Disappeared from his life. Because what else could he have thought back then?

He had been to America, but he had never been to the city of Esmeraldas, a mere six hundred kilometers to the north. It had a rough reputation—Colombian drug rings, brothels, though it was also home to several of the national footballers. At first, it seemed a crazy idea, but then he found a bus schedule, planned an itinerary: the early morning bus to Quito, a night with an old schoolmate, then out to Esmeraldas the next morning. Though how would he find her, by navigating his way to the barrio, calling her name in the streets?

Still—he was curious. And colored by an illusive nostalgia, he fantasized a life with Susi the way he'd once fantasized a life with Lucia, with half a dozen children and hot meals around a large table. But Lucia was woven into his reality now, and it struck him that even if he wanted to leave—the casita, his *tías*, the eternal blue-gray sky—there was no place for him to go. It would be good to have a break.

༺

But Lucia didn't end up going to Switzerland. Three days before she was scheduled to leave, she called from Cuenca, left a message at the main house with Mami. The casita still had no phone.

"What do you mean, she's not coming back today?" he asked.

"That's what she said," said Mami. She sat on her low stool, peeling potatoes.

"Why?"

"I don't know, *hijo*," said Mami. "She didn't say."

"What did she say?"

"Only that she was delayed in Cuenca. Had some things to do."

"Did she sound all right?"

Mami looked at him from her low stool. "I don't know, *hijo*. She didn't say much. Why, is something wrong?"

"That one," said Tía Camila. "Going here, going there, never standing still. That kind of woman is never right." She fanned her face with a dish towel. Tía Camila did not pretend to like Lucia. She didn't see the point.

Mami stood, set out a slice of honey cake and motioned for him to eat. She wrapped her arms around his shoulders, kissed him on top of his head as she had done when he was a child. "*Hijo*, you are a good man," she said. "I am glad that you are home."

Three days later, Lucia came trudging up the winding dirt path, muddy from the rains. He was drinking a beer on the front stoop. He hadn't expected her. It was dark, already night.

"I'm not going," she said, deep moons under her eyes.

"What do you mean you're not going?"

"Not going to Switzerland."

"Why not?" he said.

"It's complicated." Her voice tight and strange.

"What happened?"

"You wouldn't understand. I don't want to go anymore. I don't want to talk about it."

She went inside, slipped into bed. He was baffled, bewildered, disappointed, relieved. A short while later, he went to check on her. She was already asleep—both arms wrapped around Essy, the two of them one big ball curled up tight.

The next day it occurred to him, he had not brought the orange bottle on the high shelf to the *farmacia* in a while. It must be running low. He rummaged through the spices. It was there behind the paprika. Lucia must've gone to the pharmacy herself, because it was all the way full.

On Monday morning, she asked him to drive her to town, where she boarded the chicken bus to the city as usual. But she returned that same evening, wheeling her large, red plaid suitcase behind her.

"Mama!" said Essy. She leapt into her mother's arms, begged to ride on the suitcase as though it were some exotic horse.

"I'm back," she said.

"What's up?" he said.

She would no longer stay in the apartment in Cuenca.

"Why not?" he asked, genuinely surprised.

She said, "It's full of spiders."

༄

She seemed different. But not in that erratic way she had been for months. This was something more fragile, more volatile. He found the best strategy was to feign lighthearted approval. *Is that a new dress? I haven't seen it before. Have you noticed your fava beans growing?* On eggshells, he checked his words. She ignored him, mostly, though she lavished attention on their daughter, playing blocks or stuffed bunny tea party or pirate ship adventures. But before bed each night, when Essy called, *Mama, come! Mama, read a book!* Lucia walked away, as if she did not hear, and when Essy ran to tug at her arm, she looked through her daughter as though she were not there.

She worked in their garden. Digging and weeding and sowing and pruning, always on her knees, looking down. Mami noticed the change. Mami rarely came to the casita, but one day he saw her walk up the path, woolen shawl drawn around her shoulders.

"Essy is in school," he said.

"This is for Lucia," said Mami. She had brought a pot of *locro de papa*, potato soup. She set it down, joined them on the stoop. "Lucita, is something bothering you?"

Lucia stared up at the sky, pointed at the clouds changing shape. "They're whispering about me all the time," she said.

She sounded so far away.

Mami kissed her cheek gently, reached for her hand. Lucia sat, her gaze still fixed on the clouds. "Ma?" she said.

He walked away. He went to Fabiana that afternoon.

It was true. They whispered. At Tía Camila's birthday party, at cousin Estela's *quince*, on Día de los Difuntos and New Year's Eve, at baby Alberto's christening. They had always whispered: *What kind of woman leaves her husband and child? She goes to Cuenca, alone. Why Cuenca? In America the women do it. America! But this is not America.* Tía Camila. Tía Alba. Tía Paula. The neighbor, Roberto. His cousins on the *futbol* fields. Tío Remy, who asked after Lucia's health as he winked and nudged: *The Chinitas have the softest hands.* Even Ricky and Juan asked, "Manny, what's up with Lucia?" "She's been tired," he said. At least this was the truth.

Some days she was up at the crack of dawn, frying eggs, making pancakes. Some days she slept all afternoon. Some days she picked up Essy early from school. One morning they left the campo but did not go to school at all, and when he came home midmorning he found them outside, sailing paper boats down a trench they'd dug with Essy's toy shovels and filled with the hose. "Shouldn't she be at school?" he asked. "What?" "School," he said. "Oh, Manny," she said, breezily. "School is so silly. This is Mommy-Essy time. We're *bonding*." He swallowed. He knew he should say something, assert himself, admonish her—but the vacancy in her eyes made him cower.

One day he came home to find the bright yellow pot unattended on the stove, sizzling, boiling over, lapped by orange-blue flames. "Lucia?" he called. "Lucia!" Angry. He found them in the bedroom, on the floor, playing My Little Pony—Lucia on her knees, Essy with a brand-new butterfly barrette in her hair. "Please, you need to be more care-ful," he said. "You could have burned the whole house down."

"But Manny, you wouldn't let that happen. See? You came."

"Lucia, this behavior, it's dangerous." He gritted his teeth, lowered his voice. "I'm worried."

"Wor-ried, wor-ried, Man-ny's worried."

He did not use the word: sick. She hated that word.

"You don't seem well."

"How would you know? Are you inside my body?"

"Are you . . ."

"I'm fine. It's none of your business." Her clavicles tensed.

"I'm just asking."

"Stop asking."

"Maybe we should go to the doctor."

"We? NO," she shouted. "YOU go to the doctor. LEAVE ME ALONE."

He took his daughter outside. He felt clammy, hot and cold.

"Why is Mama so mad?" said Essy.

"Go to Abuela," he said. "Go on, *mi amor*, go stay at the house."

He began to spend his nights on the hammock outside. One night he dreamed of a woman with Fabiana's face, Luna's legs, Gua-dalupe's stubbly *pepa*. But when he rode her, he was riding Susi's heart-shaped ass. Dawn brought a sore back, sore jaw, a crick in his neck, skin riddled with fresh mosquito bites.

One evening he came home later than usual, found the screen door wide open, the house dark and empty. He figured they were at Mami's, watching TV or playing cards. But Mami's house was quiet, too. "What is it, *hijo*?" she said. "Nothing," he mumbled. He plod-ded back home. The motorbike was still there. They could not have gone far. He checked the garden, the shed, the groves behind the casita. Down by the river, he saw their clothes, laid out in the grass to dry: his T-shirts and jeans, Lucia's bras, Essy's sundresses and

Dora the Explorer underwear. *Lucia?* he called. The only sounds,
the gurgling water, the crickets, the bark of a dog. The sunlight was
fading. The water, dark. For a moment he panicked, envisioning the
worst. *Essy! Lucia!* He kicked off his boots, waded in. The mud
sludgy, warm, squishy between his toes. Small fish nipping at his
ankles. "Shit," he said. He was being ridiculous. Wasn't he? They
could be at Tía Paula's. The neighbor's. Anywhere. He sprinted back
to the casita. *Lucia? Essy?*

Finally, he heard a whimper from the direction of their bright
purple outhouse. He ran to it, yanked at the door, the flimsy hook
flying into the grass. They were there. The two of them. Squatted
on top of the toilet seat, his daughter's eyes clenched shut, pinching
her nose with her fingers. "Essy!" "Papi?" Her eyes sprang open, her
lips quivered. "We were hiding from the spies," she said. She began
to cry. She threw her skinny arms around his neck. "Papi, Papi, I was
scared. Please don't let them find us, Papi." She clung to him with
gasping sobs, her entire body shaking uncontrollably. *"Hija*, I'm here
now. I'm here." He kissed her wet cheeks, smoothed her hair. *"Hija*,
it's okay, you don't have to be scared." But his chest filled with rage.
He glared at Lucia. "Are you crazy?" he hissed. "What?" she said.
"We were playing a game. Essy, come on, silly, it was just a game."
He wanted to hit her, slap her, smash that ridiculous smirk off her
vile face. "Don't you ever dare do this again," he said. He carried his
daughter back to the casita, lay beside her as she slept in their bed.
Lucia did not come in.

He did not see her the next morning either. He didn't care. He
brought Essy to school. "Abuela will come pick you up today," he
said. The rest of the morning was spent lugging heavy hoses up the
hillside. Around lunchtime he stopped at Mami's, drenched in sweat.
Tía Camila sat on the low stool, peeling potatoes.

"Where is Mami?" he asked.

"She is not here," his *tía* answered.

"Where is she?"

Tía Camila set down the peeler, stood, washed her hands in the sink. "Your Papi took Sylvia to the doctor."

"The doctor?"

"*Sí.*"

"Why?"

"*Ay, sobrino.*" His *tía* vented a lofty sigh. "Your mother is worrying about you all the time. Worrying about your *Chinita*. Worrying about your child. Worrying so much she makes herself sick."

Mami? Sick? It sent his gut roiling, lit a fire from his chest to his face. But Mami was strong, like an ox. He could not recall her ever being sick; she rarely even went to the doctor.

Tía Camila shook her head. "You don't know what it's like for a mother, to see her own son this way. A man who cannot control his own wife. *Ay, qué vergüenza.*" Disgrace.

He blistered with humiliation, boiled all day. Dug holes, flung dirt, pounded wooden posts with a sledgehammer. His throat was dry. His tongue stuck to the roof of his mouth. He felt dizzy and had to sit down. That evening, he returned to the casita, exhausted.

Lucia was there, wearing her pink apron, standing in front of the stove, the yellow enamel pot once again at full boil. Every surface of their kitchen was covered in vegetables: zucchini, eggplants, yuca, radishes, cabbage, beets, carrots, potatoes, all diced into one-inch cubes, laid out in colorful matrices of varying sizes, six by eight, four by twelve, twenty-four by two.

"What the fuck are you doing?" he said.

She turned to him. "What does it look like?" she said. "I'm cooking. What are YOU doing?"

He punched the wall with his fist. Pain shot through his arm. The gold-framed picture of Jesus Christ clattered to the floor.

"*Basta*," he said. "Enough of this shit. You're sick. You're crazy. You need to take your pills. I need to call your sister."

"What?"

"I'm going to call your sister."

"My sister?" said Lucia.

She grabbed the bright yellow pot full of boiling water, hurled it at his face.

7

Miranda

It missed, he said, but only because he jumped out of the way. It was full of boiling water, he said. It crashed by his feet, scalded his left ankle. Made mud where the water pooled on the floor.

"Jesus Christ. Are you hurt?" said Miranda. She nearly dropped her phone. "She's angry. Scared. She's lashing out."

"Angry about what?" said Manny.

Stefan lay reading a book in bed, so she slipped out to the back porch. She stood by her wicker rocking chair but did not sit down. "Everything," she said.

"But I'm trying to help her," he said. His voice sounded clear, as though he were somewhere close, in the starry night, in the blackness of the Stöcktalersee, in the looming silhouettes of the Alps.

"I know," she said. "I'm sorry." What else could she say?

And when he'd returned, several hours later, he found Lucia sitting alone. All the vegetables were gone. The floor was clean. Her eyes glittered. And when she stood, he braced himself, ready to run, noted the cleaver in the drying rack. But then she walked to the stove. *Are you hungry?* she said. "As if nothing had happened. She handed me a bowl of soup."

"Oh God, Manny." Oh God. Oh God. Her brain in high gear, trying to fathom the progression of Lucia's thoughts.

"I'm scared," he said. "For Essy. For me. I don't know what to do. I can't talk to her. I can't control her. One minute she won't speak, the next minute she is screaming and throwing things. She's like a monster. It's really bad."

"Does she have the pills?" she asked.

"I think so."

"Is she taking them?"

"I don't know."

"She needs to take them."

"But I can't make her. Here there are no police, no hospitals, no emergency rooms. It's not like America. Please, Miranda, come help."

She heard his desperation, his fear. But she could not bring herself to tell him the truth: that she'd already been to Ecuador. Six weeks ago. She'd gone to try to make things right.

That night in Cuenca, Lucia was a complete disaster. Disheveled, agitated, she argued to herself, banging around in that tiny room. The spider, she repeated, again and again. *What spider, Lucia? What are you doing, Lucia?* But all Lucia could say was *I don't know, I don't know*, and her reply was, *Lucia, he's her father. You can't do this.*

"You're sick," she'd said. Yet Lucia refused to admit she'd stopped taking her pills. "You're lying," she'd said. Though some small part of her worried she was wrong, because she was not sure—was it the illness? Some decree from the serpents? Or could Lucia have spun herself into such a frenzy from the sheer force of her guilt? Doubts like these had never seized Miranda before. And then, her worst fear: that the line between her sister and the illness was becoming irrevocably blurred.

"Lucia, take these now." She'd tried to stay calm. Held out four of the small white pills—four, a therapeutic dose when symptoms became acute.

"Fuck you."

"Lucia, come on."

"I hate you. You're not my master."

"Stop it."

"*You* stop it."

"Lucia, please."

"*YOU* take them."

And then Lucia had lunged forward, snatched the medicine from her hand, swung at her wildly, and Miranda had fallen back against a wall.

"*YOU'RE* sick. *YOU* take them. *YOU* see how it is."

Those maniacal eyes. The outstretched hand. Clamped on Miranda's face, and then covering her mouth, and the bitter chemical taste spread across her tongue. And though she did not believe in God, she cursed him now. She spat at him. She spat and spat as she scrubbed at her tongue with her wrist.

Why her? Why her, God? Why her, why not me?

Every ounce of Miranda's being shook: her hands, her heart, her voice, her will. There was only one thing left she could think to say: *Lucia, take these. Take these, now. Or I swear, I will tell Manny what you've tried to do.*

And Lucia, at last, had downed the pills in a desolate fury, flung the bottle out the open window. *Tic-tac.* Then she flung open her ugly plaid suitcase, hurled its contents across the room: a shoe, a hair dryer, an antique brass lamp. It struck Miranda on the forehead.

In the aftermath of that brawl had come a tense, bitter silence, like a steel cage, her sister locked inside. *Let's go to the park. Let's get something to eat. How about you show me your favorite bakery? Lucia?* The next afternoon, they'd finally walked to the pharmacy, procured a refill.

And then Lucia had turned to her and issued her proclamation: *Are you satisfied? Now get out. Just get out of my fucking life.*

"She won't even go to Cuenca," said Manny. "She wasn't like this before. She was happy. Excited. Looking forward to taking Essy to Switzerland. I don't understand what happened."

He didn't know. He still didn't know. She wanted to break down then, to tell him everything, expose her sister's lies. Reveal Lucia's intentions to run off with their child. But truly, she did not know what he would do if he knew. Fly into a rage? Kick Lucia out? Forbid her from ever seeing her daughter again? To tell him the truth would poison whatever relationship he and Lucia had—and then what would happen to Lucia?

"Manny, she won't listen to me. I want to help, but I can't control her any more than you can. I can't make her do anything." This was the truth. One he could not seem to hear.

"Please," he said. "I beg of you. Please come take her. Please, Miranda, help."

She sat in the wicker rocker on her back porch, tapped furiously on her laptop, no longer noticing the clock tower in town with its copper-green cupola or the cows dotting the hillside or the Stöcktalersee or the snowy peaks of Glärnisch in the distance. She tracked down phone numbers, e-mails, names and more names, spoke in broken Spanish to clerks at the immigration office in Ecuador, found a French psychologist in Cuenca and explained the situation in broken French. But the closest psychiatric hospital was almost four hours away. She called the American embassy in Quito. *Huh?* they said. No, they could not evict an American citizen with proper papers. Not unless she was a criminal.

Sunday morning she feigned a headache—unfathomable, to face another fondue dinner with her in-laws. "Miranda, please," said Stefan.

She knew it pained him, having to make excuses for her. "You didn't come last week. It might help take your mind off things."

It was true, she had missed last Sunday's dinner, and the one before, too, and by late afternoon she'd relented, picturing the sincere look of disappointment on Grossmuti's face. She downed two Panadol, baked a strawberry tart, and when Grossmuti exclaimed, *Oh, how delicious!* it eased her guilt. *And Rafael? Is my great-grandson coming today?* and Miranda watched Stefan's gaze veer to his hands, his lower jaw protrude, *I'm sorry, he has a project to finish*, and this pained her, too.

She commented on the weather, the cheeses, the lovely new Marimekko place settings with the floral prints.

"This wine is delicious," said the sister with the pretty twin daughters.

"From Lavaux," said the brother with the petite French wife. "We were in Geneva last weekend, decided to take a detour. Have you been, Miranda?"

"What?"

"The Train des Vignes is spectacular, from Vevey to Puidoux, through the vineyards."

She nodded, the words trailing through her ears.

"You should take her, Stefan," said the petite French wife. "The gardens are breathtaking."

"Yes," said her husband. "We could use a trip."

Glancing around the table at the assortment of fair faces, harmless as vegetables, she felt like an alien. She longed for some loud, wacky aunt, some unemployed alcoholic uncle, some hint of tarnish in their normalcy that might legitimize her own strife.

"Are you all right, dear?" asked Grossmuti, her blue eyes warm.

"Oh. Yes." She smiled. "The wine is excellent. I'd love another glass."

She woke at one, at two, at four in the morning, her body buzzing like millions of microscopic bees lived in her blood. She lay awake, stomach curdled, fists tight, tornados of thoughts spinning wildly in her head. *Anxiety*, the doctor had said. *Manifestations of stress.* Her nights had been fitful these past few months, since before that trip to Ecuador. She needed sleep. Sleep was of critical importance to the brain's proper functioning—the doctor said that, too. She tried relaxation techniques. Imagined sheep. Counted backward from one hundred. Chanted sixty oms.

She was happy. Excited.

She climbed out of bed, went to the kitchen, downed a double dose of Ativan.

❧

A week passed and she had not heard from him.

"Should I go?" she asked. She asked Stefan; no one else knew.

He stared at her in disbelief.

"You were just *there*," he said.

"But this time . . ."

"What would you do? Drag her kicking and screaming? She's a grown woman."

"But *he* needs help."

"Then he can take her to a hospital."

"How can he do that? They live in the middle of nowhere."

She imagined it, dragging Lucia by the hair. She remembered the shoes, the hair dryer, the antique brass lamp flying through the air.

"He's a grown-up, Miranda. And your sister is, too."

That dispassionate face. She could slap it. Suddenly he seemed a stranger, occupying her bed.

"She has an illness, for God's sake. It's not her fault, Stefan. It's not his fault either. Please, have some compassion. You're a doctor, after all. My sister has an illness of the *brain*."

She could see him fizzing inside, resenting the accusation.

"This isn't about me," he said. "Don't take this out on me. Besides, where would you bring her? Here?"

No, not Switzerland. Mental health laws in Switzerland were as foreign to her as in Ecuador. "New York, maybe."

"Do you really think you can drag her onto an airplane with you to New York, to go to a mental hospital?"

The edge in his tone, fully realized, and now he no longer bothered to hide his exasperation.

"You could at least *try* to be helpful," she said. Rankled, up for a fight.

"*Schätzli*, please don't make this about me. I told you, tell him to get her to a doctor."

"But she's angry with *me*. Her aggression, the rages, those are meant for *me*."

"Stop it. Miranda, it's enough."

Stefan rarely raised his voice, but he raised it now. And later, much later, when she could view this part of their lives through her husband's lens, Miranda would invariably cringe—because this is what he knew: that the hospitals, Ecuador, these episodes destroyed her every time. That she would not eat or sleep; that the stomach pains would wake her at all hours of the night; that she would become angry, irritable, and any opinion he offered, regardless of how gentle or solicitous, would be wrong, dismissed, and she would snap or yell or burst into tears, and they would say things they each regretted later. That gash on her forehead—she didn't think he knew, but he did. He was not unsympathetic to the others, but in Stefan's reality, there was only one person whose well-being stood at stake: his wife. Miranda, who was good. Miranda, who tried so hard to do what was right. And if this put her in opposition to him, he hated it. Yes, he was selfish, too. Her turmoil was his. Her unhappiness, his anguish. No, he could not tell her to go to Ecuador now. But he also could not demand that she stay. It tore him up, that he loved her—he tried so hard to love her—yet how best to love her still eluded him. "You can't keep doing this to yourself," he said.

"This isn't about *me*, Stefan. It's about *her*."

"But it *is* about you. Don't you understand?"

"She's crazy. She's hurting people. She's causing them pain. And you want me to sit here and do nothing?"

"But you can't help her," he said. His tone returned to an alarming calm.

"I can try."

"You *have* tried. You've been trying, all these years."

Her eyes filled with tears.

"I love you, Miranda. Don't you understand? I love *you*."

She jerked away, bristling. "This *is* me, Stefan."

"What about *your* life, Miranda?"

But she refused to back down. He loved her. Did he? If so, the pronouncement only amplified her anger now. "This is *not* helpful, Stefan."

She threw on a robe, stormed out to the kitchen.

He sat in their bed, his pulse too fast.

She waited, shivering, slumped in her chair.

He did not go to her.

Besides, she was busy. Too busy. She was chairing a fund-raising campaign at the hospital, presenting to the board next week. And the other morning, she'd been in the middle of a meeting, had to excuse herself, suffered her first full-blown panic attack in the ladies' room. No, she could not go.

Another three days passed. She dreamed she was on an airplane, falling; her teeth fell out, clicked around in her mouth; she was thirteen years old, beating an injured bird to its death with a base-ball bat. If it died, she would no longer have to care.

Stefan was right. What more could she do for Lucia?

But for Manny.

For Esperanza.

But.

The bees buzzed in her blood.

If you need anything, I can help, I promise.

༄

"I have to, Stefan."

They were eating dinner. Lentil loaf with steamed broccoli. Ra-fael was playing video games in his bedroom.

"The awards banquet is on Saturday." Her husband was being hon-ored for his work with the community outreach program at the hospital.

"I know, I'm sorry."

"I'd really like it if you came." His tone chilly, hesitant. As if he'd had to give himself permission to ask.

"I want to come. You know I do."

"And there's Sophie's communion." His niece, whom she'd tu-tored in English up until last year, when Sophie's extracurriculars became too overwhelming.

Miranda exhaled slowly. "Come on, Stefan."

"It's an important family event."

"I'm aware of that. But Sophie is a child. And I can't take a guilt trip right now. Please."

"A guilt trip, Miranda? When have I ever stopped you from do-ing anything you wanted to do?" No, not the first time she went to Ecuador, when he thought she was meddling, and he'd expressed his concern as diplomatically as he could, and she'd stormed out of that fancy French restaurant in the middle of dinner.

But he did not sound angry now. Only cold, wounded. "You're sure you want to do this? After last time?"

"I'm not sure. Do you think I *want* to go?"

This was not the right question, they knew.

"Do you want me to tell you to go? Okay. Go."

"Stefan."

"Sophie looks up to you, Miranda. You're important to her. And she's important to me. She's my sister's daughter."

And who the fuck is that child in Ecuador?

Miranda exploded. Rocketed off her chair, threw open the front door. Stefan realized, too late, the offense of his words. She was gone before he could apologize.

"Manny, it's Miranda." Her hands were sweating. She wiped them on her skirt. "I've booked a flight. How is everything?"

She held her breath, suspended the phone several inches away from her ear, as if this would soften the impact of the blow.

His answer came swiftly.

It was not as expected.

"She is calmer now. I put the pills in her tea."

"What?"

"I crushed them into powder. Put them in her tea. Every morning for the past two weeks."

She imagined it: Lucia's back turned, his hands shaking, the clink of the spoon as he stirred.

"I'm sorry. I know this is wrong." His voice, choked.

"No, Manny, don't be sorry, please. . . ."

"I didn't know what else to do."

"I understand. Of course." She nodded into the phone. "And how is she?"

"She's been sleeping a lot. Yesterday she went to see a doctor."

He did not need her to come anymore.

"But I've already booked a ticket. Are you sure?"

"I'm sure. I think it will be okay."

Miranda set down the phone, stupefied. Whether it was awe, or horror, she could not say. But it was gratitude.

8

Manuel

He did not speak with Lucia about the incident or the pills or the new doctor she saw in Cuenca from time to time. "It's private," she said. But this was what she'd always said, and so they returned once more to this delicate dance: he, terrified of retriggering her anger, of launching her into another episode; she, resentful of his mistrust. He hated being her minder, her keeper. "You take care of it," he said, and she said, "I will." But nothing was truly different, nothing made him feel safe—only time would soften his vigilance, allow his anxiety to transition into relief.

Slowly, they slipped back into their lives. He and Essy continued to paint the casita. Polka dots. Stripes. When his daughter had turned five, they'd added two more rabbits, one on each side of the door, and then the pigs, Princess and Pea, and then Fredy, who they painted on the south-facing wall, as tall as the roof, and then a cow named Victoria.

Lucia seemed to flatten out, like a spinning coin laid to rest. She brought Essy to the river, taught her how to scrub underwear with a small rock against a bigger rock, where to lay clothes in the grass to catch the late afternoon sun. Yasmin was sent away. Lucia resumed work at the gringo newspaper, too, though in some different capacity, commuted once every other week. She would start a new book, she said. "About what?" he asked. "Healing," she said. "And El Pollo? Unheard Voices?" "No," she said.

He was glad she read again to Essy every night. Rotated through tall stacks of children's books borrowed from a used bookstore in Cuenca. *Charlotte's Web. The Mouse and the Motorcycle.* A dog-eared Spanish-English dictionary, in which she'd highlighted her favorite words. *Serendipitous. Dulcet. Vivir. Querencia.* One day she brought home a brochure for a girls' school in the city run by British expats. "What's this?" he said. "Just to look at," she said. "For when she's older, maybe. Essy is really smart."

One day she returned from a long afternoon in the woods, smiling. She had encountered a wise man, an old shaman, she said, who lived on the other side of the mountain. "You could meet him," she said. "Some other time," he said. Thereafter, she would often return with sprigs of herbs, seeds and seedlings, a vial of tincture, a crystal to hang in the window. She brewed tonics for Tío Remy's arthritis, Mami's stomach pains, Tía Alba's cataracts, prescribed motherwort and licorice root for Tía Camila's night sweats and hot flashes.

"This works?" asked Tía Camila. She poked a finger at the sediments afloat in her cup.

He could not look her in the eye, but Lucia did. "Try," she said. "You have to try, Tía, and you have to believe."

He half believed, and the half that did not humored her, downed bitter concoctions tasting of earth. "Ewww," said Essy. His daughter wrinkled her nose, zipped shut her lips, threw away the key. He recalled how he used to take her to the candy store, how their faces puckered sucking on lemon drops, how they stretched gummy worms to nearly a foot. By now, she had long finished with the village day care, wore a proper school uniform with a green plaid skirt she'd hike up past her knees whenever her mother wasn't looking. She no longer wore her hair in pigtails, rather a single braid down the middle of her back. Lucia taught her math. *How many pigs and chickens in a barnyard with twenty-four legs and eight heads?* "Four and four, of course," said Essy. One day Lucia brought home a violin she'd found at a pawnshop in Cuenca. The screeches hurt his ears. "Essy, practice out in the garden," he said. "But Papi," she said. "Music is the language of the universe. Mama says."

One day he dug into his jacket pocket and found a wrinkled bus schedule, Quito to Esmeraldas. He tossed it into a garbage can. The paper fluttered.

They spoke, occasionally, about having another child. He had always wanted more children—half a dozen, maybe more. She seemed fine. Perfectly fine. He wanted to believe it: that she was cured. Those darkest images would fade, supplanted by new memories, but the knowledge of her illness haunted him still. They made love, occasionally. He still saw Luna from time to time. Fabiana and Guadalupe had gotten married. And then Ricky, too, and Juan a few months later, to Guadalupe's younger sister, and he could not help but wonder about her *pepa*, whether it was stubbly or smooth. Soon, he would have two brand-new nieces.

One day he came home to find long yellow streamers billowing out from every window of the casita. Essy had found the rolls of crepe paper in a drawer, spent the afternoon carefully hanging them with clear tape. "Hair, Papi!" she proclaimed. "Our casita has hair!" But the sight of streamers brought the Vargas house to mind. Susi. Was she still living in Esmeraldas? The thought needled him, like the splinters lodged in the palm of his hand.

He believed they were content, most of the time. Most evenings they ate dinner, played cards outside, or slipped over to Mami's house to watch *futbol* on the new LCD television. Some nights Lucia still leafed through her narrow-ruled notebooks, carted out her old laptop. "What are you working on?" he asked. She had her own column now at the paper, could do as she liked, so it was ecotourism this month, an interview with the director of the senior center the next. "And the book?" She shook her head.

Four years passed. The dry season went. The wet season came. The animals grew and wandered and multiplied. When rains were severe, mud bubbled in through the seams of the casita and they lay down flattened cardboard and wore rain boots. Each time the tin roof started to leak again, he felt guilty for not having started work on a new house. There was always something else in need of his immediate attention. The future would have to wait.

Essy was nine years old when it happened. A cloudless spring day, ripe with lilac and chickweed and manzanilla. Essy, as tall as Mami, gangly, lithe, with a shining brown face and dark teardrop eyes. On her ninth birthday, she had insisted on cutting her hair short. It reached just below her ears.

She and Fredy were playing by the river, as they often did in the afternoons, building mud castles, digging moats, populating them with minnows and other small fish they could catch with their hands. It was one of the dogs who alerted her with its yelps and howls: Fredy had tumbled in. It wouldn't have mattered, had it not been the wettest rainy season in thirty years, turning the river into waist-deep chocolate rapids. And it shouldn't have mattered, because Fredy, though slow and thick as a dunce, was tall and knew how to swim. It was a trick, Essy thought, Gordito was playing a game, and would burst out or wave his arms or grab her by the legs and yell, "Shark!" But as she waded around, his lumbering body did not surface. She screamed for help.

Manny was close by, close enough to dive in, but the mud and sand and sediment were thick and opaque and he couldn't see. *"Dónde? Dónde?"* He screamed at his daughter as she pointed this way and that, until he stepped on the soft, bulky mass. "Go get help," he yelled. "Run and find your mother, Abuelo, Abuela, tell them to go get help." It took all his strength to drag the body out. Fredy's lips were purple. His skin was white. He lay his brother on the grass, shook him by the shoulders.

Papi arrived first. He cleared Fredy's mouth with his fingers, tilted his head, blew air into his lungs. Listened for the breath to return, and when it did not, he pumped hard on his youngest son's chest.

It seemed a lifetime that the small crowd stood gathered, watching hopelessly, Mami clutching Tía Camila's hand. Manny could see the whites of her eyes, pupils grown black, mouth gone slack. When she sagged by Fredy's feet, he ran to her, gathered her in his arms as her shoulders began to heave. *Alamar* was all she said.

He was a boy again. They were picnicking by the sea. It was not a day for mirth, but he was happy to be alive. He was a boy on the beach, belly full of fish and bread, skin hot and salty and crusted with sand. He found an orange starfish washed up by the waves. When Ricky pulled off one of its spiny arms he wailed like it was he himself who had lost a limb. "It'll grow back," Mami had said.

He wrapped his hand around his brother's ankle. The skin felt cold. "Come back," he begged.

Come back. Come back.

Essy sank to the ground, reached over to pat Fredy's bloated belly. *Please come back*, she whispered. *Gordito, I promise, I'll be the shark next time.* She clenched her teeth. She would not cry.

And then a miracle. Fredy sputtered back to life.

It took four men to carry him home, an old door covered with towels as their stretcher. Fredy was placed in his bed, warmed with lamps and blankets and hot water bottles. He shivered. Mami lay next to him, cradling his head in her bosom. Essy refused to leave his side. She told him jokes, made faces, anything to make Gordito laugh. Papi drove to Martez to find the doctor. Tía Paula peeled potatoes for soup. In the tense, uneven quiet, even Tía Camila had no words.

He brought Essy crackers. He brought corn to the hens, scraps to the dogs. He wandered in and out, bedroom to kitchen, kitchen to yard, trying to find a place to stand still. Tía Camila offered him a cup of hot coffee. He was just sitting down to drink it when a knock came at the front door.

"*Quién-es?*" called Mami.

His legs buckled as he stood.

It was Lucia, out of breath. She had run up the hill to call for help. Now, before him stood an ancient *abuelo*, face like an old record, carved with lines. He wore a crown of bright, multicolored feathers. A garland of beaded necklaces hung from his neck.

The old shaman.

"Manny," said Lucia, still huffing, "where is Fredy? I've brought help."

The shaman looked at him with bloodshot eyes.

"*Quién-es?*" called Mami, again.

He tried to block the doorway with his body. "It's nothing," he said.

But Mami had already padded out from the bedroom. One glance, and her complexion paled. "Please send that man away," she said.

He saw Lucia's confusion, her naked shame. That evening, on the front stoop of the casita, under the spring moon, holding hands, he recounted to her the story of Fredy's birth. The round, wooden tub. The shaman's words: *At best a dunce. That child is a curse.* Lucia's hands trembled. She bit her lip. "I'm sorry," she said. "I didn't know. I thought maybe he could help." She closed her eyes, fought back tears. The whole of her body shook.

He pulled her head to his shoulder, pressed his cheek to hers. She smelled like grass. He loved her then. He loved the goodness of her.

The doctor in Cuenca said it was Fredy's heart—it was getting too weak to circulate the blood through his body. Fredy had been born with this heart, a defective heart. It was a heart for a boy, not a man.

"He will need an operation."

"And if not?" asked Mami.

"If not," said the doctor, "I'm afraid he will die."

Papi was stoic. Mami, incensed. It made no difference that she'd known all her life that her son was doomed for this.

"When?" she asked.

The doctor shook his head. "Soon." But they could not perform this type of operation here in Cuenca.

"Why doesn't he go to Quito?" said Lucia. "Surely in Quito there are doctors who can perform such an operation."

It was true, things in Ecuador had changed in the two decades since Fredy's birth. Better hospitals, better technology, skilled surgeons who could fix things once thought unfixable.

"Lucita is right," said Mami. "Of course, we will try."

A rush of phone calls, appointments, and soon it was decided: Mami and Papi and Tío Remy would go with Fredy to Quito. Tío Remy's daughter, the nurse, would meet them there.

"I want to go, too," said Essy.

"No, *hija*, you stay," he said.

But he let her ride with them in the back of the truck, an hour and a half to the bus station in Cuenca. Fredy climbed on board first, pressed his nose to the grimy window. Mami sat beside him. Papi and Tío Remy behind. Essy jumped up and down, waved and waved until the bus disappeared out of sight.

He bought his daughter a soda. They sat down on a curb.

"Papi. Is Gordito going to die?" she said.

He swallowed. "I don't know," he said.

"But he can't die. He just can't. He's the only one of us who stays the same."

"What do you mean, *hija*?"

Her sigh made him feel obtuse.

"Well, he's bigger now. Much bigger than when we first came, I think. But inside, he's the same. He laughs when I tell my jokes. He loves the animals. We play the same games. I love Gordito, Papi."

"I know," he said. "We all do."

She nodded, pensive.

"And the rest of us, we're not the same?"

She shook her head. "Abuela is worrying all the time now. She forgets things, like how much flour she's already put in when she's measuring the flour for honey cake. And Mama doesn't talk the way she used to. She's much more serious now."

"And me, *hija*? Have I changed, too?"

She nodded. She pointed to his belly.

"That's all?" he said, laughing.

"You're heavier," she said. She scrunched up her nose. "But not just on the outside, Papi. Inside, too."

He studied her face, wondered how much she knew. Or if what she said was true, or if it was only that she was growing up and saw the world differently now. He had never spoken with her about her mother's illness, though he told himself he would. One day. But not now. For now, he would drink a soda with his nine-year-old wonder, and the past would stay in the past.

"Should we go to the candy store?" he said.

She grinned. Slapped him an emphatic high five.

That night he and Lucia made love in the hammock outside the casita. After, they looked up, the fronds of banana trees swaying above them. They admired the stars. "You have to believe," she said. He nodded. He prayed. He tried to believe.

Two days later, Fredy returned from Quito with his entourage. He ran to greet them.

"Can they do it?" he asked.

Tío Remy nodded.

"Yes?"

"There is a procedure," said Tío Remy.

Papi stared at the ground.

"So they can do it. That's great, right?"

"Yes," said Mami. "It's possible for the doctors to do it. But *hijo*, it's too expensive."

He hadn't even considered it, the cost, but of course, everything cost. Well, they could sell the animals. He could fix up the old tractor, sell that, too. He could find extra work in Cuenca, construction, painting, whatever it would take.

"*Hijo*, they say we don't have time," said Mami.

"They could be wrong," said Tío Remy.

"Doctors are wrong all the time," said Papi. But his voice held no conviction.

They sat at the picnic tables outside Mami's house. He watched Fredy toss watermelon rinds to Princess and Pea. Essy sprayed their snouts with the hose.

It was Lucia who asked: "How much?"

Mami glanced at Papi. They shook their heads.

"Please, how much?" said Lucia.

To him, it sounded like a staggering sum.

"I have some money," she said.

That night he and Lucia lay in the hammock, he did not want to make love. He did not notice the stars. "Are you sure?" he said, a pit in his stomach.

Lucia nodded.

"You have this kind of money?"

"I can get it," she said.

The next day she asked him to go with her to the *teléfono cabinica* in town.

"Why?" he asked.

"I need you to talk to my sister," she said.

He did not understand. To ask for money? No, no, he could not do that.

"Not about money. I need you to . . ." She bit her lip, fidgeted with her fingers.

He understood.

They went by motorbike, bumpy and loud, reeking of petrol and kicking up dust. He sat beside her in that cramped, airless booth, on a metal stool so hot it burned his thigh.

She handed him a slip of paper with the ten-digit number, but he knew it already by heart.

Hello? Manny?

Fear, locked inside those two simple words. This was what he represented to Lucia's sister.

Is everything okay?

"Lucia is fine," he said. His voice sonorous, confident. "She's perfect. She would like to speak to you."

He handed Lucia the receiver.

It was a brief conversation. Lucia did not bother with pleasantries or attempt to mince words. *This is about Fredy*, she said. Her tone terse, restrained. And when she hung up the phone she did not cheer or high-five as he might have expected of her, but said only, quietly: "Done." He felt the contradiction: on one hand, elation; on the other, Lucia's coldness, which saddened him. But these were family matters, and he would not pry.

The funds were wired the next afternoon.

This is how Fredy went to the hospital in Quito and got an operation for his heart. The eight-hour procedure was completed without complication, allaying Mami's lifetime of worry, at last. Fredy arrived home to a quiet celebration. Tía Camila baked his favorite pineapple cake. Tía Paula hung streamers. Essy added a perfectly painted red heart to his portrait on the south-facing wall of the casita, next to the cow named Victoria. And though Fredy had never fully understood what was happening, now he clung to Lucia and wouldn't let go.

"Thank you, *hija*," said Mami.

He squeezed Lucia's shoulders.

Finally, the whispers stopped.

And then one day she announced it: she was pregnant again! And when she said it her face lit up and his lit up, too, because he hadn't thought it was possible, because she was too old for this. "Yes, but I am blessed," she said.

She was buoyant, giddy. Essy, the same, bouncing on the bed, overjoyed that she would become a big sister. She pressed her ear to her mother's belly, still flat.

"What should we sing to the baby, Mama?" she asked.

"You choose," said Lucia.

He listened as they sang, their voices interwoven, almost indistinguishable now, in unison or in harmony, lullabies or boleros or American spirituals.

> *I've got peace like a river in my soul*
> *I've got a river in my soul*
> *I've got joy like a fountain in my soul*
> *I've got a fountain in my soul*

Even Mami glowed. She plodded up the dirt path in her woolen shawl, carrying tamales or *llapingachos* or *locro de papa*. Then again her reprise, the one she'd started almost a decade earlier: *You will ask her now, hijo. For the baby, you must ask her.*

So one day, he asked her. And she had a funny look on her face, but she said yes.

Mami clapped her hands, squealed like a girl. "I will tell everyone this happy news," she said. She kissed Lucia. She kissed her granddaughter. Then she pulled out her yellow measuring tape. "I will make you a dress. A wedding dress. With sheets and sheets of lace and a beaded veil. Oh, Lucita, it will be beautiful."

It satisfied him, too, the three of them together, outside after dinner, heads close and clucking like *gallinas*.

Then the doubts seeped in again—her health, the health of the baby, her health after the baby's birth. He'd kept those pamphlets given to him by that social worker; they were stored away in a trunk. He'd stored away the old yellow enamel pot, too, purchased a new one, stainless steel. But it had been years since he'd jumped out of bed to spy on her in the kitchen; he no longer knew where the orange bottle was kept. She saw the look on his face. Kissed his cheek. "Don't worry, Manny. I am taking care of this *niña*." "How do you know it's a girl?" he asked. "Well, wouldn't it be nice for Essy to have a sister?" She saw this doctor, that doctor. "I'm old," she said, laughing. Her effervescence was contagious. She hummed a bachata and asked him to dance.

She was perfect, like the girl he'd first laid eyes on at the laundromat. That girl, the *Chinita* with the perfect calves and perfect *tetas*, now this woman once more carrying his child. It felt like a dream. Each night she brewed herself a cup of herbal tea, took her vitamins, stretched to relax. She went to bed early. She rubbed her belly. And for nine more weeks they basked in each other's hazy glow, contemplating who this new creature might be who would join them, and then one night she sat in the outhouse for six hours, doubled over, and the next day the glow was gone.

She did not cry or swear or holler out in grief. She made no sounds at all.

Mami put the dress away in a closet.

Such a shame.

Unlucky.

Cursed.

Then they did not speak any more about children. She lay in bed whole days, morning till night, walled in by the mosquito net, and would not answer when he asked what was wrong. She made appearances at family parties but mingled only with the teenagers, and she did not dance and never stayed for long.

She has a hole inside of her. Gigante. Susi's words.

"Lucia, please, you need to eat something," he said.

She shook her head. She no longer worked in the garden or commuted to Cuenca or wrote in the evenings in her spiral notebook. From time to time she went for walks by herself up the steep slopes behind the casita, through the grass to the woods, though she stayed away from the old shaman now. He watched as she set off, tall rubber rain boots marking her ascent up the hillside, two bright pink dots growing smaller and smaller until they disappeared. Only when she was completely out of sight could his tension transform into sadness.

One day, as she lay sleeping, he noticed a single silvery strand of hair on her head. He could not remember how old she was. He had to think of his own age, then calculate hers.

One day their neighbor, Roberto, came to the door. There was a letter, he said. For Lucia. It had been delivered next door by mistake. A letter? What letter? They rarely received letters. Only the occasional package for Essy from Switzerland, with books or a sundress or a wide-brimmed hat, boxes of chocolates shaped like shells.

"Lucia?" he called. She climbed out of bed.

It was a large white envelope, thick and square. Embossed with fancy gold type.

"What is it?" asked Essy.

"I don't know," she said. She sat upright in the high-backed rocking chair in the corner of their bedroom. "*Hija*, you read it to me."

Essy took the envelope, ran her fingers over the fine linen paper. "It's beauuuutiful," she said.

"Is it, *hija*?"

"New York University," said Essy. "Twenty-fifth re-un-ion . . ." She glanced at her mother, who was resting again. "What's that for, Mama?"

Lucia's eyes opened slowly. She rose from her chair. "How did they find me here?" she whispered. Without opening it, she threw the envelope into the trash.

"Why is Mama so sad all the time?" asked his daughter.

"Sad?"

"She doesn't laugh anymore."

"Yes, *hija*. She is sad right now. But one day, she will feel better."

He cooked breakfast, chorizo with eggs, while Lucia slept. Essy set the table, went to the garden, returned with a papaya and two granadillas, perfectly ripe.

"When?" she asked.

He kissed the top of his daughter's head.

"Soon, *hija*. She will feel better soon. I promise." He said it to believe it. And because, well, in spite of everything—Lucia, *their* Lucia, had always come back.

And then he felt a knot in his stomach, a strange remorse. He remembered still, that promise he'd made all those years ago. *For my daughter, I will try*. He had kept the promise a long, long time. He had stuck by Lucia. This was love, or this was duty, he could no longer tell the difference.

That year, he finally laid the foundation for their new house, sixty meters to the right of the old one. Lucia sat on the front stoop of the casita, watching quietly. "Come, Mama," said Essy. A few weeks passed and Lucia would help sometimes, hauling or shoveling or setting down joists. Then they mixed the mortar, then they stacked cinder blocks, then they pieced together the Spanish-tiled roof, sawed and framed and hammered and drilled. Two bedrooms. A bathroom with a proper toilet and tub. A kitchen with porcelain tiles. They sanded and painted, installed windows and doors. One day he watched her wind up the dirt path carrying three reams of cloth: pink and orange and blue. She went to the old sewing machine Mami had passed on to her years before, showed Essy how to sew a curtain. *Like this. Like this, Mama? Not like that, like this!* He listened to them laugh.

৭৪

And then one day in the dry season, she came to him. She said, "Manny, I am going to America to visit my friend. He is dying."

She said it simply but he could sense her distress. Her clavicles tensed. He did not need to ask which friend.

He watched her take out her large, red plaid suitcase, as ugly now as the day she'd brought it home from Orchard Street. She unzipped it, pulled out a small duffel bag. This was what she packed.

"How long will you be gone?" he asked.

"I'm not sure," she said.

He did not need to hear more but she said it: "I'd like to stay until the end."

She inhaled, exhaled, long, deep breaths. Her clavicles relaxed.

Her voice sounded stronger, determined. Cancer. A few days. A few weeks. A month or two at the very most, if one had to guess.

He remembered that hospital in Westchester. They had shaken hands. But now he felt none of the animosity he'd felt back then. He felt inexplicably sad.

"Mama, why do you have to go?" asked Essy.

"It's only for a little while, *hija*. A week or two, maybe. Fourteen days. Is fourteen a lot, sweetheart?" She reached for her daughter.

"It *is*," said Essy. She threw her arms around her mother's neck.

He drove her to Cuenca in their pickup truck. Watched as she boarded the bus to Quito. She waved. He waved. She pressed her palm to the window. A lump popped into his throat. On the drive home, his head filled with memories of America: the Big Apple Laundromat. Maurice. Angel fountains spraying water from their penises. Mindy Griffin and the Vargas boys. Mrs. Gutierrez. The fires. Snow. And once more he remembered those nights with Susi, entwined inextricably with his daughter's birth. He closed his eyes, heard the clang of the radiators, low muffle of the television tuned to channel 9. The sirens wailed, he smelled smoke. He listened for Susi's footsteps, and when she came to him he let her ride until he exploded. Those days, imprinted upon him, the uncertainty and fear wore him down. But now, in the darkness, from his safe place in the campo, with his daughter sleeping soundly down the hall in her own bedroom—in the soft light of nostalgia, he could long for it now, ache for the frenzy of youth.

Where was Susi? That encounter with Nele Hernandez resurfaced in his mind. Susi flourished in his imagination. Again, he fantasized a life with her the way he'd once dreamed of a life with Lucia, with half a dozen children and hot meals around a large table.

Several weeks later, he found himself sleeping on a bus ride to Quito. It seemed the deepest sleep of his life. He did not notice the bumps or jolts or the driver's sharp swerves to avoid slamming into cows in the road. When he woke, he watched the dirt cliffs zoom by, the petrol stations and car dealerships and banana plantations, open-air taverns with dry, thatched roofs and men playing pool inside. In Quito he boarded another bus. Construction and rubble and yellow machines, iron gates and billboards, stray dogs, plastic bags, telephone poles, graffiti-plastered cinder block walls, cement buildings spray-painted with notices and signs. Rubble, dirt, cement, trash, and then mountains and valleys, the blue-gray sky. In Esmeraldas he asked the driver for the way to the barrio. Its name, stored for years in a corner of his mind, titillated as it rolled off his tongue. He was directed to another bus.

By the time he arrived, it was dusk. One dusty main road, quiet, lined with low buildings, palm trees, telephone wires. He walked, glancing back over his shoulder every few seconds. The light was fading. His stomach growled. He had eaten nothing but candy all day. He needed to find dinner—a chicken cutlet or a piece of fried fish, cabbage salad and rice or plantains. He smelled cooking from an open-air restaurant ahead. It was ramshackle, dimly lit, but he didn't care. There wasn't much else around.

As he approached, he saw her. At a rickety table outside, in plain sight, as if she'd been set there to wait for a man just like him. She wore a tight black dress. Several rings on her fingers. He looked down at the ground, shoved his hands in his pockets, headed for a large dumpster next to the low cement building. He squatted. Hid. No. It was impossible. But yes, it was really her. It was Susi. With the same too-small eyes, the dimpled smile. And a boy with her, maybe eight, maybe nine? They sat, licking Popsicles—the boy in school uniform, navy blue trousers, a short-sleeved white shirt. The brown face, with Susi's small, wide-set eyes. The grin spread from ear to ear.

He froze.

Calculated quickly in his head. No. But it was possible. Or it wasn't. Was it?

He observed them, sick with doubt and disbelief and fascination. He could've stayed in that spot by the dumpster and watched them all night, the way they waved their hands as they spoke, the way the boy's dimples flashed as he laughed.

He could stand up, walk, go to her. But he stayed, squatting. Suddenly he could not think what good it could do to move. Would he say hello, casually? Feign surprise? Apologize? Introduce himself to the boy? Would he pretend the encounter was an accident? Offer to buy them dinner? Invite them to live in the campo? About that boy, he didn't know. Couldn't be sure. But to step out would be to unravel a thread he could not sew back into place. So he stayed behind the trash, hidden.

Soon they were finished. Susi paid the bill. She stood and her dress hugged her heart-shaped ass. Her head lunged a split second ahead of her body, like a giraffe. He was not ready to let them walk away, so he followed down the main *calle*, every gland excreting sweat. Once, he thought she sensed she was being followed. She grabbed the boy by the elbow, raised her voice. They turned down an alley, disappeared into a concrete building with an iron gate.

He did not know what to do. He wanted to wait. To see them both again. He could go find a hotel, return in the morning, but his head felt too thick, his feet too heavy. He pressed his back against a wall, sat. Drifted, not quite to sleep.

He wished he had come sooner. That encounter with the sister, Nele, how long ago had it been? The boy, how old was he really? What was his name? He should've tried harder to track down Susi after she'd disappeared. Though if he'd found her, what would he have done? This was his way. All those years, bound by Mami's wishes. Terrified of *migras*. For what, he couldn't remember anymore. He had returned to his country. On his own terms. But no, they had never been his terms—they had always been Lucia's. All these years, bound by Lucia, bound to the sister who was not even around. And now here, in this alley, finally here, and it was only because Lucia was away. If she had not gone, would he have come? Was this loyalty or laziness? He could not be sure.

The clang of the gate woke him. Morning. The boy was leaving the building, so he followed him to school, studied every aspect of his gait. It was nothing like his. Was it? The boy was too young. Wasn't he? His mind, flip-flopping this way and that and he could not be sure—or perhaps, rather, it could possibly be, he was not yet willing to release it because he needed this now, wanted it desperately, to prolong the story, to cling a moment longer to this piece of another life, the life of Manuel Vargas not lived.

In the afternoon the boy reemerged from school. He trailed him to the same rickety table outside the same dingy restaurant, and there was Susi again. They ate lunch. He could not hear her words, only the breath of her voice. The boy stood, wiped his chin with a napkin. Susi stood, smiled. And one tiny sliver inside him knew—knew, already, even as he wrestled with himself still—he would do nothing now.

There was a word for this feeling; a Portuguese word he'd once learned from Lucia: *saudade*. *A vague longing for something that cannot exist again, or perhaps never existed.*

He cried into his hands.

 infinity

He returned to the campo. It felt peaceful there. He made peace, for now. He had gone and come back and made peace. He enjoyed the quiet, for now. And the comfort of his bed in his newly painted blue-gray bedroom in his newly built house. Ricky came to visit with his wife and two daughters. Juan came to visit with his wife and daughter and son. He enjoyed their company, their jokes, their allegiant admiration. He enjoyed this time with his daughter.

Days later, he would begin his worry. Weeks later, he would receive the news. In shock, he would lumber down the hall to Essy's room, raise his fist, knock-knock. Sprawled on her pink bedspread, chin propped in one hand, she chewed bubble gum while reading a book.

"*Hija*," he said. He had to say it to believe it. "Your mother is not coming back."

Part Three

✆

9

Yonah

It was a long time ago Lucia said she's gonna come for a visit, maybe six or seven years. I wait for her to call me but she doesn't call. I don't know what's going on, I don't hear from her anymore. I think, okay, she changed her mind. I try not to think about it. I don't take it personally. People say things, people do things, these two are not the same, I know that. I hope she's happy, that's all.

I could've told her when I first started having pain in the balls. But why should I tell her, I think? She lives in South America with her family, I'm not gonna make special phone call just to tell her this, and anyway if she hears it she's gonna tell me to go see a doctor and I hate doctors, and when I really need doctor I call Jie in Switzerland. Jie's husband is doctor. So Lucia doesn't come, it's okay. I know if something is really wrong, I hear from Jie.

But then the day comes when I have to pee like crazy all the time and I run to the bathroom and there is nothing, always nothing, so finally I go and get the tests. The doctors, they say I'm a man, it's prostate, and this number is very bad, this number is a little bad, and maybe I do some procedure and maybe it's gonna help me or maybe it's not, or maybe it's only going to change the numbers. I say I don't care about any stupid numbers, I want to know, will it kill me, and if so, when, and what can they do so I don't have to pee so fucking bad all the time.

They say, we watch it, so I say okay, fine, we wait, and I go build a house in Meyer, Minnesota. Minnesota, sure, because it's far away. The land is cheap, the sky here, it's like crazy forever, you've never seen anything like it, so big and clear you can see whole universe. But the winter—the winter! It's fucking cold like you can't believe it, you think New York is cold, no way, this place is freezing off your ass, and people ask do I go ice fishing and I look at them—I say, you think a Jew is gonna sit out on the ice eight hours for a fish? So in the winter I go to Israel. I have a big beautiful house there, near Haifa, and it's sunny all the time. But I can't take too much of Israelis and all the fucking politics so in summer I come back to Meyer. All the people I know, they make fun of me, look at me like this guy is crazy, and some people ask if it's near Minneapolis, or a big mall, or Lake Wobegon. No. But when I find out some time later it's not only prostate, I have testicular cancer, too, it turns out famous clinic is couple hours away.

Two months ago, the cancer shoots to my lungs. That's when I find her, Lucia, I call and I tell her everything and immediately she comes. From Ecuador.

The lungs? I can't believe it didn't start there, she says. Always, she's hated my smoking.

You see? I tell her. I never do nothing wrong with my balls.

She is a little bit fatter, rounder face, heavier middle, but she is still beautiful. Beautiful dancing eyes, beautiful smile, like a girl.

But now she's angry. She says, You tell me five years ago I would've come five years ago and now you're like this. You need a machine to help you pee. I laugh and she has to start laughing, too, because this is what me and Lucy do.

I say, Everybody's gonna die.

She says, You should've told me.

I say, You have a daughter, you have family, you have a life. I know how to take care of myself.

And she is crying and I say, It's okay, sweetie, hey, you're here with me now.

Lucia, she drives to hospital, she's demanding to know the options. More options, she says. What are the options. She's trying to save me, but the cancer starts in testicles and spreads to kidneys and lungs by now. So then she flies to New York, only for one night, and she brings back a giant suitcase.

Did you get that on Orchard Street? I say.

She says, No. Orchard Street is different now.

The suitcase is stuffed with two things—pineapple buns from my favorite bakery on Mott Street, and special Chinese herbs. You know these herbs, like dried-up sticks and weeds and bugs, not something to put in your mouth. She cooks the herbs in a special pot, boils them all day and night and the house stinks like worse than rot.

I say, I am not dead yet, are you trying to kill me? Get that shit out of my beautiful house! But I say it like Talking Heads say it, my beau-ti-ful house, and she knows I'm a little bit joking.

Just drink it, she says. She hands me a bowl of black soup, like tar for the roads, but full of twigs and tentacles and worms. I won't drink it, no way. She calls me stupid and stubborn, she is crying again, so finally I drink it, but I go to bathroom and spit it out.

The next week my son Jonny comes. Jonny and me, we have a lot of rough times for some years. In New York he tried to steal from me so many times, he makes trouble in the neighborhood, he gets his ass arrested. I say to his mother, how am I supposed to help a kid like this? I have to send him away, he's gonna get himself killed here. She says, you are not sending him back, he is teenager and she is not wanting him in the Israeli army, we have huge fights over this. Why not Israeli army, everyone does Israeli army, even sissies, even girls. But instead of Israeli army, I send him to cooking school. And you know what? He does good. But then he comes to me, he says, Dad, I want to open restaurant. I say, what do you know about running restaurant? He says, what did you know about running a store? I say, every day I work at that store, I know everything going on in the store, every delivery guy, every customer, every worker, what they do. Except Uncle Leo, he says. Jonny, my son, he knows how to hurt me, drive a stick into my balls and twist. You see, Leo, he steal from us, too. My cousin Moishe, he is partner of mine for the store. He learns about Leo, he is pissed, he blames me, he wants me to pay him back what Leo stole, so Moishe and me, we fight. I look for Leo but when I finally find him, of course the money is already gone. Money and family, it's hard to mix, but somehow we have to keep together in this country, look out for each other, this is what we have to do. So I leave New York. I don't want to fight, it's best, I'm sick of it anyway. I want quiet. I want peace. I tell Jonny, you work in restaurant business for ten years, you prove to me you know restaurants, I help you start your own. Now I don't have ten years. Jonny, I worry about him.

This time he comes to my house, he puts his feet up on the coffee table, doesn't even take off his shoes. One thing, at least he can cook now, and this is good because he takes over the kitchen and he won't let Lucia foul it up with her stinky herbs. Of course Lucia is unhappy, but she's not gonna fight with Jonny so she boils the herbs in the night. I say, *Aiyaaaa*, like Chinese people say. Lucia taught me this. But she is trying so hard. I hold my nose, I drink the soup. Then she tells me this is not enough. She says I have to *believe*.

These days I don't move so well. I have to sit in wheelchair, you can imagine how much I fucking hate this, all the time sitting on my ass.

Lucia, she takes me outside, out on the grass behind the house. It's November, Minnesota jumps into winter in November, nothing left on the trees, so we can sit and watch the lake, but I get cold so fast.

It's beautiful here, she says.

Yes. In December I am supposed to go to Israel, but this year, I don't think I'm gonna go.

You need coat, I say to her. She has flimsy purple jacket.

I have fat, she says, laughing. You, you need some fat.

She's right, I have nothing but bones. When I never am feeling hungry, that's when I know I am really sick.

We sit around, she goes inside house, comes out with blankets. Not the wool blanket from living room, because she says that one is too scratchy. She brings the blankets from the bed. I use puffy down comforter, king size. Why not? she says. You should be comfortable.

I say okay.

She sits in Adirondack chair next to me, covers herself with blanket, too. We sit, we don't say nothing for a while, this is okay for Lucia and me.

Jie, she comes, too, for a few days, all the way from Switzerland. She hasn't seen Lucia in such a long time. I see the way she is talking to her sister, suspicious, always trying to figure out if Lucia's okay. And Lucia, I see this, she doesn't want to talk to Jie. Whenever Jie comes into room, she walks out, and this is painful to see because when I first meet Lucia, all she talks about is her sister, Jie this, Jie that, me and Jie, always cutting hair together in Chinatown, they used to be so close. I ask Lucia what's going on, she gets angry, she is crying, says I wouldn't understand. I say, she is your sister, she is blood. I tell her she is making me sad. She says she is sorry, she doesn't want to make me sad. I say, okay, then don't. Past is past, let it go.

She says Jie try to control her all the time, always makes her feel bad. I know it's about the pills, and I don't like pills, I hate pills, too,

I always think Lucia's perfect, she just needs time to work things out by herself in her head. Always she keeps things locked inside. And Lucia says now her hands shake from the pills, and I can see it also, how sometimes her left eye twitches.

Why don't you stop? I say. Here is peaceful, calm, you don't need shitty pills that hurt your body. That stuff is like poison.

It's not so simple, she says.

We watch movies. I like action thrillers. I like Denzel Washington so we watch *Philadelphia* and *Malcolm X* and that movie about the running away subway train. Denzel, he is a good actor, and seeing subway, it makes me miss New York. If I could sit on that wood bench outside the store with Lucia, like old times, watching the beautiful people going by, I think, that would be nice.

When I first marry Lucia, people wonder who is this Chinese girl? I say, this is Lucia, and everybody likes Lucia. Wherever she goes she is friends with everyone. Lucia is like child in this way, without walls. Even here in Minnesota, she goes to pharmacy, pharmacist knows her now, she meets neighbor with the three nasty wolfhounds, she knows all of them by name, Ward Dunkel and Batman and Robin and Cape (that Dunkel guy, I see the way he looks at her, he likes the women, but fine, okay, men like to look at women, it works). I like people, too, but I am loud, pushy man with missing arm and thick accent. She is less loud, but she is interested in people, where they are coming from, she listens, asks questions, she doesn't pass judgment, so people, they love Lucia.

But then when she gets sick, it's different. She is fighting with me all the time, aggressive, snapping like a turtle. I know, this is not Lucia. And I think she first gets sick when we're married because we live in that small room in East Village. It's too much going on there, too much noise, too much crazy everywhere, enough to make any-body sick. Lucia needs quiet sometimes, that's all. Here it's quiet. I used to go whole day without talking. Not like now, with nurses and home health aides coming in to poke me all the time. One nurse named Sandy, she comes to my house. She is not good-looking nurse, like in the movies. She is fat, wearing big, flowery tent with matching pants. I tell her, Please Sandy, you come to my house, you can wear whatever you want, you don't need to wear uniform like that. She looks insulted. Next day she comes she is wearing same tent, you believe it? I am a dying man here, she can respect my wish.

Jie, she comes in the morning, sits on my bed. She says, I know we are family for long time now, you are like brother to me, and I know you are dying, too. But I say this, please, you cannot tell Lucia to stop her pills.

Family, we disagree. I tell her it's okay if we disagree. It's my opinion. What, a man can't have opinions? I'm a dying man, I'm gonna shove my opinions inside everybody's asses, you know me.

You can't do that, she says. You will harm her. She listens to you. Please don't do that again.

Jie, she has temper. I am not scared of her, but Lucia, I know she is scared.

She won't even talk to me, says Jie.

She loves you, I say.

Now Jie is crying, too. Shit.

How is Stefan? I say. Everything is good in Switzerland?

Good? I don't know about good.

This is also surprise to me. I am looking worried for Jie.

It's been hard, she says.

Fucking marriage, I say.

Fucking marriage, she says.

How come you never have kids? I ask.

She stares at the ceiling for long time. Always Jie is like this, thinking, thinking. Maybe I'm selfish, she finally says.

Then I thank you for coming here.

I hate airplanes, she says. But I'd rather see you alive than in a casket.

You see now why I love Jie.

My daughter, she comes to Minnesota, too. Anat, she is always my favorite, good girl, working for bank in Jerusalem now, wearing grown-up suits. Daughters and fathers, they don't crash head-to-head. Daughters, they crash with their mothers. But this time she comes in, she says, why do you stay in this cold, dark place? Why are you not coming back to Israel? There is your home. There is your family. Her mother tells her to say to me, it's ridiculous, I am crazy to die alone in middle of nowhere. I think maybe she is right, but who is to say what is right way to die?

We play cards, gin rummy. Jie wins first few games, I see she is getting embarrassed. Let's play something else, she says. So Jonny teaches us poker game, takes all our money. I say give me a break, you're gonna get everything I have soon enough! This is joke, but you know what? Jonny slams his cards on the table, walks away. *Aiya.* Oh, Dad, says Anat. She runs after him. He's just sad, says Lucia. I think how many times in my life I have been stupid like this, making my own son feel bad. And how many more times do I have left to make him feel better again.

I am coughing up blood now. I have woman doctor. She says to Lucia, if it soaks a panty liner, you call me. You believe a doctor says something like that? First time, I was scared shitless and I am thinking, those are my insides coming out, but now it's like regular, no big deal, a little blood, but Lucia, I can see she is afraid. One day I puke in toilet and Lucia says we have to call doctor. I say, come on, it's nothing, she says, are you fucking kidding me? She doesn't say the word fucking, but I know it's what she thinks and she is really mad, so I say okay, because what do I know about maxi-pad.

The doctor says we have to go to the hospital, emergency room. No fucking way, I say. I'm not going anywhere. I die, I'm dying here.

Jonny, for one time in my life he agrees with me, and Jie, I see she is not wanting to get involved, but Anat and Lucia they are yelling and screaming and calling me a stubborn fool, a selfish jackass, and then they are both crying, but this time I don't move, because I won't die in a fucking hospital. And you know what, there is no more puke, no more blood, and I turn on the TV and watch some game shows, *Price Is Right*, *Family Feud*. The next day there is no more blood, but I am in so much pain, I can't move. Lucky for me, this is the day I get a delivery. I get a brand-new hospital bed!

Where should we put it? says Jonny.

Down in the dining room, says Anat. Lots of space.

No way, I say. I like my bedroom.

But you can't move, says Anat. What about the stairs?

But they listen to me. They push my king-size bed to the wall, and this room, it's so big I can fit the hospital bed next to it.

Two beds, like a hotel, says Lucia.

Perfect, I say.

Perfect, she says.

And now I am comfortable, I am wanting shakshuka. I say, I want shakshuka! So Lucia and Jonny both make me shakshuka. They are having contest to see who's gonna make the best shakshuka, like some reality TV show and I'm gonna be celebrity judge. And then Jie says she's gonna make shakshuka, too, and she finds a recipe on the Internet. Never in my life I've had three people cooking for me, and even though the chemicals, the chemo, make so I can't taste anything right, I think, this life is pretty good.

They try to get along, I see this, the four of them. The next day I am watching action thriller in my bedroom and they are in kitchen, making so much noise. For first time, I hear Lucia and Jie laughing together, and this makes me happy, but I am also a little bit sad I am not laughing with them.

Then they come in and there is Jonny, holding crazy big cake, with a million candles, like big enough for fifty people!

You gonna set my house on fire. Is it my birthday? I say.

No, says Anat. My daughter, she is smiling so hard she is squeezing tears out of her eyes.

But it's a good day for cake, says Lucia.

Tiramisu cake, says Jonny, who is very proud of this cake that I see now is square shaped with brown and white icing like chessboard. Lucy and me, we used to play chess.

They are wearing hats on their heads, those triangle party hats for kids. They start to sing Happy Birthday song, and I laugh, and then next thing all these people are coming into my room, one and then the next and then the next. I see there is the doctor, the pharmacist, my friend who owns local hardware store, the neighbor with the three wolfhounds, other neighbors from around the lake. And the nurse with the big tent who is not wearing big tent today, only bad dress that looks like smock. Lucy, she knows I hate surprises, but she also knows only stupid fool would be mad about this.

Everyone makes small talk, and I look at them and I think, these people, most people, are nice. They don't know what to say to me, I know it can be uncomfortable, so I make small talk, too, about Denzel Washington. Smock lady loves Denzel Washington!

And then I fall asleep and when I wake up everyone is gone. No cake, no plates, no red plastic cups, just triangle birthday hat on my head. I know Lucia, she puts it there. She is so small, sleeping alone in my king-size bed.

Next day, Jie comes in to say good-bye. Lucia is taking her to airport now, she says. She gives me kiss on my forehead. I say, no crying. She nods. I love you, she says. She can't look at me. I don't look at her either. Both of us pretending like we're not gonna crack. But for first time, I feel how real it is.

When Lucia comes back I am eating dinner Jonny made, watching game show on TV. She throws herself down on king-size bed.

Everything went okay? I say.

I think so, she says.

Good.

She lets out great big sigh.

I don't bother her anymore. I close my eyes. Even dying man needs to know when to shut up.

When it's morning, I say, Tell me about Ecuador.

It's beautiful, she says. We live on a farm, you can't see anything that isn't nature. You would love it there.

How come you don't invite me? I say. I am joking, but I see it's not funny to her, she is looking sad so I shut up my big fat mouth.

They eat chicken feet.

Like Chinese?

And chicken heads. By the plateful. Only heads and feet. No body.

You can get a haircut on a truck.

What? You're kidding me.

On the back of a pickup truck, it's true.

You do that?

No. She laughs. I go to a Chinese lady who snacks on chicken feet.

You have friends there? A lot of friends?

Friends? She is looking at her hands, thinking a little bit, then raises up her shoulders. I know everyone, she says.

She climbs into my hospital bed, crawls under all those fucking plastic tubes. She pushes the buttons to raise our heads, then our feet, then she lowers the feet almost all the way.

There, isn't that comfortable? she says.

We lie like that and I fall asleep for long time, I don't know how long but when I wake up the outside is dark. Lucia is still next to me, watching action thriller on TV. She points remote to turn it off.

I want to say something, but I have to think before I say it.

What is it? she says.

Remember, a long time ago, you say you come to visit? I waited. How come you never come?

She doesn't answer me. She puts her head on my shoulder and I kiss it. I see there is some gray now, and the skin of her face, it's a little bit loose, with some lines around the eyes. I press them closed with my fingers.

All those years, you left your kids while you lived in New York, she says.

Yeah, sure, I say.

You were okay with that?

Sure. I went to New York to make good life. They were with their mom. Kids should be with their mother. Jonny, always he loves his mother like crazy.

She nods her head, rubs her eyes, blinks away the sleep. If I'd come, I never would've gone back, she says.

She shows me pictures of her daughter, Esperanza. The name means "hope." This is the first time I ever see pictures of her, so I see a lot, from time she is tiny baby to now. She has big open face with far-apart eyes, turning down at the corners like water drops.

She is beautiful like you, I say. When I meet Lucy she is twenty-eight years old, but when I remember her she is without age.

Someday I will tell her about you, she says.

What will you say?

I will tell her love is everything.

She looks at me, then down at her hands. But now, like this, I think love is just romantic way of explaining selflessness.

She sings to me. I close my eyes, and for a while she continues to sing. *Ezekiel disconnected dem dry bones.* I think it is her, but maybe it's an angel, who knows.

I am having too much pain now, too much fucking pain everywhere. They fill my plastic tubes with morphine. I can't hardly talk. I can't think. I say, I can't do this. I don't want this. I say, Lucia, you have to let me go.

She is so sad.

I tell her, You will go back to be with your family soon. Be happy.

She shakes her head, making a breeze in the room with the way her hair whips around. She shakes and shakes it, harder and harder, like she is trying to shake out everything inside.

It makes me sad, so I close my eyes.

This is life.

10

Meyer, MN

Most people of Meyer, Minnesota, had never met her in person, but they saw the reports on the news. This was December, an early winter storm. The forecasters had touted it for a week as the next Armageddon, and the entire region had scrambled to prepare. They chopped extra firewood, drained their hoses, boarded barns, cleared gutters, salted driveways, filled tubs, dug out flashlights and emergency radios. Tommy Boyle, owner of Boyle Hardware and Lumber, said he couldn't remember the last time he'd witnessed such hysteria; the store had been cleaned out of batteries seventy-two hours before the first squall even hit. Zak Barnes, veteran fire chief, urged those using candles to exercise caution, recalling how the Dixons' place went up in flames just last year.

This was what she was wearing: a pair of pink rubber rain boots. A flimsy polyester jacket with fake fur–lined hood. She was a Chinese girl from some hot-weather foreign country. She didn't know about snowstorms. At least, this was what they'd heard.

She came to town to care for the one-armed man. The one from Israel. Sandy Allsopp, hospice nurse, could attest to the girl's diligence, the tenderness with which she tucked the man's blanket around his feet, brought ice chips to his lips, gently lifted his head from his pillow as she mopped the back of his neck with a cool washcloth. The girl was devoted, Sandy said. Never flinched. She stayed right through to the end.

They didn't know much about the man either. He'd shown up one day, purchased a large parcel of land abutting Muir Lake, spent two years building a post-and-beam on top of the hill. They admired his house, its tall, arched windows visible only in wintertime, when the trees were bare, from the narrow path along the opposite side of the lake. Edie Blythe, ever the promptest widow, had brought the man hot dish after hot dish when he first arrived. He was a bit coarse, she thought, though he seemed well built, polite enough, if a touch morose. She forgave his lack of interest—it was not uncommon for outsiders.

The people of Meyer had their own ways of interpreting things.

Donny Dawes, college freshman dropout, on a double shift at the Cub Foods, said he remembered seeing her that night. She had unusually dark eyes—odd, because somehow they were also very bright. To his teenage mind, she could not be beautiful, she was beyond beautiful's age, but it registered as a prick of mortification, this older woman initiating arousal in his groin. She bought two sticks of butter. He remembered it, the two lonely sticks of butter, because he wasn't even working the express aisle, and it was way too crowded for that time of day, everyone stockpiling for the storm. He said it was her. She didn't look quite right. Sometimes people aren't quite right and you can see it in their eyes.

It was grief, some said. Clearly, the girl loved the man. She'd stayed on at the house to pack up his things, even after his two grown children had departed to bring their father's body back to Israel.

Grief drives people to recklessness, despair.

Twelve-year-old Beth Grimstad wrote in her diary: *I bet it was a broken heart.*

They remembered when it happened to Natty Brown, whose wife of thirty-one years was struck by a logging truck while she was out for her morning walk with their corgis. Five months later they'd found Natty, naked from the waist down, handcuffed to a hickory tree. The coroner's report said he'd shed his clothes before he died, as freezing victims often do—this bizarre paroxysm occurring as the body's temperature drops below eighty-five degrees. A suicide note was found, fastened to the back of Natty's neck with a safety pin.

That was gruesome, unforgettable. Madness.

It was a shame. On this they could all agree. She was young, no more than thirty-five, no, forty, maybe forty-five? The police said they'd found nothing suspicious at the house, no evidence of foul play—a mixing bowl on the kitchen counter, along with flour, sugar, eggs, the two sticks of butter. Cookies? But it could have been muffins or waffles or pound cake or scones. It could've been many different things.

She was all alone, in that big house.

But anyone can get disoriented. Lost in the woods. Caught in a bad place in a storm. The temperatures down to minus seven degrees Fahrenheit, forty below zero with the windchill factor, gusts up to seventy miles per hour. Nine local fatalities had already been directly attributed to the storm. Five elderly residents died when the ventilating units in their homes gave out. A father and his ten-year-old son died from carbon monoxide poisoning—fallen asleep in their car, overcome by fumes. A thirty-two-year-old man was found frozen on the hood of a truck. Ms. Katie Delaney, beloved twenty-four-year-old schoolteacher, was killed in a single-vehicle accident, smashed into the concrete guardrail down by the reservoir, body catapulted to the road. A tow truck fished her car from the ice, its front end crushed like an accordion.

It had happened to many of them, too. Out in the woods, caught in a storm while hiking or camping or skiing or biking or fishing or backcountry lovemaking. They were young once, too, headstrong and invincible.

It was a light snow at first. They'd commented aloud on how pretty it was, and it wasn't so cold, not at first, though forecasters had warned temperatures would drop precipitously.

Who would go out in a blizzard dressed like that?

༒

It was Sadie Dunkel, nine years old, who called out to her grandfather, "Hey, there's someone stuck in the tree!" The three Irish wolfhounds, cooped for two days, thrashed into the woods. Ward Dunkel, treading slowly, gritted his teeth each split second before the icy surface snapped under the weight of his snowshoe. It was the morning after the storm. The sun shone bright. The sky glowed a deep winter blue. He realized it now, that glint of pink he'd caught sight of earlier had been a rain boot poking out of a drift. He saw the two sugar maples loom ahead to his left. He knew the pair, their broad trunks joined together at the base to form a perfect V. Now the snow was piled high, there was room enough for a body to rest between them, and the back of the head touched one trunk while the naked foot touched the other. In between, the body lay, curled like a shrimp, knees to chest, head to knees, so all he could see was the purple polyester jacket with its fake fur–lined hood. But he did not need to see the blue-gray face with its shock-stilled eyes and blue-gray lips to know who she was: Lucia. Lucia Bok.

The tree trunks arched, tall and majestic like a grand sleigh bed, the bare branches a moody canopy. She looked peaceful there, curled in that spot, as if she'd squeezed herself into a place of safety. Only the unnatural position of her left arm, dangling stiffly, indicated she was not taking a nap. How long had it been since she'd invited the neighbors to the house for that awkward little party, served cake and tea and asked after his granddaughter? "Don't look," he said. "Sadie, sweetheart, don't look. Run and catch up with the dogs."

He touched the cheek with his palm and it was not like skin or flesh or anything housing life. It was solid. Stuck. Like a block of ice, a leg of lamb in the freezer.

Careless. People are careless. People are careless and they die.

But it was impossible to know the truth of another's interior life. Wasn't it?

They shook their heads, puffed a cigarette or adjusted their hearing aids or clutched the edges of their leather armchairs with their fingers, watched televisions blare the news.

Stefan was frying onions in the kitchen when Miranda set down the phone. He watched her face lock up, drain into blankness.

"What is it, *Schätzli*?" he said.

He dropped his spatula in the sink, switched off the stove. Her eyes, so dark, he could not see her pupils.

Manny.

"That was him?"

He hated when Manny called. It could only mean crisis, never anything good. "Miranda? Who was that?"

She shook her head.

"Was that Manny, just now?"

"No," she whispered. "It was the hospital."

"Oh, Christ. Not again." Fuck. Not again. It had been less than a month since she'd returned from that trip to Minnesota. Quiet, withdrawn. No fights, at least, was what she said, and he believed her—this was a purer sorrow. He'd mostly left her alone.

"Not again, Stefan."

"What?"

"She's dead. Lucia is dead."

There was a storm. Her body was found frozen in the snow.

❦

What came first was not the fact of the body, or the snow, or the speculations of how the body came to be in the snow, or how the body was found in the snow; that would come later. It was also not the sadness, or numbness, or grief, or release; that would come later, too. When she slumped into his arms, face in his chest, already deep in a state of shock and dissociation, what came first was this: *Manny. What will I tell Manny?* And then: *I should've gone to her after Yonah died. She was in that big house, all alone.* And: *The pills. She must have stopped taking her pills.* These thoughts would bob to the surface for years to come, the what-ifs, the whys, fueling her bleakest nightmares, unleashing the guilt and anger for all she had done or not done or tried or not tried or plain never understood—it would take its toll, test their marriage, the inexplicable eruptions, retreats, assignations of blame, minings of pasts and souls in one relentless search for meaning.

Forgiveness. That would come much later.

❦

But what came next was this: She was brisk, efficient. She sat in her wicker rocker on the back porch, pried open her laptop, booked tickets, sent e-mails, called funeral homes.

Stefan accompanied her to Minnesota. She squeezed shut her eyes for the entirety of their flights. He drove their rental car straight to the morgue. When the reporters descended, she shied away. He turned his back to the cameras, tried to shield her from their insistent probes.

The body was cremated. The remains presented to them in a cheap wooden box. "Approved for air travel," said the funeral director, with a tight-lipped smile.

It's ugly. Oh my God, it's so ugly.

The funeral director broadened his smile.

They placed the box in the middle of the backseat. Stefan drove, and she glanced at it frequently. *Miranda, which way now?* This way, that, curt, distracted, until at last they reached the rough gravel road. The barrenness of the woods. Maples and oaks. He could see the clearing now, the lake below, that vast stillness blanketed in snow.

She did not want to enter the house. He had to go first, twist the icy doorknob. It clicked, giving way to the darkness inside. It was stuffy. Sober. He could see boxes and bins, Yonah's possessions arranged in neat piles. When he flicked on a light, she let out a small cry. Muffled it quickly, her lips drawing into a tight, thin line.

On the kitchen counter, a metal mixing bowl. Beside it, flour, sugar, butter, eggs. The police had not touched anything when they inspected the house. She rummaged through the cabinets, found a garbage bag, quickly disposed of it all.

Ward Dunkel, the neighbor, came by to offer his condolences. He brought a loaf of currant bread. "I saw the lights on," he said. "I live over there." Through the tall, arched windows, across the lake, they could see a plume of smoke, rising, that distant tendril of warmth.

She made a pot of tea. They sat in the kitchen. Ward Dunkel explained about the dogs, about his granddaughter. The tree. The snow.

Stefan watched Miranda's face grow hard, like the pain had frozen up inside her and all that was left was a layer of skin. And then she did not want to listen anymore and she stood, thanked the neighbor, said they really must get going. It was not their place, this house—this was Yonah's house. They were staying at a nearby motel. They'd come to gather Lucia's things, that was all, though perhaps Mr. Dunkel could help them lock up, look in on the place every so often. Shakily, she headed up the stairs.

She disappeared for a while. When she returned, she carried her sister's clothes in two large plastic bags. "Mr. Dunkel?" she said. "Is there a Salvation Army around here?" She wanted to make a donation.

Stefan buttoned his long, wool overcoat, stepped out to the porch, a sharp bite in the midafternoon air. A squirrel scurried across the roof. Icicles hung from the gutters. The snow lay undisturbed. He popped the trunk of the rental car, set the clothing inside. Paced up and down the driveway, hands in his pockets, striving for warmth, avoiding chitchat with Ward Dunkel, who had wandered around to the side of the building to puff on a cigarette, the both of them waiting, waiting.

She emerged from the house carrying only a few additional items: a canvas travel pouch, a small duffel bag, two medium-size paintings— a globby brown duck and a yellow goose. Childish renderings, not hers, in primary colors. Stefan had not seen them before.

She placed the canvases on the backseat of the car, propped them up so they flanked either side of the lonely wooden box. She stared, biting her lip.

"Mr. Dunkel?" she called out. "Was it far from here?"

"Far?" said Ward Dunkel.

But her eyes stayed fixed on the wooden box, and Ward Dunkel understood.

"No, not far. About half a mile up the lake."

"Please, would you take me there?"

The snow was deep. The reflection bright. She raised one hand to shade her eyes, focused on lifting her feet. One step, then the next, through the forested white. Soon the house had disappeared, no discernible trail remained—only the dark maze of trees, branches, the thick wintry bareness. And three sets of footprints, marking the direction from which they had come.

Ward Dunkel chattered. *Up this way. Right through here. Not much farther now.*

It was not a long walk, twenty minutes, at most. But in a storm. Yes, one could get lost in these woods. They climbed down a hill, rounded a bend, approached a clearing where thin, purplish shadows crisscrossed their path. The sun, already low.

"There," said Ward Dunkel. He pointed ahead to the tall pair of sugar maples. Looming, stalwart, apart from the rest.

Stefan could see her breath, quick and shallow. It condensed in the cold. Her comportment, stiff, unyielding. But he did not reach for her hand or place an arm around her shoulders or attempt words of comfort. He let her go alone.

She walked up close, close enough to touch. She lingered there, examining those sugar maples, the immenseness of their trunks, each wider than her body, the way they joined to form a perfect V. She spread her arms like wings, arched her neck, tilted her chin to the sun.

A gust of wind. A bird shuttled to air.

"The finches, they stick around some winters," Ward Dunkel said. She did not seem to hear.

She turned in place, shuffling her boots. Rotated her body, surveyed from low to high. To low, again. And she continued to turn, turn, her gaze cast wide, until she had captured every detail of this scene in her mind: this chill, this hush, this illumined sky, this panorama, all three hundred and sixty degrees.

And a softening came to her eyes.

☙

She would tell Manny of that day when she met him three weeks later in Ecuador, to deliver Lucia's ashes—bequeathing them to him in the middle of a noisy airport café.

They would speak at first of other things: Esperanza; the weather; the abject ugliness of that cheap wooden box. *At least it's travel safe*, she said. This was her bungling attempt at lightness, which he readily forgave. *Like her giant plaid suitcase from Orchard Street*, he said.

She would retrieve from her purse the small orange vial, set it down on his side of the table. It rattled as he shook it in the light. *Was she taking them? Can you tell?* They engaged in conjecture, each trying clumsily to absolve the other of sins, the ones they were certain they themselves had committed. She did not tell him her composure was a gross facade—that she'd vomited on the flight, once during takeoff, again as the airplane had pulled into the gate. He did not tell her of his shame—that for years he'd been unfaithful, that he'd rushed to find Luna after receiving the news. In the end they agreed: There should be no blame, yet each would remain tortured in the years to come, unable to fend off their guilt.

He invited her to the campo. She politely declined. She could not bear to face the scrutiny of a family of strangers. He did not press. He understood.

This was a brief encounter, tender, yet strained. They would part knowing what they'd always known: that they had each loved Lucia. And this was enough, for now, neither was ready for more. In grief, the future seems impossible.

In the end, she would describe to him the best she could, that moment in Minnesota when everything else fell away. He listened closely. She watched his face as it crumpled. His body, too, sagging as though the bones had collapsed inside. And with shocking force, he would emit a long, bestial howl, shudder and sob and gasp unabashedly for air. Raw pain squeezed into fat, dripping tears.

And Miranda's would follow.

It was beautiful, Manny. It was beautiful there.

Part Four

Epilogue
Miranda

She said she would come to our apartment at noon, and at noon I was out on the balcony, watering my zinnias, as I had been every few minutes for the past half hour, peering anxiously at the street down below. She'd arrived in the city two days before, insisted on making her own way to the NYU dorms. "She's stubborn," Manny had warned. Independent. Like her mother.

She was prompt.

"Come on up," I called through the intercom. "Fourth floor." I buzzed her in.

I listened to the click-clack of her heels as she climbed the marble staircase. She was wearing heels, so I figured she must be concerned with making a favorable impression, and I found this somewhat reassuring.

"Tía Miranda," she said, slightly out of breath as she approached the wide-open door. "It's me, Esperanza, your niece."

"Esperanza, come in. Welcome, darling," I said. I kissed her cheek as we embraced. This was not a word in my day-to-day lexicon, *darling*, but with her bright blue raincoat and patent leather Mary Janes, she seemed just that. *Darling*. Lucia's daughter.

"Did you find your way? How was your trip? Are you tired? How is your dorm?" I asked, all at once. My niece and I had exchanged a few e-mails, spoken over video chat while she was submitting her college applications, but this was the extent of our communications.

"It's fine, Tía," she said, laughing, "except I didn't like the airplane. It made me feel sick. I didn't like it at all."

We had that in common, at least.

She was very beautiful, exotic, difficult to categorize, just as she had been as a baby. A healthy light brown color, luminous skin, eerily dark teardrop eyes, and one would not be able to say with certainty whether she was of Chinese descent, or a Latina, or a Filipina, or even some kind of indigenous South American Indian. She glanced around the living room, commenting on how pretty everything was: the white linen curtains, my prolific jade plants, the view over Central Park. I asked her to please sit, and she did not choose the leather recliner or the plush red couch with matching red and white throw pillows, but chose instead the piano bench, which she pulled out a few inches until it was within arm's reach of the cheese and crackers I'd set on the coffee table.

"Do you know, the last time I saw you, you were only four months old?" I said.

"Yes, that's what Papi said." Her eyes, bright. "Thank you for the books, Tía. All the English books."

"Of course. And how is your Papi? He mentioned something about a painting business?"

"Yes, he's been talking about that," she said. "But my Papi, you know, he's usually kind of . . . slow to move."

Tortoise. And Lucia, the hare.

"But he's getting married this Christmas. Her name is Daniela."

"Oh, I didn't know! I'll have to congratulate him," I said.

Though Manny and I had been in contact these past few years, it was primarily with regard to Esperanza's schooling. I would not say

we were "close," this was not the right word, but in our concern for
Lucia we'd shared an uncommon bond, and I now found myself
teary-eyed, moved. I thought: *Yes, how much he deserves this.*

"She's nice. She has three daughters, my new sisters. My Papi is
really happy."

"That's wonderful," I said. "And your Uncle Fredy, how is he?"

"Gordito is fine." She blushed. "That's what we call him. Gordito."

I opened a box of chocolates, offered them to her. She selected an
almond nougat. "My Papi loves these," she said, grinning. And then,
out of nowhere, the most jarring non sequitur: "Tía, will you tell me
about my mother?"

I was taken aback, I admit, though her abruptness was tempered
by her genuine manner, and I found myself admiring her straight-
forwardness.

She wanted to know everything, of course. A young person wants to
view a parent through another's eyes. All those years Lucia lived in
South America, she had no past, no ties, no history, no other angle
of light by which her daughter could perceive her. So I tried to tell
my niece, from the beginning, how Lucia was, even as a child—
vibrant, vivacious, a free spirit who did as she liked while somehow
remaining immensely likable. And how she and her father met, what
little I knew, and how they lived north of the city, in one of the
towns on the Hudson, until they moved to Ecuador.

"You don't remember anything about the States?" I asked.

"I was too young," she said. "Well, maybe, I remember a zoo. I
think my mother took me to a zoo."

And then there was Lucia's illness, on which the doctors could
never agree, whether it was schizophrenia or bipolar disorder or
something on the spectrum in between—this ruthless illness which
hijacks its young sufferers, evicts their souls while blinding them to
any cognizance of their own malady . . . oh, I could go on.

I asked Esperanza if she knew anything about her mother's condition and she said yes, her Papi had mentioned it and she'd read about it on the Internet. I did not probe about her life in Ecuador, though I was curious as to what kind of mother Lucia had been. Was she lax or strict, engaged or removed? Did she and Manny argue all the time? Lucia was never a good fighter; Yonah said she held too much inside, that this made her sick—but then, he never did understand her illness.

My niece did not know about Yonah, I realized, as we continued our conversation. How would she have known?

She was ten years old when her mother went to Minnesota. By then, Lucia and I had grown painfully distant, estranged, ever since that night in Cuenca. But while our few days together with Yonah failed to bring about any grand reconciliation, I now prefer to think of that time as a thaw. She had driven me to the airport—a quiet ride, but we listened to music, the Rolling Stones, sang together a few lines here and there. When it came time to part, we'd hugged at the curb, and I was not the only one fighting back tears.

"Take care of yourself," I said. And in that moment those words meant no more, no less, only a simple expression of love.

"You, too," she said. "Bye, Jie."

She was wearing her purple jacket, and she waved until I was well inside the terminal, and the sliding doors drew closed.

This is my last memory of my sister.

There was a storm. Her body was found, frozen in the snow.

I could not parse what I'd heard.

Those days after I recall as a blur. I was angry. So angry. Angry with her, angry with myself, angry with those nosy reporters in that provincial town, and outright furious with Yonah (though I'd loved him like a brother), who was already dead, who had remained ignorant of Lucia's illness, who had run his mouth loud and loose up until the very end—I thought, immediately, she had gone off her pills.

Stefan had tried to reason with me. This was his usual approach, but I refused to listen—I blamed him, too. Or rather, as part of blaming myself, I attacked him whenever he tried to acquit me of guilt. He'd criticized too harshly, refused to get involved—but I realize, now, that in essence it was this: I faulted him for not loving her the way I did.

It would take years before I could see his side.

Fourteen months after Lucia's death, I embarked on a soul-searching trip to China. A car accident, we'd been told, and I had believed without question. Our Gong-gong Po-po, no longer alive, our mother born an only child, but I was able to track down one of Ma's cousins who lived in Guilin, an old *ayi* not shy with her opinions. *Your Ba gambled,* she said. He ran with cheap women, had illicit affairs. A car accident? No. Swamped in debt, facing arrest, our father had driven off a cliff to his death, a bus full of schoolchildren as his witnesses.

His image, tarnished forever in my mind. Yet I could not say I was shocked or surprised. But if part of me had suspected, it still saddened me deeply, above all this thought: that our mother had insisted on carrying these burdens alone.

Not long afterward, I told Stefan I wanted to leave Switzerland. I could not articulate why, but whatever we said to each other, it was never right, or enough, and a bitterness had become entrenched in both of us. He was not at fault, nor his family, ever appropriate and polite; even Rafael, by then, was finishing up medical school, living with a girlfriend in Geneva, preparing their own vegan meals. I knew only that I wanted to be somewhere different, to reset my mind, and if this rendered me selfish, somehow I no longer cared. But Stefan did not attempt to dissuade me—he let me go. As Yonah had done with Lucia fifteen years earlier.

I came to New York. I came alone. I rented a tiny apartment on the Upper West Side. I was recruited by a health care firm, worked nine to five, went running, painted, cooked as I liked. I visited Tess and her family in Brooklyn Heights, occasionally babysitting for her three children on the weekends. Apart from that, I admit, I led an insular existence. But I was calm in a way I'd never been before. After two years, I decided to pursue a master's degree in arts management—at an "advanced" age, yes, but I was undeterred.

I did not know I would stay, or that Stefan and I would eventually decide to reevaluate (via hours and hours of video counseling), or that he would join me here for three months after Grossmuti died. How trite, but true: things change. Some all at once, some over a lifetime. I work for one of the museums now, managing their education department, a position I enjoy immensely. Stefan will come again next week, for six months this time. It has been nearly twenty years since we first met, playing tennis. And Rafi and his wife are expecting their first child this winter—a boy.

I still go to Chinatown, to my favorite bakery on Mott Street. But I cannot bring myself to venture to the East Village. The store is no longer, I've been told, replaced by a trendy Moroccan restaurant with a hookah lounge. One day I will summon enough courage to go check it out—though by then, perhaps it will have evolved into something else.

Sometimes I still try to imagine what it must've been like, Lucia alone in her dream-state. Perhaps, if she closed her eyes, she could still feel his presence: his raspy voice, the rough skin of his palm on top of her hand, his cindery breath mixed with aftershave. Curious (for how could one not be curious in a dead man's domain?), she floated through the house, snooped through closets for old keepsakes—a shoe box of old photos of his children, perhaps, or one perfect snapshot of their wedding day. Had he other loves? What of all those years after she'd gone away? She would've imagined it then: his life. Her life. If only she'd come back to him.

She had started to pack his belongings. A day here, a day there, at an unhurried pace—to launder his sweaters, his sweatshirts, his socks, his jeans, to organize his personal items before giving them away. *Keep. Salvation Army. Trash.* She would've needed a day, at least, just to sort through his tools. Yonah possessed little clothing, but owned dozens of screwdrivers and hammers and wrenches and pliers. One drawer contained only flashlights, another, nails and screws. In the master bedroom, I did come upon an odd sight: an ice chest full of batteries, plopped in the middle of the king-size bed. Perhaps she'd been tempted to throw them away, then heard his voice in her ear: *What?!* So she'd sat cross-legged on the bedspread, sifted through them methodically: the D's, the C's, a batch of double and triple A's. Each time, the battery tester's needle floating on its color-coded dial: *Good. Low. Replace.* She'd sorted the acceptable ones into piles, placed them inside a series of Ziploc bags. There must've been hundreds in all.

I never told Manny these details, only that after Yonah died she must've had a difficult time, and things had ended tragically. I did not attend Lucia's funeral in Ecuador; likewise, he could not come to the memorial service that Tess helped me arrange in Westchester, a simple ceremony, in a park, with a lovely view of the Tappan Zee Bridge. Though Lucia seemed to know everyone, she was close to few, so it was a handful of her friends from college, a few former colleagues, a Pakistani woman I did not know, an older woman with dyed-orange hair.

"My Papi, he can't come to this country," said my niece.

I nodded. I knew this was because he had violated the provisions of his visa many years ago—he was an illegal in this country, and would never be allowed back in. Lucia had understood this clearly.

That night in Cuenca, banging around in that tiny room, she knew it was wrong, plain wrong, to take Esperanza away from her father. But she could not bear to leave her young daughter behind.

Was I wrong? Misguided? Was I out of line? If I hadn't burst in that night, could Lucia's life have taken a different path?

I still picture her with Yonah sometimes, the two of them sitting on that dilapidated bench outside the store, chatting with the denizens of the neighborhood.

But if I hadn't stepped in, Esperanza, the sole innocent among us all, would've lost her father. In my deepest heart, I believed this to be wrong. Manny was a good father; he loved his daughter. And for Lucia to raise the child alone seemed impossible—this was what I thought at the time. But in retrospect, one could say it was Lucia's right to live the life of her own choosing, regardless of her illness, and I should never have interfered.

I don't know.

This is my secret. I never did tell Manny the truth. I will not tell Esperanza.

"My Papi is a good person," she said.

"Yes. Yes, he is. Your mother was a good person, too. A dreamer, always a dreamer, wanting to have it all. This is very American, you know."

"I'm Chi-meri-dorian," said my niece, flashing a grin. She leaned forward to touch my elbow, as if I were in some need of reassurance, and I could see it already: those NYU boys flocking to her side like rowdy pigeons.

"That's probably a good balance," I said.

"She was sad sometimes." Her gaze fell to the floor. "I remember that. My mother was sad. Why?"

I knew no clear answer to this question. She felt isolated, maybe. Constricted, misunderstood. Lucia, always chasing some happily-ever-after; she needed to be free. Or was she simply childish, self-centered, irresponsible? For a long time I saw her as the latter, I admit.

"Did she love my Papi?"

"I don't know." I sighed. "I'm sorry, Esperanza. There are a lot of things I just don't know."

She bit her lip, the way her mother often did. As if mulling the acceptability of this answer.

The cause of death was ruled "accidental." I like to think this is the truth. I picture her, alone in that kitchen, listening to the wobble of her mixing bowl on the countertop. Perhaps she went to check if she'd left the garage light on, or the car unlocked, or a snow shovel in the driveway. Perhaps she heard a dog bark or howl or glimpsed a deer through the window, cracked opened the glass sliders, smelled the wind, the pines, the smoke of a distant wood fire. She stepped outside, let the arctic gusts blast away stray images of bulky latex-gloved men carting off her Yoni's body on a stretcher. (Memories of death, those final days, forever etched in one's mind.) Tired of confinement in that somber house, she decided she needed fresh air. She enjoyed long walks. The majesty of the forest. The light snow would've offered a peaceful idyll—nature is a comfort, she always said. Or perhaps it was so much more mundane: She was missing an ingredient (baking soda? almonds?) and thought she'd go say hello to the neighbors. Ward Dunkel and his three Irish wolfhounds, acquainted with her, lived on the other side of the lake.

The storm came quickly, the police officers said. One could get lost in those woods.

The voices. It could've been the voices. Serpents, she once told me. Two. A pair. "What do the serpents tell you to do?" I asked. "They don't exactly tell me to do anything," she said. "It's more like they expose my inner state."

If only she had not been alone.

I replay those days in Minnesota. I search for clues. Was her behavior irrational? Did she seem deeply depressed? She was sad, of course, yet hadn't she flown all the way to New York City, returned with one of those ridiculously large suitcases stuffed full of Chinese herbs?

But the shock, the grief, the stress of it all.

The serpents did it—yes, this is easy to say. But I like to think that she simply went out looking for something beautiful.

"Esperanza," I said. "It's still sunny outside. Would you like to go for a walk in the park?"

"*Central* Park?" she said. Not the words, but her voice, her manner, so like Lucia.

We entered at Seventy-second Street just as the day was starting to wane, dipping into the splendorous light of magic hour. I brought her to Strawberry Fields—was she familiar with the Beatles, John Lennon, maybe the Rolling Stones? Of course, she said, and this surprised me, and we discussed music and she said she played guitar, liked to sing, though her Papi had given her strict orders to study finance or computers, something practical, but she would see first how her classes went, she might find politics or literature interesting, who knows? (I was impressed with her English, which was endearingly proper, with a slight British accent, and her grammar mostly smooth.) Our conversation continued then, beyond the past to her future, and next I noticed the sunlight had disappeared.

"It's genetic," I said, suddenly. Not to be morbid or unpleasant, but because I felt I had a responsibility to tell her, my niece, this girl on her journey to womanhood.

"This illness, it's genetic."

"I've read that," she said.

"You need to be careful. Get plenty of sleep. Stay away from drugs. Take good care of yourself."

She nodded with insufficient gravity, though correct politeness. *I'm so sorry.*

I wanted to say it, but I couldn't.

"It's getting late, Esperanza. Do you know where you are? Can I help you get back to your dorm?"

"No, no," she said. "I can find it. Though I think I'll walk a bit farther. Maybe I'll go to the zoo."

"It will be closed now."

"That's okay. But, Tía Miranda, please, there is one small thing."

"What is it?" I said, and in that moment a maternal tenderness overwhelmed me unexpectedly. She was still so much a child.

Protect this girl, God. Protect her, goddammit.

"I hope you can call me Essy."

"Essy. Yes, of course." Its lightness off the tongue suited her. "Welcome to America, Essy. Or should I say, welcome *back*. Can I take you out for dinner next week after you've settled in? Stefan is in Switzerland at the moment, but he'll be here by then. Maybe pizza, or sushi?"

"Sushi?"

"Japanese raw fish. Have you tried?"

She wrinkled her nose. "Well, my Papi says in America there is everything. But . . . maybe pizza first." She yum-yum tapped her belly, laughed, and I could not resist wrapping my arms around her slender shoulders.

"Pizza, then," I said.

My niece.

Hope.

Butterfly.

She clung to me and did not let go.

I was caught by surprise. Tears filled my eyes.

I'm here, I said. My words, barely a whisper.

I did not know what more to say, so I said nothing more, but I patted her slowly on the head. And after a long moment she pulled back and smiled, and her lightness was again restored.

Besitos! Good-bye!

I waved and she waved. And I stood, watching, as she walked away—envious of her youth, admiring of her grace, though she wobbled every few steps on her Mary Janes, catching a heel on the pavement.

Acknowledgments

Susan Golomb, for believing so passionately; Pamela Dorman, for helping me bring this story to a place where I feel truly at peace.

Lynn Buckley and Roseanne Serra, for the stunning cover; Jeramie Orton, Rebecca Marsh, Lindsay Prevette, Kate Stark, Andrea Schulz, Brian Tart, and the entire Viking Penguin team, for their relentless hard work and dedication in championing this book.

The *Missouri Review*, for publishing the short story that launched this novel. Michael Lowenthal, Celeste Ng, Lori Ostlund, Christina Thompson, Lisa Miller, Adam Stumacher, Jeanne Leiby, Brando Skyhorse, for aiding and abetting as I journeyed down my writerly path. The Grub Street Writing Center, for guidance; the Massachusetts Cultural Council, for funding; Scrivener, for a tool I could not have worked without; When Words Count Retreat, for tranquility.

NAMI Cambridge/Middlesex, for moral support through difficult times. Dr. Xavier Amador, for allowing me to paraphrase a passage from his book, *I Am Not Sick, I Don't Need Help*. Rachel Aviv, whose *New Yorker* article, "God Knows Where I Am," still inspires me to write with more grace.

To learn more about mental illness, or to find support for

individuals and families dealing with mental illness, the National Alliance on Mental Illness (NAMI) is an immensely helpful organization with local chapters in all fifty states (nami.org).

Frank, Clara, Jennifer, Sara S., Christine, Tobey, Beatriz, Jumbi, Karen S., Melissa G., Fredi, Jwyanza, the Ku-Schmitts, the Hsiung-Chais, the Standishers, Kat T., Chris C., Jade, Alison, Eran, Karine, for being early readers, consultants, and unwavering allies these past years.

My family. Close and far.

Dave, and my boys, for making everything possible.

A PENGUIN READERS GUIDE TO

EVERYTHING HERE IS BEAUTIFUL

Mira T. Lee

AN INTRODUCTION TO
EVERYTHING HERE IS BEAUTIFUL

Everything Here Is Beautiful is a tale of two sisters—as different as night and day, but tethered by an unshakable bond, even when they are half a world apart. Miranda, the older, is straitlaced and serious, responsible because she has never had another choice. Lucia, the younger, is headstrong and impulsive, prone to living life on a grand scale. Their connection, and the ways in which it is tested, is at the heart of this story.

Miranda has been her sister's protector for as long as she can remember—ever since she and her pregnant mother emigrated from Shanghai to America. Years later, after their mother's death, Lucia's impetuous nature leads her to marry an older, charismatic Israeli shopkeeper, only to leave him abruptly to have a baby with a young Latino immigrant. While Lucia is busy rushing into life-changing decisions, at times with cataclysmic results, Miranda tries to escape her caretaker role, marrying a Swiss doctor and seeking new allegiances. But when Lucia's lucidity begins to falter and she starts hearing voices, Miranda must find a way to save her sister without losing herself in the process.

Told in alternating points of view, *Everything Here Is Beautiful* spans years and continents, following Miranda and Lucia from East Coast cities to a tiny village in Ecuador to the mountains of Switzerland. The push-and-pull between the sisters, as they struggle to do the right thing for themselves and for each other, yields an intimate and powerful family drama. Lee tenderly captures Lucia's struggle, and its ripple effects on those around her, in this stirring and beautifully written tale of the ties that bind us across oceans, over time, and through chaos and heartbreak.

A Conversation with
Mira T. Lee

You have called Everything Here Is Beautiful *"a messy family drama"—one that examines our responsibilities to our loved ones, and what happens when personal fulfillment is at odds with familial obligation. Can you expand on that a little, and why you wanted to dig into this theme?*

The quick answer would be, families *are* messy, and this makes for rich storytelling. I imagine just about every family harbors its own secrets, dysfunction, stubborn patterns and hidden resentments borne in childhood that you can't ever quite escape. We don't get to choose our families, yet we're bound to them by this odd combination of love and obligation. Add to that the pressures of illness or immigration or marital strife, and you get something pretty fraught. A mentor of mine once said, "Never guess at the interior lives of others." But the writer in me wanted to do just that—explore the interior lives of my characters as they bumped up against one another. I've always been drawn to "gray areas," those difficult situations with no right or wrong answers, where good people find themselves in conflict and nobody can win without hurting someone they love. I like complexity, and family dynamics are really, really complicated.

Much of the book deals with what it is like to struggle with mental illness, or to love someone who does—yet you have said you did not want this to be a book "about" mental illness. What do you mean by that? Why did you choose to tackle this topic, and what story did you want to tell about mental illness?

Mental illness, and particularly schizophrenia, is a subject matter very close to my heart. I've seen my own family members struggle with it, and it is, in a word, devastating. But I didn't want to write a book about an illness, I wanted to write a story about *lives*—specifically, four very different lives, and how each one's trajectory was affected by Lucia's life in particular. These illnesses are unpredictable and pervasive, they screw up marriages, derail careers, jeopardize lifelong relationships with family and friends. Crises happen just as a parent gets sick, or a baby is born, or as Immigration shows up to deport an undocumented family member. And our mental health care system is riddled with intractable problems. Embedding Lucia's illness within such storylines allowed for a much broader scope and more compelling plot, which hopefully keeps readers turning pages. I like a story with lots of nuance, and the ripple effects of mental illness certainly provide for that. But it also has to move, entertain, engage.

The novel switches between perspectives, allowing the reader to access both Miranda and Lucia's points of view, as well as those of Manny and Yonah, the men in Lucia's life. What motivated this narrative choice, and did you find it challenging to get into the heads of the different characters?

I wanted to explore all the different sides of these predicaments I'd put my characters in, and having them speak from their own vantage points, each with their own stake in Lucia's well-being, made for richer characterizations. It also felt natural in terms of the way the plot moved. The tricky part was finding the right voice for each section. It was interesting though, because you'd think the men might be harder to write, since on the surface they appear less similar to me. But their voices were clear, and I could wiggle into their heads through our commonalities—like Manny's experience as the terrified parent of a newborn, or Stefan's concern over his spouse's decisions. Lucia's voice was by far the most difficult. I always envisioned her as being much more brilliant and perceptive than I am, which posed a real challenge. It's humbling to realize that a character can only be as brilliant as her creator, but I kept feeling like I was holding her back!

The book also jumps around geographically, from New York to the Swiss Alps to a tiny village in Ecuador. What compelled you about these distinct and diverse settings? How did you go about making them come alive on the page?

I think the men came before the settings. That is, the story originated in New York, but veered geographically out of necessity, because the sisters became involved with men from these other countries. Switzerland and Ecuador definitely fit with the sisters' personalities, but honestly, when I started writing, I had no idea so much of the book would take place overseas! "Going there" felt quite daunting. But I'd spent time in those places, and I researched further by reading travel blogs by expats and backpackers, as well as local news sites. I also collected photographs that I'd describe—a dirt road, or a crowded bus, for example. Having visual references was really helpful; it's the smallest details that make a place come to life.

Narratives of mental illness are often white and middle-class, yet mental illness does not discriminate—it devastates regardless of race, gender, and ethnicity. Was it important for you to challenge that narrative, and to have a wide cast of characters from different backgrounds?

It wasn't my intention to challenge the predominantly white, middle-class narrative of mental illness we most often see these days; I wrote the book with characters from all different backgrounds simply because such people have been the norm in my own life. At some point I did wonder, should I make my characters white? Cross-cultural stories in America still seem rare in fiction, but it's true—mental illnesses do not discriminate. I decided to keep my characters the way they were, and now I'm really glad I did. I think it's important to see these illnesses portrayed in communities of color, where stigma can be especially strong. And I'd argue that it's also important to see stories starring people of color that don't necessarily fit into the expected frameworks—for example, of an "Asian-American story" or a "cultural novel." I like surprises. And I don't want to have to write only what's expected of me.

At one point in the novel, Miranda and Lucia's mother says, "Immigrants are the strongest . . . Everywhere we go, we rebuild." Can you talk about the role that immigration, and cultural displacement, plays in the novel?

In my twenties and early thirties, it seemed like everyone I knew came from another country: first generation immigrants, international students, visiting scientists, musicians, programmers, small business owners, legal, illegal, you name it. And all matter of romantic entanglements were going on! So my characters, too, all go through periods of cultural displacement. I liked the off-kilter feeling it provided, how no one ever felt quite grounded, and even if one character was "home," their spouse/partner wasn't, which set up lots of natural conflicts. I also liked exploring the reasons people choose to leave their home countries, how sometimes they're moving towards something (opportunity, promises, family); but sometimes they're also running away (from their pasts, their secrets, their families, expectations).

Everything Here Is Beautiful is an intimate book about love, loss, and family. But it also revolves around larger societal and institutional concerns like mental illness, immigration, and health care. How did you balance the scope of the narrative, and tackle those big issues, while still keeping it a personal and emotionally poignant story?

I always thought of it as a small, organic story. I think if I'd thought about it as tackling "big issues," I might've felt like I was supposed to Say Something Important, which probably would've just come off as contrived or pedantic, or turned my characters into archetypes. So it was always about the narrative, about family relationships. At points, I do try to educate the reader about some of the issues involved with psychotic illnesses—anosognosia ("lack of insight"), for example, or medications, or how the mental health care system works (or doesn't)—because the reader needs an understanding of these issues in order to relate to Miranda's frustrations. To me, great fiction happens when we find the humanity in each of our characters, no matter who they are or what their situations may be. Even when we're unfamiliar with a particular experience, we can relate at an emotional level. I think that's what empathy is all about.

What do you hope readers will take away from Everything Here Is Beautiful?

I do hope readers will gain a sense of the issues surrounding schizophrenia, which is perhaps still the most severe and stigmatized of all the mental illnesses, but one deserving of just as much compassion. I also hope people see that these illnesses are only one component of a person's life, and can relate to the humanity at the core of each of these characters—as sisters, mothers, husbands, lovers, as modern women, as deeply flawed human beings who yearn for love and belonging. But I also hope readers will disagree over what these characters should or shouldn't have done. The world is gray, full of contradictions, and if I've managed to illuminate some aspect of that, then I think I've done this story justice.

QUESTIONS FOR DISCUSSION

1. Lee has described her characters as "flawed and imperfect, but all trying really hard to do the right thing." Do you agree? Which character did you sympathize/empathize with most? Least? Why? Do you have a favorite?

2. Many of the characters in the novel struggle to find balance between self-fulfillment and obligation to others. What would you have done if you were in Lucia's situation in the campo? Have you ever had to choose between what you want for yourself and what's best for someone you love (e.g., a child)?

3. Miranda has been caring for Lucia ever since she was a child, but as an adult, the role she plays in her sister's life grows murkier. What, if anything, do the sisters owe one another? What do they owe themselves? Did you find Miranda's actions caring, or meddlesome?

4. Much of the story focuses on Lucia's quest to live a rich and fulfilling life, in spite of her illness. But Lucia's decisions also impact others—Yonah, Manny, Miranda, Stefan, Essy—forcing them to adapt their lives in turn. Did you find Lucia's actions selfish, or selfless? Why?

5. Manny has to live with the brunt of Lucia's illness. At one point he reflects: "This was love, or this was duty, he could no longer tell the difference." What is the difference? When does love turn into duty and when does duty become love? Do you consider Manny loyal, or is he simply passive? Did his infidelities bother you? Do Manny and Lucia love each other?

6. In the book, Lee writes, "Immigrants are the strongest. . . . Everywhere we go, we rebuild." All the characters in the novel are immigrants, rebuilding their lives in some way. But who is running away from something, and who is running toward something? How do their immigrant experiences differ?

7. How does ethnicity/culture play into this novel? Would you consider this an ethnic novel? Why or why not? Could the same story have been told if the characters were white? What role does cultural displacement play in the character's lives and relationships?

8. Lucia points out that in our society, cancer survivors are viewed much differently from sufferers of mental illness. Do you agree? Do you know someone who has a mental illness? How does stigma affect our views of mental illness?

9. Anosognosia, or "lack of insight," is a frequent symptom of psychotic disorders such as schizophrenia and makes these illnesses especially difficult to treat. How do you help someone who doesn't realize they are ill? How did you feel about Manny putting pills in Lucia's tea?

10. "He tried so hard to love her—yet how best to love her still eluded him." The men in the book struggle with how best to love the women in their lives. Should Yonah have let Lucia walk out of their marriage so easily? Should Stefan have supported Miranda's efforts to help her sister at the expense of her own well-being? Are there right or wrong ways to love someone?

11. Who is most to blame for Lucia's end? Herself? Yonah? Miranda? Manny? Could someone have done something differently to alter the outcome? What do you think happened to Lucia?